How The Fox Runs

J.O. ELLIS

PAPERBACK HART PRESS LLC

Content Warning:
How the Fox Runs contains dark themes as well as explicit and mature content not intended for young readers. Please make note of this and read with care.

Contents

Dedicated to those who have carried the heavy weight of grief, and to those who are still looking for a place to put it.
This is where I placed mine.

Prologue

A Gift from a Fox

A CHILLING BITE IN the air meant death was coming.

Though it wasn't quite cold enough to see one's breath yet, the lush greens would soon give way to shades of brown and gray. A sacrifice to ensure that life could start anew.

A woman tightly wrapped a shawl around her shoulders as she headed to the wood pile to collect logs for the stifling cold night that was sure to come. Just as she was turning back to the house—arms full with gathered firewood—she heard a small, strange sound, from the woods behind her. She paused for a minute, evaluating what she heard—an animal perhaps, or a bird making its final call into the rapidly descending night.

She heard it again—a strange cry—unfamiliar to her, despite all her years living alongside the dense woods.

When she heard the odd sound for the third time, recognition snapped into place. It was the noise of a child—a crying child. A sound her ears had long forgotten. She dropped her logs and shuffled into the woods, with only the faint glow of twilight to guide her as she stepped cautiously over roots and vine. Ear atoned to all the familiar noises of the wilderness—singling out that misplaced sound.

With silent steps, she followed the soft crying until she reached a large pine—deep, large knots formed along its trunk. Rustling came from a lone burrow down in the entanglement of the tree's roots. She leaned in and peered closer, squinting against the dimming light.

An audible gasp left her lips when she found a full-grown fox wrapped around a very small child. No older than three, the child wore a tattered silk nightgown, and was crying into the fur of the protective fox. The fox peered at the woman as though ready to sink its sharp teeth into her if need be—its tail flicking with agitation.

With soft, hushed coaxing and outstretched hands, the woman was finally able to beckon the crying toddler away from the protection of the fox and into her arms. She wrapped her wool shawl around the dirty, and abandoned little girl, as she wept in her arms—her tiny hands clinging to the woman's overalls with tight fists. She moved to carry her back to the warm safety of the cabin but not before looking over her shoulder, back at the fox. Though the animal couldn't talk, the woman knew, from her time alongside nature, that everything had a spirit and some level of consciousness. Because of that, it felt rude to simply walk away without at least expressing some form of gratitude for the precious gift that was now nuzzled into her chest. The fox stared back at her with piercing gold eyes as wise as the trees and as shrewd as an owl.

"Thank you for keeping her warm. She'll be safe with me, now." She reassured the child's protector.

Meanwhile, somewhere far, far, away. . .

A boy cut across a wheat field, eager to get home quickly, lest he miss watching his father reheat the forge. He had slept in that morning, causing him to delay his morning chores of checking on the sheep and collecting water for his mother's wash from the nearby creek. He was anxious to get back to the workshop that rested in the valley below, adamant that he watch his father hammer metal while he kept the fires that heated it well stoked. A responsibility he enjoyed as he observed every movement of his father's hands as they manipulated his craft.

The village was a short distance ahead, just past the fields and down the hill to the valley below. He could practically smell the fire stoking to life and quickened his pace. Pails of water splashed at his sides, but, before the boy could crest the hill, a fleet of black stallions emerged from below. They charged swiftly down the dirt path, mounted by men in red military uniforms.

The boy quickly ducked below the wheat stalks, dropping his buckets of water; fearful of being seen by the men he heard stories of—men who craved only glory and death—who were happy to cleanse themselves in the blood of those who stood against them if it meant victory for their leaders.

Once the flurry of red and black passed into the woods beyond, and the boy was sure he was alone, he rose from the cover of the tall grass and looked back toward the village. Black smoke curled up into the sky, much more than any forge could produce on its own. The boy ran as fast as he could, forgetting the buckets all together, letting them lie abandoned in the field.

When his feet finally brought him to familiar soil, tears filled the boy's eyes from, not only the burn of smoke, but the scene of pure destruction before him.

Homes burned.

Livestock lay slain, along with the bodies of men, women, and . . . children. The smell of burnt flesh stung his nose and the boy covered it and his mouth with a bent arm as he stumbled through the hellish scape.

Frightening silence and the crackle of fire, was all that remained. It whispered an answer to the boy's quiet question.

Was anyone still alive?

His legs took him, stumbling, to his father's workshop, as if unaware of the interruption in his routine.

The shop was nothing but charred remains, but a familiar shape laid still in the shadows of the rubble.

Just as he mustered enough courage to go inside, to investigate further, a cry broke out across the silence—so meek he almost thought he imagined it. But it returned again, a soft, small sob. He followed the sound to a neighboring, burning house; the sound was coming from behind it. As he circled around, he found a garden in immaculate shape—untouched by the surrounding destruction. Chickens scattered about in chaos and just as he thought it must have just been them that he had heard, the cry came again from under an overturned trough.

He lifted a corner of the wooden trough to peer inside and was startled to see two big eyes staring up at him. The creature cried with fear at his presence and startled the boy, causing him to stumble backwards and onto his bottom. Hand pressed to his chest, his heart beat under his ribs like a hammer on molten steel. With a few deep breaths, he collected himself and mustered his courage to lift the trough again, now with more mettle than before. Inside, he found a small baby girl with bright red hair and emerald green eyes, staring up at him. Like a discarded doll, dirt littered her face, only broken by two lines of tears, cleansing paths down her cheeks. She did not cower but faced him with a pout and pleading eyes.

"Kareena?" the boy questioned, recognizing the small babe from his village. She was the daughter of a neighboring family. A glance over his shoulder, to the smoldering house behind, revealed a lifeless figure. Similar red hair fanned out around the body dressed in a simple brown dress darkened with blood. He wrapped the baby in his arms and made his way back through the village, up the hill and through the wheat field where he had left his buckets. The baby continued to cry without ceasing, but the boy was patient as he rocked, hushed, and cooed in an attempt to calm her.

"Shh. It's okay now. I'll keep you safe."

HOW THE FOX RUNS

Part One

A Door to Nowhere

Chapter One

ACROSS THE LAWN, THE creeping fog blocked out the light of the sun—a physical reminder of the light that had been snuffed out of my own eyes. The meds sucked all thought from me, making me feel like an empty husk of human flesh; a reprieve from the sticky, sick emotions that coated my skin like filth. Those same eyes dragged slowly to where my shadow, my only companion in this hellscape, bent at a deformed angle on the scuffed and stained wall. What was probably once white was now a collection of varying shades of brown, ivory, and creams. Left over from the ghosts of this asylum's past.

My cell door opened without announcement, as usual, and a muscularly built orderly stepped in. His hair was black and cut close to his head, his skin a warm brown, and his smile even warmer. But the friendliness of the gesture merely went through me, as I was too numb to receive it.

All I could do was count.

Count the days until the submittal of my evaluation of mental stability. My lawyer's last-ditch effort to delay the inevitable.

Count how many meals I had that day.

Count my pills.

Count the hours while I stayed locked behind these cold, white walls.

"Time for lunch," he said through his grin and I rose to follow him out the door without so much as a word. Ever the obedient little inmate.

I poked the sad, gelatinous excuse for meatloaf with my plastic spoon. No forks or knives allowed. I had no intention of eating them, but the doctors would get upset if they thought you were intentionally not eating, so I tried my best to make it look like I did—moving my food around and taking only a bite or two. It wasn't that I didn't want to eat. I loved to eat, if the food was any good. If it was anything besides the disgusting garbage they served us here. But to be honest, anything was better than getting a tube shoved down your throat. After seeing one patient rolled into the cafeteria just to be made an example of as they fed a thick liquid into a tube that traveled down her throat, I decided I wouldn't ever let it get to that.

"What do you think is in this shit?"

"What?" I asked as I turned my attention away from my tray and towards the round-faced girl sitting beside me.

"This blue drink? What's in it?" she pondered as she tapped the side of the Styrofoam cup with her plastic spoon.

"Isn't it just juice of some kind?" I speculated as I looked into my own cup of blue liquid that I definitely would not be drinking.

"I heard one of the others say the color is strong enough to dye hair. Imagine what it does to your insides." She leaned in conspiratorially as a smirk grew at the corner of her lips.

"Who cares?" I waved her off, staring back at the extremely concerning gray meat.

The rustling of a plastic wrapper brought my attention back to my fellow inmate as she procured an unadulterated honey bun from the pocket of her worn thin sweatpants. Same as mine.

I tried not to drool at the sight of it in her plump fingers as she practically waved it in my face.

"If you do what I say, I'll give this to you." Her brow lowered over beady eyes as they bore into me.

I was almost afraid to, but found myself asking anyways, "Like what?"

"Just dip those pretty blonde strands into your cup and don't take them out til I say and this is all yours." She dangled the treat in my face for emphasis.

"That's it?"

"That's it." She nodded with enthusiasm and, though her request was innocent enough, I got the creeping feeling that it meant so much more to her somehow.

"Okay. Deal." Gathering the ends of my rather long hair into one fist and without hesitation, I dipped them into the bright blue drink.

"Twenty, nineteen, eighteen, seventeen. . ." the girl began counting down. "Ten, nine, eight, seven. . ." Her excitement grew more visible on her face with each number she counted. "Five, four, three. . ." In fact, she looked as though any minute her pink cheeks would burst. Her smile painfully stretched across her face. "Two, one, OUT!" she screamed as she burst into vivacious and uncontrollable laughter. Hysteria seemed to overtake her entire body as she rolled from her seat and to the floor, grabbing her ribs as the volume of her chuckling only grew.

I stared at her in disbelief. Completely unable to understand what was so funny as she drew more and more unwanted attention our way. An orderly that stood at the corner of the common area, with crossed arms, looked our way with a narrowed glare before stomping in our direction. Swift hands pocketed the forgotten honey bun from the table before getting up and heading to discard my food and tray. As I set my tray down on the stack of others, a janitor passed by with a wheeled cart. He swiped a card that was clipped to his uniform across a gray pad, causing the door's lock to "*click*" out of place, allowing him to enter. Before the door closed behind him I snuck a brief look at the kitchen beyond.

Dull, sad eyes looked back up at me from the journal laid in my lap. Her eyes weren't always this sad. Sometimes I drew them alight with a sparkle of joy or adoration. Other times they were soft and welcoming. A comfort for my soul to look upon. But not today. Today they formed tears of their own under the cheap, No. 2 pencil in my grip.

"Alise, would you like to share anything with the group?" a voice asked from across the circle of hard, plastic chairs. I merely shook my head in response, not looking up from my task as I shaded in the hollows of cheeks.

"Alise, I asked you—"

"I heard you and no, I don't have anything to share," I interrupted rather curtly. Though this doctor in particular was much kinder and soft spoken, I couldn't stand her analyzing stare, as if she could see the truth in me if she went long enough without blinking. It was disturbing and disappointing. Because if she could see the truth I hid inside, she would know I didn't belong here. That my charges were false and she would see the proof as to why.

But, just like every other overly confident staff member here, she failed drastically at conjuring up any helpful information about me or any other inmate for that matter.

"Of course not," she huffed under her breath as she wrote something down in her notebook.

A chime echoed off the linoleum floors and vacant walls while orderlies lined up on either side of the only door in and out of the room.

"Time for exercise," the taller of the two announced and we all rose, on cue, to line up beside them. Such well-oiled little automatons.

"Remember to leave your journals on the table before you go," the female said as she rose and smoothed the wrinkles from her pencil skirt.

I reluctantly dropped mine with a careless thud onto the pile of others and shuffled toward the single-file line of other mindless drones.

Perched atop a rotted, wooden bench, I stared down at the cement walkway as blue droplets fell from my hair and splattered an abstract design below. I immediately tried to rinse out the blue stain on my ends in the bathroom, but failed to even fade the potent hue.

Unlike the other benches in the fenced-in courtyard, this one always remained vacant due to its proximity to the yard used by the more violent patients—though that never bothered me. Most often they were not out on the grounds at the same time as us, "less dangerous," patients. However, today was different.

A man in cuffs was led out into the yard, with two orderlies on each side. When they made it to the center of the sparse yard, they undid his restraints and walked back to the shade of the awning, beside the door. The orderlies on my side of the fence talked amongst themselves while they smoked. I sat alone, while others huddled around tables and benches, gathering up as much gossip and pointless chatter as they could before our free time was up.

"Hey," the man said, lifting his chin in my direction. His eyes met mine through the wired fence, making it clear he was indeed talking to me. I averted my gaze elsewhere, not in the mood for small talk.

The man gripped the wire in his tan and scarred fingers. A trail of equally alarming scars trailed up his exposed wrist before disappearing under his shirt sleeves.

"Hey," he tried again with no result, as I stared blankly back at him.

"Bitch, I'm talking to you." He shook the fence in his grip with stark agitation. The metal rattled as it clanged against itself.

His frustration was potent, creating a wave of pressure that built and grew inside me as each muscle grew more tense by the second. I should have gotten up and walked away. I shouldn't have stayed this close, where his energy was impossible to ignore. But the strength of it was so strong, it paralyzed me in place—rooted its claws in my flesh and held me in place.

"Anybody ever tell you you're stuck up?" His words, an attempt to egg me on.

Of course, they had. Every man, boy, and male I refused to give the time of day to, had. In fact, I had grown rather numb to the cutting words and vicious mood swings. Nothing like an unrequited sexual advance to turn an insincere smile into a sneer of hatred.

Still, I said nothing, just sat and stared, feeding off his anger and frustration as it welled up inside me. Fueled with every hurtful thing the opposite sex ever said to me. Relishing the fact that I was finally feeling something after weeks of numbness. Anger always felt better than sorrow.

"Come over here and I'll make you smile," he attempted one last time, but he had pressed his luck and had gotten the attention of the orderlies by the door.

"Back away from the fence," one called to him, unwilling to leave the solitude the shade provided on this muggy spring day.

"Last chance, princess," he cooed as his hands lowered from the fence to the waistband of his sweatpants.

Claws released my body from its hold at the realization of what he was about to do and I jolted upright. I daringly walked closer to the fence, just out of arms reach before saying, "Whatever you want to show me, best keep it in your pants or we'll both be disappointed." Not giving him a second more of my time I turned on a heel to walk away.

A string of curses and the chaotic rattling of the fence sounded behind me. It wasn't until I heard the shuffling of feet and the grunts of a scuffle that I looked over my shoulder to see the two orderlies wrestling the inmate to the ground. Any second, they would strap on his restraints and throw him back in a padded cell in a solitary part of the ward, and I didn't care to see a single moment of it.

I didn't need to be reminded of what it was like to be restrained to a hospital bed while an officer read you your rights. I desperately tried not to recall the memory of the man in a blue uniform telling me I was charged with the murder-suicide of James McCoy, but it surfaced anyways. The feral beast never heeded my commands to flee. Instead, it sunk its teeth into me as it reminded me of every time I so desperately tried to convince the doctors, police—even my own lawyer—that I didn't, couldn't, would never do what they claimed I did.

But they never listened. Not truly. All evidence pointed to me, apparently, and my memories of the night were spotty at best. Despite the fact that I had been drugged, almost to the point of an early grave, they still wanted answers to the events of that night. They wanted a detailed, and thorough, alibi from me when I couldn't even recall how we ended up in that bed together in the first place, and because of this I was sure to get the death penalty for a crime I knew in my soul I could never commit.

I shook the beast loose of its grip and let the dull numbness creep back into my bones. I fished out the pills I had hidden away in my pocket after pretending to take them at breakfast. The sedatives were too strong to allow me to function during the day and I found I needed extra doses at night to sleep in this hell hole that reeked of every vile emotion a human could harbor. Their stench and decay crawled on my skin like bugs while I slept, causing me to jolt from nightmare induced dreams to an even worse reality. Two, maybe three, would help me sleep that night, but I only needed one if I planned to stay up.

Just enough to take the edge off.

Chapter Two

"Alise. Alise," a soft voice whispered in the dark.

Was it night already?

I slowly opened my eyes to see a tall, lithe figure standing over me in an orderly's uniform. I jolted in surprise, before recognizing the outline before me.

Wren.

Hands rubbed at my groggy eyes. Had I slept all day?

"Are you up for a game tonight? I just checked and Victor is already asleep at his post," he whispered. The moonlight cast shadows on the sharp plains of his cheekbones and jaw.

I placed my feet upon the cold, tile floor and stretched my arms to the ceiling.

"Of course," I replied with a small sheepish grin. "I've been looking forward to it all day."

Wren replied with a prideful grin of his own.

"Me too, darling. Let's go." He offered his hand.

Guilt dug in that I was, in a way, using him. But, perhaps, he was also using me to get out of doing his work. We could both get in serious trouble if the staff discovered he was sneaking me out from my holding room almost every night. Though, he always made sure Victor, the guard down the hall, was asleep before he would come get me.

Tonight, I was beating him at a game of Texas Hold Em' that I let him believe he taught me. You can imagine his shock when, after only a couple nights of playing, I started winning and taking the pot. A decent little stash of money hid between the mattress and frame of my bed.

I placed my hand of cards on the table and giggled innocently, as I, once again, cleared the top of the makeshift table of its winnings.

"Dang girl, I can't believe you've gotten so good. You've been practicing without me, haven't you?" he teased as he took a swig from the bottle we shared. Glazed, bedroom eyes, stared pointedly at me from across the crate. They were deep, wide, and doe-like with dark fluttering lashes. One of his many charms, I supposed.

"I'm terrible. You're just letting me win." I smiled back at him and took a sip from my little paper cup. I had convinced him early on that I was a germaphobe so that we wouldn't have to drink from the same container. And since I was such a lightweight, he always poured me more than enough.

"Ahh, you caught me. I'd do anything to put a smile on that pretty face." He looked at me with slightly hooded eyes and a sloppy grin. He tended to get more confident the more he drank. I smiled back bashfully and cringed a little inside. It's not that Wren wasn't attractive. He was in a way that he would always carry his boyish features with him, even into adulthood. His nose was long and came to a point where his nostrils flared slightly, and his brows were shaped in a way that made his gaze piercing. He always appeared either angry or extremely focused. His lips were those of a pouty child and they were rather large in proportion to his soft chin.

No, it wasn't that he wasn't attractive, it was the guilt that we were friends under false pretense. If I told him the truth of my plans though, would he understand? Would he even maybe help me?

I couldn't risk telling him. I just needed to keep a sliver of distance between us. I needed him to want more, while balancing the delicate friendship we had created. If I turned him down too harshly or told him the truth, he would stop inviting me to these secret rendezvous and my plans would be ruined. So, I went along with his teasing and heated looks all while reminding him of what a good friend he was to me. And he was. He risked his job to spend time with me. And I risked everything if I didn't tread lightly.

I reached forward and gave his hand a squeeze.

"You're so good to me. Did I ever tell you that?" I asked with a sad sort of smile.

"Every day, baby girl," he replied, pulling me in for a hug over the crate we used as a table. I allowed him to hold me and then quickly pulled back as soon as his grip lightened.

The awkwardness was finally broken when he looked at his watch and said, "Well, I better get you back before they notice you're gone." He sighed deeply as he rose to his feet. As he turned around, I took the opportunity to take out some tightly folded clothes I had been hiding under my baggy shirt and slid them under a dusty shelf. I sat there and waited for him to realize I didn't rise behind him. As Wren turned around, he saw my distraught expression. Head hung low, staring at my hands in my lap.

"Don't be sad, sweetheart." He was insistent on calling me everything *but* my actual name. "I'll come back for you before you know it and I'll let you win every game. Okay?" Nodding, I let him take my hand to pull me up off the dirty floor.

The following morning, after breakfast, I found myself seated in the office of Dr. Aaron Carpenter, as was engraved on the nameplate on the desk before me. He had not yet arrived for our scheduled session so I took the time to observe the room, to distract myself from the jittery chill of anxiousness. Papers and files cluttered his desk along with half-drunk mugs of coffee. The back of a worn leather chair was to a window overlooking the courtyard and was encased in bookshelves. I skimmed over the books only to find they were completely dull and expected. Volumes of medical journals and other psychological research. There were no pictures of family or a single personal item to be found in the entirety of the office. It could have belonged to anyone. An anonymous room where the person residing could be interchanged on a whim. Which I assumed they were since I had never met with Dr. Carpenter before. The door clicked open behind me and a sharp tinge of guilt pricked my skin for spying around his office, even though there was nothing to find.

The warm, welcoming scent of vetiver and coffee, along with something else I couldn't quite discern, engulfed the small space as Dr. Carpenter strode into the room with not even so much as a look of acknowledgement in my direction. He held a steaming mug in one hand. His face buried in a book.

No, not a book. A journal. My journal. The one my lead psychiatrist gave me upon arrival here. Standard protocol, he had said. Everyone got one to write in that any member of the resident's team could look through at any time. It was intended to be a type of diary, but mine was mostly filled with sketches, poems, and random quotes. All meant to appease the doctors with my participation while never giving any real insight.

Without being told, I moved out from behind his desk and took a seat.

"This is quite good," he said as he approached the desk. I was taken aback as he looked up at me. He seemed rather young to be a doctor. At least, much younger than the ones I had previously met with. His skin was still smooth with youth. His hair, full and without a trace of gray.

"Excuse me?" Not sure what he was referring to, my journal or the mug of coffee he seemed to worship before him. He responded by handing me my journal on the page he was viewing. There laid an all too familiar sketch. One I drew several times over through the years and couldn't let go of: the image of a queen or a goddess. I still hadn't decided. Crystals adorned her long wavy hair like raindrops and a gown flowed over her figure in cascading silk. She was a character from my dreams that always brought me a sense of calm and comfort as I drew her. On the adjacent page, quotes and lines from Robert Frost were scribbled.

"Oh. Thanks, I guess," I replied and handed the journal back to him. Most people would be embarrassed to have a stranger reading through something so personal. I had no such luxury here.

"Did you sleep well last night?" he asked, looking me over.

"Yes," I lied. Though I suspected the darkened circles under my eyes and the pale pallor of my skin gave me away. However, I wasn't about to tell him I'd been up all-night playing cards with an orderly. He stared directly at me with an evaluating gaze as if reading the lies written on my face. For a moment I thought he would call me out on my bluff. Instead, he abruptly stood from his desk, causing me to flinch, and walked over to a file cabinet.

"I want to show you something," he said as he withdrew a small wrinkled paper from the cabinet and handed it to me.

"I've been advised not to show you this, but I think you have a right to see it." I took the paper from him with a perplexed crease in my brow. "As it is yours, after all."

I read with shaking hands. Never before had I seen the damning letter yet, it was to be my noose, my smoking gun. The piece of evidence that would, without a doubt, proclaim my guilt.

My suicide note.

Discovered by police in the same bedroom that James and I had been found. I had been told of its existence but was never allowed to see it for myself. Until now. My lawyer and psychiatric team feared I would have some kind of outlandish, feminine breakdown, if I read it.

It appeared to have been written hastily. The script, light and loopy. I had thought the words would spark recollection of what happened that night. But nothing stirred as I scanned over the generic and almost cliché writing—the wording foreign to me. The letter told the story of a scorned lover whose insecurities and jealousy drove her to kill a man she felt she was losing her hold on. Apparently, I thought James would break up with me and I was suffering from the whole, "If I can't have him no one can" melodrama. Yet, there were no deep feelings I could identify within the writing. The confession was bland and emotionless.

"How do you feel reading this for the first time?" Dr. Carpenter asked as he started back toward his desk.

"A little confused to be honest. This writing doesn't sound like me and I can't imagine myself wanting any harm to come to James." Or wanting anyone to die over something as petty as jealousy. I slid the letter back onto the desk but instead of taking it he brought my journal forward, lining it up beside the letter.

"Anything else?" he questioned.

A little confused why he was asking, but curious, I read over the letter, and the random words from my journal, again. The crease in my brow deepened. I couldn't believe what I was seeing and that I didn't notice it at first. It was wrong. The whole letter was wrong. The words were not words I would typically use and the a's—I had a very unique way of writing my a's, but the a's in the letter were the standard, common kind with a tail. I never wrote my lowercase a's with a tail but instead with a hook over top. As could be seen in the journal.

"This wasn't me," I said softly, sliding the letter closer toward his end of the table. Then with more conviction I looked him in the eyes, I found, already trained on me. "I didn't write this letter!"

Chapter Three

THE REST OF THE day I felt the shaking tension of anxiety tighten around my bones. Our session ended shortly after I exclaimed that the letter was not mine. Dr. Aaron Carpenter kept my journal, for now, but he did not confirm whether he believed me or not. Just simply stated that he would look into it for my sake. I guess he was attempting to be neutral since he was my psychologist and not my lawyer.

Or maybe he thought I was suffering with a case of denial.

That simpleminded, backwoods lawyer!

He didn't even think to have the handwriting evaluated. Since I had no money, he was court appointed to me and, from our previous conversations, I got the feeling he truly thought I was guilty to some degree. My hands tingled as I paced back and forth in my room—though it was more like a cell. My body screamed for me to run, to do something. I couldn't sit by and let a broken legal system destroy my life more than it already had. There was no doubt in my mind that I did not hurt James in any way, let alone kill him. And now I was furious that I was led to consider otherwise.

The clock on my time here was ticking down and I knew the end had come sooner than I originally anticipated. I wasn't going to wait any longer for my lawyer, or the staff of doctors leading my evaluation to help me. I had no faith in their competency. If anyone had a shred of intelligence in them, it was Dr. Carpenter for noticing the difference in handwriting before anyone else. But he was just a resident psychologist aiding in my evaluation—not the final say. Nor did I even know if he believed me or would help my case. No. I needed to take action if I wanted to have the final say in how my story played out.

I lifted a corner of the fitted sheet on my too thin bed to reveal a small slit in the mattress's seam. Digging my finger into the small slit I coaxed out four yellow and white capsules, methodically emptied their powdered contents into a used candy wrapper, and rolled the open end closed before placing it into my ill-fitted bra. Then, I raised the mattress up to remove the winnings—from playing cards with Wren—that were taped to the bottom, before placing them in my sock. Then, with a racing mind, I laid down and waited on the worn mattress, knowing sleep would not come that night.

I prayed and begged for Wren to come to my room, for time to speed up and release me from its slow torture. My heart raced. Every ounce of my being wanted to run, to move, to do something other than lay here on my bed and wait. Several times I thought of trying to beat the locked door down, or rip the bars off the window, but it would be fruitless and cause unwanted attention, possibly adding extra security that I worked so hard to keep at a minimum. Instead, I sat on the edge of my bed, bouncing my legs and kneading my hands.

Just as I thought I was going to rub my flesh raw; a soft click came from the entry to my cell and a familiar face peeked around the corner. It took everything in me not to leap up and hug Wren in grateful relief. But I didn't need to, he could see the worry etched on my face.

"Rough day, kitten?" he asked with a mock pout.

"You could say that," I replied with a sigh, rising to follow him out into the hall.

Upon entering the old, moldy supply room—that no one during the night shift seemed to use—I quickly snatched a random dusty item from the shelf by the door and hid it behind my back. It felt cylindrical and slightly weighted in my hand. Before we sat down around our makeshift crate table that laid on the cold floor, I tucked the item into my waistband and pulled the hem of my shirt over it, seamlessly. As I sat, I made a silent wish, that everything would go smoothly.

Halfway through his shuffling of cards, Wren sighed and looked up at me with a focused force. A small grin tipped the corner of his lips.

"There's something I've been meaning to tell you, Alise," he said. I stiffened at the sudden, unusual use of my actual name. Frozen, I waited for his response, hoping my reaction didn't show.

"We've met before," he continued.

"We . . . we have?" I sputtered. "When?" Hoping I hadn't greatly offended him for not realizing it myself.

"At the university's library last year." He smiled, possibly sensing my embarrassment. "You wouldn't have remembered. We bumped into each other. You were distracted, talking to James and almost dropped your books when you walked straight into me. Don't worry," he continued, noticing the cringe in my expression, "you weren't rude or anything and it was brief. I didn't expect you to remember. But, that day, you were the most beautiful thing I'd ever seen and I knew I'd never forget you."

I was instantly filled with shock at his confession.

"You can imagine how surprised I was to see you here, that day in the courtyard, when you tried to bum a smoke off of me." He chuckled, lightly. In truth, I didn't ask him for a cigarette, because I did not, in fact, smoke them, but I did remember him approaching me in those early morning hours, most likely at the end of his shift, offering me one that I refused. As he went to walk away, I told him he could sit by me while he smoked and we talked for, what I thought, was the first time. That was the start of this delicate balance we had. It wasn't long after those early morning conversations that he started sneaking me out of my quarters at night to play games and drink in this very room. This whole time I thought I had been the one to seek him out, but it turned out it was him who sought me out first all along. I felt a little stupid, but relieved that it worked out in my favor.

"I'm so sorry I didn't recognize you, Wren," I said as he dealt out our cards. "You must think I'm such a snob."

"Not at all, darling. A pretty thing like you couldn't possibly remember a dull guy like me." Half of the time I couldn't take what came out of his mouth seriously. He was such a flirt. He then produced a whiskey bottle from within his jumpsuit and poured each of us a cup.

"Not drinking from the bottle tonight?" I teased back.

"Thought I'd class things up a bit." He threw me a sly grin from across the crate. I chuckled at the ridiculousness of considering sipping whiskey from paper cups while sitting on a hard, cold floor as "classy."

"No hard feelings, darling, fate has once again brought us together." He really was ridiculous and almost charming.

"Cheers," we toasted, tapping together our paper cups. I tried not to spill as I sipped from behind a forced smile.

Midway through our game and conversation, the slight warmth from the whiskey faded as quickly as it came. The realization that I needed to make my move now, before time ran out, sobered me to action. With Wren's focus buried deep in his hand of cards I discreetly removed the item hidden in my waistband and slowly lowered it to the floor. Holding my breath, I rolled the item hard across the floor towards the door where it slammed with a noticeable thud. Wren's head jerked up. Shock lit up his eyes as they grew wide.

"W—what was that?" I asked with feigned caution. Doing my best to copy his own expression. "Did you lock the door?" I fearfully whispered.

"Shit." He stood up on slightly unsteady feet to check.

In seconds I removed the wrapper from my bra and emptied its powdered contents into his cup before he turned back around. He lifted the can I rolled, off the floor and looked at it in confusion. He then placed it back on the shelf by the door.

"No need to fret, love. I think this dusty old fool just fell off the shelf and startled us. Tricky wanker," he drawled as he waved a disapproving finger at the can. He always seemed to start talking like an old British man when he felt the effects of his drink. Another humorous, yet charming, quality.

I sighed in mock relief and giggled at his remark.

It only took a few sips for the sleeping aid to take effect. The alcohol helped too. And in just a few minutes, Wren was laying his head down on the crate, closing his eyes while his words trailed off and died on his lips.

"Wren?" I tested. "Are you drunk, sleepy head?" I reached over the crate and touched his cheek in an attempt to discreetly check his breathing, and to see if he would stir. I ran my fingers through his soft, brown waves in a last attempt to see if he would respond. He was in a deep, restful, medicated sleep. I gently slid my hand down to his chest and, with certain hands, I unclipped his key card from his breast pocket and clutched it tightly.

I rose slowly to my feet, all effects of the whiskey disappearing with a sudden rush of adrenaline. I padded silently around the room to where I had stashed clothes the other night. I placed them in a garbage bag along with the money in my sock and tucked them under a trash bin attached to a discarded janitor's cleaning cart. I inserted a fresh bag around the rim of the bin, concealing the bag of clothing and money below. Taking down a jumpsuit from a hook on the wall, I quickly changed out of my patient clothing. And before rolling the cart out of the room, I grabbed a cap off the shelf and tucked the noticeable ends of my blue-tinted hair into it, pulling the cap down low over my brow.

On a last-minute impulse, I looked in the direction of Wren's peacefully sleeping form and whispered quietly, "Sorry, friend. You really were good to me. Goodbye." And rolled the cart forward, out of the musky supply room and into the first phase of my planned escape.

Chapter Four

THERE WERE BENEFITS TO being a small, unimposing female. One was that I could easily go unnoticed and appear harmless upon first impression. Not to mention, most assumed I was uneducated when they learned about my upbringing, or lack thereof. This was another misconception I used to my advantage, because no one suspected that an orphan from the Pacific Northwest, a flight risk—a troubled child—could find her way into one of the most sought-after universities in the southern United States. In less than a year I managed to gather enough money for books and board, as well as meet the GPA requirements to secure multiple scholarships. But if history was any indicator to the pattern of human behavior, then it was no surprise that they *always* underestimated me.

The security staff were unjustly confident in their safety measures. The building was old and had yet to be outfitted with cameras. Just a guard, at the end of the hall, if he could even rightly be called that, kept post at all hours. Furthermore, areas that only staff had access to, like the pharmaceutical supply room and kitchen, were accessed with a key card that they carried on their person at all times. The cards were nondescript though and all staff seemed to have access to all areas with no hierarchy of clearance.

As I walked past a sleepy-eyed Victor at the guard post I nodded my head low in greeting, concealing most of my face as I used Wren's key card to open the access door to the common area. I held my breath as I walked through the threshold, thinking any second Victor would realize I didn't belong. But, as the door clicked shut behind me, I was greeted with only silence as I exhaled and made my way forward, towards the cafeteria, making sure to empty trash bins into mine along the way. I was almost dizzy with anticipation, my stomach threatening to relinquish every meager drop of alcohol I had consumed. I reached the kitchen access door and swiped Wren's keycard. A green light flashed and the door clicked open. I only needed to steal a knife before I went through the back door and then I would be out of the building.

My breath caught in my throat and my heart stopped as I caught sight of someone in my peripheral. A cook, with his back turned, was washing dishes, including all the knives. Their shining blades glinting on the metal countertop in front of him. I glanced around quickly to see if there were any still in sight but I couldn't hope to be so lucky. There would be no chance of getting a knife unnoticed now. The man was too buried in his task to so much as glance at the janitor who entered, so I cut my losses and continued to the back door as I tossed the stolen key card on the floor.

My intentions were never to get Wren in any kind of trouble, or to incriminate him in any way. I wasn't going to do more damage than had already been done. So, instead of Wren being accused of aiding in the escape of an inmate, he would simply be a sloppy orderly who lost his keycard, that would later be found in the kitchen. With that a loose end was tied and a bridge was burned. I could only hope that Wren wasn't sharp enough to put the pieces of tonight together. Or if he did, he would find it in his heart to forgive me. To understand my desperation and see that I left him without the knowledge of my plan to protect him. Yes, I did use him but there was no going back. Nor was there any regret when it came to the choice of my freedom, my very life, over his sure-to-be-wounded pride.

The cart rolled through the back door that was, as expected, left ajar by a rubber door stop, and I breathed in the night air. A chill ran over my body and my hands shook as I removed the bag of trash from the bin and tied it before throwing it into the dumpster. The pair of orderlies on a smoke break were too immersed in their complaints to pay me any mind. With one last look I turned a sharp corner and pressed my back against the brick exterior of the asylum and waited until I heard the assuring "click" of the back door as the orderlies returned to their duties inside.

Lifting the bag of clothes and money from the bottom of the bin, I tucked it into my jumpsuit before zipping it back up. Around the corner was an unlocked gate. Another unintentional piece of information Wren gave to me during one of our drunken talks. I passed through the gate without hesitation and turned to face the options before me. To the right was the staff parking lot that led out to a road, a road that would lead to a bus stop no more than a few miles down. To the left, were the woods.

My feet charged toward the dark embrace of the forest. When I was just a few steps from the consuming shadows of the trees I let myself run. I ran until that feeling of being watched stopped searing the back of my neck. Ran until I heard the soft rush of a car driving by on the opposite side of the woods—where the road started but couldn't yet be seen.

Even though the cold night air was making me shiver even more than I already was, I quickly stripped off the jumpsuit and changed into the clothes I had stashed in the trash bag. A plain white t-shirt and a forgotten pair of too-large sweatpants that, thankfully, still retained their drawstring. I planned to keep the hat on until I could cut or wash the blue out of my hair and silently cursed myself for my impulsive slip-up. The honey bun was worth it though and I would not regret licking its sweet contents from my fingers. I would never understand why it brought her such joy to watch me go through with it. Perhaps it was the thrill of having control over another human being. Like a master who balanced a treat on their dog's nose and refused them from eating until commanded to do so.

There was no jacket to shield me from the cold. It would have been impossible to conceal anyway, and I would have never been so lucky as to find one in my weeks of scavenging the laundry room on my service days. So, after tucking the money into my shoe, I wrapped my arms around myself and made my way to the road, leaving everything but what was on me, behind.

Never looking back.

When I could see the road through the piney woods, I turned and headed south. Following alongside the road but still remaining concealed by the woods and dark. After walking for what felt like an hour, lights of the bus station illuminated ahead. It wasn't until then that I decided it was safe to step out from the tree's protective cover.

It was colder than I anticipated and it did nothing for my already shaking hands. I could see my breath in the air as I took big, slow breaths to tamp down the adrenaline in my veins. Though the darkness of night was my friend, I never wanted the warmth of the morning sun more in my entire life. It must have been close to 5 a.m. In just a few hours, the orderlies would make their rounds to let inmates and patients out of their cells and would notice I was gone. It would be several more hours, maybe even a day, until Wren would wake from his sleep and realize what I had done. A sharp blade of guilt and the finality of everything cut into my lungs. Or maybe it was just the icy night air as I approached the mostly stagnant bus station.

Despite a few cars in the parking lot, no one seemed to be there beyond the attendant at the window. With the cash in my shoe, I bought a ticket for the longest route I could afford, making sure to tip my hat low. I had just enough left over for a bottle of water and muffin from the vending machine. I didn't have much of a plan after this. When the bus route ended, I would have to get off.

All I knew for certain was I wanted to bite into the earth, consume life, and drink freedom like I never had before. It was all I had ever wanted and it was so close to finally being mine.

Maybe I would find somewhere to work. Where I could get paid under the table and make enough cash to get a plane ticket out of the country. Or maybe I would find a small remote town in the mountains to live alone and unbothered for the rest of my life. I tried not to dwell too much in the excitement of hope as I stared out the window of the moving bus. I had been the first to board, allowing me to hide my face from the rest of the passengers by leaning my head against the bus's tinted window. Not daring to look toward any of them. My heart lurched forward as the bus pulled away from the station and a small amount of tension left my shoulders with each crackle of gravel under the tires.

As several miles passed and the sun made its slow appearance on the horizon, I realized how bone-achingly tired I had become. Most likely, coming down from the surge of adrenaline. I fought a yawn and tried my best to keep my traitorously heavy eyelids open. Just as I started drifting into that realm between sleeping and wakefulness, I felt the heavy weight of something soft laid over me. Its warmth brought a small smile to my lips as I inhaled the scent of vetiver and coffee and . . .

Chapter Five

E YES FLYING OPEN, I twisted my head to the side to see a verdant gaze staring back at me. Lips pressed into an angry thin line and wavy, tawny hair. My mouth opened in horror to speak, to give an excuse for why I was there—anything—but nothing came out. Instead that cold, hard, glare froze me solid as he hissed, "If you don't want to be turned into the police, I advise you keep quiet and do exactly as I say."

With that, I clamped my mouth shut. Change of plans, this was a very large, very unexpected obstacle, and if I was going to navigate my way around it, I would have to be smart. *Think, think*, I told myself. *Find a window of opportunity and take back control as soon as you can.*

His eyes roamed over me and down to the jacket he had draped over my lap. "Put it on," Dr. Carpenter commanded.

I did as he instructed, knowing most of the time, it was better not to fight back when you weren't in the position of power. Not until you could regain it.

"How did you recognize me?" I murmured as I shuffled into the oversized blazer. He scoffed at my apparently ridiculous question.

"I'm no idiot," he huffed, facing forward and crossing his arms over his chest, a slight scowl still on his face. I thought I had concealed my face and hair completely. My fingers grazed the caps rim as I felt for loose strands. There was no telling what other staff members were on this bus and who else might have recognized me.

"We're getting off at the first stop," he continued. Feeling my plan fall apart and every tiny ounce of control over my life slip away, I retorted back without thought.

"I'm not—" but before I could finish, he swiftly turned and clutched my wrist, pulling me closer to him, as he spoke so softly and cruelly into my ear.

"You have found yourself in quite the predicament, Miss Fox, and you are in no position to be making demands or rejecting requests. Until then, you will do exactly as I say." Just as quickly, he released me. The heat of his grip still throbbed on my wrist. I rubbed at the lingering warmth while inhaling a deep breath, refusing to look at him while I collected myself. Who was this man? His demeanor was so different from the gentle, curious psychologist from our session. Never could I have anticipated this kind of menacing dominance from him.

The rest of the journey felt as quick as a heartbeat while thoughts and scenarios raced through my head. Ones of me running, fighting, making a scene—anything to get away from him and to take back the upper hand. All ended in me being arrested by the police, or worse. There was no lie, no twist I could come up with in that moment to get me out of this scenario. And when the bus came to a stop, jolting me out of my dizzying haze, I felt the man beside me stand and offer his hand as he said to me, "This is our stop."

He noticed my hesitation and began to loosen my sweaty grip on the arm rest one finger at a time and pulled me up from my seat. As he dragged me down the aisle by the hand, I kept my gaze down toward my feet as I shuffled behind him. The bus had stopped at a rather obscure location. A simple bench lit by a single lamp post on a road to nowhere. The only thing to be seen was a desolate two-way fenced in by the surrounding forest. Sentinel pines watched over us as they towered high above.

The bus doors closed and the vehicle pulled away and off down the long stretch of pavement and into the early promise of morning—along with all my hopes. Once the bus was out of sight Dr. Carpenter released my hand and before he could face me to give his instructions, I took my chance and bolted toward the darkness of the tree line.

If I could just get into the dense forest, I could run until I found a place to hide. I was stealthy and fast. The woods were my beacon. The thick brush was as familiar to me as if it were my own home. How many times had the wilderness offered me safety as a child? Whether to play or hide in—to escape the monsters of my harsh reality or to play with the imaginings of my fantasies. My heart leaped as I crossed the invisible border into the tree line. No sounds of pursuit from behind.

Keep running. Keep running. Keep running. I commanded my legs with each heartbeat. I only spared a quick glance over my shoulder to confirm I was alone. Clumsily, I tripped over a root, causing myself to fall to my hands and knees. Without hesitation I crawled behind a large pine and scurried up the trunk to a standing position. My back pressed against rough bark, head lifted to the canopy as I reeled in my rapid breaths. When the thrumming of blood in my ears finally subsided enough to hear more clearly, I carefully slid to the side, glancing around the tree to the direction I came from. Still, no one in sight. No sound of crunching leaves or footsteps to be heard.

A high-pitched yelp escaped me. Dr. Carpenter stood in front of me, only a hair's breadth away. Arm braced beside my head. My heart fluttered like a caged bird. Startled by his sudden appearance, I willed my knees not to give beneath me. While my brow glistened with effort from my escape, his was dry as a bone. He didn't even pant from exertion, as I was.

Without wearing a doctor's coat or jacket, which still draped my slim shoulders, I could see more of his build. He was surprisingly fit. Hard muscles corded his forearms, exposed by his rolled-up shirt sleeves and the fabric tugged tight from the broadness of his chest as he pinned me in a cage of arms against the tree. He was much taller than myself, though most were compared to my below-average stature. His head lowered to look down at me, his hair a plethora of golden tones. Somewhere between wet sand and sunshine. It was disheveled from the chase. His stare, predatory. It was impossible to believe this was the same man in the hospital who complimented my drawings and gave me soft pitying smiles during our session. It seemed I had completely underestimated and misjudged him. How did he remain out of sight? How did I not hear his footsteps following behind?

"Please. Don't run from me again." He grabbed my wrist and dragged me out of the shelter of the woods, back towards the road. This time he didn't let go. After we reached the road's edge and were back under the light of the lamp post, he turned toward me. I flinched in reaction to his touch but he simply reached out to tuck a loose strand of blue hair into my cap. His touch was surprisingly soft for how infuriated he must have been with me. Then without a word, he turned back around facing the road.

We stood in silence for a long moment and just as I was going to ask him what we were waiting for, a truck appeared on the horizon. Dr. Carpenter stuck his hand out in the universal signal used for hitching a ride. I figured there was no way the vehicle would stop for two random people on the side of the road in the early morning hours. But I was proven wrong as brakes squealed to a stop beside us and the driver rolled down his passenger window.

"What is a pair of kids like y'all doing way out here?" the wrinkled and sun-worn man asked. The smell of stale cigarettes wafted from his vehicle. His grin was stained, but friendly. As were his brown, crinkled, eyes.

Like a performer on cue, Dr. Carpenter smiled a toothy grin dripping in charm as he leaned into the open window frame.

"Morning, sir. My wife and I missed our bus. The next one isn't for hours and this ole girl here is already exhausted from our journey," he drawled so casually as if he were one of the locals himself. Was he? I wondered while sneering at the back of his head.

Wife indeed.

"Is that so?" the driver asked, looking us over.

No! No! It's not! I wanted to scream before thinking better of it. Dr. Carpenter could easily have told the truth and had the man contact the police, but he didn't. If I protested now, he would have every motivation to reveal me.

Concern laced the driver's eyes as he looked over me and to Dr. Carpenter's hand wrapped around my wrist. Seeming to notice the man's attention, Dr. Carpenter swiftly pulled me toward him as he wrapped the same arm around my tiny waist. Practically consuming me whole against him. I believed he found me smaller than he first assumed under all the ill fitted clothing.

"Yes, sir," Dr. Carpenter replied with that easy smile. "We would be eternally grateful if you could give us a ride."

"Where y'all headed?" the older man asked. Taking that as an invitation, my captor opened the passenger door and slid me in, onto the bench seat.

"Just a few miles south to the preserve, if you don't mind," he said as he climbed in and closed the door to the cabin. "Thank you so much for helping us out, sir," he continued, speaking over my head to the driver.

I was starting to feel a little more than annoyed at being treated as though I wasn't even present in the truck while Dr. Carpenter and the driver spoke on the trip to this preserve. Turns out the man's name was R.J. of all things and he loved to talk about his grandbabies. Dr. Carpenter encouraged him with dozens of questions about them and his line of work. He was, in fact, a day laborer, as I suspected by the worn look of his hands and the grease stains on his jeans. A kind of do-it-all handyman.

At some point in their conversation, I spaced out, staring at the road ahead. Counting the lamp posts. I had counted thirty-two since departing from the bus stop. If I could keep count of them all until we reached our destination, then maybe I could back-track my way to the bus stop. That was if I could get away from Dr. Carpenter successfully. Which seemed unlikely at this point. Now that I got a good look at him, I knew I couldn't fight him off or outrun him. And I used all my money for the first ticket I had bought.

How would I get back on another bus?

I thought to plead with the man driving us. To tell him I was kidnapped and that I didn't know my captor. But that would lead to the cops being called or worse, Dr. Carpenter would retort my claim and R.J. would believe him over me. I was fuming in my seat with frustration. Once again there was no scenario that ended in my favor and I was starting to feel like an idiot for attempting to run so soon—for showing my hand too early. I would get no leniency from Dr. Carpenter. He would be on alert from now on, watching me like a hawk with that predatory stare.

Lost in my task of counting lamp posts and turns, I barely registered we had stopped.

One hundred sixty-two. Right, right, left.

My faux husband had already exited the truck and was offering his hand to help me out. I didn't take it as I slid out and leapt down on the gravel path. The path wound into a state park with cleared underbrush and a small wood cabin with a sign reading, "Visitor Center," nailed to its exterior.

"Take care of yourself," the man shouted from the vehicle before taking off back down the road. Dr. Carpenter waved farewell. But, as soon as the driver was out of sight, he grabbed my wrist again and dragged me behind him down a dirt path.

"You don't have to drag me along everywhere like a child," I protested.

"Don't I?" he countered.

After only a few moments of following the path Dr. Carpenter made a sharp turn off into the forest. All the while pulling me behind like a horse being led by the reins. As the sun rose higher so did the temperature and I found myself uncomfortable in more ways than one. I had an unrelenting need to get his jacket off. I tried to jerk my arm free from his grip just to have him turn on his heels and scowl at me.

"I'm hot," I protested as I yanked my wrist free. I slid the blazer off, wrapped it around my waist and matched his glare with my own defiant one. He stood there staring, his scowl searing me as harshly as the sun, before deciding to continue onward. This time not reaching for my wrist. It felt oddly bare without the vise of his fingers wrapped around it.

"Let's go," he commanded over his shoulder. "We still have a ways to go until we reach our destination and I'll advise you not to attempt to flee again."

With a grunt I begrudgingly followed him deeper into the woods. We weren't following any noticeable path and the brush only got thicker and more tangled the further we traveled. Where was he taking me? And what for? Was he going to hurt me? Kill me? Or worse. Make me do something I didn't want in exchange for him not turning me in? The fear of the questions made my feet stop in his wake. I bit my lip, wondering if I should attempt to run again or if that would just make him more upset with me. If he did have ill intentions, then I needed him to see me as a person. To sway his better nature toward that of compassion.

"Where are we going?" I asked, wearily, hand twisting the sleeves of his blazer that hugged my waist. He stopped and looked over his shoulder toward me.

"Somewhere safe."

Safe for him or safe for me? I wondered.

"You can understand why I am hesitant to trust you right?" I questioned again, unable to move.

Of all the responses he could have given me, he gave the least expected. He chuckled—a deep soft rumble in his throat followed by a sigh.

"I can't imagine why you wouldn't trust me when you're the accused criminal who ran away," he smirked.

"Then why didn't you turn me in? Right then and there? I've no choice but to assume you're planning to use it against me in some way. Probably to get what you want from me, only turning me in once you're done. Am I right?" I said with arms crossed over my chest. I was ready to run again. Ready to fight. Whatever I needed to do. Even if it meant my life instead of the violation of my body, if that was the case.

His amusement turned to a sneer of disgust as he took in the implications of my words.

"No. I'm not going to use it against you, Miss Fox. And I would never use someone in the way you are implying. For you to assume so is insulting." Heat bloomed on my cheeks that wasn't from the sun.

Well, that's reassuring, I guess.

"Now may we continue? We have a long way to go, and I'd like to get there before noon." I noticed the local drawl he used on the ride here was gone and was now replaced by a slight accent I couldn't quite put my finger on. He continued on as he headed forward without looking back at me. I quickly scrambled to keep up with his long strides.

Chapter Six

A**S THE EARLY MORNING** grew into late, I was grateful for my earlier purchase of the water bottle. After taking a gulp I offered it to Aaron in an attempt to appease, but he shook his head in refusal. Fine, let him dehydrate. We trekked for several hours through uncleared terrain. Though I was starting to feel fatigued from lack of sleep, I didn't dare ask for a break. I needed to save my favors for later, after I won Aaron over some and convinced him I wasn't going to run again. Then I could use whatever leniency he granted me to my advantage.

We entered an area where the brush grew thinner and the trees were more spaced out. Pine needles and moss muffled our steps and tall, branched birch trees towered overhead. I could see further ahead to a drooping slope. As if noticing where my attention strayed, Aaron instructed, "When we descend the slope be cautious. It can be slippery. Use the branches to help you."

My eyes rolled at his assumption that I had never hiked uncleared terrain before and hence had no idea what I was doing and needed his advice, let alone help.

Men.

When we reached the crest of the slope, I saw a shape in the distance. A small cabin, enclosed by maple and pine, laid in wait in the valley below.

"Is that where we are staying?" I asked.

"Yes," he said before descending down toward the valley. His sure steps, annoyingly effortless.

The cabin reminded me of a place my body had long forgotten but my mind and heart never could. A little hidden treasure in the woods, away from the world and all its harsh realities. At the thought I felt slightly giddy, almost forgetting I was dragged here against my will by a mere stranger.

Almost.

The descent was easy enough and at one point I caught Aaron giving me a side-eyed look of surprise at my ease. The rest of the way to the cabin I made sure to walk beside him. No longer behind.

When we entered the cabin, the first thing I noticed was how quaint it was. The space only contained one room with everything visible upon entering. There was also only one bed. As if noticing where my gaze had gone, Aaron said I could have the bed and he would take the couch that sat across from the fireplace.

"I'll be on watch most of the night anyways," he reasoned. "Bathroom is through that door." He gestured with his chin. And just like that he was out the door we entered, leaving me alone in the cozy interior, but he didn't go far. I saw him pass by each window as he encased the perimeter, like a wolf prowling about their territory. A few hours later he brought in firewood while I rummaged through the cupboards, but he didn't say a word before leaving again.

There was a well-stocked pantry of nonperishables, but only eggs and butter in the small fridge. The kitchen had all the basics needed to cook a meal and no frills or gadgets to make it easier. There were men's clothes in a dresser by the bed. All seemed rather too large for myself and I pouted at the thought of having to wear the stolen, and already dirty, clothes I had on for the duration of this visit.

How long would we be here anyways? For only a short time or indefinitely? I shook the thought from my head. I would be here for as long as I determined. Until I was able to escape, successfully.

The irony did not evade me that I quite literally escaped one prison just to find myself in a new one, the very same day. But at least this one was more pleasant than the former and mostly solitary, excluding my captor.

I made my way to the bathroom. One toothbrush lay by the sink and one towel hung on the rack by the tiny curtained shower. There was a narrow, slim window at the top of the wall connected to the shower. Far too small for me to shimmy through.

A thought occurred to me. Was someone, the good Dr. Aaron Carpenter perhaps, already living here? Or was our arrival somehow planned or anticipated? Surely kidnapping me wasn't planned. He couldn't have possibly known when I was planning to escape for I did not know it myself, let alone that I had plans to at all. No dust or musky smell was found upon my observation of the cabin and everything was in such an organized state it made the space feel unlived in but well kept. Nothing was tossed aside or out of place. There were no wet towels on the floor or bed left unmade. It made it impossible to tell if the dwelling was regularly inhabited or not. Not a single sentimental item on the fireplace mantle or even a framed picture. Who did this cabin belong to? And what was it doing hidden deep in government owned land? To be honest, I wasn't sure if we were even inside the boundaries of the state park anymore.

Outside the kitchen window was the most welcoming view. A wall of mature pines and maples clustered together. Cardinals and robins danced with each other from branch to branch. The brush was thinner this time of year from the cold nights and comfortably warm days. Thus, more of the forest could be seen beyond. If it wasn't for the fact I was brought here against my will, I might have said I found my place. This little cabin in the woods, away from any large cities where I could start over in anonymity, was quiet, secluded, and peaceful. A strange paradox to my actual situation. It was perfect, yet the circumstances were not.

That evening I heated up some soup I found in the cupboard and left a bowl out for Aaron. Still trying to get on his good side for my own sake. My first prerogative was to convince him I had no intentions of running again. In the meantime, I had enough motivation to stay. As long as we were out here, hidden, then I was safe from being found by the authorities. At the least, I was given time to develop a new plan. Maybe I could find a way to work out a deal with Aaron. Where I could stay here in secrecy, but in exchange for what? Besides the usual thing men always wanted from women, which Aaron made clear on the way here he would not want from me, what else could I barter with? I had literally nothing but the clothes on my back.

We had barely spoken all day. Aaron came and went from the cabin like a haunting spirit. If it wasn't for the fact that the cabin was so small, and technically only one room, I never would have known he came at all. Everything he touched, everything he used, he put exactly back in its place. Looking as though it was never used or touched in the first place. No remnants of pressed lips lingered on glasses or water splashes on counter tops. He was painstakingly clean and organized, whereas I was not.

My mind didn't want to sleep but my body begged for rest as I crawled into the cold bed. I let my thoughts plot and plan and scheme while my eyes fluttered shut and my body melted into the flannel sheets. I had no idea if Aaron ever came back inside or not to sleep that night. But the entire time I sensed his presence. An annoying itch on my skin I couldn't scratch. A constant tickle of hair on my neck, causing me to startle every time I edged closer to sleep. I could feel the weight and pressure of the anxiety I had been dodging all day since he ruined my plans. It would only be a matter of time before it burst forth from its confines. Until then my muscles tensed and my jaw clenched until it stifled the worry enough to sleep.

The next day I talked Aaron into letting me forage. With his supervision of course. But foraging for mushrooms and berries wasn't my true motive. I needed an opportunity to survey the area. To search for a path or stream that I could follow later, when I found the opportunity. As we traveled past ancient trees covered in soft green and brown moss my eyes focused on the ground looking for edible plants to collect and a path to retrace. Meanwhile, Aaron's gaze focused only on me—burrowing holes into the back of my head and shooting arrows down my back. Worried he may realize what I was actually doing, I decided to try and distract him, disarm him even, with questions.

"Where are you from?" I started with.

"Far from here," he answered curtly. Clearly not interested in talking.

Ignoring his tone, I continued, unphased.

"Are you from a different state or country?" Bending down I inspected a cluster of mushrooms growing on the side of an oak. Oyster mushrooms by the look of their white caps and short stems. Safe to eat.

"Why do you ask?" Clearly attempting to divert my questions with his own.

"It's your accent. It's faint but I noticed it the other day. I can't quite place it." I pondered while gently breaking off a few mushrooms to place in the bowl I had brought for just that purpose. When I stood, I faced him with all the patience I could muster, making it clear I was waiting for an answer. With a sigh, he wearily rubbed the back of his neck.

"My family was from a small village on the outskirts of France," he rushed the words before crossing his arms over his broad chest. "No more questions, okay?" he asked, eyebrow raised.

Humming, I tapped my fingers on my chin in mocked contemplation. "No deal," I sang, and continued further into the woods.

A resolute sigh and reluctant footsteps followed me.

"Do you visit your family often?" Not bothering to face him. Since he was behind me, he couldn't see my fingers silently mark another yard counted from the cabin. Twelve so far.

Before me a bush of white flowers and jagged leaves accented with red clusters of berries appeared. A stream of light from a gap in the canopy shone down upon it like a beacon.

Baneberry.

Poisonous.

A morbidly wretched idea struck me. Perhaps I could roast and grind them into Aaron's frequently needed coffee grounds. Not enough to kill but to make him sick enough to open up a window of escape in which he would be too weak to chase. Though his eyes were constantly upon me, most likely he wouldn't know they were poisonous, as it was not common knowledge, and I could slip a few clusters into my basket. I reached out toward the ruby hued berries as I made to snap a bunch from its stem.

"Not those." A hand came to rest upon my shoulder before turning me around. "This way." He beckoned with a tilt of his head. Maybe he was on to me and deserved more credit than I gave him when it came to being observant. I reluctantly followed as he threw me off course, headed north now instead of east. Feeling defeated and wondering if I would have a chance to sneak out and find the bush again, I dared to ask another question.

"How come you don't visit your family?"

"Next question," he replied without hesitation.

When I finally caught up to walk beside him, I glanced quickly at his profile. He kept his eyes forward. An emotionless mask.

"I ask because I don't have a family of my own. I would like to think that if I did, I would be with them as much as possible." Sharing a piece of myself in hopes he'd open up. It occurred to me that he might have already known though. He was the psychologist assigned to my case, after all. He had access to my file which was certain to hold all my records and housing history. The several foster homes and group homes I ran away from. Every time I was arrested for a fight I hadn't started or petty theft. Honestly, I didn't have any new information to offer him that he didn't, most likely, already know. But he was such a mystery to me. I continued to scan the fields and trees looking for more edible forage, counting my steps, anything to keep from looking at Aaron's face and the look of pity that was sure to be there.

"I know," he whispered back. I felt his stare burn into me. "What does *hiraeth* mean to you?"

Looking over my shoulder, I faced him, surprised, yet, not sure what he was asking me. Noting my questioning stare, he clarified.

"I saw you had written it in the journal you kept at the hospital."

"It means to miss a place you cannot return to. A home that is gone or never existed at all." His silence told me to continue. "It is a way I've always felt. Even

48

before my parents died. I would draw pictures of fantastical lands and write childish stories, where people could talk to the animals. I know it was silly and just childhood imagination, but a part of me misses that world I built in my mind. I always wished it was real and that I could live there, instead of here." I gauged his reaction, certain he would think me ridiculous.

"But it is just a feeling. I had to face the reality that there is no home for me. Not anymore, and I can never go back to the one I once had," I exhaled deeply. Attempting to shed the weight of truth those words held.

"Is that why you took me? Because you knew no one, beyond the authorities, would be looking for me? That no one would miss me?" I swallowed hard, cramming the hurt of disappointment into an already too full pit, deep inside.

Aaron looked down at me, stunned, as if he were insulted again by my assumptions. But in a blink the emotionless mask slid back in place and he changed course again. Continuing to trek forward into the woods.

"It is not as you think," he threw over his shoulder.

"Then explain it to me. Help me understand," I demanded as I, once again, was forced to follow after him like a puppy.

"I don't fully understand it myself." And without another word he headed in a beeline back to the cabin only looking over his shoulder a few times to make sure I wasn't far behind.

Chapter Seven

THE FOLLOWING DAYS MELTED together. In fact, I was starting to lose track of time, altogether. Was it Monday or Wednesday? Did it rain yesterday or three days ago? Aaron must have been sneaking off to the store while I slept because every other morning I would wake to a replenished refrigerator and cabinet of food—new boxes of tea or a fresh jar of honey. In an attempt to confirm my suspicions and find a window of opportunity, I stayed up through all hours of the night waiting for him to leave; staring him down as he read on the couch by the fire until my eyes became heavy with sleep. Only to wake up the next morning with a dozen fresh eggs or loaf of bread, waiting for me. Cursing myself over cups of hot tea, as I was starting to suspect the cabin was enchanted.

"What are you reading?" I asked from my nestled spot on the bed.

"Just a bit of fiction," he mumbled, waving me off. I huffed out an exasperated sigh of boredom.

I had found some paper and pencils in a drawer and was sketching the scene before me. I sketched to keep my mind and hands busy. To keep paranoid thoughts and restlessness at bay. Papers lay scattered on the small night stand. Random musings of birds, flowers, the cabin, anything I saw and observed, that I had tried to recreate onto paper. The pencils were not artist grade graphite, but they worked just fine.

Blowing a stray hair out of my eyes, I attempted to capture the highlights of flame in Aaron's hair. Antique gold, brass, and bronze intermixed, bringing forth the gold highlights in his pine green eyes. If only I had colored pencils, I could capture the hues as well. I couldn't deny my subject was handsome, even beautiful, in some ways. I shook the foggy, confusing thought loose. To start thinking like that was dangerous.

"Where does the food come from?" An attempt to redirect my train of thoughts.

"The store," he answered. Again, eyes never leaving his book.

"Obviously," I huffed in frustration.

"Then why ask?" he countered, only building my frustration.

Eraser dust fell away with the brush of my hand.

"I meant if you are here the whole time, then how is there new food in the refrigerator when I wake in the morning?" I was baiting him, trying to get him to confirm what I already suspected.

To my annoyance, he answered, "Magic."

A mock laugh huffed out of my lungs, finally drawing his attention away from his book. His focus challenged me from across the room. *Was that an attempt at humor?*

"Would you rather know the truth or have food to eat?"

"Why can't I have both?" I crossed my arms over my chest in defiance.

"I would think you, of all people, would know by now, Miss Fox, that we cannot have everything we want from life."

"It's Alise," I insisted. The formality like nails on a chalkboard to my senses.

"And actually," I continued, raising to my knees on the firm bed, the hem of an oversized tee shirt I had changed into skimmed just above them—"I'm pretty sufficient at getting what I want."

Aaron's evaluating stare roamed over me—from my face to my knees and back again.

"I'm sure you are." Sarcasm dripped from his tongue. He returned to his reading and I collapsed in defeat, turning my focus to the moonlit woods from the window beside me.

"Read to me," I requested. An eyebrow arched perfectly over his gaze in response.

"Like a child?"

My eyes stared back at him, waiting. As did his. But I refused to cave so easily.

"Come here." He beckoned with the curl of his fingers. Giddiness at my victory, yet suspicion at the ease of his surrender to my request caused butterflies to flap in my chest. I eased off the bed and padded across the cold floor. I sank deep into the cushions and wrapped a worn, fleece blanket around my shoulders, waiting for him to start. Instead, a pressing stare greeted me, as if I were a talking toad that came to perch beside him.

"What?"

"Care to exercise your manners?" he asked.

I sighed deeply. How many small victories was I willing to hand over for my purposes?

"I'll wait." Calm expectancy laced his tone. Clearly, he was more practiced in patience than I was.

My options were to contend to his strange insistence on manners, or crawl back into bed and miss the opportunity to catch him sneaking out tonight. Swallowing my pride, I gave him what he wanted.

"Please," I all but whispered.

"That's a good girl," he chuckled. "That wasn't so hard now, was it?"

"Shut up." My socked foot playfully kicked his leg. I couldn't understand why my face felt hot. Perhaps it was the proximity to the fireplace and its burning hearth.

"Shut up or read to you? Which is it?"

A grumble of curses fumbled from my mouth as I sunk deeper into the cushions.

"Quite the mouth you have," Aaron muttered through a chuckle and crooked grin, making me want to punch him for looking so charmingly irresistible while teasing me.

"Please, just read before I hit you over the head with that book for being so insufferable."

"Two 'pleases' in less than ten minutes and it's not even my birthday, Miss Fox."

Pulling the blanket over my head, I groaned in annoyance and smothered my growing frustration in darkness and silence. Blocking out how devilishly delicious he looked while entertained at my expense.

A moment later his voice returned in a calm steady pattern as he began to read. I poked my head out from under the blanket and stared at the fire as his lulling rhythmic voice soothed any lingering frustration away. His cadence was almost song-like and I wondered if he could also sing. What it would sound like if he did. If I could ever convince him to, for me.

"I've seen you around before, haven't I?" the tall gorgeous man before me asks—a guitar strapped across his back.

"Probably. I've seen you quite a few times playing out on the lawn to your many adoring fans," I say back, mockingly, as I clasp my hands together while dramatically batting my lashes.

"Oh. Yeah, that," he says uncomfortably rubbing the back of his neck.

I almost laugh at his feigned humility. "I'm sure it's just so unbearable. Having all those girls pine over you."

"I actually don't like the attention to be honest," he retorts, surprising me while looking completely serious. Maybe the humility wasn't fake. "But it's not really beneficial to have stage fright if you're an aspiring artist," he continues with a

grimace. "I'm working on it though. Hence the public practice sessions on the lawn. My performance coach said it would help desensitize me to performing in front of an audience."

"Well, you looked pretty comfortable with all the charming smiles you passed around." I thought of how naturally he seemed to beam and sing around so many staring eyes under the shade of the large oak in the university courtyard.

"I smile when I'm nervous."

Well, that explained it. In fact, he's doing it now. Giving me one of those all too beautiful smiles. Does that mean I make him nervous?

"I guess that's a trait that would benefit a musician," I reply as I find myself entranced by that smile. It's so friendly and full of familiarity that shouldn't be there.

"I'm James," he says while extending a hand.

I stare at his hand for a long minute but his anticipating grin never falters. I huff out a breath of disbelief. Is this guy for real? Just like that, I'm supposed to believe this spiel he gives me about being shy and hating all that female attention. I don't know what game he's trying to play with me but I'm not joining in. Not today, I think as I turn and walk away.

"See you around, rockstar," I quickly throw over my shoulder as I flash him a smile of my own, before heading off to class.

I awoke alone. The cabin was still chilled by the night air, not yet warmed by the slowly rising sun. Only a cluster of dying embers remained in the hearth. Aaron was nowhere in sight. The dredges of a dream, or perhaps it was a memory, fade from the reach of my consciousness until it's beyond recollection. Feeling parched, I planted my feet on the cold wood floors and padded across the small cabin to the kitchen. On the counter, a note, written in surprisingly elegant handwriting, awaited me:

I'll be back soon. Don't do anything reckless.

Was all that was written. No sign off or estimated time of return.

This was it. This was my chance to run. I'd run until I found a path or a stream that would hopefully lead me to a road or civilization. From the closet I removed a backpack. I filled it hastily with clothing, the money I had stuffed into a sock the day before—after swiping it from Aaron's wallet—matches, a blanket, and some nonperishables. Lastly, I filled a canteen from the kitchen cupboard with water and flew out the door. It didn't matter that I had left the cabin in complete disarray in my haste. When Aaron returned to find I was gone, it would be too late.

A sudden sound alerted me that I wasn't alone. Frozen I stood in silence, holding my breath and waiting. Again, the rustling sound of footsteps crunching leaves and twigs tickled my ears. There was no way Aaron was back already and on my trail. It couldn't have been more than fifteen minutes since I left. My plan was to find the path again, where we veered off when we came through the park on that first day. With another solid crunch of leaves under foot I crouched down. Another sound sent me crawling behind a wide tree surrounded by dense brush. Through the cover of the brush, I peered through to spy who was approaching.

It wasn't Aaron, but two men in camouflage, most likely hunters. I debated stepping out to make my presence known and maybe ask for directions. Play the role of lost hiker. However, there were two of them and only one, small me. They carried guns on their backs and knives at their waists. We were most likely far enough out and away from another stirring body for anyone to hear a gunshot let alone a cry for help.

A soft hushed voice came from over my shoulder. "My note clearly stated *not* to do anything reckless." A hand came over my mouth as I yelped in surprise. The hunters paused in their chatting.

"Did you hear that?" one asked the other.

They paused a moment longer before the other replied. "Most likely a bird." And continued on their way.

Aaron released his hold on me and I turned back to face him, crouched beside me in all seriousness.

"How did you—" he silenced me with a finger pressed to his own lips.

"You have two choices," he whispered, barely audible over the returning forest sounds. "You can go to them and hope they don't mean you harm, hope they believe your story and don't remember your face. . ." he glanced down at the ends of my ponytail draped over my shoulder. In a rush I had forgotten to grab a hat to hide my still faintly blue hair. "Or your hair," he continued with a disapproving shake of his head. "Or you can come back to the cabin with me. Either way the choice is yours and so are the consequences."

I couldn't believe he was actually giving me a choice. Why was he willing to let me go now? Was his offer genuine or would he chase after me again as soon as the hunters were out of sight? And how had he found me? How did he stalk without any detection?

"I won't chase you this time," he muttered as if reading my mind. "I promise."

Already weary of the two strangers, my choice seemed simple but no less difficult to make. He was right. I couldn't risk them seeing me. They could already have heard of my escape from the asylum, seen my face on television or heard my description on the radio. What would stop them then from turning me in? And I wouldn't be able to overpower them or get away if they grabbed me. Defeated, I turned to face Aaron with my answer.

"Let's go."

Chapter Eight

A HOUSE BURNED BEFORE me. *Muffled cries came from inside. I ran to the windows and tried to open them. The only people in my life who had ever truly loved me, besides possibly one other, screamed inside, but the window wouldn't budge. It was melted shut, and no matter how hard I pounded on the glass with my fist, it wouldn't break. Hot, acidic tears rolled down my cheeks causing me to squeeze my eyes shut against the pain of their burn. I wanted so badly to save them just this once. And if I couldn't then I would prefer to die alongside them, rather than to keep living this dim life with only their ghosts to keep me company.*

As if a sadistic genie granted my wish, I opened my eyes to find myself in the burning cottage. Everything, every memory and room was completely engulfed in flames. Including myself.

An agonizing scream erupted from my lungs as pain laced every inch of my body. I shot up out of bed, drenched in sweat and tears as panting hot air seared in and out of my burning lungs. I knew it was just a nightmare. I reassured myself repeatedly that I wasn't even there that day the house burned down. I was deep in the woods, located on the back of our property. Sent to forage for herbs for my mother's tinctures and syrups. It was only when I smelled smoke and saw a black cloud looming above the tree line, too large to be a controlled burn pile, that I ran back home. But I was too late.

I was not in the house when it happened and a part of me would always wish that I had been.

A loud thud broke me from my daze and fully pulled me back to the realm of consciousness. Aaron stood by the door in an alert state. Confused, his eyes scanned the cabin's interior. When his sight connected with mine, he held it with a puzzled look. As if trying to remember who and why I was there. He ran a hand through his hair, releasing the visible tension in his shoulders with a deep exhale.

"Are you alright?" he asked as his tensed shoulders dropped slightly.

I jumped out of the bed and briskly walked to the kitchen sink. I turned on the faucet and splashed icy cold water on my face and neck. Immediately regretting doing so as the cold caused me to shiver. I needed to rein in my body and thoughts.

In through your nose, out through your mouth, I thought to myself, over and over until some of the bone deep tension laxed and the shivers weakened.

"I heard cries coming from inside the house and thought—" he paused, walking over to a rustic wooden dresser.

"I'm fine." I sighed. "Just a bad dream."

Aaron turned toward me with a set of flannel pajamas in his hands.

"Looked like more than just a bad dream." His eyes searched me with concern and curiosity. I suddenly became very aware that my clothes were soaked through with sweat. The cold night air puckered my skin and I quickly crossed my arms over my chest. Aaron turned his head away, looking at the bed now blotched with my sweat and tears.

"Here," he murmured, handing me the flannel pajamas, "you should take a hot shower. It'll help you warm up."

Without any objection I took the offered clothing and headed into the bathroom with what dignity I had left. The bathroom was tiny at best. With a stall shower. But the water was hot and I took my time under it, washing out the last of the blue from my hair and letting the pressure of the showerhead beat the tension from my muscles. When I finally stepped out of the sauna-like room with two dripping wet braids in my hair, I noticed Aaron asleep on the couch. A peaceful sleeping boy in front of an all too welcoming fireplace.

The still sweat-soaked sheets were anything but appealing and the cold night air beckoned me to the fire, as it gently crackled in the hearth. Giving in to comfort, I laid down on the small rug on the floor between the couch and the fireplace. With my back to Aaron, I folded my arm under my head and drifted off to the sound of crackling embers but, instead of fire, I dreamt of rain.

Body aching, I stirred and readjusted my position. My arm tingled with sleep. A weight laid around my waist where my flannel top had scrunched up. I was no longer on the hard floor but somewhere soft and warm. Feather light touches rhythmically skimmed the skin on my lower back. It danced in slow idle swirls, playing a soothing song on my flesh, lulling me swiftly back to sleep.

When I woke, it was slow and gradual. It took several moments to get my bearings as I stared hazily at the dying embers in the fireplace. A sense of missing something came over me as I realized the spot beside me was cold and empty. I debated if I had dreamt up the entire night. But I was still wearing the flannel pajamas that were not mine. The shadowed touch of fingers echoed on my skin like a memory. I rose gently to see Aarons back turned toward me while he faced out the kitchen window, mug of coffee in hand. Still feeling a bit groggy, I stared at the back of his head for what felt like an awkward eternity. Taking in the shape of him—how his shirt hugged his shoulders but loosened toward his waist—I found myself curious to know what he looked like under it. I quickly brushed the idea away.

"Sorry for stealing the couch," I yawned, playing at nonchalance. Though I was pretty sure he was the one who moved me, considering I started off on the floor. A part of me wanted him to turn around and break the still morning silence. To admit it was him. But he didn't. I got up and busied myself with rummaging through the kitchen cabinets looking for a mug and a kettle.

"Are you feeling better?" Aaron grumbled, possibly still tired.

"Yes. I'll be fine. You don't have to worry about me," I rambled while pouring water into a soot-stained kettle. I tried not to get too physically close to him, again, as I busied myself in the narrow kitchen. Denying the strange urge to touch him. To accidentally brush his arm. To grace his fingers while handing him another cup of coffee. To be close. I didn't understand it.

"What about you?" I dared ask with a glance at his profile. He continued to stare out the window. If I broke his concentration, would he snap out of his daze and throw his guard back up?

"I've just been thinking." He huffed out in an exhale. I dared to push a little more.

"Of what?"

"Something I think I want to do."

"What do you want?" I asked and cringed internally at the intimate tone. A tick in his jaw told me it wasn't lost on him.

"It doesn't matter." He sighed.

"If it's what you want. If it makes you happy, then it does matter. It matters to—"

He cut me off with a piercing look that froze my thoughts in place. His body hummed with an energy I couldn't define—making the air between us thick and hard to take in.

The kettle whistled in protest on the stove and jolted us, breaking his intense focus. He swiftly took the tea pot off the stove and turned back to me with a slightly lighter demeanor.

"It does not matter because I cannot have things the way that I want them. I do not make the rules," he carefully poured hot water into a mug over a teabag.

Before I could say thank you or ask him to clarify what it was, we were truly talking about, he curtly stated he was going to patrol the area and left the cabin in less than two blinks. I was left alone again with my growing thoughts and growling stomach.

About an hour later I was sitting on the kitchen counter, finishing my tea with a happy, full belly. Aaron returned and marched straight to the bathroom without a word. A second later I heard the shower turn on, water slapping against tiles. Another empty teacup later, he came strolling out of the steaming bathroom running a hand through his damp hair. Water dripped on the shoulders of his white t-shirt.

"There's some breakfast in the microwave," I stated casually as I jumped down from the counter and made my way outside to the deck. Content to enjoy the rest of my morning in solitude.

The late morning sun wasn't quite over the treetops yet and every bird imaginable was singing its praise to the early light. Branches and brush rustled as leaves and twigs were disturbed by the comings and goings of woodland creatures. All could be heard but not seen through the thick, low-lying brush.

My heart was reminded of everything I loved about home, before foster care, group homes, and endless uprooting. I had learned quickly not to place roots anywhere else ever again. Ripping them out over and over again only promised pain. It was easier to not get too close and not stay long. I closed my eyes and took a deep breath of the fresh pine air. Behind me, I heard the door to the cabin open and shut. The banister I was perched on gave slightly under his weight. The strength of his presence was demanding yet hard to describe. It was like the pull of a magnet or the warmth of the sun on your face. He didn't say a word until I acknowledged him. With his back against the railing, elbows propped up on the banister, he faced me with an amused smile.

"What?" I asked, concerning the uncommon grin on his face.

"You look like a little bird."

"Thank you, I guess," I responded before returning my focus to the scenery before me. Aaron's presence seemed to quiet the woods morning song.

"Listen," he said, commanding my eyes back to him. "Yesterday I went to the hospital to keep up appearances and check on your case."

So that's where he was.

"They didn't report your escape yet but they will soon. They can't hide their fault in security and your absence for much longer. We can thank their pride for the time we've had so far." His golden hair waved slightly as it dried in the sun. Intent eyes focused in on mine. "I believe you, Alise," he said, "I know you didn't write that confession and I don't believe you had anything to do with James's death."

Looking away from him, a painful knot gathered in my throat and I blinked back threatening tears. This was the first time someone ever said they believed me to be not guilty. Not my lawyer, not my case workers, not even Wren said it outright.

"Look at me." Aaron gently cupped my chin and turned it back to face him. "I'm going to keep you safe and I'm going to do my best to help you."

"Why?" I rasped out. Ever-present doubt clinched my chest. He released my chin.

"Because it's not fair or just that a person be wrongly charged with something as serious as murder and I cannot sit idly by and watch it happen." He paused for a moment in contemplation. "I need you to trust me or this won't work."

"That's a tall order," I replied, tucking my knees in tight against my chest.

"I know it's asking a lot from you but honestly, you don't have much of a choice." Harshness returned to his face, erasing all traces of warmth from the moment.

"Yeah, I guess you're right, but why can't I stay here?" I dared to question.

"It's not as far out as you think and most likely the locals have figured out that I've been staying here. It won't be long before they come searching for you or realize my absence and put two and two together." He pushed himself off the railing.

Disappointment cloaked over me. A soaking, heavy feeling in my bones.

"I have a vehicle nearby. We can stay one more night to pack and plan but we need to leave by sunrise. The more space we put between you and that *hospital*, the better."

Without waiting for a reply, he went back inside, leaving me to say goodbye to another place I'd never see again. Goodbye to the protective, watchful pines. Goodbye to the chipper, lively birds, the rustling leaves and encroaching vines. Goodbye to the reflection of a long since passed life. A life of both dreams and nightmares.

Chapter Nine

"**A**LISE, WAKE UP!"

Aaron shook me awake from my accidental nap on the couch. The ill-angled position of my neck on the armrest caused a painful ach that I rubbed away, lazily. The fog of a forgotten dream disoriented my thoughts. Aaron had no patience for my slow rise from the soft cushions and lifted me by my waist to unstable feet.

"Is it dawn already?" I yawned, noticing that no hint of light shone through the windows.

"No, but we must go, now." He threw a pack on my shoulders before grabbing his own by the door and ushering me through. I followed his lead as we stealthily crouched behind the cabin's back entrance and made our way to the brush line.

A grunt of protest escaped as Aaron shoved my head down behind a cluster of bushes. Flashing red and blue lights leaked from between the gaps of pines and beams from flashlights, and spotlights shone upon the cabin as bright as day.

"Stay close now, Little Fox," I heard Aaron murmur under his breath, only loud enough for my ears to hear as he knelt close beside me, our thighs kissed one another's. It appeared we had less time than Aaron had originally predicted as we silently watched police officers descend upon the cabin, their flashlights shining through the window panes while they searched. There was a tug on my hand and I looked up to see Aaron pressing a finger to his lips and beckoning me to follow into the dark wood beyond.

By the time we were deep into our trek through the quiet forest I had convinced myself that everything Aaron was doing for me was entirely too good to be true. Too selfless to be believable. What was he getting out of this?

"Why are you risking so much for me? You know aiding and harboring a fugitive is a felony, right? You'll end up in just as much trouble as I'm in or worse," I finally said aloud now that I felt we were far enough from the cabin to be out of earshot.

"Then I guess we better not get caught." His tone did nothing to reassure me. "And in order to do so I'll need your complete obedience," he continued.

"I'm sure you have noticed," I said as I stepped over a protruding tree root, "but obedience isn't really my thing."

"I have noticed," Aaron replied, extending a hand out to help me over a crumbling log. Instead of taking my hand though he grabbed my waist and lifted me over it in a surprisingly strong grip. I cursed myself for gasping before he slowly lowered me down. My chest lightly grazed his for only a second, though we both seemed to notice. Aaron gently set me back down and continued forward. I was grateful for the darkness of night that concealed my, most likely, flushed cheeks.

"That is why I know I am asking a lot from you, Miss Fox. If we are to make it to our destination unnoticed, we will need to trust each other. Try to remember I am helping you." He glanced over his shoulder. "Let me."

That was the part I struggled with most. I had trouble believing his sense of justice was so strong that he was truly willing to risk committing a felony, just to help one of his patients. A practical stranger. But I couldn't pin down an ulterior motive. The cynic in me wanted to doubt every intention and every good deed. However, I remembered James and what he had said to me once during one of my melancholy rants.

Just ride it out, babe. Sooner or later, people will show you who they really are. All you have to do is give them the opportunity.

I would try to follow suit, though I was still guarded.

The sun was a shy lover in the early hours of dawn. Light hung low on the horizon. Rays of gold flashed between the bodies of pine trees. The air warmed as the night merged into day. We had been hiking for hours when we approached an old, dilapidated bridge that crossed over a brush filled ditch. Upon closer inspection however, the brush seemed unnatural. Heaped in piles that appeared staged.

Aaron jumped down into the ditch and started tossing away branches until the faded hood of a worn car peeked through. How long had this been here? Had he been using it this whole time and hiding it under this bridge? From the look of it we would be lucky if it even ran. The tires were almost bald and the paint was faded. The headlights were fogged from long amounts of time in the sun. Once a side door was revealed from under the staged brush, Aaron beckoned me to toss him my pack. He climbed into the vehicle and I waited as he made several attempts to turn over the engine. At last, it sputtered upon ignition and he waved at me to join him.

To my surprise and horror, Aaron planned on driving the car through the ditch itself. Branches smacked against the windshield, making me flinch in anticipation of splintered glass in my face, though it held up against the onslaught, in the end. All the while, the tires found every rock and dip, causing me to bounce uncontrollably in my seat.

"Brace yourself," was all Aaron said after I hit my head on the cabin roof. I shot him a frustrated scowl.

"Are you insane? At this rate we will likely have a flat tire before we even reach the road."

"Navigating through the trees is almost impossible. This is the clearest route," he replied, never taking his eyes off the path.

We truly weren't as far away from the main road as I had originally thought. In just a few short minutes we reached it. After making sure no one was coming or going, Aaron gunned the car's engine, giving it the boost it needed to lurch out of the ditch. Looking out the rearview mirror one last time to say a silent goodbye to my hopeful and pathetic plans, I then looked over at Aaron and wondered what lay before us. A shuddering breath trembled on my lips. Shaking my head in protest I attempted to distract myself from the unknown by finding something decent on the radio.

"So, where exactly are we going?" I finally asked hours later. The woods had cleared away as we drove through one small town after another.

"West," was all Aaron said.

"How far west?"

"To the coast."

"What's out there?" I pressed.

"Somewhere safe." He was quite skilled at the art of only giving short, vague answers.

I sighed with resignation.

"It's going to be a long drive. We might as well communicate."

"Isn't that what we are doing now?" His eyes were tired and cold as he focused on the road ahead.

Trees and the occasional farmhouse flew past. Some near unlivable but with cars in the driveway all the same. Others were landscaped with an abundance of potted plants and colorful yard décor. I wondered what the inside of each one looked like, as we passed them by. Daydreaming of who lived inside. Were they a young family with too many kids to count or an older, retired couple with nothing but time?

Sorrow draped over my shoulders like a heavy blanket at the memory of warm hands on mine. The smell of soil and herbs in a cluttered kitchen. Foggy windows framed in rustic wood. The long-forgotten feel of a worn rug under my bare feet. A house that no longer existed, as well as the family that once resided in it.

"Want to play a game?" I asked after a long pause of silence, needing the distraction from my memories.

"Not particularly," Aaron replied.

I huffed an overtly audible sigh, that blew loose strands of hair from my face.

"But if it'll keep you from fussing like a child, then sure." I shot him a glare just to see him grin slightly at my slouched posture and crossed arms. Self-consciously I straighten myself.

"How about twenty-one questions?"

He audibly groaned.

"What? That way we can get to know each other better," I encouraged.

"There's nothing to know."

"Oh, I highly doubt that," I said while turning the volume on the radio down.

"I'll go first. What's your favorite color?" I started off light, to avoid scaring him off from the idea completely.

"Red. You?"

"Green."

"Where were you born?"

He hesitated before curtly replying. "Les Rousses." With a perfect accent.

"Parles-tu Français?" I all but bounced in my seat, giddy to have someone to practice with.

"Non."

Like water poured on a candle, my smile was snuffed out.

"But you just–"

"And that was two questions, so now I get to ask two." His eyes gave me an almost regretful look at my sudden disappointment.

"Where were you born?"

"You can't just keep asking me the same questions I ask you."

"I didn't realize there were rules to this game." A slight crease formed between his brows.

I waited for him to ask a different question but within the moment of a few breaths I caved.

"I don't know," I huffed.

"What do you mean you don't know?"

"I mean I honestly don't know. My adoptive mother found me in the woods behind our house." The memory of leaves and dirt crunching under my bare feet washed over me. So vivid I could almost smell the earth. "No one ever came for me. So, she kept me and made the day she found me, my birthday. She said I was a gift from a fox and that it was a sign I was meant to be with them since her and my father's last name was Fox."

A solemn pause grew between us and I worried I had said too much. I had not intended this game to become so personal so quickly.

"Did she give you your first name as well?" Aaron asked.

"No, actually. Though I was too young to remember much about where I came from or how I had ended up lost in those woods, I apparently recalled my name when I was asked." Of course this was all based on what I had been told by the same people who claimed truth to the fanciful story that I was given to them by a fox.

A grumbling echoed in the silence, causing Aaron and mine's gazes to lock in speculation of whose stomach was the culprit. I pressed my hands to my own, noticing the hollowness there. Aaron let out a breathy chuckle. His lips kicked up to the side to reveal a single dimple, before turning his focus back to the road ahead.

"Are you hungry?"

"That was three questions and yes—always," I stated without hesitation and smiled weakly back at him.

We drove straight through the day and into the following night, not wanting to risk staying in one place for too long yet. Aaron and I took turns driving once I convinced him I did, in fact, know how to drive a car. His body was tense and eyes anxious as if he anticipated that at any moment, I would run us off the road. Finally, after several minutes of side-seat driving and many reassurances on my end, exhaustion got the best of him. Mid-sentence I looked over to see his head lulling to the side, eyes shut.

As dawn approached, I was feeling more than a little ripe. I pulled into a rest stop, not bothering to wake Aaron who was still asleep in the passenger seat. I left the car running and headed for the restrooms. At such an early hour the place was mostly deserted. Only a few other vehicles parked under the flickering light posts.

Upon entering the women's restroom, I glanced below each stall to make sure I was alone. After confirming so I headed to one of the many sinks and proceeded to splash water on my face and neck. The cool water refreshed my warm sticky skin. I gripped the sink with both hands and stared at the reflection before me. In just the few days since being out of the asylum my appearance had somewhat improved. Fullness had started to form back into my cheeks. My eyes were once again an icy blue compared to the sullen gray they took on in captivity.

However, I was still not satisfied with what I saw: a scrawny, childish body, smothered in clothes that were several sizes too big. At my age I should have been developed, or well into a full woman's body, yet I was not. I put the blame on my unknown genetics or the several years of living off noodles and tea while in college. I splashed my face again to blur the sight before me. With eyes closed and water running, I took several deep relaxing breaths, letting the sound of the running water drown out every sound around me—every invasive thought in my head.

A large hand closed over my mouth, tightly. Another wrapped around my arms and waist, pinning them down to my sides. My eyes flew open in a flurry as my yelp of surprise was smothered. Long strong arms gripped me tight against a hard chest and started dragging me backwards. My feet tripped out beneath me. I attempted to get a glance at my captor in the mirror. Water dripped into my eyes, distorting my vision. Dark eyes looked back at me from the reflection of the mirror. From what I could make out, a black hood was pulled over their head and a face mask covered the rest of their features from view.

My breath quickened. My feet kicked out as I was continually pulled back, deeper into the bathroom. Not the exit. I could only imagine what his plans for me were if he got me into a stall alone. Desperation fueled me. Instinct took over, like a cornered animal. A sharp elbow slammed back into his ribs causing his grip to lighten slightly. It gave me just enough space to lean forward before slamming my head into his face. The back of my skull connected with his nose. Shocked, he released me completely. Taking full advantage of the moment, I ran towards the restroom exit. Halfway to the door my feet slipped on the slick floor. I came, crashing down on my hip. I hissed through gritted teeth. At the back of the room a deep voice moaned beneath cupped, bloody, hands.

He muttered a curse as his vengeful glare narrowed down on me.

Scurrying back onto my feet, I ran. Ran like the devil was chasing. Ran like that day in the woods. Ran until I was seated back in the car with the door locked. Panting wildly, I threw the car into reverse, throwing Aaron forward and startling him awake. He was immediately thrown back into his seat as I floored the vehicle into drive.

"What are you—" He cut off at the sight of my bloody hair. Eyes widened before narrowing into slits, mouth drawn tight. "What happened?"

My breathing was too rapid to respond. He gave me just a few more seconds to catch my breath before questioning me again.

"Are you hurt?"

I reached up and touched the back of my head, pressing lightly. Only a dull pain flared in response. I hid my cringe.

"No. No, I don't think so," I rasped.

"Good. Now slow down before you lose control of the vehicle."

Becoming aware that my foot was still pressed, pedal to floor, I raised it slightly until the car coasted back to the speed limit. A glance in the rearview mirror confirmed no car trailed behind. We were alone on the vacant road. Slowly I released a shaking breath from my lungs.

"Now. Tell me what happened," Aaron demanded.

Chapter Ten

AARON BECAME EXTREMELY PARANOID after I told him the details of the attack at the rest stop. Though I assumed the incident was random, he apparently thought we were being closely followed. When I finally calmed enough to relinquish my iron grip on the steering wheel, Aaron convinced me to let him drive. He decided to change our route and drove several miles out our way, to get onto a northbound highway.

"You should try to get some sleep now," he encouraged.

But I couldn't, adrenaline still coursed through my body. Hands buzzed with tremors and my jaw clenched. He reached over and handed me a water bottle.

"Drink," he ordered. Hesitating, I worried I wouldn't be able to keep the liquid down. "It'll help. I promise." He nudged the bottle toward me.

Nodding I took the offering and unscrewed the cap with clumsy fingers before taking a few cautious sips.

"Try to eat this too, if you can." He reached behind his seat and pulled out a chocolate bar from his pack.

"I don't think I can." Nausea rolled over me at just the thought of food.

"You haven't eaten since yesterday. Trust me it will take the edge off the crash you're about to experience."

With a deep sigh, I accepted the offered food. Only daring to take a small nibble.

"Let's see if we can find some music." Swift hands pressed buttons and turned knobs on the outdated dash. After several stations of nothing but static, old, yet familiar, big band style music came streaming through the radio. Aaron left it at that.

He was being awfully and unusually attentive. Almost doting over me instead of reprimanding me for not waking him at the rest stop. At not being more alert and less reckless.

"You're not mad?" I asked, almost regretting I had.

Confusion creased his brow as he dared a quick glance at me.

"Why should I be mad?" he asked.

"I . . . I don't know," I mumbled, not wanting to give him a reason to be.

"Are you used to others getting upset with you about things that are outside of your control?"

"Please don't play psychologist with me right now." I rubbed my temples, feeling a headache coming on. I took a few more sips of water before resting my head on the window.

"And yes," I whispered after a long moment of silence, "I guess I am."

Every blink became slower and heavier with each passing second. My mouth mindlessly lip-synced the words to a song as it resonated from the speakers. Out the window I counted the passing trees until I drifted off. But not before I heard a low soft voice sing along to the tune. Dazed and unable to decipher it from dream from reality. Memory from present. Serenading me into the clutches of sleep.

You're just too good to be true. Can't take my eyes off of you.

Our route was uncharted and somewhat haphazard after that. We often headed north or south for hours out of our way, for the sake of throwing a ghost off our trail. I never once noticed any sign that we were being followed while we were on the road, and only felt the blanket of dread the few times a police officer was nearby. Whether that be in a passing vehicle or crossing paths with one while passing through a town to stop to rest and eat. I found myself ducking my head and steering out of view.

Sometimes I would drive. Other times we wouldn't stop at all and drove straight through the night. Aaron always seemed to be looking over his shoulder, feeling some undetectable force that I could not. I wondered what he saw—what he heard. Several times I asked him what he was looking for or if he thought we were being followed. His answers were always short and indirect, as usual.

"*Possibly,*" or "*Someone,*" he would say.

"Do you think it's the same person who attacked me at the rest stop?" I finally mustered the courage to ask.

"Maybe."

Aaron shot me a scornful yet inquisitive look.

"What did you do?" he asked.

"Nothing," I lied as I made to stuff a rogue pant leg back into my oversized, protruding jacket. He grabbed the loose item and gave it a firm yank, causing every piece of clothing I stashed within to spill out over the vehicle. I opened my mouth to protest but was cut off.

"Very reckless," he said outside the strip center. A disappointed crease formed between his brow. "We need to be laying low. Not drawing attention to ourselves by committing petty crime."

"I was careful," I retorted. This wasn't my first time stealing what I needed and though I was no master criminal I was a little insulted at the disbelieving look on his face. He looked down at the clothes scattered about, as I desperately tried to gather them up again.

"You don't need to steal, Alise. I have plenty of money to get you whatever you want, you need only ask"—I made to speak, just to get cut off again— "and I'm sorry I didn't notice that you have been wearing my clothes this entire time. Of course, you would be more comfortable in something that fit you properly."

His sweat pants hung off my hips, threatening to fall at any moment despite the several times I had rolled the waistband. I didn't mind that his shirt was more like a dress on my slight frame but I was self-conscious every time I leaned forward, as the neckline hung open for all to see the absolute lack of anything worth seeing beneath.

Feeling defensive despite his apology, I pulled my lip between my teeth.

"It's just, I'm really small and they are way too big for me." I held out my arms for effect. I felt like a pathetic sight as Aaron's eyes seemed to take in my small form. I thought I saw curiosity in that once over. A sigh of resignation left his lips as he rubbed the bridge of his nose.

"There's no reason they need to know what you took. Let's just go back in. Pick something out and I'll overpay to make up for what you stole." He held the door open for me as I gaped, a little unsure if he was serious until Aaron beckoned me inside.

Later that night, I sat cross-legged on a bed in our hotel room. After several hours of debate, I was finally able to convince Aaron it would be safer to spend the night in one place instead of spending it driving.

Clicking through the channels I looked for any mention of my escape. Either it wasn't making the news or I wasn't lucky enough to have stumbled upon reports of it. Or even better, we were far enough away that it didn't reach the concern of our recent towns local station. I hoped for the latter. Perhaps they tracked me to the woods and assumed I didn't survive. No one would know of my experience and skill in such environments. Being underestimated played to my benefit once again.

"Come with me," Aaron said upon entering the room. He insisted on clearing the perimeter despite circling several motel parking lots before choosing this location. "There's something I want to show you."

I changed out of Aarons sweats and into the, new to me, jeans he bought at the thrift store I so sloppily stole from. Aaron more than made up for my actions. He drew most of the cashier's attention toward himself, so as not to let her get too many chances to view my wanted face and left her blinking with shock at the extra change he left on the counter. She protested as we briskly walked out and purposefully ignored her calls to us for forgetting our change.

A moment later we stood in front of an empty pool at the back of the hotel. Cracks and fissures ran along its sides like a dried-out bone—a skeleton of what once was. Clearly it was meant to be off limits. The fence around it was locked forcing us to climb over to get inside.

It was late. The stars and a single light post shone down on us in the desolate quiet of the night.

"It's a pool," I said, stating the obvious.

"It's perfect for our use." Aaron made his way down a ladder attached to the side of the pool, jumping down the rest of the way and landing almost elegantly before extending his hand out to help me down. He caught me by the waist and lowered me gently down. I turned in his arms to face him.

"And of what use is that?" I playfully, tried and failed, to mock his accent.

He was silent and for a moment I thought I might have offended him. About to apologize my heart jumped as I met his eyes. The way they were focused on me was almost tender. Not the predatory or scornful stare and glances I come to expect from him.

"You're vulnerable," he breathed, hand still on my waist. Chewing my lip, I wondered what I was doing down here, in an empty, abandoned pool, at night, with Aaron's hands around my waist. He blinked at the gesture, seeming to remember himself and removed his hands. The cold air was a stark contrast to the warmth of him.

"What I mean is you need to learn how to protect yourself. How to get away and escape capture."

"I think history would prove I'm already capable of escaping imprisonment."

"That's not what I meant," he countered, running a hand through his hair. "If you are going to run off like a little fox, then you need to know how to get away if you are physically overpowered. Using your wits was smart but you need to know how to break free if someone grabs you, such as your wrist," he said, doing just that. I yanked my arm in reflex, with no success.

"Not like that"—he tapped the top of his hand that braced my wrist—"up towards the palm then down towards the fingers. Don't just pull away," he instructed plainly, as though it were that simple. I gave him a skeptical look before doing just as he said.

With a swift tug up then down, my wrist slipped through his grip as he said it would.

"You let me break free," I objected.

"Try it again," he offered out his hand.

Again, it worked.

"Now try it with my hand in different positions. Remember always towards the palm then the fingers no matter their placement."

For several minutes I practiced the move. Every time my wrist was able to break from his grip. Aaron constantly changed the placement of his hand on my arm and gradually applied more pressure to his hold.

"Very good," he finally said after several rounds. "You're a fast learner. From now on, every night, we will train in a secluded space like this. I'll teach you everything you need to know to get out of a situation where your opponent is larger or stronger than yourself."

Basically everyone, I thought to myself as my excitement grew at the idea.

"Sounds great. What's next?" I asked, bouncing on my heels with enthusiasm. An eager smile curved my lips.

A soft chuckle and gleaming eyes were his only response, my eagerness to learn seemed to please him, before he continued with his instruction.

I enjoyed my *lessons* as we called them and I think Aaron did too. He never grew tired, nor impatient. I never had such a playful instructor. Sometimes, he would get much closer than needed to throw me off in a hold; his breath hot on my neck causing me to falter. Or he'd tease me into frustration until I cried "*give*" and did the move his way.

"You have a fighter's spirit, Little Fox"—the nickname was growing on me—"but I'm afraid most of your energy is misplaced. It makes you sloppy and predictable." I glared back at him from across a grassy clearing. Not knowing if he meant to instruct or insult me.

The blades of grass danced in the cool night wind. A whispered chill ran across my damp brow. The parked car's headlights shined in my eyes. I blocked the light with my hand only to find Aaron gone from sight.

A tickling breath danced on my exposed ear. Startled, I turned to see him standing behind me. He crossed his arms and looked down at me with a satisfied, smug smile.

"Rule five. Always be aware of your opponent's position."

"What about rules one through four? Care to tell me what those are first?" I asked, giving him an annoyed glare in return. "Also, the light was in my eyes."

"Excuses will not do you any favors, Little Fox. *Also*," he slurred mockingly, "it's not my fault that you haven't been paying attention. If you had, you would already know rules one through four."

"Or perhaps you are not as good of an instructor as you think," I retorted, matching his posture.

"And what's with this, '*Little Fox*,' nickname you insist on calling me?"

He shrugged a shoulder in response. "It suits you." And strode back towards the car.

"Let's call it a night. I can tell you are tired."

"No, I'm not," I yawned as I followed him toward the car, betraying the validity of my words.

"Come, let's find a place to sleep. You earned a soft bed tonight."

My feet became heavy with exhaustion and the idea of a warm bed as they dragged through the grass and to the car, before I collapsed in the passenger seat.

Before we started training regularly, being pent up in the car for hours on the road would cause my body to become restless. Most nights I was finding it hard to sleep. Unspent energy caused my limbs to toss and turn. But after we started training, where we sometimes spent all night in empty pools, abandoned parking lots, and desolate clearings, my body all but crashed into slumber. No matter if it were on the back bench of the car or a motel bed. I was grateful for the nights we did manage to find a place Aaron deemed safe enough for us to rent a room.

They were always motels where the rooms faced the parking lot. Never an interior room inside a building. Too many chances to be seen, not as easy to escape from, Aaron said. He would always pay in the office, always cash, and meet me outside after getting a key. The car was always parked behind the building. Directly behind our room, in case we needed to escape through the bathroom window. And also, so no one would see our car out front in passing. He thought of everything it seemed. Even more so than my anxious mind did.

"Bad news," he said as he approached me waiting outside the car.

"They only had a room with one bed left and there isn't another motel for miles."

"Oh," was my only response since I honestly didn't mind.

He brought me around the front and unlocked the door to our room. Sure enough there was only one bed in the small room and it wasn't king sized, but a full at best.

"I'll sleep on the floor," he said as he strutted into the dark room, turning on a table lamp. I waited until he cleared the room, nodding at me that it was safe, before I entered and closed the door behind me and set the deadbolt. I cringed as I scanned the damp looking floor. A chair sat next to the table but it wouldn't be much better than the floor, which I couldn't possibly let him sleep on either.

Nor would I.

"It's fine. Honestly. We can share," I offered.

I stifled a giggle at the scandalized look he shot me—as though I just stripped naked before him.

"Seriously Aaron, it's fine. And unless I dreamt it, we both slept on the couch in the cabin, that one night." Unless I did just dream it, but this was the first time I dared to bring it up.

He ran a contemplative hand through his hair.

"Are you sure?" he asked.

"Yes. Don't look so frightened. I promise I won't bite," I snapped my teeth at him with a teasing smile as I strode towards the bathroom.

By the time I showered and changed into Aaron's boxers and t-shirt, my body felt laden with exhaustion. Aaron must have felt the same because he was already in a deep, still sleep. A table lamp's light shone gently on his peaceful face. Feeling brazen I allowed my eyes to roam his features. From his thick lashes, soft full lips, and strong jaw to his bare, broad chest. It slowly rose and descended with each steady breath. My own tightened at the sight. Normally he slept with a shirt on. The one I was currently wearing. My fingers itched to touch his smooth skin. To caress his face tenderly while marveling at his build.

Shaking my head of all thoughts I took a deep breath before I climbed into bed, taking care not to let it squeak under my shifting weight as I turned off the lamp and pulled the covers up to my chin.

Chapter Eleven

DEAD EYES STARED AT me from across the bed.

I jolted up as a silent scream stretched my lips. Roaring filled my ears until they felt as though they would bleed. My body went numb as I tried to shake James awake. My hands felt as though they were not my own. Though my lips moved, no sound came out as I begged, "Please, please wake up!"

Hot tears filled my eyes and burned my cheeks. I shook and shook but he still didn't stir. I willed my legs to move. To run. To do *anything*. But they only grew sluggish and heavier with each failed attempt. I collapsed back onto the bed beside him, unable to even move my head away from his haunting stare. All control left my body. I couldn't scream, couldn't move an inch. Only tears fell as I blinked at the once beautiful face before me—now pale and lifeless.

Why did you leave me? I thought. *What am I supposed to do without you now?* His death tore a hole in the earth so singularly devastating that cracks of darkness spread from it. I felt it everywhere and in everything. I carried that darkness in my shadow where it was always in my peripheral and even on the sunniest of days, I knew it would follow me.

James's arm flung forward and grabbed my shoulder as his milky dead eyes blinked at me. And this time I could hear the scream that escaped.

"Alise, wake up!" He shouted down at me, but his voice was all wrong. Not the melodic tone I had loved but something gruff and deep.

Strong hands pulled me up out of the nightmare and I found Aaron across from me, eyes wide with concern, hand resting on my shoulder. I rubbed at my damp face and wiped away the still-falling tears.

"He's gone," I whimpered. Fresh tears painfully pushed at the back of my eyes. Aaron didn't hesitate to pull me close against his chest.

"It's alright. I'm still here," he whispered into my hair. "I won't leave you."

Tears were beyond my control as they continued to fall and trickle down his warm skin. He said nothing more as he stroked my back. Didn't ask me what happened or try to stop my crying. Aaron stayed in this moment with me and only offered comfort in the firm hold of his embrace and the steadying beat of his heart.

"When you are ready, we can talk about it." He placed a small kiss atop my head. The rest of the night he never once loosened his grip on me. Even as I drifted back into an exhausted sleep with my head resting on his steadily rising chest.

We continued our question game on the road the next morning. I devoured what little information he was willing to part with, giving me a foggy and gapped picture of the man I was traveling with. That I was, essentially, trusting my life with. For one, he had a heavy and somewhat concerning codependency for coffee—sometimes drinking six cups a day. Yet, he still seemed exhausted most of the time and was quick to fall asleep when it was my turn to drive. I wondered if it was all those long nights he stayed up patrolling the cabin, finally catching up with him.

Because Aaron previously had access to my file and, I assumed, already knew a good deal about my past and how I ended up at the asylum, I felt somewhat patronized when he would ask questions about my past anyways. I would play along though and answer as vaguely as possible in conjunction to his own mostly cryptic replies.

"It's your turn," I stated after he half-answered my question about his ability to read and understand several languages, but apparently, not speak them.

Sure.

"Did you fake your psychosis while in the asylum?" the question burst from his mouth as though he'd been holding it in for days.

"What do you mean?" I fiddled with the ends of my hair, attempting to dampen the accusation in my tone.

"I read your file."

Of course, he did.

"And according to its contents, you claimed to have felt others' emotions on your skin and body. Feelings, you claimed, were not your own, but projections of others around you." He glanced at me from the side of his eye before focusing back on the road.

I contemplated how to respond. I wanted to tell him the truth, but I didn't want him to look at me the way the others did. The way my lawyer did when he decided to use this odd curse as a way to avoid getting the death penalty. The pitiful and clinical way the doctors did when I was forced to spill a secret, intimate part about myself to them in an attempt to save my pathetic life. My strange weakness laid bare for them to dissect like a fascinating specimen.

"I wasn't faking," I murmured, focus still fixated on my split ends. "It's true. It is something I've always dealt with since I could remember. Sometimes it's a small minor sensation that I can brush off, like the tickle of a spider web or the buzz of a fly landing on my skin. Other times it's much, much worse."

He didn't say a word. The silence, my invitation to continue. I looked over at him to gauge his expression. Worried what I would see written on his face and dreaded the pity or disbelief that would be etched upon it. But he remained unmoved, unwavering in his focus on driving. It was almost as though I was speaking to an inanimate object. It was as though he were a sponge that absorbed my words and digested them without judgment or condescension.

"There have been times when the feelings are so overwhelming, I feel sick to my stomach and I can't eat. Or I shake. Or have an anxiety attack." I looked back down at my fingers as they nervously twisted my hair into ropes. "Those times are the worst. My mother called it a strong sense of empathy, and had taught me about certain plants that could calm my nerves when the attacks happened, but since she is . . . well, I haven't really had access to them lately." And I left it at that.

"I agree with your mother," was all he said, grabbing my attention with his concurrence. "Empathic abilities could manifest in that way or"—my heart skipped a beat—"there could be another reason." And my heart sank. I didn't want to be sick. I didn't want to be crazy.

"And what is that?" I asked, not really wanting to know. Certain he would say it was because I truly was insane on some level.

"I'm not sure." He clearly did not want to make me feel worse in my vulnerability and I, myself, did not want to face the harsh reality of a possibly decaying mind.

Though defiant to his lead at first, we now operated in sync. Our body language was a tool we used to navigate our terrain as we traveled cross country toward the west coast. A raised brow directed the other to speak soft and vaguely while out in public or around others. The clearing of the throat indicated it was time to leave. A wink meant to play along with whatever story was being told to an unsuspecting gas attendant or waitress.

We were quite the outlaws. Outlaws who didn't steal, apparently. One of the honed skills I had gained over the course of my life was now off limits. I wondered about Aaron's strange code. He was obviously okay with helping fugitives escape the long arm of the law but bristled at the idea of stealing so much as a bag of chips.

"Hand them over." An outstretched arm indicated to the bag I had stuffed into my hoodie. Reluctantly I pulled them out, handing them to him and sticking out my tongue.

"Nice try," he said and smirked at where the bag had been hidden.

"We have one more thing to do before we continue on the road, so please try to be on your best behavior." Aaron looked over at me in defiance. I met him with my own.

"What are we doing?" I asked.

"Getting a different vehicle," he answered, only after paying the attendant and exiting the gas station. "We are far enough out of state and I haven't seen our tail in days. Now is the perfect time to switch vehicles."

"Who are you?" I asked, smiling up at him in admiration and curiosity. This person before me, who seemed to think of anything and everything when it came to avoiding notice. A perfect actor who assimilated into any role that best suited our false narrative. I found it harder and harder to believe he hadn't done something like this before.

His lips dipped slightly and he fully ignored the question. I entered the vehicle and shut the cabin door before turning to him to ask, "What does our tail look like?"

"A red jeep. He appears to be male and alone," he reported to me like a soldier debriefing a comrade.

"I see," was my only response.

"I'm curious. . ." he continued, to my surprise, "why we haven't seen any reports of your escape on the news nor radio scanners reporting it to the police. It is possible the hospital hired a third party to find and retrieve you to avoid having to report your slip through their embarrassingly weak security measures," he paused in contemplation. "But even that is a weak theory at best."

"Who else could possibly be looking for me?" I wondered out loud.

"I don't know. And as much as I don't like knowing, I don't plan to find out." Aaron put the car in gear and pulled out onto the highway.

Chapter Twelve

WE DROVE OFF FROM the dealership in an old, tan station wagon. More room for sleeping, Aaron reasoned, and very inconspicuous. This way we could camp out more and no one we might come across would think twice about it as opposed to the green, beat-up sedan. He even grabbed an air mattress from a local general store and set it up in the back, along with some well-loved blankets and pillows we had taken from the cabin.

Ever since that night in the hotel, sleeping in the same bed wasn't an issue. Aaron was always a gentleman, never making a move, sometimes to my own disappointment. For, while he was the pinnacle of self-control, I found myself aching and restless some nights—wishing the pillow barricade between us was gone but instead, I would sneak off to the bathroom while he slept to make use of the shower head's high-water pressure.

I was grateful when that phase of my hormone cycle had passed, for there would be no sneaking off when we slept in the close quarters of the station wagon. At first we mostly parked at the back of empty store parking lots or public parks. That is until we approached the coast.

My heart sang along to the melody of crashing waves and crying seagulls. I wiggled my toes in the sand, relishing every tiny grain that tickled my skin. My hands ached from clutching the blanket tightly around me, blocking the bite of the chilly coastal winds. It was worth it though, to see the sunset in an array of pinks and golds. Making its slow descent into the ocean, moments before the moon welcomed the stars to its night court.

Aaron shouted for me from atop the seawall. Damp, jagged rocks climbed up to a parking lot for day use and overnight campers, like ourselves. We had befriended, or should I say Aaron had charmed, a couple with an RV traveling along the coast and they invited us to have dinner with them earlier that evening. As it was with everyone we encountered on the road, Aaron crafted false names for us and spun together intricate, yet ridiculous, stories of our travels. Always a perfect blend of truth with fantasy.

Sometimes we were brother and sister. Sometimes newly engaged. Other times partners on a business venture gone awry. Tonight, we were lovers, who recently sold all our belongings to move to the golden coast from Vermont and brought nothing but ourselves and a rusted old station wagon on the start of our new beginning. This tale was my favorite. Perhaps because it was so similar to the plans I had made for myself. Except I wasn't alone in this version.

Belly full and eyes shining, I ascended the weather-worn, wooden stairs toward Aaron. He sat at the opening of the wagons' hatch beckoning me inside, away from the cold and damp night air. I crawled in behind him, draping my arms over his shoulders and rested my cheek on his back. He stared ahead at the setting sun. His hair ruffled by the ocean breeze. His golden strands captured the sun's last rays and his eyes glowed bronze.

"I never want to leave this place," I sighed into him.

A soft sigh of his own responded.

"Tell me something about where we are going next."

"What do you want to know?" *Always with the vague answers*. A question for a question. I held back my grunt of annoyance.

"Are there other people there, like me?"

He peered at me over his hunched shoulders.

"There's no one like you, Alise."

I playfully slapped his back. A mischievous smile graced his lips and he beckoned me inside with a tilt of chin.

As I crawled deeper inside, he closed the hutch door behind me. His body draped lazily across the air mattress and pillows we set up in the back of the wagon.

"Come here," he rasped, ushering me to lay beside him.

We laid side by side gazing out the back window at the star strung sky for several long moments. The cold night air encouraged me to wiggle closer into Aaron's heat. His warm presence was like the sun. Aaron lifted my hand and held it against his own—palm to palm.

"So small," he observantly teased. Each of his large fingers interlaced, one by one, into mine.

It was hard to trust that we had gotten to this point in such a short amount of time. I went from suspecting he would try to kill me, turn me in, or worse, to now trusting him completely. We communicated almost telekinetically through body language. Often only needing to grunt or sigh, throw a glance or lift a brow, to convey a response or warning. Our minds now like one. We had gotten to know each other more and more over the long days of driving and he was slowly shedding the cold, indifferent skin he wore those first nights at the cabin.

That time felt like a century ago, yet James's death felt like only yesterday. Music from a strumming guitar echoed in my head. From deep in the corners of my mind, James looked up at me from his writing with that perfect charming smile, gracing his face. Only I knew it meant he was nervous or worried. He wore smiles like a collection of masks that hid all his secrets from the world around him. Except from me.

The pain of missing him tightened my throat. My eyes turned glassy.

"What are you thinking," Aaron asked, noticing the change in my demeanor. He noticed everything.

I sighed and sat up on my elbows to face him. I couldn't bear carrying every secret alone anymore but, I promised James I wouldn't tell anyone his. No, that was his choice to make, not mine and not until he was ready. Which now meant never. No one would ever know and both him and I would take it to the grave.

"I wish I could tell you," I whispered. "But I made a promise."

"I understand." Aaron's eyes studied our still joined hands. "I know a thing or two about keeping secrets and the burden it weighs."

Wasn't that an understatement.

"If it makes you feel better, you can tell me what you feel without giving the secret away."

I nodded and took a deep breath. After all those weeks of questioning by police, my lawyer, even Aaron and my assigned team of doctors, I never said anything to make them believe otherwise, in their assumptions about me and James's relationship. Until now.

"James and I were not romantically involved," I paused to gauge Aaron's reaction but his eyes were still fixated on our hands as his thumb brushed over my knuckles.

"It was just something we allowed others to believe, a game we played to protect him from unwanted attention." I approached my next words cautiously. "And from the truth." I was toeing the line and silenced myself before I could say anything else that would give James away. Even in death I would cherish his trust. Even these few words felt like a betrayal. And though they could have possibly freed me, I still kept his secrets.

"I understand," Aaron replied and rolled back onto his back. He pulled me down by my hand to lay my head on his chest.

"I also have a complicated relationship with someone," he admitted.

I lifted my head and looked at him pointedly, to our clasped hands, to our physical closeness. An airy chuckle rumbled in Aaron's chest as he read the plainly displayed concern on my face.

"It is not what you think. I call her my sister though she isn't, at least not by blood, but that doesn't make it any less real. Legally we are siblings though."

"Are you adopted?" I asked.

Like me?

Like I was?

"Yes. We both are. We were adopted by the same man but we knew each other before." I understood. They were probably in the same orphanage or foster home before being adopted. Reassured, I laid my head back down and stared out the window beyond.

"There is no doubt in my mind that what you and James had, romantic or not, was real. If it felt real to you, then that's all that matters." Fingers brushed back loose strands of hair from my forehead.

"Our friendship was real," I breathed. "He was my best friend." I swallowed hard against the threat of tears. Strong fingers cupped my chin and turned my face towards his.

"You don't have to hide your tears from me, Alise. You don't have to hide anything from me." A soft reassuring smile curved his lips.

"I know." But did he know the same applied to him? "You know you can always be honest with me too." I hoped I could encourage something he was perhaps keeping hidden, out. Maybe one of the secrets he hid in his eyes.

Aaron released his grip on my chin. Gentle fingers pushed aside a cornsilk strand from my face. A combination of defeat and longing swirled in his pine green eyes.

"I wish I could tell you everything, but not yet. Not until I'm sure you are safe." Confusion creased my brow.

"I'm safe with you," I countered.

"If only you were." For a long moment we stayed there, trying to put the puzzle of each other together and coming up short. How was I not safe with him? He never harmed me, though he had plenty of opportunities to. He never even tried to make a move on me despite the times we were close, just like this.

I didn't want to admit the small frustration his self-control brought out in me. As if reading my mind, feeling the hum of my body against his, his lids lowered and his thumb reached up to swipe gently across my bottom lip—back and forth.

"Let me guess. You want to tell me why, but you don't make the rules. Am I right?" I whispered against his touch and savored every delicious graze. His eyes lowered to my mouth.

"Right." The breathy word was hot against my cheek. My own gaze lowered to his hand; the touch twisted me from the inside out. Another hand cupped my face and I rested against it. It took every effort not to press into him completely. To not give in to that churning urge to feel every inch of him against me. An uncontrollable shuttered breath left my mouth and my lips slowly parted under his touch. Aaron's eyes flung back up to mine. Then he released me completely.

"Goodnight, Alise," he said before firmly placing me back into the crook of his arm and closing his eyes.

Did I misread him? Within minutes he was asleep or at least, pretended to be. All the while my head swam as I wondered what secrets held him back. I swore he wanted to close the space between us in that moment. I couldn't have been so delusional as to misinterpret the dark cast of his eyes upon my lips. What was wrapped so tightly around him that it pulled him further from me with every attempt to tug closer?

My panting breath clouded my hearing as I ran faster and faster through the maze of redwoods. Occasionally I would stop behind one to wait and listen. The cracking of a branch sending me off again. I felt my pursuer on my heels. Felt the presence of his breath on the back of my neck. He wanted me to know he was close. Every sound made intentionally, to scare me into flight like a rabbit scurrying from a den of brush. I was grateful for the muggy air as it coated my throat with every gulping breath.

The sound of rushing water approached. I sought it out and discovered a small waterfall pouring off a cliff's edge. The dark shadow of an alcove hid behind the wall of water—the perfect hiding spot. My wet soles nearly slipped on the mossy rocks as I slid behind the mass of water. Its white noise blocked out my panting as I readied myself to flee again.

My hand flew over my mouth as a tall dark shadow passed in front of the water wall. My knees buckled at the thought that he would find me. How did he track me so well despite my haphazard path and the rushing water that should have hidden my scent? For what felt like a long moment, the shadow stood at the edge of the falls, before giving up and walking away.

I sighed in relief but knew better than to step out too soon. After a count of one hundred, I reeled in the courage to leave the alcove with one large inhale and exhale. A plastic knife I kept from one of my takeout meals bedded its prickly edge into the palm of my hand and suddenly I felt silly for still carrying it. The stream the waterfall fed into was shallow and soaked my shoes through to the ankle as I surveyed my surroundings before I decided which direction to head next.

The plopping sound of a pebble falling into the water had my attention darting to the cliff above and behind me, just in time to see a dark figure leap from its edge. This time I did not flee, but instead, braced my legs a little further apart and prepared myself for a fight. The figure was descending right above me as though to collapse on me. Instead, I used his own weight against him. Flipped his shoulders so he landed on his back with me on top. My silly plastic knife pressed against his artery, ready to saw it open if need be.

Aaron chuckled with amusement as he looked up at me. His clothes were soaked through and his cheeks pinked with effort and a mischievous glint in his eyes. He almost looked boyish, though I knew better of it.

"Why did you go easy on me?" I accused, as my knife pressed in to emphasize my annoyance.

"I did no such thing," he lied through a wicked smile.

"You made yourself known several times as you pursued me. And then again at the end. Or else I wouldn't have known you were behind me." I lifted my knee from his chest and removed my knife. "How am I supposed to learn if you let me win?" I sighed before offering him my hand.

"Perhaps I made my approach known to instill urgency. There was more than one instance where I was close enough to touch you."

I thought of the bark that tugged lightly at my hair as I hid behind a tree. Was it in fact his fingers that tangled my ends instead? Had he dared to reach out and touch the stray strands of my ponytail as I paused to catch my breath? The thought sent a shiver along my spine. Though I couldn't say the dread of him being close enough to touch was the cause.

Still, I pouted like a child who'd been cheated in a board game as Aaron righted himself. Roaming drops from his soaked clothes trickled along with the waterfall's cadence. Pride shined in his eyes, directed at me.

"You were swift and certain in your movements. In the end you subdued me and that is all that matters." His smile was a gift I felt undeserving of. Yet, I wanted it all the same. So I drank it in and recorded it to memory as he looked down at me. The moon glinted behind his head. Illuminating his golden strands in a halo of light. Though he was no angel, perhaps he could be mine.

If only for a little while.

Chapter Thirteen

"W HERE ARE WE?" AN abandoned, brick, building stood before us. Windows were fogged over with dirt and large fissures ran along the exterior walls. Tall weeds and grasses sprouted from the concrete. Vines curved and climbed up the three-story building. A rouge flower here and there sprouted in no clear pattern. It was a sure sign that nature was determined to take back its rightful place.

"It is not what it seems. Trust me, wait until we get inside and I will show you." Aaron rubbed the back of his neck. I don't think I had ever seen him so nervous.

"Let me clear the building first and then I'll come back for you," he continued as he hopped out of the car and slammed the door shut behind him. He braced his forearms on the open window. "Just wait here." I nodded before he sauntered off, disappearing into the darkness of the building. A rusted metal door clicked shut behind him.

This was it. He was going to kill me.

Why else would he have taken me to this abandoned building at the edge of town. It was so far from where I was last seen that it would take months, if not years, for them to ever find me. Was this some sick game of his? Get me to trust him on this long road trip to his chosen killing site so he could catch me off guard? I swallowed my anxious thoughts down into the pit of my stomach. No. It would be too much effort. What would his motive be? It was just my imagination running away with me, I told myself.

The building was very nondescript, a simple square shape with no signage or ornamentation, making it hard to determine what it was previously used for. An annoying ache grew in my lower stomach, causing me to shift uncomfortably in my seat. My bladder grew impatient as seconds turned to minutes. Twilight made its slow emergence. A single lamp post flickered to life.

Submitting to my body's demands I left the vehicle and looked for a place with some semblance of privacy. I doubted the building still had a functioning restroom and that it would be one worth the search to use. Instead, I opted for a tree, not too far from sight of the car.

I considered the relevance of my earlier concerns. There were so many times he could have harmed me before now. That first time I ran from him into the woods for one. He had caught up so quickly and with minimal effort. If he wanted to do something menacing, then that would have been the perfect time to strike. And why teach me how to defend myself if he intended to hurt me? But what was this place and why had we traveled halfway across the country to stop here?

I quieted my racing mind with deep steady breaths.

As I pulled my pants back up, I started at a rustling sound from behind. I turned in a crouch, cautiously, and peered around a tree. Crunching echoed through the still air as tires rolled over fallen branches and leaves.

I was not alone.

A red jeep came to a stop just behind our vehicle, blocking it in. Tension racked my body and I froze, too terrified to move and risk notice. Not daring to even breathe too deeply. They found us. Had they still been trailing us even after we switched to the station wagon?

What appeared to be a male with dark hair stepped out of the jeep. His average frame strutted around our vehicle before peering in. After seeing that it was empty, he pulled a black hood over his head and jogged to the same door Aaron had entered the building through.

Aaron.

I had to warn him. Find him before this guy did and hopefully get out undetected.

He stuck his head in first before entering completely, closing the door behind him. Shallow, quick breaths escaped my lungs in an unsteady rhythm as my hands shook. The first dose of adrenaline surging through me.

"Be brave. Remember what Aaron has taught you," I told myself. One last long inhale and I headed for the building, crouching low below the windows. Only when I gathered the courage did I finally peek through a window. The lack of light and excessive filth coating the glass pane blocked whatever insight I was hoping for. I continued around the building's exterior, looking for another way in as I didn't dare use the same entrance as our stalker. It was then I realized we had pulled up to the back of the building.

I turned a corner to find two heavy glass doors. The kind that would have been used for a business or a school. One of the door's interior glass panes was missing. Tiny shards littered the ground around it. Careful not to snag a jagged edge, I stepped over the metal frame and through to the dark vastness beyond.

I squinted my eyes as they adjusted to the dark. Trace remnants of day, pouring weakly through the windows, provided light. Ahead of me an abandoned, broken desk, littered with leaves and debris, appeared. The walls were peeling like rotting skin and speckled in dark, moldy stains. Dust coated every surface and flitted in the air. The floors caked in places with animal feces and mud. I covered my nose with the hem of my shirt when I passed those particular patches. Each step was sure and light, careful not to disturb anything in my path. Not to leave a trace of my presence as I became the hunter of these desolate halls. I paused momentarily, listening for the footsteps of the others, with no success.

Aaron, where are you?

Urgency tried to take hold of my nerves. Every muscle in my body screamed to run, but I forced it back. Ahead I heard a loud clang, like that of a heavy door shutting. I followed the direction of the sound to a narrowed hall. I felt utterly exposed. Shivers ran down my spine and every hair stood on end. All around me papers bristled on a phantom breeze, the source undeterminable. Had Aaron just come through this way? Or the one who sought us out? Doors stood like soldiers, at attention, along the hallway. Some remained open while others locked shut. A small, narrow window adorned each door. I rubbed my sleeve over filthy glass before looking through. Within the rooms stood rows of desks and chairs, similar to what would be found in a classroom. Still no sight of Aaron or our pursuer.

After surveying most of the bottom floor my nerves were shot. Square linoleum flooring echoed under my steps in a large opening with nothing but a few broken chairs to greet me. Large floor to ceiling windows consumed the wall to my right entirely. Night was only minutes away and if I didn't find Aaron and get out of this building soon, I would be traversing it in total darkness.

My hands shook uncontrollably and at any moment I feared my knees would give out from sheer dread. Another shudder crawled down my spine. This place was something out of a horror film. Why had Aaron brought me here? I so desperately wanted to call out for him. To scream his name at the top of my lungs until he found me, but I couldn't risk gaining any unwanted notice. Besides, if I cried out, my courage would fail and I knew I would become nothing but a terrified sniveling child.

A wind stirred the leaves around me, causing me to startle. My eyes traced their source to a pair of doors just as they were swinging shut. The realization that I was no longer alone, that I was getting close, blanketed me. Reminding myself it was two against one, I made my way as quickly and quietly as possible through the doors. The handle was still warm from a recent touch. I pushed open the heavy door and beheld twin, enclosed, staircases to both my left and right. I stood as still and quiet as death, waiting for a sound, a foot step, a breath, anything that would indicate which set to take. Dead silence greeted me. I hadn't noticed at first, but this entire building was far too quiet for the amount of nature that had overtaken it. No birds chirped nearby. No flutter of wings or rustle of critters coming and going to be heard. It felt unnatural. Even the air felt strange, as if electrified—thick and oppressive.

A soft moan snapped me to attention. Gasping, I turned my head toward the right staircase before charging up slick steps. I approached a small landing and instantly collapsed to my knees. Aaron's body lay motionless before me. A large gash on his head leaked crimson into his golden hair. His eyes were closed and his body still.

No. No. No.

I rolled him over on his back. His chest rose slowly as it expanded and contracted with air.

"Aaron," I hissed. "Aaron. Wake up. Please wake up. We have to get out of here. He's here. Aaron please," my words became rushed as I slipped my arms under his and tried to drag him towards the descending steps. Tried and failed. If I wasn't careful, we would both go tumbling down the stairs and incur further injury.

Something grazed my knee, startling me. I looked down to see a thickly rusted pipe. A trail of blood in the wake of its path. He did this. Whoever followed us here must have found him and did this. No longer cautious about the volume of my voice, I shook Aaron frantically.

"Aaron! I can't carry you. Please, you have to wake up. We have to go now!"

A scream tore through my throat as I was yanked up by the back of my shirt. A grip so strong it lifted me to my feet. A force struck me from the side, causing me to fall down the slick, hard, stairs. The steps bludgeoned my body as I tumbled erratically. Red flashed before my eyes, immediately followed by unending darkness.

Chapter Fourteen

"Did you know this building used to be a school?" a voice with a thick, English accent pulled me forward from the edge of darkness.

"In the 1950s they shut it down after a cafeteria worker sauntered into the freezer and never returned." A blurry figure, impossible to define through heavy, fluttering lashes, leaned into my line of sight as it spoke. Rows of shelves with canned goods towered behind, doubling as my vision blurred.

"The authorities reported it as a natural gas leak that caused the staff to have erratic hallucinations. Quite clever," the voice echoed in varying volumes in my pounding head. Prickling stung my limbs as I lay on what felt like stone and ice.

"I should have known he would bring you here. With it being one of the few forgotten and unguarded portals in the First Realm, it would be easy to smuggle someone through."

I must have still been blacked out and having some strange nightmare. His words made no sense to my thrumming skull.

I propped myself up on my elbows and rolled onto my side, immediately regretting the movement when my head beat my body back into still submission. A hand came down on my side pinning me in place.

"Now, now darling. Hold still. You took quite a tumble." Fingers stroked my cheek.

"Aaron?"

"Is that what he's calling himself here?" Confusion willed my eyes to fully open and see the face before me.

"Wren?" I couldn't believe it. "Wren, what's going on?"

"I'll be the one asking the questions, sweetheart. Now first things first. What are you doing traveling across the country with Articus Desaius?"

Fingers pressed to my throbbing skull, just to find the spot tender to the touch.

"Who?" I winced.

"Of course, he wouldn't use his real name," he muttered to himself. Then, as if speaking to a child, he said, "The blonde twit you've been traversing the better part of North America with, darling. Ring a bell?"

"I think you're confused," I groaned, rubbing a sore shoulder. Feeling as though I had been run over by a truck, or more accurately, thrown down a flight of stairs.

"No. It's you that is confused." He tapped the barrel of a sleek black gun to his head for emphasis. I hadn't noticed it in his hand until then. The sight was followed by a splash of cold alertness.

"Wren," I sat up scooting back against the wall, "What are you doing here?"

"I've come to collect you. Obviously," his tone condescending. The implication that I was merely some object of his that he lost, didn't go unnoticed.

"You're going to turn me in," I stated more than questioned.

Wren brought the gun to his chin in contemplation. The way he waved it around as if it were a second appendage was unsettling.

"I could. I could return you and watch you lose your mind in a cell until they execute you. Or. . ."

He drew out the word just to watch me squirm. Anticipating my will to break and ask first. I held fast, never taking my eyes off him and that gun in his hand.

Growing impatient he continued, "Or I could just keep you for myself. My prize," he emphasized.

"What?" I rasped. My eyes darted around for something, anything I could use to defend myself.

"Didn't you ever wonder who it was that poisoned you and James that night? Who laid out the path to death that you so quickly found yourself on? It was me, Alise. Though it was never my intention for you to die as well. No. You are worth much more to me alive." A switch flipped in his demeanor and his voice grew deep.

"You're just a means to an end. A loose end that never got tied off, unfortunately." He glared at me with scornful eyes. I let him keep talking while my hand inched closer to its target.

"The sad part is we could have been together, you and I. At least I thought so until I saw you with him. That musician boyfriend of yours. You didn't spare me a single thought then. No. Not until you saw me at the asylum. I now realize that was only because you intended to use me for your own ambitions." A scowl formed between his brow.

I didn't recognize this person. This was not Wren. Not the man with sweet pet names and generous smile I had come to know. Before my eyes he shed his skin like a snake—peeling away the mask of Wren with every word he spoke. The cheery smile that would greet me across our makeshift cards table, transformed to a scowl. Warm, soft eyes gone cold and hard. His voice, usually dripping with charm in a slow drawl now replaced with that strange accent I would hear him sometimes use when he drank too much whiskey.

"It really is a shame"—his hand reached up to touch a strand of my hair and I flinched—"We had something good going, didn't we?" I tilted my head away from his touch.

"And then you *ruined it*!" he shouted, startling me. My skin hummed with the energy of his charged rage. "By running off with *him*! Of all people! Stealing what is mine!" He pointed the barrel down at me and aimed directly between my eyes. I sucked in a breath through gritted teeth and clamped them shut as hot tears crested my lashes.

"Open your eyes, Alise. I want to see the look in them when I tell you the truth of it all."

I forced myself to look at him through damp lashes. If anything, just to feed him the lie that I wasn't as scared as I appeared.

A gunshot reverberated in my ears and I fell to the floor with my arm thrown over my head. Silence followed. Had I been shot? I felt no new pain beside the sting of aching cold from slamming sideways onto the hard floor and the sharp ringing in my ears. After several rapid breathes, I dared enough to open my eyes and took in the scene before me.

Aaron stood over Wren's limp body, a bloody pipe in hand.

"Close your eyes, Alise," he deadpanned. Yet, I didn't. Couldn't.

Blood sprayed his unrecognizable face, livid with primal rage as he brought the pipe down again, delivering a fatal blow upon Wren's skull. I cowered into the corner, not believing what I was seeing, who I was seeing and what he had just done. A hellish nightmare of crimson and carnage. I didn't know these men before me. Not the one lying motionless on the ground, bleeding out, nor the one standing over him, knuckles white over the slowly dripping pipe.

A swift hand removed the gun from a limp one and kicked it away. His chest still heaved with exertion as verdant eyes snapped in my direction. I gaped at him, lips trembling.

"What did you do?" I screamed, voice cracking. I tried desperately to regain my breathing but my lungs heaved rapidly out of control.

The now stranger knelt before me, reaching to clasp my face before noticing the blood on his hands and the fear welling in my eyes. He thought better of it and pulled away.

"You, you—" I stuttered, unable to get the words out. The truth of what lay before me was too ugly to let out of its cage.

"It was him, Alise. He's the one who was following us. And most likely the one who attacked you at the rest stop as well." He sneered at the limp form beside him. As if that were proper reasoning for what he had just done to Wren. As if that excused him from the murder he just committed before my own eyes.

"He can't hurt you now."

I felt the truth in his words but I didn't let myself find comfort in them. Not when the man left standing was a much more formidable beast than the one slain.

"Who are you?" I asked for the final time.

Aaron abandoned the pipe and turned away from the scene to yank on the metal door of the commercial sized freezer, to no avail. A padlock secured on the handle.

"Tell me the truth," I demanded, inching my way across the blood slick floor. "Tell me. Now!"

Aaron rummaged through the shelves, tossing aside random kitchen appliances. Dusty cans rolled across the floor.

"My name is not Aaron Carpenter. That's just an alias I used while visiting the First Realm. My true name is Articus Desaius and I'm an inhabitant of the Second Realm. Any other questions?" he replied without ceasing his search.

"It's true then. What—" My eyes trailed to the bleeding body on the floor.

"Don't," Aaron warned, bringing my focus to him instead. "I don't know what he told you, but if you are referring to the body between us, I can assure you, he is not who he told you he was." He brought forth a pair of bolt cutters and made a beeline for the padlock. "His name is—was—Brenton Drexar. He is also a citizen of the Second Realm and is in no way whatsoever supposed to be here." There was that word again, realm. He grunted with effort as he attempted to cut the padlock with the bolt cutters.

Finally, within reach, my shaking, blood slick hands wrapped around the handle of the discarded gun. Tremors vibrated through my arms as I rose to aim.

"What's behind that door?"

Aaron, or should I say, Articus, turned toward me, eyes widening at the sight of what I held. Of what I aimed in his direction. He raised his hands, bolt cutters falling from his grip.

"Alise—"

"Answer me!" I shouted. Hot tears streamed down my face. "No more lies."

Articus sighed deeply before responding, "Beyond this door is a portal. A portal that can take us to another dimension, but not if we don't hurry. It's unstable and about to collapse."

"You're insane," I choked out on a sob. "Both of you are fucking insane! How can I believe a word you say?" This had to be a nightmare. Any minute Aaron would shake me awake and I would tell him of the ridiculousness of it. We would laugh it off and I would forget every horrid detail by breakfast.

"Listen to me, Alise," he continued gently.

"What if that feeling you had—of missing a place that doesn't exist—what if it was more than a feeling?"

I slowly lowered my aim as he stepped closer to me. My strength and will drained with each small step he took toward me, approaching cautiously, as though I were a feral animal he didn't wish to startle.

"What if I told you that beyond that door is a place where you could start over? A reflection of this world, yet different. Where there is no past for Alise Fox to run from. You could have a clean slate and a fresh start. And I could keep you safe. It could be the place your soul has been missing."

I shook my head, willing this sick dream to end. He was a breath away, his hand clasped over mine as he slowly removed the gun from my grasp—finger by finger. The sound of steel hitting the floor, echoed in finality, and I knew I wouldn't wake up.

"We could find your true home," he whispered, inspecting me, before turning back to the metal door. Leaving me still and speechless.

Steel bolt cutters did their job and with one last grunt of effort the rusted lock fell to the floor. Articus pulled the cumbersome metal door open wide. Heat from a warm hand wrapped around my wrist and tugged me toward the commercial sized refrigerator.

The depths beyond were an abysmal black, all-consuming, like a bottomless pit turned on its side. Wind pulled toward the darkness like a vacuum. A portal, they had called it. Though it lay plainly before my very eyes, I still couldn't trust what they saw. I couldn't trust him. Couldn't trust my own senses. Couldn't trust any of it as I pulled away.

"I'm not going anywhere with you. You both have been lying to me about who you are this whole time." I grunted as I finally wretched my wrist free.

"I have done nothing but tell you the truth, Alise. Every time you have asked, I have told you what I could." He wiped a hand over his bloody face. Blood that wasn't his smeared across his sharp cheekbones. Like the blood that now coated my own hands.

"I have never gotten a straight answer from you. You killed him right in front of me! How can I ever trust you again?" My voice raised over the roaring in my ears and my legs threatened to give out. I pieced together the chaos around me. The strange conversations and behaviors over the past weeks and every little thing I had dismissed started playing through my mind like a reel in an effort to piece together the puzzle.

"Besides from my name I've never lied to you. As far as he goes," Aaron said, gesturing his chin to the body on the floor. "It was him or you. Do you wish I chose differently?"

Yes, I thought but dare not say aloud.

Death would be preferable to this new nightmare I found myself in. Where I recognized no one and nothing and even my reality was being flipped on its head.

Aaron extended his hand. Pleading eyes refused to leave mine. "I'm sorry, Alise. I wish I could have told you everything from the start, but I had to be sure. I knew you would need to see the portal for yourself or you would never believe me. I had to be sure and I am now. I know in my bones you don't belong here and if you come with me and we make it out on the other side I promise I'll tell you everything I know."

He was all but begging and losing the grip on his leashed desperation as his hand remained extended. Unwavering, yet shaking. A soft, almost regretful murmur, left his lips, "There's nothing here for you."

The sharp cut of truth pierced my heart. I crossed my arms and sank into myself with foggy eyes and a shuddering exhale. Looking back over my shoulder at the man who laid on the floor, I knew he was dead. Undeniably, irrevocably, dead. I bit my lip to redirect the pain. The loss. The loss of everyone I had ever cared for and loved. I lost them to tragedy. Lost them to betrayal. Lost them to lies.

The delusion of our friendship was just that—a figment. A false skin both him and I wore. There was no one left. Aaron, I mean Articus, was right and I wondered, for a second, if he meant for his words to hurt as much as they did.

For the purifying fires of truth did indeed burn.

"You'll tell me everything," I stated more than asked. Strands of hair fluttered across my face from a phantom breeze coming from the mouth of the portal.

"Yes! Yes. And if I don't know the answers, I'll do everything I can to find them for you. I promise you Alise, but we have to go through now. The portal is. . . " A loud thunderous crack sounded from the black, emptiness behind us. The ground shook and a whirl of wind sucked loose debris into the portal's gaping mouth. The vacuum grew stronger. Larger objects scuttled towards its pull. Even the bolt cutters shifted closer to the bleak darkness, inch by inch.

"It's closing!" he shouted over the roar of wind. "I'm sorry. I didn't intend for it to go this way. I wanted you to have a choice."

The wind gust grew stronger, whipping my hair across my face, violently. He was right, I had no choice. If I stayed the authorities would pin the blame of not only James's but now, Wren's—*Brenton's*—murder on me. There truly was nothing left for me here but fear and more death.

A hesitant hand reached out for his. He pulled me swiftly to his chest, wrapping me in a strong grip, as a can flew off a shelf and passed our heads. He stumbled backward, through a door to nowhere and nothingness as I molded into him—into a black hole. Into the uncertainty of all I did and did not know.

To the path before and the life behind. Becoming nothing and everything. Falling into nothingness I landed in him.

As we tumbled through the darkness, a warm breath tickled my ear. "I should have kissed you that night on the beach."

Part Two

THE WOLF OF THE COLONY

Chapter Fifteen

10 YEARS AGO...

CRASHING, COMBINED WITH THE sound of shattering glass and shouting, thundered above the heads of the house servants. Some scattered from the kitchens to spy on the havoc. Others, mostly the elders, merely continued with their work, mumbling their grievances. One gave a sad shake of a head while their hands returned to washing dishes.

"I reckoned the young master would be upset this morning," a light voice chided.

"Upset is an understatement. If this continues, he'll tear the entire house down brick by brick and us with it," an older male voice countered as he hacked a knife through what would be, the day's supper.

"Lord, have mercy on us all," the woman prayed, crossing her dripping hands over her chest and forehead.

"Amen to that," the male agreed as he wiped bloody hands on his apron.

In one of the many bedrooms on the floor above, a young boy yelled out his demands to anyone within earshot, "Bring her back!" The boy's eyes were glassy—a fiery, verdant that burned with fury as he wrecked anything he could get his hands on. His chest rose and fell with quick pants of exertion.

"Sir, I cannot. Your father—"

A lamp shattered against the wall beside the butler's head, cutting his words short.

"*Get out!*" the boy screamed as more items from the luxuriously decorated room came crashing to the ground.

The boy stomped over to the wall where the butler stood by the door. Though the boy was several inches shorter than the man, it did not stop him from flinching in fear as the boy reached up toward him, just to rip a painting from its hanging wire and smash it in an uncontrolled rage beneath his feet. The crumpled face of a beautiful man in military dress looked up at the boy in disappointment as his foot came down on his face, repeatedly.

"Bring her back or I'll tear this bloody house to shreds!" the boy screamed to the butler before the man slipped out the door, not wanting to become the next victim, should the boy run out of inanimate objects to let his fury out on.

Most children would not be allowed to have such violent, temper tantrums in a family of high standing. But this was not some aristocratic young man. This child was that of a wolf. He was plucked straight from the wilds themselves, along with the sweet, soft girl, who was now missing from the house, to the boy's great displeasure. To even attempt disciplining or containing such a creature would surely end in a fatal wound to any who dare try. Only the general knew how to control the little beast. Only he held the key to manipulate the child's will. Said key was now the cause of the current bout of chaotic rage in the young master.

The boy, now done with the previous room's demise, was making his way down the hall with destruction following in his wake. He stomped with determination in every step, as he made his way towards a thick wooden door. A servant waved his hands in an attempt to deter the young master from disturbing its occupant. However, the servant quickly leapt to the side as the boy boomed a command for him to move out of his way. His own will to guard the door crumpled under the rage, evident in the young master's sneer. The heavy wooden door flung open, causing it to slam against the wall and rebound, as the boy hollered at the occupant inside.

"Where is she?"

The man inside looked up from the papers at his desk with utter boredom etched in his features as he looked toward the wild, disheveled child before him. He did not leave his seat, nor did he show an ounce of concern as he ignored the boy's question.

"I did not fill this house with nice things just for you to break them in one of your fits."

"*Where is she*?" the boy demanded, lungs at risk of bursting from his screaming and panting.

"Is that what this is about?" the general asked calmly, as if the fit of rage that started merely walls away was a common occurrence in the house and of no concern to himself.

He turned his attention back to the papers before him, finishing off a letter with complete calm and collectedness. Ever the unmoving, unflinching, unwavering, cold and calculated, general. Even in his own home. Even toward his own children. The boy panted in the stillness.

"We have discussed this already, Articus. I had Ms. Paddington escort Kareena to Chateau Mont-Choisi, where she will have the finest education a young lady of her class can obtain. She will need to be polished into an impeccable debutant if she is to acquire an advantageous marriage for this family. Surely her running about the grounds with you all day isn't going to prepare her for that," the general sneered.

"She's mine," the boy seethed. "She's not your doll to dress up and sell to the highest bidder!" Heat crawled up his neck in red blotches. "Bring her back," he growled.

The general looked up. An eyebrow raised at the boy's audacity to make such demands.

"It has been done and I have no intention of changing course, no matter how intense your possessiveness may be toward her. You two are, in fact, my wards and I will do as I see fit with the both of you. That includes you attending the Academy and her attending finishing school as planned, and I've grown rather tired of this discussion."

Though the general was a lethal force, he was still young to be in command of so many men, with so much sway and power, and he had not anticipated the press of sharp, cold metal at his throat. Seething, feral eyes stared down from atop his desk. The boy crouched on its surface—the tip of a letter opener pressed to the man's neck. A flutter of disturbed pages flinted delicately to the floor. Without the chain of the girl to bind the boy to the man's will, the little beast had no leash for which the man to tug.

The general merely smiled at the threat in front of him. Just as he did at every opposing army on any battlefield. In fact, he relished the challenge and grew more alive with the threat to his life. He chuckled softly, being careful not to make any sudden movement.

"No need for such dramatics," the general said with a challenge in his cold eyes. To overpower the boy as usual, wrangle the weapon from his hand and beat him into submission, would be too easy. And would wrinkle his coat. No, he had something far more profitable and long-term in mind for his young ward who was so full of lethal potential. He knew if he sent Articus away to the Academy, separated the boy from what he held most dear, that he would merely run away after the girl. And the endless cycle of retrieval and reprimand would only distract from the young boy's training. Make him indignant and unfocused. He needed the boy willing and motivated, if he was to harness his untapped potential as his heir and right hand. As his weapon.

Nothing would get in the way of the general's goal. Instead, he grinned, almost charmingly, and said to the wild creature, "Let us make a deal."

Chapter Sixteen

I FELL THROUGH A door to nowhere.

Weightlessness overcame me and my eyes flew open. Though Aaron, or was it Articus now, held me as we fell, I found myself alone. A dark, milky sky full of stars surrounded me, yet, never had I felt more alone and lost in my entire life. It was only a blink, only a heartbeat, before the universe melted away and an ominous weight pressed against me from all directions. Gasping, a cold, heavy weight gripped my lungs.

No air.

There was no air.

With another blink, I was floating in a dark pool of water, unable to distinguish up from down. Darting around furiously, I looked for a light source, trying to find the surface.

Several odd-shaped pieces of sun-bleached driftwood came into focus. Panic took over and I choked down another gulp of water as a beam of moonlight illuminated the shapes' true forms. Skulls, femurs, and finger bones of different sizes crowded the sandy floor like a morbid mosaic. The horrifying realization that I was to contribute to these dark waters' collection squeezed my throat tighter. My chest seized with its protest for air.

My body thrashed in panic, with a fury to survive. Each hasty movement grew more tired and lax. The kicking of my feet slowed as they attempted to push me to the surface, far away from the bones below. Yet, I was so tired—so very tired. My thoughts grew quiet and my panic turned to something like peace. It would be nice, I decided, to float amongst the lost. To sink to the watery graveyard below and no longer be alone and so tired.

From far away, so muffled I could barely hear, a voice called out my name. Was it death? Did I outrun him for far too long and he finally caught up? Was he coming to claim me? Death felt colder than I imagined. Too cold as it wrapped its lulling hands around my chest and pulled me further down. Nothing but darkness and the solitary moon, glinting above, were with me now. It was indeed, peaceful, down here with the dead. With the others who fell through that gaping black hole and ended up here. In this watery crypt.

The only sound was that distant calling of my name. Strangely enough, it felt like home, and I wanted to answer.

Maybe what happened before was only a dream. Perhaps Wren, or was it Brenton, shot me after all. Or was it possible I was still in the asylum? Finally losing my grip on reality.

The moonlight was suddenly blinding and cool air kissed my face. My name boomed in my ears. A tight grip wrapped around my waist. With my next involuntary breath, all the water I had swallowed came up. I vomited it back into the dark body of water as the arm around my waist pulled me from behind. When I stopped heaving enough to breathe properly, I witnessed my surroundings through burning watery eyes.

Black, star-flecked water, touched by the shimmering moonlight, stretched for miles before me.

"Alise!"

Articus desperately swam, with me in tow, toward a not-so-distant shore. His eyes wide with alarm and effort as he dragged me along.

"Can you swim?" His breaths were labored with his effort to keep us both above water. The weight of our soaking clothes only added to the drag and resistance.

Nodding, my throat too wrecked to speak, the arm wrapped around me adjusted so he could launch me ahead of him. Nothing but pure fear and determination drove me to swim harder than I ever had in my life, to get to shore and out of this dark, strange, limitless water and the dead below. A lure, I was shocked to realize, I so willingly almost succumbed to. That death hypnotized me with his false sense of peace. My will playing right into his beckoning arms.

I all but crawled onto land. My hands and knees sank into the muddy shore line, but each step was a reassurance as I put more and more distance between myself and the haunting waters. After several ragged breaths, my arms and legs gave out and I collapsed onto my back and gazed up at the star-strung sky. The stars winked at me, as if to say, "*Remember us?*" Instantly I was taken back to the few seconds, or was it hours, that I was floating in that milky universe, alone.

Shooting up onto my elbows, I found Articus panting beside me on all fours.

"Thanks for the warning," I huffed out between labored breaths.

Articus sat up on his knees. "I had no idea that the portal would transport us to the middle of a lake, but you're welcome for saving your life. Again." He ran a hand through his hair and over his face before rising to his feet.

Ignoring his begrudging tone, I asked, "Where are we?"

"The Second Realm. My home." Water dripped from his thoroughly soaked clothing. A cold breeze reminded me, with an icy shiver, that I too, was thoroughly soaked. I wrapped my arms around myself in an attempt to stave off the cold as I watched Articus tramp off toward a dense tree line in the distance. He turned around to find me still sitting, soaked through and in shock on the shoreline.

He made his way back over, his wet clothing ladened his steps, and extended a hand to me. "Come. We still have a ways to go until we reach the Academy and only a few hours of night left to get there."

I stared at his hand as if it were a foreign object. Shaking my head, he retracted his hand with a frown before running it over the back of his neck, looking put off and annoyed.

"There were bones, human bones, at the bottom of that lake," I grit out through chattering teeth.

"I saw them as well."

"Do you think. . ."

"Yes. They are most likely those who unknowingly entered the receiving portal. Hopefully it will fully collapse and we will be the last to ever use it."

A fresh wave of shivers overtook me. How easily it would have been for us to end up like the others resting below. Sharpness pierced my chest, making my eyes water as I recalled Wren—*Brenton*—saying that the building used to be a school. The people who went missing, most likely dead or lost forever. Women. . . and children.

"Receiving portal?" My attention caught on to the term like a life raft for my sanity.

"Yes. A receiving portal in an entrance from one realm to the next. And like all portals, they only open at certain times."

Articus's body hummed with anxiousness. His foot all but tapped in place as he surveyed the shoreline. He wanted to put just as much distance between the water and himself as I did and his patience was growing thin with my questions.

"I know this is a lot to process and I wish I had more time to explain, but right now I need to get you back to the Academy and out of those wet clothes."

His words brought reality back to my consciousness like a slap to the face. My mind rushed to recall everything that had happened in the last moments before falling into the lake. To before entering the portal. Images skittered across my memory like a fast-forwarding replay.

Aaron bringing that bloody pipe down on Wren's skull.

No, not Aaron—*Articus*.

He wasn't the man from the bus or the cabin or who I shared those long hours on the road with. If anything, he was the man who chased me down in the woods all those weeks ago and the one who killed Wren.

"I'm not going anywhere with you," I spat as I rose, my limbs slowly regaining their strength.

What did you do?

A sharp stitch cinched in my chest. "You killed Wren. And. . . and we just left him there." Pain burned the back of my eyes.

"As I told you before, his name was Brenton Drexar, not Wren as you called him. And his death was not intentional. For Christ's sake he had a gun pointed to your head, Alise. Do you have no sense of self-preservation?" Fury and confusion glazed his eyes and fists clenched at his sides.

A part of me knew Articus was right. Wren. . . Brenton, did threaten my life, as he had said. Someone I thought I knew, someone I trusted to some degree. Somebody I had actually felt guilt over using the way I did, and yet, he turned on me and showed his true self and his true nature and. . . wanted to kill me for my betrayal. Not to mention he attempted to kill Articus.

I recalled his body lying motionless in the stairwell. How my chest seized with panic as I begged him to wake up. And yet when I saw him again standing over Brenton with that bloody pipe drooping from his hand and falling to the floor, I felt a strange combination of relief and fear. Not fear of him hurting me, but of the unknown. Of the fact that I didn't recognize the man I knew as Aaron anymore. There was no question in my mind though that the blow Articus delivered was the only thing that spared me from that bullet. Knocking it off its intended course as Brenton pulled the trigger.

But what was it Wren said right before? He wanted to confess. To tell me the truth before he killed me. What truth?

In my state of stubbornness and confusion, Articus grew impatient.

"So be it," he barked before ducking down to scoop me up, throwing me over his shoulder, effortlessly. A yelp of surprise escaped me as I kicked against his grip. I pounded my fists on his chest, and protested his intentions to carry me off to who knew where like a disobedient child.

"Let me down! I can walk!" I shouted.

"Forgive me if I don't believe you, but you have already made it clear you have no intentions of complying."

"Fine! Fine!" I said in an effort to appease him. "I promise I won't run off. Just tell me where we are going." Swallowing deeply, I prepared to strike him with his own vow. "You promised! You promised me, you would answer all my questions." I knew they hit their mark. He paused a second before sliding me down before him.

"I did, didn't I," he recalled more than asked. I nodded my head anyways. Before my eyes I saw his demeanor change to one of calculation and indifference. A mask I had seen him don before.

"Alright then, Miss Fox," he said coldly, clasping his hands behind his back. "I'll answer all your questions to the best of my ability until we reach our destination. In the meantime, I request you stay close and follow me." We trekked forward into the woods. A worn and well-traveled path appeared and I followed closely behind.

"Are you going to tell me where we are going first?" I asked after a beat of silence.

"As I said, the Academy."

A breath of frustration escaped my pouting lips.

"Can you elaborate . . . please?" Surrendering that last word reluctantly.

"Lovely," I heard him whisper under his breath.

"The Academy is where young men, usually from well-to-do families, go to further their militant education." His steps crunched rock and twig under foot.

"Like a university?"

"In a way, yes. Not only do men receive training that will aid them in their future military careers, the Academy is also an institution of knowledge and research."

"And why are we going there?"

"It's my home. I can keep you safe there until we decide what to do with you next."

He spoke as if I were a stray he found on the street.

Charming.

"We?" I pressed.

"You, Clouden and I. We will need his help. As soon as we get there, we'll seek out his council on your situation. Watch your step," he added, indicating a pot hole in the path that was waiting for an unsuspecting ankle to twist. I sidestepped it and, through the tree line, thought I saw the twinkle of lights.

"You called this the Second Realm," I paused, assuming my statement alone would be indication enough to elaborate. "I don't understand what that means," I added after a few moments, thinking of the galaxy I hovered in only moments ago. "Are we still on Earth? I mean it looks the same, but after what happened in that portal I just..." my words trailed off as my mind tried to piece sense together. Looking at the ground, my eyes confirmed it was indeed dirt under my feet, water squishing out of my soaked shoes, trees that surrounded me, air filling my lungs.

"Yes. This is Earth, just not the one you are familiar with. It's a different plane than the reality you know. A different version of events occurred here that molded this dimension into what it is now."

I still couldn't comprehend or believe what I was hearing. Another plane of reality? Dimensions?

"Why do you call it the Second Realm?"

"Because it is the second layer in the Four Realms. I can explain in better detail when we reach the Academy. It contains the world's largest archive with the greatest collection of research journals and articles on the Four Known Realms. We'll be certain to find more than enough material to help you better understand and answer whatever questions you may have about this realm, as well as the others."

"Oh," I whispered as I tried not to collapse from my suddenly weak knees. There were others, four total, according to Articus. He spoke as if each one was its own unique interpretation. A reimagined version of the reality I had always known, in what he referred to, as the First Realm. If what he said was true then why didn't anyone from my realm speak about the other realms? Was it a secret? I chewed on these questions and decided to hold back on demanding more details until we reached the archives of this "Academy" he was taking me to. Articus paused and turned to face me, as though expectant in my reaction to all this new information.

"I understand this is all very new, and possibly terrifying for you. The authority of the First Realm has decided to withhold all information on the Four Known Realms from its citizens, and has even denied the existence of the other realms for hundreds of years."

My head swam. Was I even walking or just stumbling through time? I felt as nauseously weightless as I had moments ago when I was floating in that sea of stars. After physically shaking it loose, traces of disbelief still clung like cobwebs.

"Wait this . . . this doesn't make any sense. You're talking about alternate dimensions and realities. That can't be true. I—" Articus strode forward, closing the space between us in a few strides. He clasped my face in his hands and forced my gaze to lock with his.

"I'm telling you the truth, Alise. You cannot possibly believe that the world you lived in was the only one. I know you didn't. I saw the doubt of it in your journal and in our talks. Look at me," he gently demanded when my eyes wandered away. "Is it so hard to believe that there's more than what you know? More than what you have been told?"

I paused, considering the truth in his words. Hadn't I always felt lost? As if my body—my very soul—had never fit comfortably in my environment. The constant illnesses that wore me down and the empathic curse that coated my skin. At one point I felt that even my mind grew toxic from the air I breathed. Would it be different somewhere else? Wasn't that what I had been looking for, deep down, all these years?

I nodded and Articus slowly released his hold on me before returning to the path.

"I feel I must warn you, Miss Fox," Articus continued. "This realm is not like the one you grew up in, in more ways than one. The culture is vastly different, especially when it comes to the roles of the sexes. Especially for females," Articus gritted out.

"How so?" I urged him on.

"Let's just say the culture here is similar to that of your realm's distant past. It is nowhere near as progressive here," he quipped as he spun and continued forward.

The past? Which past? How far back was he indicating?

"Is this the past? Did we time travel?" Still fishing for a way to make sense of this all.

Articus scuffed back what sounded like a potential laugh.

"No, we did not time travel, nor is such a thing possible. We are on the same field of time as we were before. I just wanted to prepare you for the similarities you may see, between the First Realm's early-nineteenth century customs, and here. Though you'll soon see there are quite a few differences as well. The formalities for one can be quite rigid, therefore, I will continue to call you Miss Fox in public settings as you should also refer to me by my last name."

As he spoke, the trees parted before us, and the once-distant sparkling lights came clearly into view. A vast city lay miles before us. Smaller buildings with gray, sloped roofs mingled with the golden domes of cathedrals. A stone bridge joined the side we stood on with the city below. It curved elegantly over a sparkling river that snaked around the distant city, hugging it securely. The muffled thrum of engines, shouts too far away to decipher and bells chiming the time, sounded from the city's interior. The faint smell of smoke mingled with the damp breeze coming from the river. Breathing deeply, I soaked it all in.

A horn blared from the sky above and I was startled, looking up to see an aircraft, unlike any I had ever seen, float lazily between the clouds. Several aircrafts to be exact, all varying in shape and size. Some had large balloons atop them, while others had sails like a ship at sea would.

"Those are airships," Articus murmured in my ear, seeming to follow my gaze. My mouth hung open as I took in all my eyes could consume. Grabbing my attention, he leaned in and pointed ahead of me to the right.

"Over there, on the edge of the city, is the Academy. Do you see it?" My eyes tracked his gesture to a set of towering spires that seemed to kiss the night sky. The Academy was immense and looked more like a church than any college I had ever seen.

"Come. We need to get you in, unseen, before dawn breaks."

Too dumbfounded to resist, I let him take my hand and drag me away towards the sparkling city and all its luring beauty.

Chapter Seventeen

ARTICUS AND I MANAGED to skirt around the city's edge, unseen. I followed closely on his heel, and, reluctantly, obeyed every hushed order until we reached a cellar door, behind the grand opulence that was the Academy. A monstrous, neo-gothic castle with spires and stone statues that climbed toward the sky, cloaked beneath the heavy cloud cover. Though I was more than apprehensive to enter the dark, underground confines, I did so, as instructed, and waited for Articus to return with clean, dry clothes for me to change into.

"What the—" I muttered as I inspected the old-fashioned garments. A woolen brown skirt and a white, cotton, button-up blouse were draped in my arms, along with over-the-knee stockings and heeled boots with button closures.

"You can't be serious," I rasped, trying to keep my shock at bay.

"They are all I could get a hold of at the last minute. I wasn't expecting to have a woman accompanying me back and you can't very well be seen in the clothing we came in." Slim slivers of light leaked from the cellar door, casting the final beams of moonlight on Articus's thick, wavy hair. I took in his own change of attire. He wore dark gray trousers with a matching vest over a white collared shirt. The sleeves were rolled up to his elbows, exposing bare forearms. On his feet were dark, polished, oxford style shoes that appeared to be leather. He looked more like the psychologist I originally met all those weeks ago and yet, this version of him felt so foreign. Even though I loathed to admit it, he looked quite handsome. Especially in the dim moonlight. His warm features battled in contrast to our cool-toned surroundings.

He was a splash of golden sun against a gray background.

His hands slid into his pockets. "Please be quick," he said before turning his back to me for privacy. I wanted to protest him even being in the same space while I changed, but I couldn't deny that, despite it all, his presence was still a comfort to me. But that was the Aaron I trusted and grew close to. Not this stranger who spoke so eloquently in his old-fashioned clothing. Not this . . . Articus.

How much of what he told me about himself, back there, in the First Realm, was even true? The man I thought I knew, he wasn't real, he was a fever dream I had before being tossed into a cold lake and waking up to this strange new world. No—this man, Articus, I did not know or trust.

I changed quickly as the silence grew thick in the cellar. The only sound was the shuffling of cloth on skin. Dust tickled my nose and an uncontrollable sneeze erupted.

"Lord, bless," I heard Articus say softly, with his back still turned.

"You mean, 'bless you,'" I corrected as I slid on a boot, hoping it would fit.

"*No*. I meant, 'Lord, bless,'" he countered as he turned to find me rising and dusting dirt from my skirt.

A sort of curiosity glimmered in his eye and I wondered what I looked like at that moment. Most likely nothing that I would recognize in the mirror. I felt different in so many ways. So completely out of control of my own life, or even the understanding of it. My gaze trailed to the spot on Articus's head where, only a few hours ago, he was bleeding.

"Does it still hurt?" My hand absentmindedly gravitated to touch that tender spot.

Articus flinched from my touch like a skittish animal.

"I'm fine. Ready?" He lowered my hand by the wrist. I nodded my response.

Before we entered the Academy, Articus threw our old, still damp clothes into a lit, outdoor stove. The smoke rose into the starry sky like the burning of a sacrificial lamb as the last remnants of my past life turned to nothing but ash.

My eyes took in everything they could as we passed through a large, rather ancient kitchen, where copper pots and drying herbs hung from various rafters. Through several winding halls, lined with too many doors to count, at some point I became completely, and utterly, lost, and I was convinced that I could never retrace my steps out of this labyrinth. More twists and turns emerged through an alcove in a large corridor, and floors cased in black and white marble appeared, along with arches and pillars adorning every encasing. We paused before a large set of double doors, decorated in intricate molding. They were overwhelmingly ornate in design and detail.

"This is the Academy's library, where the archives are stored," Articus whispered as he opened the doors and ushered me in. Air left my lungs as I took in the large moonlit space. Though it was hard to make out any details in the dim light just before dawn, what I did manage to see nodded towards the gothic.

Towering bookshelves, ladened with leathery tomes covered every wall, and layered every aisle. Iron, spiral staircases held up a second story, filled with even more shelves of books, with a thick ornate railing, the only thing separating it from the rest of the space. My heeled boots echoed off the combination of wood and marble floors until a carpeted runner appeared beneath our feet and muffled the sound. Along my peripheral I spotted alcoves with desks and chairs. The small nooks looked rather cozy and private compared to the vastness of the library. Narrow, leaded glass windows let in the early dawn light.

"Clouden will most likely be in his office at this hour," Articus said, to no one in particular, as he headed up a narrow hall with a wooden staircase, lit by a faint light that glowed from above. The words *Prof. Clouden Archives* were painted on the fogged, glass door that illuminated the stairwell. Articus hesitated a moment with one foot on the steps.

"You better wait here," he suggested, before heading up the stairs and entering the room above, leaving me completely alone in the faint, gray glow of the library. From behind the door above, Articus was greeted by a muffled voice, exclaiming his name in a questioning tone as if he were not expected.

Anxiously, I bounced on my toes and clutched my arms. Voices beyond the door grew too quiet for me to decipher. I took the time alone to absorb in every detail of the magnificent space around me. An enormous globe, larger than one I had ever seen, sat in bronze casing at one end of the library. It looked more like a piece of artwork than an actual study aid. My fingers itched to spin it on its axis, to study its design for any differences in continent structure and country borders.

Each bookcase, embedded into the surrounding walls, was topped with a lustrous filigree molding that clasped roman numerals in its center. Simple wooden ladders, shaped more like staircases lined the tall bookshelves to their peaks. I followed their height to the second-floor railing, up to an ornately decorated, domed ceiling. Every stunning detail stole my breath.

If this was all just a nightmare, it was a beautiful one.

I felt the urge to lay on the cold hard floor and stare up at the ceiling and to drink in every mural, and molding, for hours and hours until I had my fill.

Just as I was about to surrender to the floor, a soft click sounded from the top of the stairs. I turned to see a dark haired, slightly matured, male, assessing me like an apparition. A hushed curse escaped his lips. Articus's stoic expression hovered behind the older man's shoulder, before the door slammed shut, causing me to flinch. Voices rose from behind the door. Louder this time, so that I couldn't help but overhear.

"Articus, what have you done?" the unfamiliar male's voice demanded—Clouden, I presumed.

"She can benefit our campaign—our research," Articus's voice countered, ignoring the other male's question. "Imagine the wealth of information we could gain. The proof in her existence alone."

"She is a girl, Articus, not an artifact." A slight sting accompanied the word "girl" and "artifact," making me feel inferior, as if I were a small toy.

"I know that," Articus's voice hissed.

"You must send her back," Clouden ordered, coldly.

No. No, I couldn't go back. Not now. Not so soon after everything that happened back there. Surely the event of . . . Brenton's body being found, and my escape, along with Articus's sudden absence, would lead to assumptions. It wouldn't be long before authorities put two and two together.

A shiver raised the hair on my skin and a sickening knot twisted in my stomach at the thought of Brenton's body laying cold and pale on the dirty tiled flooring.

Close your eyes.

I wish I had.

"If I brought her back, she would be hunted down and killed for a crime she didn't commit. Or worse, for my own actions," Articus retaliated. A wave of relief washed over me to hear Articus defend me on this matter.

"Must you be so blinded by her?" Clouden growled in reprimand. "You go off on a mission to gather information and instead *illegally* smuggle a First Realm citizen into our dimension, putting both your life, and hers, in serious danger. And for what? A pair of pretty eyes?" Heat from a combination of anger and embarrassment flushed my cheeks.

"It wasn't like that!" Articus's voice roared along with a deep thud, as though something fell to the ground. "It's not like that," he repeated, softer but just as firmly. My skin buzzed with the energy of the argument and charged me into a frenzy of my own. My body soaked in their fury like a sponge, it made me frantic and restless. I had heard enough to know the direction this conversation was going in.

Clouden had said Articus smuggled me here *illegally*. What would happen then if this was discovered? If I was found to not be from here, the Second Realm, but, instead, the First, as they called it.

Why was it illegal for me to be here? And why did Articus take such a risk in bringing me?

Confusing questions swirled in a toxic concoction in my mind as I paced the rows upon rows of bookshelves before finding myself in an alcove, staring out a leaded window to the sunlit gardens beyond. Morning finally made her debut.

I replayed every word I heard, trying to piece together a puzzle I couldn't begin to understand. Articus spoke of a campaign, one that I could be used to aid them in. Also, Clouden said, Articus was in my realm on a mission to gather information. What exactly were they trying to prove, and how were they intending to use me?

"There you are," a soft low voice startled me from my thoughts. I turned to see Articus at the end of the aisle, Clouden hovering over his shoulder. The man was indeed older than us, though the only indication of his age was the light peppering of gray hair at the temples of his shoulder-length, dark chestnut hair. His beard was short and well groomed, framing his sharp jaw. His eyes were also dark like his hair, brown like fresh coffee. My first impression was that he was quite handsome for a man who stayed sequestered in an office above a library in the early dawn hours. And not at all what I had imagined or expected.

"Here is the plan," Clouden started without so much as an introduction or greeting. "If anyone asks"—he indicated toward me with a glare—"you are my charge who has come to live with me, temporarily, at the Academy. I can offer you protection in this way but no other. The discovery of who you really are, where you are from, depends completely on yourselves and your own discretion." He turned abruptly to Artiucs. "You escorted her here on my behalf and have been traveling from the outer village provinces. Am I understood?"

I was startled by the authority in his voice and the realization that he was now addressing both of us. I nodded silently as Articus simultaneously hummed in agreement.

"For now, Articus will arrange your sleeping quarters. You will assist him, and myself, in our research as needed. I expect your full cooperation. If you fail to comply in any way, I will not hesitate to send you back where you came from. Also, it is crucial that no one else, beyond the three of us, know of your true origins." Without waiting for a response, Clouden turned on his heel and strode off, muttering under his breath, "I'm going to lie down."

Articus relaxed his tense posture and released his hands from behind his back, sliding them into his trouser pockets. He opened his mouth but I cut him off before he could speak.

"I overheard your conversation. You can't just use me for your little experiment like some guinea pig." Frustration creased my brow and I found myself striding up to him in defiance as all of my pent-up anger bubbled over.

Articus turned his head away, side-eyeing me in disgust. A muscle ticked in his jaw. "If you refuse to make yourself useful and comply, then you leave us no choice but to return you to the First Realm." He crossed his arms over his chest. "Clouden is not accustomed to taking in stray girls."

Stray.

His indifference sliced through me, the word "stray," was salt to the wound. I felt my bravado faltering.

"But you are the one who dragged me here," I threw back.

"Quite by mistake, I'm afraid. I see that now," his response was full of casual boredom as he scratched his jaw.

"So, you would have just left me, knowing what would happen to me if you did?"

"All I know, Miss Fox is that I'm completely exhausted by your utter lack of gratitude." That side-eye measured me up and down once again, but instead of disgust I saw hints of frustration, felt his desperation in my bones. It caused me to feel fatigued—utterly exhausted. Or was it the hour? The fact that we had swam and hiked through the night finally weighed down on me.

"Since I have no choice in the matter, just take me somewhere where I can sleep off this nightmare," I huffed, letting my defiant stance melt into a tired one as I rubbed my face.

Articus turned to lead me out of the library, and halfway to the grand double doors I thought I heard him mutter, "You always have a choice."

Chapter Eighteen

MY FEET WERE PRACTICALLY dragging through the Academy halls as the last tendrils of adrenaline left my bones and my eyes became too heavy to lift beyond the ornately tiled floors and the larger set of feet before me. Mindlessly, I followed, turn by turn—utterly lost in so many ways. Ways I was determined to tally and assess after some much-needed sleep. A groan of frustration was knocked from my chest as I bumped into Articus's hard back. He had stopped dead in his tracks. I looked up, surprised to see him smiling like a child, a glint of sheer joy in the corner of his eye. My gaze followed his to the end of the hall where a young woman stood, hands cupped over her mouth in exuberant surprise.

Multifaceted hair in shades of copper fell loose from her bun, framing her heart-shaped face. Piercing emerald eyes glittered across the distance between us, solely fixed on Articus, as if nothing else existed around her but the man several feet ahead of her. A squeal escaped behind her covered mouth before she charged toward us and jumped, with complete abandon, into Articus's outstretched arms. She clutched tightly around his neck as he spun her with a soft chuckle. "I missed you too," he said into her hair.

I took a step back from the intimate scene before me, feeling slightly uncomfortable with the unfamiliar display. The young woman reached up to cup Articus's face in her hands. "I had no earthly idea when you would be returning and, of course, Clouden was an absolute vault when I would inquire into your whereabouts, as usual."

The way she spoke, it sounded so proper, and reminded me of something I might hear from a woman in England, centuries ago. Even her clothing was unlike anything I had seen. She wore a simple, light gray, long-sleeved dress with white cuffs and collar under her apron, with a crown-like hat atop her head to match. Although, now slightly askew from being twirled around so fervently. My eyes darted between the two in confusion as my sleepy mind tried to understand the persons before me. Just then the young woman seemed to notice my presence and released Articus's neck.

"Oh, hello there," she beamed, straightening her hat and running her hands down her skirt. "You must excuse my emotional outburst. See, it has been several months since I've seen my brother and I hate to be parted from him for so long and oh my . . ." She giggled, looking back and forth between myself and Articus as she rambled, "Excuse my manners. My name is Kareena Desaius. I'm Articus's younger sister." She sketched a quick curtsy and bowed her head slightly, in greeting. "And you must be. . ." I opened my mouth only to be cut off by Articus.

"This is Miss Alise Fox, she is Clouden's ward. He sent me to escort her back to the Academy for him. Hence the secrecy, dear sister. You know how private he is." Articus shot me an encouraging look to play along. I curtsied and bowed my head as Kareena had done.

"I'm so pleased to meet you, Miss Desaius. You may call me Alise, if you wish," I said, introducing myself with every ounce of decorum I could muster. Stunning performance, if I may say so. I am nothing if not adaptable.

Kareena squealed again, causing me to flinch in surprise. Her hands clapped joyously before her arms wrapped around me in a tight embrace.

"Oh goodness, I am just so happy to have another young lady here. I know we will be the best of friends and you must call me Kareena."

"Yes, well . . ." Articus coughed in interruption. Kareena released her vise-like grip and held me by the shoulders at arm's length, inspecting me with kind eyes.

"We have just arrived back from our travels, sister, and I'm sure Miss Fox is exhausted from her long journey. Now if you wouldn't mind, I was just showing our guest to her new sleeping quarters—"

"She can stay in my suite!" Kareena grinned wide, with all the hope and excitement of a child, despite her womanly figure that would argue otherwise. I wanted to live in that smile. Wanted to knit it into a blanket and wrap it around myself on cold nights. It shined like the sun and felt just as warm when directed towards me.

"Oh no I couldn't—" I started to protest.

"Nonsense. I have an extra room and my suite is much more spacious than the guest quarters. It would be no trouble. In fact, I would love the company. It would be a privilege to have you stay with me."

"Kareena," Articus gently chided. I shot him a venomous look, immediately hating his attempts to reign in her enthusiasm.

"Of course, only if you would like. I understand if you would prefer your own space, especially after such a long excursion." This close I could see a splash of freckles across her face. So perfectly, yet naturally, positioned, as if an artist flicked a brush of watered down, tawny paint across an ivory canvas and called it a masterpiece.

"That would be lovely and so undeservingly generous of you, thank you," I answered confidently, taking both Kareena and Articus by surprise.

"I must say, Brother," Kareena continued, turning her attention to Articus, "you look worse for wear. And where is your luggage, Alise?" she directed back to me.

I felt dumbstruck by her sudden keen observation. We must have looked like two drowned rats after what we went through.

"Well. . . um—"

"You see, Sister," Articus cut in, "Alise has no luggage. We were robbed by outlaws while on the road."

"Such ridiculousness," she chided and slapped her brother on the arm. Articus chuckled at her affectionate touch.

"Quite the truth, Sister. We barely made it with the clothes on our backs. Perhaps you have some garments you could lend Miss Fox, until appropriate ones can be procured? And I beg of you not to tell the general about our little mishap. I don't need another reason for him to be cross with me."

Kareena inspected him with suspicion.

"If you say so, Brother." A breath of awkward silence grew between the three of us in the immense, echoing space.

"Wonderful! Yes, well I'm on my way to the infirmary now for my shift, but Articus knows the way to my suite and can see you there. You may rest and I could show you the grounds when I return, if you wish."

"Thank you. That would be lovely," I said.

"Well then," Kareena said, before she turned to Articus, raised up to her toes, and planted a chaste kiss on his cheek. "Behave yourself, Brother, and try to get some rest yourself. You look dreadful."

Articus stood, hands in his pockets, unphased. "Ever the flatterer, dear Sister."

Kareena ignored his remark and turned back towards me. "Again Miss Fox, I mean Alise, it was a pleasure meeting you. I'm sure we are going to enjoy getting to know each other very soon." She carried on down the hall, almost skipping.

"She's. . . just. . ." I started, stumbling on my words in her wake. A buzzing energy fizzled and popped across the atmosphere in her lingering wake.

"The sun," Articus finished for me. If she was his sun, then Articus absorbed every ounce of her light. For just a moment his face glowed in a way I had never seen. But only for a blink before indifference, and perhaps a bit of distress, arrived to wipe any trace of happiness away.

"Congratulations, Miss Fox, it now seems we will both be lying to my sister for the unforeseeable future." Without further explanation, he continued on in our original direction, hands clasped behind his back. "This way please," he said absentmindedly. Realizing I was still caught up in the force of nature that was Kareena Desaius, I shook my thoughts loose and shuffled after him.

We traveled through grand halls with arched ceilings, intricate tiled floors, and thick columns. Every bit of the Academy was opulent and ornate. Especially compared to the stale simple buildings I was accustomed to. Alcoves with leaded glass windows could be found randomly throughout the building and each new space we entered had me lagging behind Articus's swift stride as I gawked in awe. I felt grateful that Kareena offered to show me around later since Articus did not deign to say a single word about any of the spectacular areas we passed through.

The sun peeked over the walls around a lush, manicured courtyard as we traversed its stone paths. A few people shuffled about the grounds, only stopping to nod their head in greeting to Articus. Some referred to him as "Sir" while others simply said, "Good morning," before carrying on with nothing more than a simple tip of the head from Articus. There were very few women, and the ones we passed did not greet Articus at all, but rather, kept their heads and eyes lowered. All appeared demure and, in a hurry, as they shuffled by in muted, matching uniforms.

Finally, after what felt like miles of walking through a maze of breathtaking architecture, we arrived at the living quarters where the higher-level staff, such as professors, stayed if they required accommodations, according to Articus's brief description. He opened a heavy, wooden door for me, clasping it firmly by its ornate crystal knob before ushering me in with a wave of his hand.

"Normally, I would not be permitted to be alone with you in a room, unchaperoned, let alone your bedchambers. However, since this is my sister's suite it will be easier for me to come and go without suspicion." He closed the door with a soft click and leaned against it, arms folded across his broad chest as I took in the room before us.

Spinning around the space, I observed every fairytale element. A seating area held two light pink high-back, upholstered armchairs in front of a massive carved, stone fireplace. Beautiful pastoral and floral art decorated the mantle and walls. Simple padded chairs sat across from each other beside a small white table in one corner. Twin console tables, in a dark, rich wood flanked both sides of the entrance with matching vases containing matching flowers within them and across the living space, large bay windows were nestled around padded bench seating and a floor to ceiling bookcase with more decoration than books on its shelves.

"To the right is Kareena's bedroom and to the left is where you will be sleeping." Articus strode toward the door on the left and opened it with an encouraging look for me to explore inside. As I stepped into the quaint room he continued, "Each room has its own washroom with its own shower."

"Showers? You have showers here?"

Articus smirked. "Yes, Miss Fox, this is not the Dark Ages. Try to have an open mind and reserve your assumptions."

"Honestly, I don't know what to expect anymore," I muttered, more to myself, as I took in the tiny, yet lavish, room. Before me was a full, and well-appointed, four poster bed with sheer, sky-blue fabric draped from post to post. One matching upholstered chair sat to its right, next to a small night stand and across from a beautifully carved, Queen Anne-style armoire, with speckled mirrors embedded in each of its doors. The wall to the right housed a decent sized window, above a small upholstered bench with, once again, matching sky-blue fabric. To the left was a door that I assumed led to the washroom.

I was curious to see what a Second Realm shower looked like and rushed into the adjoining room. I was greeted by complete darkness.

Was there a candle or did they have electricity here?

"Umm, Articus. How do I make it light in here?" I asked, feeling completely idiotic for having to ask such a thing.

"Here," a soft voice said beside me as he pressed a brass button on the wall by the door.

"Oh," I said by way of thanks.

The washroom, as it was called, was small as well, with only a glass-encased shower, pedestal sink and gold framed mirror above it. And a toilet. I gave thanks to the universe for running water and plumbing in this realm.

"Let me show you how the shower works." Articus reached past me into the shower stall. On the tiled wall beside a set of knobs was a glass like panel.

"What is this for?" I asked, indicating the rectangle of glass.

Articus said nothing as he lifted a brass lever up from a tilted bottom facing position to a top facing one.

"This one releases a stream of water as you lift it up and cuts off the flow, as you press it back down. This dial controls the temperature of the water," he slowly turned the dial, clockwise. As he did, a small fire appeared and grew with each turn in the glass window. I reached my hand out to test the water. It was in fact warm and growing hotter with each turn of the dial.

"Fascinating," I murmured to myself. "An individual heat source. Does every washroom have this?" I asked.

"Just in this building. The Academy is very old and only recently has this building been renovated with the latest accommodations. However, the dorms in the main building, where the cadets stay, has a central boiler for their showers, as does the kitchen and servant quarters."

My mind thought back to earlier this morning, when we first entered the Academy. That must have been the kitchen, and the small halls lined with doors must have been the servant quarters he spoke of. Making the people that we passed by, the staff.

A long pause grew between us in the shower stall. A space so small, we almost touched as we both avoided the spray of the water. One large breath, one millimeter forward and our limbs would graze. My skin grew tight and my thoughts fogged along with the shower's glass walls. I took a step back only to meet its damp touch.

An ache grew in my chest at the memory of how he touched me before. How he held me in the back of an old station wagon as the sound of crashing waves lulled us to sleep. At the loss of the young man who opened up to me on that long drive to the coast. Had we become friends then? Or was I just deluding myself with someone who only showed me kindness in order to use me? As I did Brenton.

Either way, I wanted that time back. I wanted to hear him sing along to those old-fashioned songs that played over the radio, again. I wanted to sip tea while we talked over his third cup of coffee. I wanted Aaron back, not this stranger, this proper young man with his hands always where they belonged. This unremorseful murderer who intended to use me for his own agenda.

I noticed the water was still running and reached over to turn it off. Articus kept his eyes fixed straight ahead as a muscle fluttered in his tight jaw.

"I think I've got it from here." I turned to step out of the stall, but was stopped by a strong arm braced across the threshold. I turned to reprimand him just to be met with pine green eyes, searing into me. His mouth opened and closed. Words seemingly lost on his tongue, he sighed and his mouth stretched into a fine line.

"I am not your enemy." His stare was unwavering as those gorgeous eyes burned a hole into me, making me feel small and wanting to grab any sense of control or power I could from him.

"That's not for you to decide," I said a bit too softly as my bravado weakened under the pressure building in the small space.

Articus merely dropped his arm. A silent dismissal.

Chapter Nineteen

As promised, Kareena gave me a tour of the Academy grounds after her early morning shift in the infirmary, where she worked under the tutelage of the head nurse as her apprentice. In between explaining the uses of the various spaces we passed through, she would interject amusing stories of injuries and illnesses she had treated since her time in the infirmary. It seemed that even into young adulthood men were reckless and arrogant. Some believed themselves to be invincible enough to achieve a leap from one roof top to another. Or skilled enough to ditch wooden practice swords for real ones in sparring practice.

"The boy arrived looking like bloody ribbon candy." Kareena chuckled, ignoring the looks we received from several of the cadets we passed. "Of course, he was in no mortal harm, just several cuts that I'm sure stung. But not as much as the punishment I'm certain the weapons master will administer." Kareena stopped, noticing my attention stray to all the men in impeccable uniforms, giving us once overs.

"Oh, don't pay them any mind," she fussed as she wrapped my arm in hers. "Women are rare here. Besides you and I, there are only a few staff members. To say the boys are rather desperate for female attention would be an understatement, but do not fret, you are the professor's ward. No one would dare make unwanted advances toward you." Her eyes looked me up and down as she continued. "Though I don't blame them. You are quite beautiful."

Heat flushed my cheeks. "You're too kind. But I'm sure it is you they are feasting their eyes upon," I redirected. Kareena merely laughed. The sound was akin to windchimes caught in an autumn breeze and gained us many more looks in return.

"Oh, if only what you said were true, dear. No, I'm afraid I'm as good as a leper on these grounds. In this city, in fact." Shock slapped me in the face. I forced us to stop and faced her.

"You can't be serious. What makes you say such a thing?"

"I'm completely serious," she responded, steering us back onto our path. "No one would dare touch, let alone speak to the daughter of the general and if they were ever to gain an ounce of courage to so much as greet me, then my brother would be more than happy to remind them that their bravery was far better used on the battlefield than on an attempt to court me."

"That seems a bit overly protective." An understatement, yet, I approached with caution.

"Yes, they can be but I'm actually grateful for it most days. It keeps me from getting distracted from my goals. No man will get in the way of my ambitions." She tilted her chin slightly up.

"May I ask what those are? Your goals I mean." I was trying my best to imitate Kareena's language style. Remembering I was under the pretense of being from this realm myself. But it felt awkward and unnaturally forced compared to the casual style I was used to.

"I aspire to be a doctor one day." She paused and looked at me, assessing my reaction.

What kind of response was she expecting? Did she expect me to scoff at her admission?

"Well, that sounds lovely, Kareena."

She blinked back at me.

"What?" I asked.

"You don't think it is too ambitious?"

"Not at all. You seem quite intelligent. I'm sure it's attainable for you to achieve. Why do you ask?" Was it really so far-fetched for a woman to be a doctor in this realm?

"To be honest, intelligence or not, it wouldn't even be a possibility if it were not for my father's approval and influence." She grasped my arm and continued us forward through an area that looked to be a dining hall. Several wooden tables and chairs arranged in rows with wide aisles on a black and white marble floor. Thick, leaded, glass windows, topped with pointed arcs were spaced evenly across the ivory stone walls.

"Of course, Articus had to convince him of my cause but, once he did so my father then saw my dream as a challenge of his own. He takes pride in the idea of having the first female doctor of our region be his own daughter. The pressure can be a bit unbearable at times, but I'd much rather feel the pressure of my own ambition than that of being someone's prize."

Oh, I liked her. I liked her so much that I wished her to be my own sister.

"Men," I said under my breath.

"Men, indeed," Kareena concurred with a giggle.

Apparently, Mass on Sunday mornings was mandatory. No exceptions except for the fatally injured or ill. The clothing I had been given by Articus the previous day was also not deemed suitable for the occasion, according to Kareena. After bedecking me in several layers of undergarments—enough to make my head spin—chemise, stockings, corset, corset cover, she shook out a light pink dress from the back corner of her wardrobe.

"Luckily, for you, I have kept several of my older dresses from when I was . . . smaller," she said hesitantly, as though thinking of the least offensive term to describe my frail, meek, body. "They may fit you, but if not, perhaps we can cinch the waist with a bow."

I inspected the dress she laid out on her bed. It was finer and more intricate than anything I had ever worn. Several layers of ruffles decorated its skirts, making it appear even fuller over the petticoat tied to my hips. The sleeves puffed out in a similar fashion to the dress Kareena wore and tapered to a slim fit at the wrists. The collar was also modestly high and snug around my neck, and delicate satin rosettes adorned the bodice in small clusters. I felt like a cupcake with strawberry frosting and imagined I looked just as tooth-achingly sweet and fluffy.

Kareena, surprisingly, was silent as she helped me dress, after I told her I was more accustomed to simple fashions. She even styled my hair without question as to why I couldn't do it myself. I watched her every move keenly so as to replicate the hairstyle myself later. In the end she decided to braid both sides of my head to meet in the back where a long single braid was wrapped into a bun at the nape of my neck and secured with several pins and even a few flowers that matched the color of the light pink dress. It was more beautiful than anything I could think of for myself, yet simple enough to replicate.

She wore a similar hairstyle and a dress, with rouge auburn curls framing her face. However, her dress was made of a sage-colored satin that brought out her green eyes. Her hair, like the many colors of fallen leaves, stood out in stark contrast. I envied her easy beauty. Though I knew her and Articus had no blood relation, there was no denying the similarities in those gorgeous, pine-green eyes. However, while Articus's was that of a dark forest at sunset, flecks of gold in the irises, Kareenas were emeralds cut and polished to perfection. Rare and beautiful.

I stared back at my reflection in Kareena's vanity for several uncounted seconds. My own, usually blue eyes had faded to an icy shade of gray. Darkness rimmed under them with exhaustion. Signs that the emotional and physical toll was becoming too much. I desperately wanted to crawl back into bed and sleep for three days straight, but even the thought of undressing was exhausting. It would probably take thirty minutes alone, just to strip down to the undergarments. The color of the dress did nothing for my pallor, though one would expect the rosy tone to bring pink back to my cheeks. Instead, it harshly contrasted the paleness of my skin and the ash of my hair. I had decided early in my teen years that only black and white suited my phantom-like traits.

We made our way, by foot, to the cathedral that was thankfully located just outside the Academy grounds. We passed by immaculately dressed young men and women, some in bright, beautiful dresses similar to Kareena and mine. While others wore more simple garments in neutral shades of gray and brown with matching hats pinned to their hair. Some men wore uniforms of red and gold, while others wore suits in varying shades of black, gray, and brown. All with shoes that shined, as if freshly polished.

Towering, twin spires, touched the hazy morning sky and kissed the clouds with bronze crosses that jutted from the cathedral's peaks. In true opulence, like every building in this realm, it seemed its heavy, wooden doors were encased with grand columns on either side and an archway to match. As we took stone steps up and through the entrance, I craned my neck to the vaulted ceilings that were even more ornate than those at the Academy. Inside, the ceiling was painted with intricate detail, depicting scenes of angels floating on clouds, mostly nude with strong masculine forms, with robe-wearing men in prayer, pleading eyes averted to the sky above and a young woman, her head covered, backlit with an infant in her arms.

"A bit more grandiose than what you are used to, I assume?" Kareena whispered beside me as we made our way down the main aisle. Our heeled boots clicked an echo through the vast nave as they tapped against ancient stone, inlaid in intricate designs. Some were engraved with words written in a language I did not know. I nodded my head in silent answer and was utterly speechless.

The truth was that I had never been in a church. What little I did know of theology was gleaned from one of my father's old art books. A thick tome that harbored a collection of theological paintings dating back from the twelfth century to nineteenth. I would flip the pages, one by one, and read the little descriptions below each depiction as I curled up in a knitted blanket on a worn rug in his office.

The Temptation of Christ on the Mountain, Duccio di Buoninsegna, circa 1255–1319.
The Resurrection, Piero Della Francesca, circa 1420–1492.
Christ Crucified, Diego Velasquez, circa 1599–1660.
Madonna and Child by Giovanni Battista.

All names and dates that held no purpose beyond its pages, until now. I understood, in this moment, the inspiration and feeling each painting was meant to stir in a place of worship such as this one. Whether it be divine inspiration or propaganda, that was to be decided by the viewer.

My parents never taught, or pressed, any kind of religious practices upon me as a child. We never spoke about God or went to church, and we never celebrated some of the holidays others did—as I found out later. It wasn't until I was in foster care that I had a traditional Christmas, with carols and displays of the nativity. The feasts of heavy meats and almost sickly, sweet desserts that charity organizations would sometimes put on for us, underprivileged orphans, was one of my first experiences with the unusual holiday. We celebrated during the time my mother would usually burn a yule log and have me help make ornaments made of seeds and honey to put on a tree outside for the birds. It was a ritual we always did on the shortest day of winter. My mouth watered at the recollection of the rare and delicious feast, and I wondered how long Mass would be this morning as my stomach grumbled.

Kareena ushered me to a wooden pew to sit. Upon seeing the spot she had chosen for us, my hands became clammy with nerves. Our seats were so close to the front.

Wonderful.

I slid in beside her on the hard, mostly empty, bench. Behind us, a few pews back, I noticed only women sat on this side of the church, while the pews to my right were filled with men—a lot of them—each with a head of hair combed impeccably into place. Even the older gentlemen, who didn't have much left on their heads, tamed what remained. I internally giggled at the ridiculous sight of five single strands combed perfectly across a bald scalp. Kareena elbowed me in the side, snagging my attention back to the front of the church.

As my eyes roamed back toward a slightly raised platform with what looked like an altar upon it, I caught sight of familiar, wheat-colored locks in the first row. Articus sat beside Clouden, along with some other, older men I didn't recognize. His eyes were fixed on the altar ahead. Or was it the cross on the wall behind it?

A rather large sculpture of a man hung before it. Upheld by nails in his hands and feet. A crown of thorns sat on his head. Red was painted as blood from the wounds and his eyes were positioned on the ceiling, as if looking to the very clouds and depictions of heaven painted above, in longing misery.

I jolted to attention at the blaring of organ pipes as everyone rose to their feet and a man in black and white robes entered the space. After bowing before the bleeding man on the cross, he ascended a small staircase to a slightly elevated podium in the corner of the stage, raised above the gathering before him where all could see.

As he raised his arms in a kind of greeting, the congregation started to recite a sort of chanting prayer in unison. I kept my lips sealed, having no idea what was being said or how everyone seemed to know what to say.

The rest of the service was a blur of much of the same—a song or prayer that everyone, besides myself, seemed to know, and a lot of sitting and standing. Thankfully it was easy enough to follow Kareena's lead. Occasionally, during the long readings from the priest, I would sneak glances at Articus and find his face quite serious, focused, and almost in reverence during some of the prayers.

Did he actually believe in this kind of thing?

My eyes wandered over the gaudy space. Alcoves accented with arched, stained-glass windows decorated the walls on both sides. Each seemed to illustrate a scene from a story. One of an urn pouring out water across the earth, followed by the next which depicted a large ship with a man aboard. His arms were stretched out to an approaching dove. Though I was confused by the context of the images, as an artist I respected the time and craftsmanship that must have gone into each window.

After what felt like over two hours of rising, sitting, and kneeling, everyone rose to their feet, yet again, as an organ bellowed another soulful tune. The priest descended from his raised platform and gracefully exited through a discrete side door as the attendants sang what I hoped would be the final song of the morning. Afterwards some mingled with others to chatter before filing out the doors.

Others bustled out immediately as they too were anxious or possibly as hungry as I was.

"Well, I don't know about you but I am famished," Kareena said. "I really must remember to eat a heartier breakfast on Sundays or I fear I'll faint during the benediction."

My shoulders shook with a silent chuckle as I watched her blow a strand of hair from her face and fan herself dramatically.

"We couldn't have that, now could we." I snickered behind my hand.

"I insist you join me in filling our stomachs to the brim until we fall into a food-induced coma for the rest of the day," she demanded as she took my hand and led me out of the pew towards the aisle.

"That would be divine," I responded before glancing over my shoulder.

Articus leaned in towards the man in robes, speaking conspiratorially. The priest nodded his head and the two discreetly stepped away from the chattering crowd, passed a nondescript wooden door and out of sight.

What was he up to?

Chapter Twenty

I WOKE TO THE taste of bitter pills—my mouth, dry as cotton. My head felt weighed down, so heavy I couldn't lift it, I could only roll it from side to side as my blurry vision tried to take in my surroundings.

White ceiling.

White walls with a lattice pattern of sunshine on one.

So much white.

I had the inclination that my head was on a thin pillow, and stiff, thin, cotton rubbed my skin. Lifting a hand to rub the throbbing from behind my eyes, I found my wrist restrained. Cuffed with a leather restraint, fastened to a small metal bed frame.

No.

No.

No.

This couldn't be right.

I was sleeping in a bedroom at the Academy, in a suite I shared with Kareena Desaius in the Second Realm . . . Not in this hell.

Not again.

But the taste of sedatives lingered on my tongue—the bitter chalk of too many pills, and not enough water to wash them down. I looked down at my body, clothed in a thin hospital gown. The kind they gave the high-risk patients, instead of the t-shirt and sweats I had worn during my stay. It itched my skin. Cold, stale air unrelentingly leaked through the thin material, making my skin prickle.

Why was I back here? Had they found me with Brenton's dead body and brought me back? Was that why I was restrained and sedated? But what happened between then and now?

Thoughts of a dark freezer room, sucking all the air into it like a black hole, and a young man with golden hair pulling me out of a lake of stars and bone, resurfaced. Wasn't that memory the truth? Or was it just a medicated dream? That a mysterious man, one I knew as a psychologist here at the asylum, brought me to another dimension for a fresh start.

The thought alone sounded too far-fetched. Wasn't this the more plausible reality? This room, these cuffs, and the inevitable future where I would be charged with not only James's death, but that of Wren's as well.

Or was it, Brenton?

Two orderlies walked into the room, their faces indiscernible under the fog of the sedatives I was sure to have flowing through my bloodstream. An older looking man in a long, white coat stood at the corner of the door frame, looking down at me.

I tried to ask what was happening but only an incoherent moan came out, for my tongue was too thick and dry to form words.

"Here she is, officers," the doctor said as the two entered the room, cuffs in hand.

"She's been sedated since we found her and I advise you to keep her that way," the doctor advised as the orderlies unfastened my cuffs.

"She can be quite violent, this one."

Once the restraints from the bed were removed, one of the orderlies raised me up to a sitting position by the arms. My head rolled to the side, resting on my shoulder. I had no control of my body. I was a ragdoll manipulated by a child and contorted like a play thing, as the orderlies placed my legs over the edge of the bed.

"Call for a wheelchair, she's not going to be able to walk in this state," one of the orderlies said to the other.

I attempted to talk, to ask what was happening. Where was I being taken? Anything. But only a humiliating stream of drool leaked from my lax mouth.

This was living, breathing, hell, to be awake and conscious in your body with no control over it. To be completely at the mercy and will of those around you with no means to protest.

Despite the sedatives that made me so immobile, my heart started racing with panic. Breath quickening as I was placed into a wheelchair and cuffed to its armrest before being wheeled out of the room and down a vast, never-ending hall.

Suddenly there wasn't enough oxygen in my lungs. I was breathing faster than ever before. Taking large gulps of air as my heart pounded against my chest, but it did nothing for me. The air coming in flooded my lungs, choking me like water. I was drowning in it. I wanted to claw at my chest and throat, wanted to open my chest cavity wide to free the rapid, fluttering bird from the cage of my ribs. But, of course, my hands were uselessly cuffed to the wheelchair.

A cold wet sensation stung my neck and my eyes darted to the side to see the doctor with a readied syringe.

"Just to be safe," he said as he removed the alcohol wipe from my flesh and plunged the needle into my neck.

I shot up, eyes wide as I panted. Sweat coated the cotton night dress I wore and the silky, smooth sheets around me. My hands frantically grazed the bedding and trailed to my chest, the back of my neck, and my face as I took in as much of my surroundings as my eyes could absorb.

Furniture in calming shades of blue greeted me in the luxuriously appointed room. I was back at the Academy, in the suite I shared with Kareena, I assured myself. To be certain, I all but leapt out of bed and padded to the adjoined washroom. I quickly turned on the light and faced myself in the mirror.

Hollow gray blue eyes stared back at me. Full lips and cornsilk hair, damp with sweat, were a welcomed reassurance. I wrapped my arms around myself and squeezed my arms tightly until my nails dug into flesh to the point of dull pain. I could feel it. I could move my body. No longer a limp sack of bones and flesh.

I turned the faucet on and let the sound of running water drown out the last remaining panic of the nightmare before splashing icy water on my face. This was real. This was my reality now, despite how bizarre it seemed. I was no longer in the hospital, let alone that realm, I told myself.

This is real.

I recited a list of truths—the things I knew were undeniable.

"My name is Alise Fox."

"My mother and father were Petra and Clifton Fox."

"They died in a fire."

Tears born of terror and sorrow rolled down my cheeks and combined with the water dripping down my chin, falling into the sink as my truths turned into desperate convictions.

"I'm in the Second Realm."

"I'm in a suite at the Academy."

"Articus Desaius is real."

"This is real," my voice cracked and my hands clutched the edge of the porcelain sink.

"This is real. This is real. This is real," I chanted again and again until my breathing slowed as well as my heart.

I was not going back to sleep.

I rubbed my eyes and yawned for possibly the hundredth time since we started our trek into the city. Kareena assured me it was a short distance to the boutiques, and an easy trip on foot, but I was beginning to see her definition of "short and easy" was far different from mine. Especially when I was running off a single piece of toast and only two hours of sleep.

Our booted feet clanked along the surprisingly clean, cobbled streets and walkways. Its uneven surface caused me to stumble a few times as we made our way. Mercifully, no one seemed to pay any mind to the two young ladies traversing about town on their day off.

I, however, noticed everything.

Poised young ladies, appearing close in age to ourselves, were also milling about the city in long skirts and variously colored, high-collared blouses. Gracefully they glided into shops of all kinds. Some hosted displays in their windows of satin and lace ribbons in a variety of colors and exuberantly decorated hats with feathers, cherries and more ribbons.

Others entered patisseries. The delicious smell of baked bread and sugar wafted by every time someone entered or exited. Patrons entered with eager grins and walked out carrying pastries dusted with powdered sugar in their gloved hands.

Hatless boys ran down the street chasing after a dog with cans tied to its tail while a slightly older boy rode some sort of motor bike I had never seen before. His messenger bag flapped against his back, full of rolled papers and packages while his page-boy hat threatened to fly off his head as he gained speed.

All the sounds of the city, everything my eyes took in, disoriented me. It was as if I had stepped back in time yet to a place elsewhere. To a different version of the past. Contradictions confronted me at every corner. Something old-fashioned and something new and inventive mingled together.

A woman sold roses to passersby while a bronze, mechanical street sweeper scuttled down the road and appeared to be operating on its own. Its gears churned and groaned while its mechanical brooms spun debris into a gaping hole at its front, so as to gobble up rocks, trash, and the like.

The occasional, vintage-style automobile would appear around a corner before almost silently accelerating away. Their round, shining curves reflected the sunlight and it glared back into my eyes as they passed by. I would be sure to ask Articus how they operated later, but for the most part people seemed to travel on foot or bicycle. Though the bicycles were unlike any I had ever seen, one I observed had a larger wheel in the front than the back and looked rather uncomfortable to ride. Another, ridden by a postal worker, had what appeared to be a small engine attached to it that softly purred without emitting any exhaust. Exposed gears of various metals churned at one side of the back wheel.

Beautiful Parisian buildings I had only seen in history books lined the streets, white-washed with sloping gray roofs, as airships of every shape and style hoovered across the skyline. Some kept afloat with enormous hot air balloons while others glided on wings made of wood and cloth. Others even sported sails that caught the wind like a ship gliding on an invisible sea.

Pain struck me suddenly, and shocked me to attention. I had rammed straight into a street lamp in all my gawking. I rubbed the soreness in my shoulder, certain it would bruise and caught notice of a sign on the lamp post. The black and white poster was of three young men in soldier uniforms. Their hands in salute as they gazed off the page. Below the image, bold type read:

PREPARE FOR DRAFT DAY. ENSURE YOU ARE REGISTERED AND READY TO SERVE THE COLONY.

Kareena took notice of my distraction and paused in her trail of words I had been paying no attention to, to come to my side.

"Alise, are you okay? You must be more careful where you are walking." She folded her arm into mine. "I know this must be a lot to take in with you being from a small village. Have you ever visited the cities before?" she asked.

"No. Never." My attention was still fixed to the poster as she dragged me along.

"Well, I'm honored to be the one to take you on your first outing. You are in for such a treat." She beamed. Her voice grew higher with enthusiasm.

"First, we will design an entire wardrobe for you. You can't possibly carry on in the clothes my brother scavenged for you. Then we shall reward ourselves for all our efforts by gorging ourselves at the confectionery. I know a shop that makes the most delicious truffles."

"Kareena, I couldn't possibly have you make such a fuss over me and to be honest I don't have any money." I blushed with shame.

"Nonsense! Neither do I," she exclaimed and shot me a sly expression.

"But my father does and he holds credit at almost all the shops in the city. Don't you dare feel an ounce of guilt for spending it with me. I know I shall not." The tension left my body as she pulled me along. "Come, come. We're almost there." My heavy feet shuffled alongside her.

"I thank the Lord every day that I live in a French state of the Colony. They truly have the most beautiful fashions," Kareena said, mostly to herself, as she held a bolt of olive-green satin to her chest and swayed before a tall, gilded three-faced mirror. She paused and gave a critical glare at her backside.

"And the most decadent food, I'm afraid." She sighed and turned to face me. "What do you think?" she asked.

"I think the color looks beautiful on you."

Kareena chuckled at my response. "No silly. Not me. I mean you. How do you like the designs Madame Clarisse has chosen for you?"

I felt hesitant to respond since said Madame was presently at my feet, hemming what would be one of my new skirts, as I stood as still as possible on a raised pedestal. Bolts of fabric in every shade and design imaginable, leaned against one another. Spoils of ribbon and lace trim lay beside a stack of fabrics Kareena and Madame Clarisse picked out for me. Some claimed to brighten my eyes while others warmed my complexion. Or so, I was told.

After sliding the last pin into the skirt's fabric, Madame Clarisse reached into her pocket and retrieved a small, bronze rabbit with oversized ears that appeared sharp in the center, like two small knives. She clipped the tiny metallic rabbit to the edge of my skirt, and it hummed along its roadmap of pins as its sharp ears cut off the excess fabric. It made a full cycle before stopping to drop back into Madame Clarisse's hand. A perfectly cut and stitched hem was left behind.

"Marvelous," I found myself saying.

Madame Clarisse merely smiled up at me before rising and dusting off her skirts.

"What do you think?" she asked, her accent thick and airy, hands gesturing to my garment.

I looked in the mirror and swished side to side, admiring the seamstress's craft.

"It's quite lovely," I said. "One of the nicest pieces I have ever worn." At that Kareena giggled. One of the many sounds she made when she thought me ridiculous.

"There will be much finer garments than even this skirt, Alise. Just wait till you see the rest of your wardrobe." She beamed at me, hands clasped together, almost giddy with anticipation. And for the first time, I let myself soak it in—let myself enjoy the indulgence of having clothing made specifically for my body; skirts and pants that actually held to my slim waist and bodices that did not gape at the bust, but instead felt like a perfectly-fitted glove against my frame.

And I felt not an ounce of guilt while Kareena and I stuffed ourselves sick, sampling every flavor of truffle the confectionery had to offer. The space was illuminated by tiny gold and crystal chandeliers. We sat in polished, white, wooden chairs across from each other at a small glass top table. Rows upon rows of chocolates, truffles, and other sweets lined a golden-framed glass counter behind Kareena. The walls were bedecked in pink and cream striped wallpaper.

As I gazed out the window of the chocolate shop, I noticed another poster on the lamp post beyond. Same as I had seen on our way to the seamstress. I waved off Kareena who offered up yet another truffle and asked, "That poster on the lamp posts. I've seen several of them today. What are they about?"

Kareena followed my line of sight out the window.

"Oh, yes, those hideous draft notices they plaster all over the city this time of year. As if we could forget that, every year, every boy who turns eighteen is to be sent off to serve in the military—leaving young girls across the Colony to pine over their absence." She gave me a puzzled look from over the rim of her tea cup. "Do they not have the draft in the village you are from?"

Oops.

This must have been a topic I was supposed to have known about, and what Articus meant when he told me to direct all my questions to him. I would have to be more careful.

Quickly correcting my miss step I replied, "Yes, of course. I just have never seen posters for it before and there are not many men in my village as it is." My fingers fidgeted in the fabric of my skirt; my eyes casted down.

When I looked up a moment later, wondering why Kareena had gone unusually quiet, I saw pity in her eyes from across our spread of sweets. She reached for my hand and took it into her own.

"We need not speak of it again," she said sympathetically.

Guilt and confusion followed me the rest of the day, stealing what joy I had earlier. In those brief moments when I felt, almost, like a normal girl. Not one with secrets and lies draped over me like heavy armor.

Chapter Twenty One

D ETERMINED TO LEARN AS much as I could about the Second Realm, I shuffled behind Articus, as he led the way to the archives with a renewed sense of purpose. Perhaps I could acclimate to this realm and start a new life here, as Articus had offered all those days ago. Like adjusting to the seasons, I only needed to wear a new layer—one of knowledge and adaptability and I was sure I could find a place to fit.

For now, that place was in a dim alcove in a corner of the library, seated at a massive, heavy wooden desk with volumes and scrolls of all kinds laid out before me. Articus picked the location, deep in the back for its quiet and privacy, assuring me others rarely came to this part of the immense library. Articus swiftly gathered materials for me to look over and study, before he studied me himself.

Some texts held pictures of airships, dissected in diagrams that identified their parts and functions. It perplexed me how many variations there were of the aircraft, and that inventors were still designing and building more aerodynamic and efficient designs.

After consuming my fill of the subject, I shifted over a heavy tome from my stack and opened the leather binding to a section about politics, hoping to glean more information about the draft that Kareena had spoken of. The text confirmed what she told me. Boys from across the boundaries of the Colony were drafted to serve at age eighteen. They would first spend a few years in training at one of the many military academies across the Colony, before being sent off to serve for a minimum of four years. After which they were free to start lives of their own, if they still lived, or continue their military careers, if they so wished.

"Articus?" I whispered, catching his attention from across the table. He sat with his feet propped up on the polished wood, a stack of books and scrolls of his own, piled by his feet as he scribbled notes in a journal.

His brows rose and his eyes locked with mine from above his tortoise and gold-rimmed reading glasses. A strand of hair fell across his brow.

"Is this country—the Colony—currently at war?"

"No. At least, not in the typical sense."

"Then why is the draft in place? I saw posters for it while out with Kareena yesterday."

Articus let down his feet and rested the journal in his lap before continuing, "Though the Colony is not currently at war, per se, it is constantly pushing its borders of power and control. As a result, it is mandatory that every male citizen of the Colony be trained in military combat in order to secure its power in numbers. It is the strength of its empire as well as an insurance against any who would think to oppose it."

So, the Colony used its male citizens as a protection of sorts, for who would dare to come against an army as large as half the population? Trained and with experience.

I continued reading the texts on government and policies of the Colony as

Articus continued his note taking. It was all rather droll until I scrolled over something about a theological style government and a group of mostly clergy who ran everything, fittingly called the Council, when another question popped into my mind.

"Where did you go with that priest the other day, after Mass?" I asked, looking back up to where Articus sat, now hunched over a map.

"Quite observant, aren't you, Little Fox," he responded without looking up from the scroll. I waited for his response. The silence demanding someone speak first as I wondered if he was in fact going to respond or ignore me all together.

"I went with him to confess," he finally answered, sounding annoyed as he was once again pulled away from his task.

"Confess?" A chill shivered down my spine at the indication of what he could have been confessing to.

"Confess what?" I hissed.

"The sin of murder," he deadpanned. His expression silently said to my confused one, "Obviously."

No. He didn't. He couldn't. Why would he implicate himself and possibly us?

"What?" I rose from my seat, hands pressed on the table before me, shocked at his cavalier tone. As if he wasn't just telling me that he told someone our secret.

"You told him you killed Brenton?"

"No, of course I didn't tell him the details of who or when or even where. Father Gerard knows better than to ask about such things."

"So, you just confessed murder to him." I shook my head as I collapsed back into my chair.

"It wouldn't be the first time," he said. A sick heat rushed down my spine, causing me to gape at the man across the table from me.

"First time to confess?" I speculated, though I knew, that wasn't what he had meant.

"The first time I've killed someone, Alise. Don't forget where you are, this is a military academy. These men will likely be sent to fight at some point, if they haven't already, and it will not be long before they are faced with the choice of kill or be killed. What do you think I have done to be in the position I am today?" Frustration rose in his voice as he broke my stare and pinched the bridge of his nose.

I froze as another piece of the old facade I had conjured, when he was Aaron to me, chipped away. Though I didn't think Articus was entirely innocent, I never stopped to imagine he had familiarity with taking a life before he took Brenton's. I recalled how he struck him without hesitation—with swift surety and no remorse. He had been showing me all along who he really was, but I chose not to see.

"Please, don't look at me that way," he pleaded, breaking my thoughts. I had been gaping in horror and quickly clamped my jaw shut and looked away.

I thought I heard an exhausted sigh from across the table when suddenly loud footsteps echoed towards us.

"There you are," Clouden said. His voice booming, compared to our earlier hushed conversation and the silence of the library.

"Have you gone over realm travel with her yet?" he addressed Articus—ignoring my presence completely.

"We were just grazing over politics before you arrived and have not broached the topic yet," Articus answered as he stretched his arms above his head.

His white shirtsleeves were cuffed at his forearms, layered under a steel gray sweater vest that matched his trousers and made the forest green of his eyes that much more verdant. Though he was finely dressed, the small details were sloppy and effortless. His collar was left unbuttoned and his hair disheveled as he ran his fingers through it, pushing it off his handsome brow.

"I require Alise down in the lab." I jolted at the sound of my name and Clouden's sudden attention.

"I will give you a brief run-down of portal travel on our way," he continued.

I merely nodded my reply and rushed to follow after him as he turned briskly on his heel. Sure, strong steps surrounded me from in front and behind. A quick glance over my shoulder confirmed Articus's pursuit. His glasses hung hazardously on his vest, barely holding on with each stride. Hands buried casually in his pockets as he strode, and when my gaze rose to his face he acknowledged my attention with an agitated smirk. His full mouth stretched thin.

"The first thing you should know"—Clouden said to no one in particular but brought my focus to the back of his head, all the same — "is that one cannot skip realms in portal travel. Each portal takes its traveler to either the realm above or below it. Hence why the realms are numbered and portals are either receiving or exiting, depending on the realm in which they are entered." I thought of the one in the abandoned building that we had taken to get here. Brenton, had said that one in particular, had been locked up and abandoned. Forgotten with time. Were there many unknown portals in the First Realm or were they all accounted for? And who all knew of them? Used them?

Before I could ask, Clouden continued his lecture, as he descended a set of narrow stairs in a dark corridor. His voice bounced off the cavernous walls as we followed. Steps clacked together out of rhythm.

"There are four realms that we know of and here in the archives, myself and every researcher before me has made it our life's work to study everything we can of them, and their native-born citizens, and document it for future researchers."

Clouden fumbled through a ring of keys before unlocking the steel door before us. The temperature was much cooler here and I rubbed my arms to stifle the chill. The thin, cotton sleeves of my blouse were not enough to combat the temperate change.

The cavernous room was filled with lab equipment of various kinds. Though some looked familiar, other items were unidentifiable to me. Beakers bubbled with unknown substances, mechanisms with gears and screws laid half-finished in abandoned heaps like dissected carcasses. The walls were dark stone, the only light coming from Edison bulbs hanging from an industrial style chandelier and the odd pharmacy lamp. An architect style table sat below the lamp, parchment with unfinished sketches, and inkwells with their caps left open laid, haphazardly, upon its surface.

"Articus, with the approval of the Council, has been secretly entering the First Realm, undercover, to aid me in my research." I stole a glance toward Articus at this revelation. His eyes stayed fixed ahead where Clouden rummaged through a shelf of documents—avoiding my gaze.

"Here it is," Clouden said to himself before placing the found items on a zinc tabletop in the cluttered laboratory.

Clouden ushered us over to his side as he unfolded an expanse of parchment before him and ran his hand down his short-trimmed beard. The image depicted was a diagram of sorts with the structure of the Four Known Realms, and their relation to each other.

Structured like a staircase, the bottom left step was labeled "The First Realm." The step up from that, the Second, then the Third, with the final step in the top right-hand side reading "The Fourth Realm."

Clouden's finger dragged lightly across the parchment as he explained the diagram. Between each step—or realm—was a black oval, indicating a portal. He explained that most portals in the Second Realm were accounted for and labeled as either doorways to the First Realm—therefore illegal to enter—or an entrance to the Third Realm, which was often used for exploration and trade. On the step that indicated a portal to the First Realm, a red "X" was drawn through its oval symbol. Clouden continued, his focus now solely on me and no longer on the diagram before us.

"Now that you are here, Alise, I can, at last, explore a theory of mine that I have been cultivating over the years, but have never been able to prove without a subject." His use of the word indicated that I was said "subject" and it made me feel a little less human. When I looked to Articus for his reaction, he simply nodded as he stared off at nothing in particular.

"My theory is that each realm holds a frequency. One that is then embedded into its native-born citizens, present in say, their aura, or even their genetic makeup. I've never been able to prove this theory since I have never had a native born of another realm to study—until now." Clouden's gaze fell on me. His brown eyes felt cold in the stale dark space, his tone doing nothing to warm them. A shiver that had nothing to do with the temperature skittered over me, causing my skin to prickle.

"You need a sample of my blood," I stated, more than asked, feeling I already knew the answer.

"Only if you are willing to give it freely," Articus answered before Clouden could and stared him down from over my head with a glare of certainty. "And only when you are ready," he directed at me, though his eyes were still fixed on Clouden. Clouden stared back, his jaw ticked before seeming to give in and turned away.

He approached a bronze chamber I hadn't noticed earlier. On its door was a wheel like an airlocked door on a submarine would have, with a small, round window above that. Beside it, to the right, were control panels and instruments that, I assumed, read data.

"There is also the frequency chamber. It reads the energy a human's body puts off—its' aura. And it can also concentrate the Second Realm's magnetic waves within its confines. But I am not confident in its accuracy yet," Clouden said, gesturing to the bronze chamber.

"So far, I have only been able to obtain energy readings from Second Realm citizens, and nothing to compare the data against in order to validate its accuracy. It still needs work."

"Why have you not been able to test others' auras from the First or Third realms? Are there no volunteers?" I asked.

"Third Realm citizens refuse to leave their mother realm for spiritual reasons, and centuries ago the First Realm closed all its known portals and made it illegal for others to travel to and from them—hence the secrecy in Articus's work."

I immediately thought of the red "X" drawn through the single portal symbol in the diagram. That must have been what it meant, that the realm was closed off to all, and why Articus and I would be implicated in more than just murder if we were found out.

"That just leaves me then," I said. I was smuggled goods for Clouden's science experiment. This is what they had intended for me from the beginning, it seemed.

Was this the only reason Articus brought me here? Was everything else he said about keeping me safe and finding me a home just a ploy to get me to come with him? A boon to please Clouden.

Articus's warm breath hit my ear as he leaned in and said, "If you're not ready yet, if you need more time, take it," before straightening to glance at an obscene grandfather clock with a face of constellations that moved like water with each ticking second. Zodiac signs oddly replaced the position where numbers would be and a moon in a slowly waxing phase decorated its center.

"Thank you greatly for the brief physics lesson, Clouden, but I'm afraid Alise and I are running behind and I have much more work for her. So, if you will kindly, excuse us." Articus clasped my elbow and steered me toward the steel door, not waiting for Clouden's dismissal. An exasperated expression trailed us up the tunneled stairs before the steel door slammed shut behind us.

"I have something much more entertaining than monotonous tests in mind for you," he said over his shoulder as a wolfish grin kicked up the corners of his mouth.

Chapter Twenty Two

I FELT RIDICULOUS IN the lacey bonnet and apron that comprised a cleaning maid's uniform, and also pity for every woman who had to wear it before me. It was something out of a period-piece film, much like everything else here. Trying to wear a complete sense of nonchalance and belonging, I fumbled with the key that Articus also retrieved for me, in my pocket.

I'm supposed to be here, I'm meant to be here, I repeated to myself, attempting to settle my shaking hands.

Once inside, I let out an exhale. I locked the door and made haste, determined to search as quickly as possible for anything that could give us information on how Brenton was getting to and from the First and Second Realm, and to what end.

It had been Articus's idea that I impersonate a staff member with the uniform and key he had acquired in order to gain access to the dorms while the cadets were in classes, under the guise that I was merely performing cleaning rounds. I was hesitant to the idea at first, the fear of being caught somewhere I shouldn't was heavy on my conscience, but after placing the key in my hand, Articus held on for a few more unnecessary seconds as he tilted my chin up to face his gaze and said, "The devil we face is always smaller than the devil we fear." My curiosity won in the end. I condemned his encouraging words that sprouted newfound courage in me as the lace trim of the borrowed uniform itched my neck, mercilessly.

Brenton's dorm lay in total disarray. Clothing of all kinds hung from the back of a chair and the small bed frame. Half emptied cups lay abandoned on a writing desk and nightstand, one even so much as tipped over as I accidentally bumped my hip into the corner of the feeble desk, while attempting to avoid stepping on a pair of filthy, discarded boots.

Men.

I started with the nightstand drawers and moved on to the closet with no luck in my search. After a couple minutes of throwing the small, simple room into further chaos, I paused, empty-handed, not even sure what exactly I was even looking for.

Articus's words played like a tape recorder in my mind.

"You'll know it when you see it. Just trust your instincts and take anything that may be of use."

If I was hiding something, something secret or personal, that I didn't want anyone to find, where would it be? For me there was only one answer. I lifted the twin mattress at each corner until my heart both jumped, and sank, at the discovery beneath it. It seemed Brenton and I preferred the same hiding places.

A small collection of folded papers lay between the mattress and frame.

Could this be something of use?

The edges were worn as though they had been folded and refolded several times. I carefully unfolded the stash only for my stomach to drop with disappointment. Further inspection confirmed it, each sheet was only a raunchy flyer for a gentlemen's club, with a lewd and completely unrealistic sketch of an extremely disproportionate female body, or a page that seemed to be torn from an article, describing a somewhat violent sex scene. Though we held preference in hiding places, our tastes in art and literature could not be more different.

Alas, my efforts were fruitless.

A defeated sigh left my lungs. I straightened up as much as I could before casually relocking the door behind me. As I turned back around to head down the hall, my face slammed into a broad chest. A baritone chuckle radiated from it. I shuffled back against the door and looked up to see a stunningly handsome face staring down at me.

"A bit clumsy, are we?" he spoke between the teeth of a dazzling smile.

"If by *we*, you mean yourself, then yes," I retorted, rubbing my cheek. An amused laugh left his lips again. It was a sensual dark sound, similar to his hair, like melted chocolate, it curled and coiled atop his head and bounced with his laughter, while somehow still remaining tamed. Quicksilver eyes looked down at me, from atop a perfectly straight nose.

"I'm sorry to have startled you. I was looking for someone and was surprised to see you leaving this room. I haven't seen anyone come or go from it in weeks." His hand rubbed the perfectly groomed stubble on his chin.

"Well, you must have just missed them, because the room was in complete shambles before I cleaned it," I lied.

A curve hitched up the side of full, yet skeptical lips.

"If you'll excuse me, I have more rooms to clean," I continued as I made to slide past him. An arm came down, resting on the wall, blocking my path.

"May I ask your name, ma'am?"

"I'm no one of importance, and I am not a 'ma'am,'" I said as I tried to avoid his approach again, feeling more than a little annoyed that he wouldn't let me pass. He lowered his head down to meet me at eye level.

"Miss, then." He paused for a long moment, waiting for my reply, never looking away. Unflinchingly, I returned his challenging stare. He looked so comfortable in his skin. Confidence radiated from him and he wasn't the least bit phased that we were locked in a staring contest, while he had me pinned to a wall, in a highly-trafficked hallway.

"Has anyone ever told you, you have the most beautiful eyes?" he asked.

I rolled said eyes so hard they could have fallen from my skull. "Yes, actually," I replied as I ducked under his arm and scurried down the hall as swiftly as possible.

"What about that name?" he shouted.

My only response was a curt wave over my shoulder and a secretive smile on my lips.

"What has you so giddy?" Articus asked. His verdant green eyes surveyed me as I entered the dark office located precisely above the library. A rod iron, spiral staircase, located in the darkest corner of the archives, led to a small landing and a very old wooden door that could use a fresh coat of paint.

What little light there was came from the single, lead-glass window and a single lamp, adjacent a heavy wooden desk, where Articus was clearly working. Bookcases lined the wall behind him. Their shelves were filled with more than just leather tomes. Trinkets and busts, picture frames and the odd animal skull occupied them as well as volumes on everything from poetry and warfare—all pieces of the man sitting before me.

His worn, leather, wing-back moaned as he shifted in his seat, resting an ankle on his knee.

"Nothing," I replied, trying my best to stifle the pounding in my chest and flush on my cheeks that was either from rushing up the stairs or my encounter with the handsome stranger. I was going with the stairs.

"Oh, Little Fox, how sweetly you lie," he tsked, while his eyes remained fixated on the book in hand.

"I do not. And how about it's none of your business?" I strode forward, swishing my skirt, hands clasped behind my back, suddenly feeling playful in the ridiculous maid's uniform.

"Did you find anything?" Articus asked, still not looking up.

"Unfortunately, no." I sighed. "Well besides some very concerning depictions of women in compromising sexual situations and painfully engorged breasts."

His eyes quickly glanced up and darted away as if caught looking where they shouldn't. Only he was too late. A small secret smile pulled at my lips. His refusal to maintain eye contact frustrated, yet, emboldened me.

I approached him until my knees touched his, erasing all distance between us.

"Articus," I all but whispered.

He hummed a noncommittal response, still refusing to acknowledge me or the fact that we were now touching.

"Look at me," I commanded softly, my voice low and lush.

He played as though he didn't hear me, as though he were transfixed by whatever he was reading. I leaned forward, bracing one hand on the arm of the wing-backed chair as the other gently removed the book from his hands before dropping it carelessly. Feeling guilty for the innocent hardback's abuse, I silently pleaded forgiveness as it clattered to the hardwood floor.

"I was reading that," he all but growled. His voice was rough and low, and his brow furrowed with a crease. My skirt hitched ever so slightly as I climbed slowly, gracefully, into his lap. Legs straddling on either side of his waist, between his own thighs and the armrests.

I refused to remove my stare from his. A game of who would break it first played out in the small breathes of space between us. I made to remove his glasses next but his hand quickly grasped my wrist, halting it before I could touch the gold frames.

"Don't," he gritted through his teeth, not at all meaning the removal of his glasses.

My hand withdrew in obedience but as soon as he released it I quickly swiped the frames from his face anyways, and flicked them away, probably breaking them as they clattered to the floor.

I didn't care.

Everything in his look, from the mischievous tilt of his lips to the cunning in his burning, verdant eyes, told me he was wholly familiar with the rules of our exchange and possibly had a few tricks of his own.

"Don't ignore me when I speak to you!" I snapped through clenched teeth.

Just as quickly as the words leapt from my lips, he retaliated. A surprised yelp escaped me. Sweeping me off his lap and carrying me to a dark green, velvet lounge he deposited me on its soft cushions as though I weighed nothing. The air in my lungs knocked out in a gasp. His eyes darkened as he looked down on me, his hands swiftly braced my wrists above my head. He buried his face into the crook of my neck as he whispered, "How could I possibly ignore you in this utterly, unholy outfit." Lips tickled my flesh as he spoke, causing my hips to roll against him. He released one of his hands from my wrist only to drag it slowly up my bent knee, past the lace trim of my stocking to where it ended and bare skin began.

"I think you are mistaking my restraint for indifference. In truth, I want nothing more right now than to watch you squirm from between these sweet thighs." His thumb circled lazily as his fingers slid under the lace seam. His touch was teasing as it approached closer and closer to its desired target, with each pass. My breath quickened at the delicate yet torturous touch.

"Would you let me, Alise? Would you allow me to do as I pleased with you?" A tightening in my core grew. A moan, pleading to get out, bloomed in my chest. "Just say the word. I need to hear you say it." Warm breath titillated my skin as he spoke and caused it to prickle with goose bumps.

This game of mercy had gone too far. Would he truly do as he said, or were they just tempting words to reduce me to begging? Surely, he would sit up and laugh the moment I caved and said yes. It was just a ruse—a ploy for dominance as we both tugged at each end. I knew better than to give in so easily.

Tucking my leg behind his knee, I knocked him off balance and sent him tumbling to the floor. His clumsy weight did the rest. In a blink I straddled him with a leg pinning each arm as I jerked his head back by a tuff of sandy hair, forcing him to bare his throat to me as I pressed the sharp point of a confiscated fountain pen beneath his jaw.

His eyes were wild as they met mine. A wolfish grin grew slowly from his full lips as he took me in, from where my legs straddled his chest to the loose strands of hair that stuck to my lips.

"Exquisite," he breathed, as his hands flexed and fisted beside his head. "You're quite the fast learner, Little Fox. I wonder what other notorious skills I could teach you?"

A whole parade of indecent thoughts flooded through my mind and I suddenly didn't feel like the one in control anymore. I hopped off his broad chest, heat rising up my neck, past my collar, and with trembling hands smoothed out the creases of my skirt.

"If you're not already occupied, we can continue your training tonight. That is if you still wish to," Articus said as he rose from the ground and dusted off his trousers. I gathered my nerve and returned the fountain pen to its hiding place in the pocket of my apron.

Blinking, I turned my focus back to him. He leaned against the bulky and worn wooden desk. Legs crossed at the ankles as he cleaned his reading glasses that were, graciously, not broken, with a handkerchief. As he awaited my reply, his eyes searched me from head to toe and back to my face. He bit the corner of his lip in an attempt to hold back a smile. Probably at the sight of me looking so flustered in this ridiculous outfit.

Though several parts of me raged against spending more time with Articus and his games than absolutely necessary, another small part was eager to learn all I could in defending myself.

"That will be fine." The answer was stale on my tongue.

"I'll inspect Brenton's dorm room for myself, in case there is anything you might have overlooked," he stated as I made to leave. Feeling much too awkward to stay even a moment longer. After he spoke, however, I turned to glare at him accusingly.

"If you could have searched the room yourself, then what was the point of me wearing this ridiculous disguise and going to look in the first place?"

"And miss the opportunity to see you in that uniform?" He chuckled. "I'm far too indulgent to pass on such a sight."

Scoundrel.

"I'm so pleased I could be of entertainment to you, sir." Sarcasm dripped like venom from every syllable. Too sweetly I smiled and made a show of curtsying before turning on a heel to leave. Entirely filled with more than my share of Articus Desaius for the day, as the echo of a chuckle followed me down the spiral steps.

Chapter Twenty Three

T HAT NIGHT I ANXIOUSLY paced my room, unable to relax despite my best efforts.

During dinner, I wasn't able to eat much. Kareena attempted to hide her looks of concern over my lack of appetite before finally asking me if I was feeling alright. Looking up from my plate of meatloaf and roasted vegetables, I used the opportunity to excuse myself, claiming I was rather tired, before slinking off to my room to be alone.

In honesty, I couldn't pinpoint what exactly was causing me to have this particular wave of anxiety. Was it the energy around me or my own doing? My stomach was in knots. Waves of sudden nausea rolled over me unpredictably. My skin felt hot and damp one moment, while chills had me rubbing my arms and the back of my neck, the next.

Was it the excitement of the day? The disappointment of not finding anything of use in Brenton's dorm room? Or was it the energy of the staff and cadets living at the Academy humming against my skin? It had been weeks since I'd been around such a large group of people on a regular basis, let alone lived with someone—every emotion and mood casted off by them touched me. Now multiply that by a hundred living, breathing beings and I'm left feeling disoriented in every way. The sensation made me want to curl up into a tiny ball under the covers. To go numb from it all. And like every time before, when I've felt ill for no rational reason, I became frustrated with being so weak, affected, and vulnerable. Having a theory as to what caused it now, did not help. It only made me feel crazy and isolated.

Why are you so afraid of the truth? A wicked, soft voice mocked in the back of my mind.

"I am not afraid!" I whisper-yelled back into the ether.

Who was I trying to convince though, beyond myself? Would the full knowledge of Brenton's true intentions in our friendship ease the loss or would it only make his betrayal and death that much more painful and confusing? I had too much on my mind. Too much to chew over, alone, into the long hours of night.

My hands fidgeted in the pockets of my skirts. My teeth worried my bottom lip raw.

A soft knock on my bedroom door broke my spiraling thoughts, followed by a soft rustle as a piece of paper slid under my door, catching at the edge of the Parisian rug I was currently wearing a path in.

Unfolding its smooth edges, there was a single line written.

Meet me in the woods behind the gardens at your earliest convenience.

There was no signature, but it was not needed.

My feet absentmindedly carried me to the bay window that overlooked the gardens below. Looking up from the letter, I peered across the moonlit grounds where just days ago, Kareena and I had strolled. As my gaze trailed toward the dark wood beyond, a tall figure caught my attention standing just beyond the border of where the garden met a clearing. His features were obscured by the night, with only the glistening glow of the moon lighting the top of his head like some anointed shadow. He slowly raised a hand from his pocket and beckoned me to follow before turning to the forest beyond and disappearing between its dark prison of tree trunks.

"Your problem," Articus stated, "is you fear the sound. So in turn, you fear the weapon." Without warning he fired off another shot above our heads, causing me to flinch and throw my hands over my ears.

"Won't people be concerned there are gunshots going off this late at night?" I shouted over my cupped, ringing ears.

"Do not fear the weapon or the sound it makes, Alise. If you must fear something," he continued, ignoring my concerns, as he strutted towards me, "fear its wielder. Here," he said, offering the still warm pistol to me. "Once you become familiar with it, you will no longer be afraid."

I hesitated.

"It is just a tool," Articus encouraged. My hands shook, for more reasons than the cold night air, as I reached for the weapon.

"I'll show you." Gently he arranged my fingers over the pistol grip, putting them in proper placement. Articus stepped behind me and his hands locked my elbows straight before me.

"A little wider," he indicated with the light tap of my ankle with his foot. I widened my stance.

"Bend your knees, slightly."

His face hovered over my shoulder as his palm splayed across my core. Another hand reaching around to point to a tiny notch that sat on the top of the barrel.

"Line your sight up with this to aim." Hot breath warmed my ear, causing my body to relax slightly. "When you aim, inhale and pull the trigger on a slow exhale . . . it will help steady you." The warmth of his presence left me. "Go ahead and give it a try," I heard him say from further behind me.

My vision strained as I aimed for a large knot in a tree trunk some distance away. Its bark was marred by several previous assaults. Every inch of my body stiffened until I was ridged as a statue.

"Breathe out slowly," Articus reminded me, noticing I held my breath with anticipation. His voice carried through the still night air. My thoughts grew silent and my vision dimmed, until all that was left was a tunneled view of my target and my increasing heart rate in my ears.

A deafening explosion sounded, consuming me completely and almost causing me to drop the pistol to cover my ears against the painful shock. Articus swooped in to retrieve the gun before it could tumble from my grip.

"You did quite well for your first time. Do you want to try again? Perhaps this time don't drop the gun afterwards." His face was alight, clearly enjoying this exercise much more than me.

"No," I replied, hands clutched to my queasy stomach. "I think that's enough excitement for one night." My head swam and my limbs shivered. I was going to be sick.

"It's just the adrenaline. The more you do it the less of an effect it'll have on you," Articus reassured. "I want you to observe one of my classes tomorrow. It will help desensitize you, at least to the sound."

I nodded in agreement, too queasy to open my mouth and potentially lose what little dinner I managed to have eaten. I felt stupid and weak for my body's reaction and the continuous lack of control I had over it.

"For now," he continued, holstering his weapon, "let's work off that adrenaline coursing through you." A devilish grin grew across his full mouth.

"What do you have in mind?" I countered between deep, steadying breaths.

"No better way to burn off adrenaline than physical exertion," he said as I eyed him suspiciously. "Run, Little Fox," he commanded in a low and rough voice, before unholstering his weapon and firing it in the air, causing my feet to, instinctively, take action.

Deeper and deeper into the woods I ran. My skirt and heeled boots made it much more difficult to navigate the uneven terrain and dodge roots. Anticipating another gunshot behind me or a strong hand reaching out to capture me at any moment, only fueled my pace. It wasn't until exhaustion took over and my limbs went numb that I collapsed on the damp grass and wondered if we could have rid my tension in a more enjoyable way. A smirk that was not my own responded overhead to my unspoken thoughts.

Damn, how was he so fast?

"Better?" Articus asked as he extended a hand to help me up. I reached for it, but instead of using it to pull myself up, I swiped a leg against his footing, causing him to tumble as I yanked him down to the ground with me. His eyes grew wide midair, only making me that much more satisfied to see the surprise on his face before he fell in a heap beside me, chuckling.

"Better."

The following morning, I woke slightly more refreshed than usual, only to find Kareena was already gone from our shared suite. Most likely already starting her shift in the infirmary. It wasn't until several hours later that I was finally dressed and showered—ready for a light breakfast of croissants and various jams and curds. Decking on the several layers of garments and arranging my hair into something appropriate took, frustratingly, most of the morning. But overall, I thought I did pretty well for myself as I scampered down to the training yard where Articus had instructed me to meet him. I found him already present, inspecting rifles that had been laid out on a wooden folding table. His demeanor was back to that of cold seriousness as he barely registered my presence.

"Stay back there, away from the range," he bluntly commanded with not so much as a good morning or how are you. He must have only had one cup of coffee that morning. Striding back to where he indicated, not wanting any part of his mood to rub off on mine, he interrupted my steps with, "And Alise, please try not to distract my students." I turned to find him glancing at me from over his shoulder with a dissecting glare. Quickly I turned back in time to hide my exaggerated eye roll before sitting down on a stone bench, still cool from the early morning hours.

"Yes, sir," I whispered, mostly to myself.

Bells chimed from the cathedral not too far off, summoning several young men in red academy uniforms into the training yard. They lined up at the table where the rifles were placed and stood in orderly rows as though awaiting orders. It was then I noticed many, if not all, of them appeared similar in age to Articus. How odd it must be to instruct and command a group of peers.

A wonton gaze caught my attention from the line of men. Recognizable gray eyes stared from under a neat mop of curly burnished hair. The stranger's lips parted to silently form the words, "Good morning." Not wanting to be rude, I lifted a clasped hand from my lap to give a small wave. The movement did not go unnoticed.

Articus glanced between us before barking out, "Da Romano," causing the onlooker to stiffen and turn his attention to him. "Finding yourself distracted this morning, cadet?"

"No, sir," Da Romano replied.

"Good, then take a rifle to the range line and await my instruction."

Articus was a firm and unrelenting master. Quick to call out any misstep, whether it be in posture, placement, or form. Not a single flaw slipped by his notice and I wondered how many he saw in me each day, grateful that he did not bring them up, for surely, they were many.

A knee bounced in anticipation as I watched several cadets follow Articus's instructions. By the time the first round of shots went off my skin hummed, still sensitive to the sound as each shot sent me lurching slightly in my seat. Every deafening boom cut off whatever thought tried to form in my mind. Meanwhile, Articus made his way to each shooter, critiquing and adjusting here and there as needed. An air of cold arrogance and boredom never leaving his features.

My mind wandered to a dark study, above a flight of spiraled, iron stairs, and the things I could do to attempt to wipe that expression from his face. Every idea, once again, was interrupted and torn from my reach with each firing of a rifle.

From the pocket of my skirt, I removed a folded scratch of paper and the nub of a pencil I had found that morning buried in a bureau drawer. With it, I tried to distract myself with sketching small details from the golden morning. A small bird that took flight with the ring of a gunshot, the curve of a skilled hand as its fingers wrapped around a rifle's trigger. Each attempt to capture the life before me, resulted in an unintended line here; a too firm press of the pencil there. All a result of my persistent flinching.

Starting to feel tension in my jaw and shoulders, I took a long steading breath, mindfully letting the sounds of gunfire ring through me instead of against me. The more I accepted the sound, just as one would anticipate and endure thunder in a lightning storm, the less I found I would flinch. I repeated this initiative over and over, watching as fingers pulled back on their triggers and timed a slow exhale in correspondence.

By the time training was coming to an end, I felt as though I had been meditating for hours. The sounds of gunfire became ambient noise. My mind grew calmer, almost quiet. Taking in my sketches I noticed the most recent ones held fewer mistakes.

As I looked up from my sketches, Da Romano caught my attention. He set his rifle back down on the table with the others and made a beeline for me. Articus pretended to be too busy with another cadet to notice, though a quick glance from the corner of his eye told me otherwise. In the span of a breath, Da Romano stood before me. An aristocratic smile was topped by a heart shaped cupid's bow. Utterly charming in every way. He swiftly, yet gently, took my hand in his own without hesitation.

"I believe we have met before, but I have failed to formally introduce myself. I am Dante Da Romano," he stated, lifting my hand to his mouth for a chaste kiss before fixing those sterling silver eyes back on me through dark thick lashes. "And what might your name be, miss?" Completely thrown by his ancient and formal gesture I stumbled over my response.

"A-Alise Fox."

"Miss Fox," he repeated, with a drawl savoring the sound as though it were a piece of candy. Cool breath danced on my fingers. His eyes strolled slowly across me until noticing the scrap of paper still clutched in my other hand. "You are quite talented," he remarked. Quickly I stuffed the sketches back into my skirt pocket as my words rushed to make little of the artwork.

"You are kind to say so, but it is just something I do to pass the time." Noticing my embarrassment, a small smile teased the corner of his lips. An eyebrow shot up with curiosity.

"Not playing chambermaid today?"

A moment passed in confusion before understanding his meaning, remembering the first time he saw me was outside Brenton's dorm room, in a uniform that was not mine. Whereas today I was dressed in a ruffled lace blouse with billowing sleeves gracing my slender arms. While a high-waisted skirt of woolen tweed poured down my hips to just above my heeled boots. Two rows of brass buttons lined its front, ending in two pleats below.

"It was a one-time experience." I slowly pulled my hand away from his grip, utterly entranced by his perfectly-formed features and the charm that dripped from his voice like honey.

"Unfortunate. My heart breaks, along with every man's in the Colony, I'm sure," he contended as his eyes continued to trail me from head to toe. The memory of myself in said uniform clearly written on his face. While the other cadets I encountered while traversing the halls of the Academy hid their stares and kept to themselves—as though they'd be punished for so much as looking my way, let alone speaking to me—Dante held so much confidence in his words and gestures towards me. Or perhaps it was arrogance. I tried to play at indifference, as though his bluntness had no effect on me. However, I was certain a tingling sensation in my cheeks betrayed my unimpressed demeanor.

"Don't worry, Miss Fox," he whispered, leaning in conspiratorially, "your secret is safe with me." He winked and turned on his heel to join the other cadets back inside the Academy's stone walls.

Chapter Twenty Four

A FTER ANSWERING SEVERAL OF Articus's predetermined questions about the function of a hand-held hair dryer, we sat in silence, immersed in our own research. I was deeply engrossed in a diagram labeling the mechanisms of an airship, with a description of their functions for flight as well as sailing the sea. They were one of the Second Realm's novelties I wish had existed in the First. How beautiful and magical it would have been to see one sail across the sky as a child—coasting from one puffy cloud to the next. Though perhaps Second Realm citizens would find it just as magical to see a First Realm airplane soaring through the sky. I looked toward the single leaded window in our private little nook, deep in the library's archives in hopes to see one of the intricate airships again but was, instead, disappointed with a foggy gray view.

"What are the other realms like?" I suddenly found myself asking.

"Very different from this one, I can assure you," was all Articus said as he continued writing down notes in a small leather notebook.

I huffed a sigh and continued to stare out the window. Once again, defeated and put off by his curt and vague response.

I jumped in my chair as a heavy tome slammed down in front of me. Articus suddenly over my shoulder, flipping through pages until he found a section titled, "The Savage Beauty of the Third Realm".

"I've never been there myself, but I'm told that a lifetime ago Clouden would frequently travel to the Third Realm and had even formed tentative relationships with the native citizens." He indicated with the tilt of his chin for me to explore the passages laid out before me.

Pages upon pages recounted a lush landscape, devoid of modern technology. A vicious paradise that would no sooner dazzle you then chew you to pieces and spit you out. Depictions of animals twice the common size, slaughtering miniscule humans within their enormous jaws laid side by side with renderings of exotic plants and flowers, most suspected of having multiple medicinal purposes used by the natives, as well as severely toxic chemical components.

Governing structure was listed as currently unknown, with nothing beyond a spiritual leader or healer and a dismantled kind of monarchy.

"Did Clouden write this?"

"Some of it I am certain he contributed to, but the rest is an accumulation of decades of research from our predecessors." Articus set down his notes and retrieved a scroll before unrolling it before him on the desk we shared.

"Will you ever go see it for yourself?" I asked.

Articus merely huffed a sound of resignation. A small smile tugged at his lips as he shook his head as though I just told him a joke of sorts.

"What's so funny?"

"The freedom you think I have here. As though I could travel anywhere I so wish."

"Well . . . couldn't you?"

"One can only enter the Third Realm with expressed permission from the Council. The only exception being for the purpose of trade. Until the general finds a strong enough need for him to convince the rest of the Council to allow me to travel there, I am limited to only enter the First at their command."

"So, let me get this straight. If it benefits them, a couple of powerful men, behind closed doors, will decide to break the very laws they impose on others." Without looking up, Articus tapped his nose in confirmation.

"I see," was all I could manage to say, understanding all too well what it felt like to be told when and where to go. The tug on the leash of control had a constant, aching pressure I wanted to snap. A sensation I craved so deeply as a child, it fueled my feet as I fled one foster home and later group home after another. The act branded me a flight risk to all future potential caretakers. They didn't know, or must not have understood that you couldn't take away something as delicious as freedom from a child weaned on it and not expect insatiable cravings.

From across the table Articus caught my attention by clearing his throat. I dragged my gaze to meet his.

"How does one typically show affection in the First Realm?" he asked.

A little surprised by the turn of the subject, it was a far cry from the morning's focus on the operational function of common First Realm devices, I pondered all the possible options. Hugging and kissing of course but also words of affirmation and playful touch could be considered affectionate. It didn't occur to me that an expression that came so naturally could be different to another culture, even one in a different dimension. But then again it had only been days since I've discovered different realms even existed. Anything was a possibility at this point.

"Well, there are several ways," I finally answered.

Articus didn't respond but merely focused on me intently, indicating for me to continue.

"There are hugs for example, mostly for friends and family."

"Yes. Of course," he said softly and removed his reading glasses to clean them with a handkerchief.

"And there's kisses," I continued.

The whisper of a smile touched his mouth as he put his clean glasses into a hidden coat pocket. "Are those also for friends and family?" he asked.

"Yes, but you wouldn't kiss them the same way you would someone else." My teeth worried my lip with the direction the conversation was headed.

"Someone else?" Articus asks with feigned innocence. A touch of mischief curved his mouth. It radiated off him like giddy butterflies tickling my skin.

"Yes. Like someone you care about . . . romantically."

"A lover," he deadpanned. "And how would this kiss be different from how one would kiss a friend or family member?"

"Well, it's deeper for one . . . and usually . . . longer and sometimes well . . . often times . . ." I fidget in my seat, cringing at the innuendo of my misguided words. Why was I struggling to answer this simple question? Suddenly I felt as uncomfortable as a child getting the talk while a rush of heat flushed my chest all at once.

"Continue," Articus encouraged, hiding a full grin behind a fist and looking every bit amused at my discomfort.

Damn him.

"You would use your tongue," I rushed out. My cheeks most definitely reddened. "I assume it's the same here."

"I cannot assume anything when it comes to my research," he countered my attempt to end the subject. My mind tumbled for a response. Anything to break the silence that grew thick in the space between his stare and myself.

"It's called French kissing," I blurted out.

"French kissing?" He pondered thoughtfully rubbing his chin as he rose from seat. "I don't believe I've ever heard of such a thing."

"You do kiss here, don't you?" Thinking of the times I wanted him to do just that. Of the several times I was disappointed with his lack of reciprocation. Though I had seen Kareena kiss Articus on the cheek in greeting, and Dante had kissed my hand, maybe mouth-to-mouth kisses weren't culturally practiced in this realm.

"Of course, we do, but I'm not convinced it's quite the same as this French kissing you speak of," he said, putting an over emphasis on the French part before sliding his hands in his pockets and stalking slowly around the table. "Perhaps if I had a demonstration, I could better understand this culturally romantic gesture you are attempting to describe." I stiffen in my seat at his words. His proximity towered above me as his grin disappeared into an expression of seriousness.

Don't look at his mouth. Don't look at his mouth, I begged my eyes.

"How will that happen if no one here knows what it is, let alone how to do it?" I asked, though I already knew the solution as soon as the question left my lips and I cringed at my misstep.

Articus bent at the waist and spoke softly, "You could show me. I assume you know how." My eyes betrayed me yet again with a glance at those plush lips of his.

This wasn't playing fair.

I let out a nervous, breathy, chuckle, seeing the game laid out before me—the trap he set. Waiting for me to nibble at the bait.

"Very clever," I said, about to rise and leave. Articus caused me to pause with a light clasp around my wrist.

"Not at all. I take my research very seriously. I would never want to record something inaccurately. Besides"—a glimmer of that mischief in his eyes reappeared—"I trust you not to mislead me on this."

Was he offering me an out? An invitation? A chance to get a taste of what I never received from him in the First Realm? Or was it truly academic curiosity? Perhaps both. And with no strings attached. "Just a demonstration?" I hesitated.

"Strictly for research purposes," he reassured.

Looking away I contemplated my decision. I couldn't deny that I had wanted to kiss him on more than one occasion, during our time together in the First Realm. But after everything that happened, I decided it wouldn't be safe for my heart to continue down that path any longer. From the moment he struck Brenton I built up a wall of distrust and suspicion to separate us. If I did this, it would need to be emotionless. Sensing my hesitation, he released my wrist and stuffed his hands back in his trouser pockets.

"Only if you're comfortable, of course. I wouldn't want to impose—"

Swallowing my courage, I pulled him by his lapels with shaking hands and pressed a soft kiss against his lips.

Why shouldn't I get what I wanted for once? Even if it would mean nothing between us.

His lips were surprisingly warm, as though he had a fever, causing a melting sensation to flow through my very bones with every second they pressed against mine. The sensation washed away any remaining hesitation. My grip on his jacket loosened until my palms were laid flat against his chest. I pulled back to slightly adjust the angle of my approach and felt his head tilt accordingly. My hands slid up to his neck by their own fruition, strumming the soft hairs at the base of his head. When our lips connected again, I brushed his bottom lip with my tongue. A gentle request, encouraging him to open for me. He obeyed eagerly. Our tongues and lips fell into a dance in which he let me take the lead. His movements became a mirror to my own. A flick for a flick. A languish stroke for another in return. The entire time his hands fisted in his pockets, unable or unwilling to touch any other part of me.

The heat within me grew so strong I could no longer tell whose lust was fueling it. I found myself arguing with my desire. Just one more taste. Just one more stroke and then I'll end it. Every kiss he let me take from him made me feel lighter, powerful, and more confident. And the fact that we were in the shared space of the library, where anyone could pass by and see us, only added to the fluttering thrill that grew in my chest.

Though he didn't lay a single finger on me, I could feel his enjoyment through every reciprocated movement. He never pulled back—never lightened the pressure. He let me take my time, giving him a thorough demonstration indeed. I hadn't noticed our breaths quicken. Hadn't sensed the rising moan in my chest until it almost escaped. I jerked back quickly, releasing him as my fingers flew to my lips.

Though his chest heaved from under his button down, he looked calm and composed. His slightly parted lips appeared glossed and swollen, the only lingering indication of what had just transpired.

"So, that was what you call a *French kiss*," he said, as he pressed his mouth in a thin line.

I nodded in response, suddenly unable to find my voice after shoving that rouge moan down my throat. Feeling flustered I smoothed my hands down my skirt, trying to banish the lingering sensation of his hair between my fingers.

"I have to say it's not too different from how we kiss here." A devilish smirk kicked up the corner of his mouth with his admission. My eyes went wide. "Of course, I've made use of my tongue while kissing before but I've certainly never known the gesture to be called French kissing." He started to turn away—to leave me in the wake of his conclusive thoughts on our kiss. As though he didn't just slap me into shock with his confession.

The scoundrel.

My face flamed with annoyance and embarrassment. He was definitely playing a game with me and I had fallen into it so easily. Was he silently laughing at me behind those lips the entire time? Thinking how foolish I was to give in to his manipulation so easily and desperately. I picked up the closest thing within reach, which happened to be a rather dense book, and threw it towards the back of Articus' head.

"You jerk," I grunted, missing my target by several inches. "You tricked me into kissing you knowing full well what kind of kiss I was talking about!"

Articus looked over his shoulder at me and then the book on the floor before picking it up. "Little Fox, I would never make you do something you didn't want to do." He turned to face me fully, taking me in from head to toe, making me feel vulnerable under his scrutiny. "Admit it. You wanted to kiss me for some time now. I just merely presented you with the opportunity to do so without repercussions." Standing mere inches before me he bent slightly to look me in the eye as he said, "Your aim still needs work, sweetheart." My jaw dropped at his audacity.

He all but slammed the book down on the table to make his point. That mischievous grin returned. My hands uncontrollably clenched at my sides as his shoulders shook with a chuckle.

"You're quite cute when you're angry, all pink and flustered." He flicked my nose before turning to walk away.

"I'm not your sweetheart!" I shouted at the back of his head. My hand mindlessly grabbed another book from the table.

"Please, don't throw any more books," he said without turning around. "They are rather old and valuable."

An enraged grunt escaped me as I made another attempt to connect the book to his head. But he swiftly turned a corner behind a bookcase, just in time for it to take the full force of the book's blow instead. The act left me feeling more foolish than ever. Like a child throwing a tantrum. He truly brought the worse out of me.

Running fingers through my hair, I yanked at the base of my skull as I closed my eyes tight and moaned internally. With a long sigh, I bottled my frustration away for later. Fingers, however, found their way back to my still tingling lips. The ghost of a smile, curved beneath their caress.

"What in the heavens is going on between you two?" a light feminine voice questioned, fluttering into view like a songbird. Startled, I turned to see Kareena standing at the far end of the same aisle of books Articus had disappeared behind, arms crossed and a knowing smile on her adorably freckled face.

"Oh, never mind." She sighed, uncrossing her arms and approaching me. "I want you to meet someone. Come along." When her soft hand took mine to lead me out, my frustration was all but forgotten and replaced with cheery anticipation. As if injected right into my veins, her delight sunk into my skin and became my own.

Chapter Twenty Five

W E QUICKLY DASHED DOWN narrow halls and through several unmarked doors before descending a familiar staircase into the servants' quarters. I wondered what she could possibly have wanted to show me that was down here, as she continued telling me about her shift in the infirmary that morning. Apparently, some medicinal powders had gone unaccounted for and Kareena was left to recount the entire inventory for the duration of her shift.

"I swear, Nurse Petit blames me for every mishap that occurs in that infirmary, even though records indicated the misplacement, clearly, could not have happened during my last shift." Kareena let out an exasperated sound as I shuffled to keep up.

"However, I'm always the one to take the blame and make things right." She paused as we approached an arc leading into the large kitchen Articus and I previously used to enter into the Academy.

"Here we are. Now I'll warn you she can be a bit . . . direct, but she truly is the warmest, most honest soul you could ever hope to meet," Kareena warned me. Before I could ask whom, she was referring to a boisterous voice radiated through the space.

"Kareena, are you going to dawdle by the door, girl? Or are you going to come in here and give me a hand?"

As we turned the corner into the kitchen, a stout woman hauling a rather large crate of produce came into view. She clearly struggled against the weight of the load as Kareena rushed to help her lift it onto the counter by the large copper sink.

"Indeed, all the energy of the Four Known Realms is wasted on the youth. No doubt by the end of the day I'll regret giving Fredrick the day off," the older woman grunted in a thick accent. Her words were made even more wispy by her labored breaths.

"Ms. Hazel, I brought—"

"Now girl, come here and let me get a proper look at you," the woman interrupted as she took Kareenas's face in her worn, yet nimble, hands. She smiled at what she saw and pecked Kareena on each cheek before releasing her and returning to her vegetables.

"I assume that Nurse is giving you grief again? I've heard from the staff about the missing inventory this morning. A bunch of chattering, gossiping children with far too much time on their hands," Ms. Hazel rambled on, completely unaware of my presence.

"She had me counting inventory my entire shift and when I had no—" Kareena turned to me, seeming to suddenly remember her purpose in dragging me down here. She grabbed my hand and pulled me further into the warm kitchen where the inviting scent of herbs and lemon calmed my nerves as it surrounded me like a comforting blanket.

"Ms. Hazel, I'd like you to meet someone," she said, placing a hand on the woman's shoulder.

As she turned away from her work to face me, her inscrutable gaze took me in from head to toe. She seemed to peer right through me, leaving me vulnerable and revealed, as though she saw the truth of me and everything I truly was, and had done.

It was terrifying to feel so transparent.

"My dear child, you are a twig," she exclaimed, coming toward me to take my thin wrist in her hand.

I tried not to cringe. To flinch away from her firm grasp and scrutinization of my body. Unfortunately, I was used to these kinds of comments. Where others would gasp in horror or shame for a person making a comment about another's size being "too large," no one had ever batted an eye when criticisms about my "too skinny" build were made. A double standard that I had learned to accept like a slap from an infuriated guardian. However, the sting had never lessened.

"I'll see that you get double portions of protein for your meals."

My head bowed a little as it usually did with the common comment about my weight but nonetheless, I softly thanked her for her concern.

"Now, now, Ms. Hazel, this is Miss Fox, Professor Clouden's ward and our new guest here at the Academy—" Kareena introduced us with all the eloquence of a royal emissary.

"I know who she is, child," Ms. Hazel cut in. "You think I don't know all the coming and going-ons in this institution? The staff here keeps me more than well informed with the amount of talk that goes on. One could drown in the gossip." Ms. Hazel turned to Kareena and clasped her hands as she looked at her with utmost affection. Her change of demeanor was so abrupt it was starting to give me whiplash.

"Now tell me, my girl, how is my sweet boy doing? He hasn't come to visit in months and you know how I worry for him." Her eyes all but pleaded.

"Oh, he is as busy and self-important as always. If he's not drowning away in his work, he's off with Father, and the lord knows where else." Kareena paused as she looked back at me, as though catching herself.

"In fact, he just returned from escorting Miss Fox for the Professor. Alise is from the village of Peillon."

"Is that so?" asked Ms. Hazel. Kareena's pointed look in my direction urged me to speak.

"Yes, ma'am," I lied.

"I'm not familiar with Peillon but I'm sure if you are here as a ward, it cannot be for a good reason that you have left."

This was the part I hated. The part where I receive pity that was not deserved. And even though in the First Realm my parents were truly dead, for some reason, pretending I had deceased parents in this realm felt like a betrayal to all of those who actually suffered such loss. Kareena and I had only known each other for a short time, but already I felt close to her. Already she felt like a friend or even a sister I never had, and I hated lying to her. Even now as she introduced me to someone who clearly meant very much to her and Articus.

To my relief though, not an ounce of pity lingered in Ms. Hazel's expression. Just a look of knowing. That same revealing gaze that cut to the core of a person and made me feel as crystalline as a window pane.

"Such is life to experience sorrow," she said, before returning to her work. I couldn't bring myself to glance back at Kareena. To meet the sadness that would inevitably be in her eyes from understanding. Instead, I fixated on how Ms. Hazel made quick work of slicing carrots as the sound of her knife chopping echoed off the kitchen walls. I envied the monotony of it. The way time could pass in mindlessness as dough was kneaded and vegetables prepared.

"Could you perhaps use some help?" I asked, the words escaped me on impulse before I could think better of it. Ms. Hazel threw me a cautionary look from over her shoulder.

"The Professor would have my head if he found out I had a non-staff member, let alone his ward, down here, helping me in the kitchens. Such work is only reserved for punishment of the cadets."

"No one need know, ma'am. Right, Kareena?" I turned to find Kareena gaping, yet her expression quickly turned to a conspiratorial grin as she eagerly nodded her head in agreement.

"Yes, I see no reason to let Clouden, or anyone for that matter, know everything Alise is up to while she is staying with us. We can keep it a secret. And if the staff gossips, as they do, we will laugh it off as rumor."

"I could use the extra help in the mornings. Can you bake, girl?" Ms. Hazel asked me.

"Yes, ma'am. I've been cooking and baking most of my life." A half-truth but truth enough to not feel like a lie. Ever since I was placed in foster care, and even after I exited out of the program, I had cooked for myself and sometimes others. I knew enough to get by, and then some, which was more than most my age, thanks to the knowledge my adoptive mother handed down to me about wild edible plants, and how to prepare them.

"After the dough rises, we knead it like this." My mother's fingers and fists massage into the puffy blob.

"Let me try!" My eager, young-self begs as I climb up on a wooden stool and mimic her movements.

"Great work, darling." Her warm smile lit up my core of childhood pride.

"Very well then, meet me down here at dawn and be prepared to work," Ms. Hazel's voice interrupted my thoughts, pulling me from my memories.

Gratitude flooded me to know that I now had something to occupy my time besides being summoned by Articus for his questioning and training. To have something to wear me down enough to keep the nightmares away. When my hands were busy, my mind was no longer free to wander.

I drank in the silence like a prisoner desperate for water. Farther from the clatter of polished boots and the rumble of hundreds of deep male voices; words indiscernible, lost in the chaos of their tones intermingling, I could finally take in a lung full of air. A bit of tension easing from my shoulders and jaw with each step away from the symphony of voices that harbored in the dining hall as I made my way towards the building that housed our suite.

She stayed behind to converse with other nurses from the infirmary while I excused myself, claiming exhaustion and the need for some fresh air. Not a complete lie given the vise of energy the crowd of cadets and staff had woven around my chest.

I would have given anything to have the cheery, bubbly, center-stage kind of personality Kareena had—that James also had. But every attempt to try left me feeling depleted, used up, and utterly exhausted. Leaving me with the impending fear that everyone saw straight through my act and thought me a complete fool for even attempting to be anything other than the quiet, skittish, girl I *truly* was.

I twisted my fingers in my palms. A slight relief harbored in my chest, like a hole punched in an airtight lid, that no one seemed to mind that I was turning in so soon. And now I was a ghost, wandering these enormous grounds. With no one else around to give me an inquisitive stare or strike-up small talk I didn't feel up to having.

A sharp crack like lighting caused me to flinch and turn my attention to a row of opened, arched windows that overlooked an empty courtyard. Though it wasn't in fact empty. Two tall, dark figures seemed to move in an intricate dance of give and take. Push and pull. Clanking came from the primitive looking poles each held in their hands as they stroked their opponent's. My hands grasped the stone ledge as I peered down to get a better look. The dwindling evening light made the two men's features difficult to discern.

A breeze carried the scent of earth and grass as it tickled the loose strands of my hair and made me content to spy a while as a ghost of the Academy would.

"Cheeky cheat you are," the darker figure said.

"There are no rules in warfare. You know this," a familiar voice countered back. I gasped with recognition, instantly darting behind the gap between two windows before thinking better of it and feeling rather silly. With them engrossed in their sparring and with my view out of their line of sight, certainly they could not see me watching from above.

Upon second glance I could more clearly make out the features of the lighter figure. My mind filling in the details my eyes could not see, from memory. The other had rich, bronze skin and a plum of tight dark curls atop his head. Though their builds were similar in height and strength, the darker male's shoulders appeared wider, his chest broader. It peeked through the opening of his white button-up, his skin soaked up the darkness. Defined shadows creased the muscles of his exposed forearms with every strike of his weapon. But where he held the advantage in strength, Articus was faster and more calculating.

He used that vicious speed to duck and dodge his opponent's heavy blows before becoming arrogant and clumsy. His partner in combat swiftly knocked him to the ground with a hit behind the knee. The dark, broad man, snatched up Articus's discarded weapon and held it against his neck as if it were a sword, ready to decapitate he who bowed before him.

The top of Articus's golden head caught the shine of twilight like a crown upon his brow. As he looked up at the victor, the horizon glowed red with its descent into night.

"Though, you know how much I love seeing you prostrate before me, you have to stop letting me win like this," his opponent said as he glared down at Articus on his hands and knees. "Do you surrender?"

"Fuck you," Articus grunted from his spot on the ground. Though his words were harsh they were accompanied with a smug grin and a light tone to match. His opponent sighed before offering Articus an outstretched hand to pull him upright.

"Had enough abuse for today?" the other asked as he tossed the pole back to his sparring partner. Articus caught it midair. A single dry laugh escaped his lips before they parted into a challenging smile.

"Not even close," he said and righted himself in a defensive stance. A greedy smile returned to his partner's own expression as Articus said, "This time don't hold back."

"Wouldn't dream of it," his partner replied.

For several moments they went back and forth, tit for tat as they swung their weapons in wide arches and low swipes. Seeking to sweep their opponents feet from under them or to strike an unprotected spot, both were ferocious fighters. Yet, I found their movements elegant and entrancing as one would find in a dance. I struggled to pull my focus away as a small nagging voice in the back of mind told me it was time to leave before I was discovered spying. But I couldn't.

"This new level of frustration wouldn't happen to be over a certain young lady, would it, Art?" His opponent's tone was light but lined with concern.

"If you are referring to the newest thorn in my side, you would be correct," Articus huffed out between breaths as he blocked blow after blow, before attempting a few offensive moves of his own. This was the most winded I had ever seen him.

"I don't believe I have ever seen a woman get so far under your skin like this," the other observed. "Want to talk about it?"

"I'd rather not," Articus said as he arched his staff in one wide swoop, bringing it down on his opponents with a thunderous crack. Frustration, the force behind the act.

"Of course not. How foolish of me to ask." The man used the strength behind his wide arms to slide both of their staffs back into a defensive position.

"Though I enjoy our little therapy sessions, I do have other responsibilities too—"

His words were cut off by a quick intake of breath as he quickly made to block Articus's frantic blow. This time he moved swifter and more relentlessly than before, as if a lid was opened on the jar that held his frustration, allowing it to spill over.

"She's unimaginably beautiful," Articus huffed out. "Yet she carries herself as though she thinks she's the most undesirable person in the room. She constantly plays hot and cold with me and though I do enjoy our games, I never know if I have won or lost."

"Sounds like you two are perfect for each other. Both self-degrading and dense." The other grunted as his feet gave several steps back from the force of Articus' strength.

"Everything about her is . . ." Articus's staff slid against the other's before smacking to the ground. He relaxed his stance, his staff hung loosely at his side, and took a long inhale as he pushed strands of hair back from his glistening brow. "Distracting."

His companion leaned in and threw an arm over Articus's shoulder then they started speaking too quietly for my ears to hear. I took it as my sign to leave, unnoticed, while I still could.

Chapter Twenty Six

A S THE NIGHT GREW late, I only grew more and more restless. Images of a well-honed body, flexing with every sharp maneuver intruded upon my thoughts. Recalling certain raw and vicious movements from the earlier sparring match caused an unexpected tight, heaviness in my chest that shortened my breaths. Every glance at the washroom spurred fantasies of a certain golden-haired, pain in my backside. Running water drowned out the world beyond the shower stall's glass walls. Only the sound of matching, quick breaths, and sodden clothing smacking the wet tiled floors, accompanied it.

I shook my head free of the indecent fantasy and debated seeing if Kareena was still awake. Ultimately deciding against possibly waking her since she worked so early in the morning, I sauntered over to the sparse bookcase. Feet padded silently against the plush rug. After scanning a few spines, all with rather romantic titles, I decided against reading all together, as I was unable to choose a book from the unfamiliar collection. Instead, I intended to distract myself with more sketching. After plucking my newly-gifted sketch pad and pencils, I nestled into the overstuffed, wingback chair, prepared to draw into the night until exhaustion made it impossible to see straight.

When Kareena and I had returned from our evening meal and after checking in with Ms. Hazel so Kareena could retrieve the latest Academy gossip, a parcel wrapped in brown paper and twine awaited us with a simple note addressed to myself.

The note did not say Dante was the sender, but I was able to guess as much from the two lines written in it.

Praying to see you in that delicious maid's uniform again.
In the near future, I hope.

The teasing remark, reminiscent of our earlier conversation.

As I went to turn on the delicate, hurricane glass lamp I noticed it was not plugged in. In fact, there was no cord at all. However, the lamp still turned on as I rotated the switch at its base. I did this several times in an attempt to appease my curiosity. I lifted the lamp, feeling its weight. Were there possibly batteries inside? The lamp didn't feel unusually heavy for its size. There was no place for batteries to even be stored. Its milky glass shade, decorated in water-colored flowers, sat atop an antique gold stem that tapered into feet shaped like petals and leaves and nothing else. I looked it over thoroughly from top to base turning it every which way as the wheels turned in my head.

"How on earth?" I muttered, making a mental note to ask Articus about its function first thing tomorrow.

I wiggled back down into the comfortably padded chair and started sketching a familiar face from my dreams. She lived eternally in my mind like a daydream of a fictional fairy queen. Long, silken strands cascaded from her circlet crown and a whimsical dress, that I suspected, would be made of spider silk, billowed like water down past her toes.

I put pencil to paper to start an outline, or at least, I tried to. My mind struggled to focus on the task. Catching myself distracted by other images. One of a girl on her tip-toes, kissing a prince with golden hair and his hands in his pockets. I chuckled to myself. Articus was no prince. I shook my head to clear my thoughts. My eyes continuously strayed from the sketch pad in my lap to peek over at that annoying lamp. It mocked me with its curious glow and stillness.

"Stop distracting me," I hissed, realizing how crazed I probably looked talking to a lamp. In the middle of the night. Alone.

It only took three attempts to continue my sketch until I was slamming the pad down on the table and tip-toeing out of our shared suite and across the grounds to the main building of the Academy with lamp in tow.

From across the gardens, I could see the faint glow of light from a small, singular window above the library, and knew Articus must still be up, working in his office late into the night. I would ask him about the stupid lamp and he would tell me how it worked and I would finally be able to rid myself of my curiosity and sleep.

I made every effort to go unnoticed on my way through the Academy grounds. I kept my slippers on, making my steps softer than they would have been had I wore my heeled boots, and I listened for voices and footsteps, around every corner. With the library entrance within sight, I dashed like a fawn through the woods.

A surprised scream escaped my lungs as I collided into a firm, stiff chest.

A wide, soft hand clasped over my mouth, as another hand pulled me closer around the waist. I lifted the lamp in my hand to strike my captor but was stopped by a tight grip around my arm.

"Death by lamp was not at all what I was expecting tonight, Miss Fox," a familiar voice said. I looked up from that strong chest to a wicked, lazy smile and silver eyes.

"Dan– I mean Mr. Da Romano, you frightened me," I whispered, taking a step back from his hold on me. "What are you doing about so late," I asked, accusingly, making sure to speak more formally.

"I could ask the same of you," he countered, releasing his hold and looking me over in suspicion. He was not in his usual cadet uniform of red, gold, and black but instead looked rather charming and approachable in a knitted, charcoal sweater over a white-collared shirt and tan slacks. Velvet loafers with a crest embroidered on the toes, adorned his feet.

"My lamp," I stumbled, trying to think of a legitimate reason that didn't involve me sneaking off to visit another man in the middle of the night. "It's broken and I was hoping one of the servants could fix it for me. I was heading that way and wasn't expecting to run into anyone this late." I paused, waiting for him to give me a reason for his lingering in return. Instead, Dante merely reached over and turned the dial on the lamp. It faintly Illuminated the hall with its warm light.

"Looks as though it's in fine working order to me." Heat flushed my cheeks.

"This fickle contraption. One moment it refuses to turn on, the next it's working fine. How odd," I stammered, flipping the lamp on its side in mock inspection.

"Odd indeed," Dante's eyes inspected me in return, searching like I was some riddle to be solved.

"Where are you from, Miss Fox."

I froze at the unexpectedness of his question. Clouden warned me about laying low and here I was, in the middle of the night, alone with a man, asking me where I was from and standing much too close for propriety.

"Oh, just some small village far from here. I doubt you would be familiar with it."

"Try me," he challenged. And though his hands were now clasped behind his back, he leaned into the space between us. It made it hard to focus, but I needed to come up with an answer, and quickly.

Where was it Clouden said I was to tell people I was from? Hadn't I told this same lie to Ms. Hazel, just this morning? Something with a P—Pelling?

"Peillon!" I said a bit too enthusiastically and hoped I was pronouncing it like a native. "Very small," I continued.

Dante's face lit up in recognition and my heart sank. "Oh yes, Peillon. I have distant relatives there. Unfortunately, it has been several years since I've traversed its stone alleyways and streets. Do you know the Riccis?" he was practically elated. I could do this, I could play along. I pretended to ponder on his question. Even pressed my free hand to my chin and opened my mouth in sudden realization.

"Yes. Yes, the Riccis. Wonderful people. I cannot say I knew them personally, but they are very well-known in our humble village. I must say it would not be what it is today without the Riccis," I added, laying it on thick, hoping it was just enough to not question me further.

A clever little grin hitched the corner of his handsome mouth. He was, in fact, handsome in the most classic of ways—there was no denying it. He was the kind that exuded class and wealth. Even his tousled curls had a shine and tameness to them that was completely unnatural, but appealing, all the same. I imagined twirling them around my fingers in tight loops before releasing them to spring back in place.

A soft sound broke me from my wanton thoughts. To my horror I had been staring at said curls for two seconds too long. Remembering myself and my rather indecent situation, I slipped back into character, with forged propriety.

"I'm sorry Mr. Da Romano, but I must go. As you know, it is late and well . . ." I gestured between us. Dante only stepped in closer. As if I hadn't just hinted at our current inappropriate situation. I froze as he lifted my free hand to his lips. Placing a soft kiss on my knuckles. His other hand was still tucked behind his back. He looked like a prince straight from a fairytale. This man was unreal.

"Sweet dreams then, Alise," he whispered my name like a sin. As I made to pass by him, he grabbed my elbow, stopping me.

"The servant quarters are that way," he indicated pointedly with a tilt of his head in the opposite direction.

"Oh, you are right. Thank you." I offered a quick curtsy and headed away from the library, only stopping to see if Dante was still behind me, watching. He was, like a vigilant royal guard. When I turned a corner, I stopped and waited.

Waited for the click of footsteps on marble.

Waited until the sound grew too faint to hear before turning back and continuing on my intended path.

I thanked the mother above when the heavy wooden doors swung open without a sound and thanked every star in the sky for its vacancy. Tip-toeing up the iron stairwell to Articus's office, I was relieved to see a faint glow of lamp light still leaking from under the door. I knocked lightly, calling to Articus with a loud whisper. I rocked on my heels in anticipation as papers and feet shuffled from behind the door. It slowly whined open and my stomach sank in dread.

I made a mistake.

Articus stood before me in nothing but his trousers. His perfect body, on display before me—something I only saw the frame of while he sparred earlier. Unfortunately for me, it was all so much more enticingly beautiful than my imagination could have conjured. I most definitely made a mistake in coming here so late at night.

I opened my mouth to apologize, to make up an excuse to leave, but I only gaped. Appearing disheveled and vulnerable only made him even more appealing, while the moonlight accentuated every ridge and plane of his torso and the dips that disappeared below his waist band. The lamps glow backlit his form as though he were some unholy angel.

"Did anyone see you come up here?" he asked, bringing my attention back to the surface of reality. I looked over my shoulder to check.

"Umm, no I—"

Firm hands pulled me into the room. The door slamming shut behind my back. Before I could so much as blink I was caged in between the door and strong, bare, arms. His hand rested on the frame—a mischievous smile pulling at his full lips.

Was that a dimple threatening to emerge?

"What a stealthy Little Fox." Amusement glittered in his darkened eyes, making it suddenly hard to breathe. I don't know what I expected coming up here, but it wasn't this. An electric current tensed every muscle in my body, making me rigid and unmoving, unable to think as my back pressed into the door. My mouth still hung open and I made an effort to shut it without mewing like a frightened kitten.

Articus leaned in closer. A hair's breadth away from my chest grazing the top of his perfect torso if I breathed too deeply. His fingers grazed my arm, trailing down, slowly, torturously gentle and I jolted with a sharp intake of breath.

"Alise," he breathed.

"Yes," I barely spoke, unwilling to look up into those eyes. Afraid of what might reflect back at me in them. His hand folded around mine and one by one untangled the stem of the lamp from my fingers before inspecting it curiously.

"Why are you carrying a lamp?"

My breath broke free. The tension shattered like glass. I fell back into the reality of why I was up here in the first place and the fact that, while we were alone, I didn't have to speak so formally.

"Oh yeah, I was going to ask you how it works." The mask slipped off effortlessly, to be replaced by another I saved just for him. An eyebrow raised into his messy mop of sandy hair at my question all while, seeming unphased by my sudden change in tone and demeanor.

"How it works?"

"Yes. Did I stutter?" I questioned rather starkly and crossed my arms, trying to bury the embarrassing fluster this man brought out of me with his surprising half-nakedness. Articus chuckled, examining the lamp again.

"All this way in the middle of the night for a bloody lamp," he mused to himself more than me. The soft, low rumble of laughter radiated from his chest. I wanted to place my hand upon it. To feel its current through my fingertips. Let it travel to my limbs and comfort every muscle with its harmony. Thoughts of dripping wet lips, caressing soaked and scorching skin, invaded my thoughts. Those pesky fantasies. I fought them back into the depths. Smothered them someplace deep where they would suffocate and die.

"I think I made it perfectly clear I did indeed come up here, in the middle of the night, to ask you about this lamp." Stepping aside to gain some distance between us. Articus looked me over, eyes stopping at my tapping foot before releasing a resigned sigh.

"You turn the switch to the on position and it lights up," he said curtly as he demonstrated such. I grabbed the lamp from his hand.

"I know that, obviously, I've used a lamp before, but how does it work? There's no cord. Where does the electricity come from? It doesn't seem to have a place for batteries." I turned the lamp upside down to indicate such.

"The power source is wireless, like all other electronic mechanisms," he said as if it were common knowledge. It probably was, but, clearly not to me.

"I forget sometimes that this is all very new for you," he sighed, seeming to have read the ignorance on my face. I continued studying the lamp in my hand.

"Come." He ushered me to a small window by the lone black stove in the corner. Its soft glow combating the chilled night air. "See that tower over there?" He gestured to a spindly looking structure. Similar to that of images I had seen of the Eiffel tower in design but slightly narrower and with a long slim antenna atop it. I nodded in reply.

"That tower emits a frequency that powers all electric utilities for hundreds of miles. Whether it be a light bulb in a lamp, or a radio, or a car. It powers everything without the need for wires or cables."

"Wireless electricity," I breathed quietly to myself.

Articus turned his full attention on me. We were standing so close I could feel the heat radiating from him. Even back in the First Realm, I noticed he tended to run hot. With the moonlight pouring through the window and across his body like liquid silver, I noticed, for the first time, a large scar that ran along the side of his torso and another down his shoulder and over his collar bone. Wincing at the thought of how painful injuries so severe must have felt, I found myself reaching toward his abdomen, fingers barely brushed his skin before I jerked them back. Realizing where my attention had roamed, Articus registered his state of dress, or lack thereof and grabbed a shirt from the back of his desk chair before sliding it on only to leave the top half buttons undone. Now instead of getting a full view of what lay beneath, I was teased with the sharp cut of his collar bones peeking out from his open collar.

Why was every piece of him so appealing? And distracting? And infuriating?

Wanting to ease the tension, I asked, "Is it customary for a man to kiss a woman's hand in greeting or farewell here?" Recalling not just once but both times Dante kissed my hand in such a way.

"Only in the case of addressing clergy or high-ranking members of the opposite sex. Why do you ask?" Articus eyed me with suspicion from his spot across the small threshold with his arms braced behind him on the heavy wooden desk.

"No reason," I lied, chewing on my bottom lip.

"You are referring to Dante, are you not?"

My stomach sank.

"What do you mean?" I turned back to the window, mocking ignorance. There's no way he could have—

"Out in the training court, I saw him kiss your hand," he continued and a sigh of relief flooded out of me. I hadn't realized he had been watching so closely. I assumed he was too busy with the other cadets to note the interaction.

"I didn't know you even noticed," I confessed.

"I notice everything, Alise." When I turned to face him again, I tried not to flinch. He was mere inches away. Towering over me with a look in his eyes that I could not decipher. "You didn't just come up here to ask me irrelevant questions about a lamp and chaste kisses, did you?" His question was a challenge that made my hackles rise. I felt cornered as I stared back at the wolf who stared down at me.

"As ridiculous as it may seem, that is exactly why—" Making to turn my head away, his finger and thumb clasped my chin and gently directed my focus back to him—clearly undeterred.

"You are restless tonight," he spoke gently yet certain. Gaze falling to my fingers as they mindlessly tapped on my skirts. They froze at his notice.

"I couldn't sleep," I confessed, as softly as sin, but I refused to elaborate as to why.

"Tell me how I can help, Little Fox." His attention fell to my mouth as his thumb danced delicately across my bottom lip.

How tempting and easy it would have been, to press a kiss to that small bit of flesh. To lean in—to allow something more to happen. Isn't that what I really wanted? Why I truly couldn't wait till the morning to ask him about the stupid lamp? And though every fiber of me ached to close the gap between us, I stubbornly shoved that down somewhere dark to let it starve and hopefully die off. As much as my body wanted to give him everything, my heart grabbed the reins and yielded nothing.

"Trust me, if I needed help falling asleep, you're the last person I would seek out," I bit back. His hand dropped to his side as though I had actually bitten him and I immediately regretted the venom in my words. A flash of something like hurt was quickly masked from his face.

"Of course," he concurred with a show of indifference. "Why would you when you have someone like Dante Da Romano nipping at your heels."

A shove for a shove.

"And what's wrong with that? Why do you care if he's pursuing me or not?"

Articus pinched the bridge of his nose. "Dante is a spoiled Elite who spends most of his time drunk, chasing girls with his fellow goons, and has never been told 'no' in the entirety of his life. Pardon me if I don't see him as your equal."

"Sounds like a good time to me," I threw back at him, though somewhat sarcastically, just to see the shock it could deliver. Unfortunately, I didn't get the reaction I sought. Instead, fierce eyes pierced me, telling me without words that he was in fact, serious. "I don't need your concern or jealousy. I'm a big girl and can decide what I want for myself," I said, brushing off the tension in the room.

"I never said you couldn't," he countered as he collapsed back in the worn chair behind his desk, back to the papers haphazardly strewn across it. A single huff of laughter left my lips in retaliation.

"It seems you couldn't sleep either. Too much coffee perhaps?" I chided like a concerned mother.

"Good night, Miss Fox," was all he said in dismissal. His eyes refused to leave the papers before him.

I huffed at his bluntness and the cold, formal use of my surname. "Sorry to have disturbed you at such a late hour," I said, a bit too formally in return, as I made my way to the door.

"Always a pleasure," he replied coolly. I wanted to throw the lamp at his head. "Oh, and one more thing," his voice softened and grew deeper, causing me to pause over the threshold. "Try not to dwell on scandalous thoughts of me too late into the night. I have a very long session of questioning planned for you tomorrow morning and you will be no good to me . . . fatigued."

My mind instantly went to the gutter and willingly bathed in its filth. Heat crawled from my neck to my cheeks, making me grateful my back was turned away from Articus's prying eyes. Warm, deep, and sinful every word was an innuendo to something more than just questioning. My thoughts conjured up images of him pulling me back into his office and thoroughly questioning me atop his messy desk. What was wrong with me? He knew exactly what he was doing. He was just trying to get a reaction from me. To regain control of this battle of wills.

I slammed the door behind me a bit too forcefully, and my feet clamored down iron stairs. I all but marched straight to the suite I shared with Kareena before stripping every layer of clothing from my hot, tight skin and jumping into the similarly scorching hot water, spraying from the shower head.

Sleep didn't find me until after I stifled my moans of relief into a pillow. My own finger's ministrations reeling back control of my urges, with every caress. Though the entire time they danced between my thighs, I wished and fantasized that they were someone else's. I chose to visualize a devilishly perfect smile that belonged to none other than a fairytale prince himself, yet those silver eyes changed, as if of their own fruition, into a deep shade of pine green. The ghost of gentle kisses on my neck grew fierce with more pressure before switching to playful nips on my flesh and I found myself back on that velvet settee, letting Articus do as he threatened to me instead of wrestling him to the ground as I had. With each thrumming stroke, I fell deeper into the sweet waking dream. My self-control swept away with the idea of what his mouth would feel like against my swollen, aching, center. Trembling legs clenched together involuntarily as a moan escaped from deep within my chest. As my breaths slowed and deepened into rest, I rolled listlessly to the side, and cursed the familiar voice that whispered me to sleep.

"Why do you run from me, Little Fox?"

Chapter Twenty Seven

Music greeted me, along with the sun's early-dawn light, shining through the sheer panels draped along the bedroom's large bay window. My eyes fluttered open and took in its dim rays as they drew patterns on the walls. Everything felt surreal, as though I was still in a half-forgotten dream. The unusual clock on the nightstand chimed a tune as a music box would. Its cheery melody repeated in a loop as tiny, animated birds chirped along atop it. The contraption was a stunning work of craftsmanship. Its porcelain case, painted with bright flowers and trimmed in gold detail. I closed the gilded lid to stop the loop of music. Iridescent birds disappeared below.

Kareena had shown me how to set it the previous night so I would not be late meeting Ms. Hazel in the kitchens as promised.

"Did you not have clocks of your own back home?" Kareena asked, clearly puzzled when I came to ask her how to operate the intricate and ancient looking clock.

"Father always said clocks were the thieves of time." And I smiled at the truth of it. My adoptive father's voice echoed in my mind as I repeated his words. A vision of him in his worn cardigan, staring out the window of his study for hours as if time didn't exist at all, formed my thoughts. His actions were of someone who truly knew how to squeeze every ounce of pleasure from a day. He would always fly through his work at a maddening pace, grading papers and researching his thesis as if the load of responsibilities was unexpected. My adoptive mother would then chide him for dawdling all day. The two were opposites in every way.

After getting ready for the long day ahead, I made my way towards the door where a gorgeous bouquet of flowers sat on the foyer table. Another note with my name on it was positioned upon the heaps of pink flowers. I plucked the note from its perch and read:

Based on my observation of the dress you wore Sunday,
I assume pink is your favorite color. Please correct me if I'm wrong over tea this
afternoon.
Presumptuously,
Dante

A grin snuck its way across my lips.

"Oh, how lovely." Kareena's voice startled me as she came around to inspect the note still in my hands. "Dante Da Romano?" she questioned with shock upon seeing his name scrawled on the note.

"What do you know of him?" I asked as I quickly stuffed the note in my pocket.

"Only that he is one of the most eligible bachelors in the Colony!" She squealed giddily, like we were two young girls planning our hypothetical weddings.

"His father is a councilman and his family is very influential. Our father works quite a bit with his, as they are both on the Council together. Oh, and they have the most beautiful estate in Venice!" She twirled for emphasis and clasped her hands as her mind wandered off to some distant vision of a long-ago memory.

"You've been?" I stated more than asked.

"Well, just once, when I was much younger and father wanted to debut me to some of the Elite families and their sons. But I do remember they had the most beautiful gardens and a ballroom unlike any other and more servants than I could count. The women in Venice were so beautifully dressed. It's the only city that comes close to Paris's level of exquisite fashion and cuisine."

Kareena frowned down at her nurse's uniform which was clearly the least favorite of her attire.

"So, you would say he's a good catch?" I asked cautiously. By the way she spoke of him I couldn't help but wonder if she had a crush on him. Perhaps intended him for herself. Seeming to read the unspoken question Kareena quickly interjected a reassurance.

"Yes, of course, but you need not worry about my intentions. I have—" she paused, abruptly. "Look at the sun! I must go or I'll be late for my shift. As should you or you'll procure the wrath of Ms. Hazel," she quickly stammered, practically shoving me through the door with her.

Pine green eyes looked up at me from behind gold-rimmed reading glasses. Another one of his quirks I secretly thought was adorable, though I'd never let him know so.

"Are those for me?" he chuckled behind a teasing smirk as he referred to the bouquet in my arms. As an apology for being late I had brought the bouquet with me to give to Ms. Hazel. However, she was not the slightest bit impressed.

"What am I to do with these, girl? When what I could use are your hands in this kitchen, on time."

Thus, I was forced to keep them with me until I could make it back to my room. Unfortunately, because I was late to the kitchens, I was then also late in meeting Articus in the library for our session. Feeling like a fool as I carried the enormous bouquet with me down the Academy's halls.

"No," I teased back, sticking my tongue out. "They're from an admirer," I said with a dignified raise of my chin before setting them down on the table in front of Articus.

"Oh. I see. Another young man who wishes to do unspeakable things to you." A flush and tightness came to my cheeks and I bit my lip to stop a smile. I hoped all the indecent things I imagined him doing to me last night didn't show on my face.

"Now, Articus," I retaliated. "We don't know what his intentions are, yet." Turning to face him, I found him already standing close by my side. Damn his stealth. The boy moved like a phantom. His height difference made itself known. This close, my shoulder brushed his arm as he leaned in. He looked down at me with an expression of hunger.

"When it comes to you, Little Fox, all men's intentions are indecent." I could feel the flush try to return to my cheeks but I refused to behave like some giddy school girl.

"Let me tell you a secret," I whispered. As I cupped my hand toward his ear and leaned in, I thought I saw a wash of confusion across his face for only a blink before I spoke into his ear, "I can handle myself."

"Is that how you tell a secret where you're from?" He leaned back appalled by the gesture. As if I just offered him a dead fish. Before I could respond he turned me around with my still-cupped hand so that my back was pressed into his chest. His head loomed over my shoulder as he draped an arm across my chest. A hand clasped my shoulder as a close friend or protective lover would. His hot breath warmed my neck as he leaned in and whispered, "Here, when we want to tell a secret, we embrace the receiver and speak over their shoulder. That way we are both looking at the subject we are whispering about." I tried my hardest to keep my eyes fixed forward on the archive shelves before us. My heart beat a little too hard and I counted the aisles of books to distract myself as he drawled on in some nonchalant cadence. This felt like a test—as if to call my bluff because in his arms like this, I felt like I couldn't handle myself after all. Swallowing hard, I barely spoke the words, "This all seems rather intimate."

Just to have his daring lips reply, "Isn't that the nature of whispers and secrets?" His hand released my arm and slowly descended down mine. My traitorous body shivered at the slight touch.

"Intimate?" I absentmindedly repeated.

"Yes," he whispered. It took everything in me to hold my ground and not jolt away from his grasp as soon as he released me. I felt like an animal frantically skittering away from a hunter's trap. That is what this was, a trap. He was the hunter and I, prey—engaged in a game we both loved to play. When I faced him, his eyes darkened with a slight edge of concern. That breath of a moment dripped on like cooled honey while we both debated whether to draw closer, or pull back. A stalemate between two players waiting for the other's move.

"Are you cold?" he spoke first. I wrapped my arms across my chest and rubbed my arms in an attempt to settle my puckered skin.

"Yes," I lied.

"Alise," a baritone voice that could only be Clouden's, jerked us apart. "May I see you in my lab for a moment?" Clouden took us in—his gaze all-knowing. I felt as guilty as a child who was caught stealing a cookie, though technically we hadn't done anything untoward. "Alone," he added, inspecting Articus coolly. Articus's demeanor was now that of a bored prince.

"As you wish," he shrugged. Clouden's hand guided me towards the lab before the words could finish leaving Articus's mouth.

Once in his underground lab, Clouden asked for a sample of my blood to test and I obliged willingly. After procuring a few vials he advised me to remain seated while he tinkered with his lab equipment. Unfamiliar mechanisms of brass and glass bubbled and ticked through their functions.

"How are you going to test my blood?" I asked, partly from curiosity, partly from a need to break the uncomfortable cold silence that filled the already chilly, cavernous space.

"I'm going to run samples under different frequencies and see how your cells react," he replied without looking up from his task. "Since all things born of a certain realm vibrate in harmony to their birth realm, my theory is a foreign object, such as the cells of a person born from another realm, will not flow in harmony with a realm they were not created from. It is Articus's theory that you are not, in fact, native born of the First Realm." I watched as he inserted a drop of my blood into two, flat, pieces of glass before sliding them under a microscope.

"And do you agree with his theory?" I dared ask.

"Yes," he said curtly and without further explanation. "The only trouble is that I don't have the exact frequency sequence for all the known realms, just the Second. I'm working to obtain the others but for now all we can test is if your blood moves in harmony with the Second Realm's frequency or retaliates. This will determine if the Second Realm is your native-born home or not. Here, have a look." He gestured to the microscope.

I peered into it and saw tiny red misshapened blobs bouncing, almost violently, into each other.

"Now take a look at my own cells." He slid a different glass tray in and I observed similar red blobs moving gracefully like a slow flowing river.

"As you can see, if my theory is correct, then we can conclude that you do not originate from the Second Realm, based on your cell's reaction. But I cannot know for sure which realm you are native to until I can gain the other realms frequency sequences and test your cells in the controlled environment of the frequency chamber. Only then Miss Fox, may we be able to solidify the truth of your origin." Clouden looked at me pointedly. Or perhaps he was observing me like one of his specimens. Dissecting me with his eyes.

"Is it dangerous that my blood shakes like that in reaction to being here?" I worried my lip with the thought that my blood cells were essentially buzzing inside me like bees.

"I would consider your cell's reaction a mild one, which I theorize is because the Second Realm's frequency is not far off from your origin realm's. However long-term exposure, over time, could lead to a shortened life span and other physical and mental repercussions." Nausea rolled in my stomach.

"Such as what?" I dared to ask.

"Possible psychosis, anxiety, depression, paranoid delusions, possibly even cancer, to name some of the worst, but nausea, tremors, and fatigue are assumed more common for a mild, short-term case such as yours." I sensed a piece of the puzzle click into place.

"When I was living back there, back in the First Realm, I was much more frequently ill than I am now. Honestly, I've almost felt better here than I have in my entire life. Does that mean the frequency there was even further off from my origin realm than it is here?"

"If my theory is correct then yes, we can assume that the frequency here is, in fact, closer to that of your origin. Articus believed so himself anyway, and it played a part in his reasoning for bringing you here in the first place. However, the real question is which realm is your origin realm, Miss Fox. From where were you truly born?"

His question sank into me like heavy stone as he turned back to the beakers and notes. If I wasn't born in the First Realm or here either, if I was to believe Clouden's theory, then that left only the Third and Fourth Realm. But there were only four known realms to begin with. What if there were others that had yet to be discovered? Could I be from one of them instead? If so, then I may never find my birth realm and I would always feel this way. I would always feel sick or tired or displaced for the rest of my life until my body failed.

Suddenly, I became very aware of my shaking hands and smoothed them on my skirts while taking a long deep breath. Looking for a distraction, my gaze strayed across the scientific instruments back to the man beside me. His brown hair was tied back, revealing slightly peppered strands at his temples. The only indication of his age. As he studied what was before him, head tilted, his glasses slid to the edge of his nose. He pushed them back up, absentmindedly. It was then I caught sight of a long, thin scar across his jaw line.

"This," he said, seeming to have noticed my attention, as he tilted his head. "Was a gift from our mutual friend. A lifetime ago." My eyes widened as I registered his meaning. Quickly, I attempted to hide my shock by studying the table before me. Feeling as though I was prying into something personal.

"Seems no one is an exception to his rage," I murmured to myself as I thought of Articus bringing a rusted pipe down on Brenton's skull. If Articus wounded his own mentor so permanently, then who wouldn't he hurt if he was in one of his rageful moods? If he snapped and lost control? Silence tingled my skin and I turned to see honey brown eyes looking down at me. The disappointment in Clouden's stare caused me to internally cringe. He held it there for several seconds before sighing deeply and removing his glasses.

"When I found him that day, I could see the wolf that consumed him." His hand scratched the scruff of his chin. "I felt shame for letting it get to that point. Instead of being a father to Articus, my brother had created a tool for his disposal that had been left unchecked for far too many years." Hands gently folded his glasses before returning them to his jacket pocket.

"No one was going to save the boy drowning inside. No one had nurtured him or showed him any kind of life besides the one my brother had. So that day I stood my ground and ripped the knife from his hand and every day since I've been trying to help him control his anger. To be something more than the wolf."

"Was he going to hurt someone?" I asked.

"Only someone he saw as a threat to himself or Kareena which, unfortunately in his erratic state, was everyone at that moment." He turned away from the zinc table top to rummage through a cluttered drawer of tools. "Shortly after, I convinced my brother to let him work with me, as my apprentice. He was reluctant but agreed. Mostly because he could no longer deny how out of control Articus had gotten." Clouden's face grew grim as he paused and stared forward at nothing in particular.

"I was too late to help my own brother, to prevent him from becoming the power hungry, selfish ass he is today but, it is not too late for Articus. There is still hope for him yet. He needs only to make the decision himself now. I fear I've done all I can do for him at this point." He raked a hand through his hair before returning to the zinc top empty-handed, pushing loose strands from his brow. "There is still a part of that wolf inside of him, Miss Fox. It is what motivates him to protect others." I glanced down at the glass bottles before me, distractedly running my finger around the rims as I tried to imagine the kind of childhood Articus must have had and the guilt Clouden felt for it.

"And you," he rasped, causing my attention to snap back to him. "I don't know what happened between you two before he brought you here but, it has . . .

changed him. He's different in some hidden way I cannot quite place." With that he gave me a forced smile, not reaching his eyes as though he were not accustomed to the gesture. An expression of both appreciation and yet, concern. "But I am all the more grateful for it—for you and what you may mean to him." My mouth gaped open and then shut with all the words I choked on, lodged in my throat.

My mind clamored to correct him but my voice failed. I meant nothing to Articus beyond someone to serve a purpose to his cause. A means to an end. And when he was done with me, with what knowledge I could offer him, he would let me go, I was sure, and move on with his life. Perhaps Clouden was getting Articus's hope for progress confused with something else. Articus didn't care for me.

"You . . . you can't truly believe that he values me as anything more than a relic."

"I do," he quipped. "But what does an old, jaded man know of these things?"

A soft pass of laughter escaped me.

"You're not old." A small, more natural curve to his lips formed.

"Ah but I am jaded," he deadpanned, causing my shoulders to lax with a sigh.

Chapter Twenty Eight

MY DOUBTS ABOUT THE validity of Clouden's claims were confirmed as I made my way to the infirmary.

Hushed voices, and the sound of stifled cries leaked from an alcove where a door led to the servants' quarters. Stunned by the intimate scene I stumbled upon I quickly ducked behind an adjoining wall. However, my curiosity got the best of me and I peeked for a second, confirmed, glance.

Articus embraced a girl I had never seen before. From my viewpoint I could only make out the wide, pleading look in her eyes, and the deep rich color of her hair as strands slipped from a low bun at the nape of her neck. Strands that

Articus's fingers were presently buried in as he held her against his chest. His lips whispered what I could only assume were sweet promises into her ear. In a moment the girl wrapped her arms around his neck and raised to her tippy toes. Her wide doe-like eyes approached closer to his own. I turned away, knowing what was to come next.

Clouden was wrong in his misguided assumption about Articus and I. Obviously, Articus was in some kind of relationship with this girl. Or enjoying himself with her at the very least. A strange, sick feeling twisted my stomach at the thought of what they might do together when they were alone. How he might kiss her lips and other parts of her body in secret hidden places. The sounds she might make when he touches her.

I compartmentalized. Pushed it down into that bottle I kept all my undesirable thoughts and feelings in and shook myself free of it before swiftly heading back on my path.

"What should I wear to tea?" I whispered to Kareena as she shuffled around the infirmary, trying not to gain the harsh attention of Nurse Petit. "Please, Kareena, I'm utterly hopeless without your aid in this department. Come back to our rooms with me and help me get ready." I plastered on my widest, sweetest grin.

"I would absolutely love to, but . . ." she threw a cautionary glance in Nurse Petit's direction. "You know who is in one of her moods today and has me replenishing all the ready-made medicines. It's going to be at least another hour or longer until I finish."

"I can help!" I said a little too loudly and Kareena giggled as she shushed me.

"Fine, but just be quiet," she chided playfully before leading me into a back room full of powders and herbs. At the back wall stood a lone table with a single pharmacy lamp shining down on it.

"If you can follow a recipe, it's all rather easy and tedious work," she said before closing the door behind us.

She assigned me the easiest of tasks, putting a mineral powder she already blended into empty capsules. It was mind-numbing work but if it allowed Kareena to get off her shift sooner, I was more than willing to help. The idle chatter back and forth while we worked did wonders, distracting me from my growing anxiousness about having tea with Dante.

When all inventory was accounted for and capsules made, before heading back to our suite, I purposefully left my bouquet behind in hopes it would lighten the infamously grouchy nurse's mood. Kareena giggled into her hands as I quickly scrolled an anonymous note of my own.

> *To my rose in a garden of thorns.*
> *Lovingly,*
> *Your admirer.*

"You are absolutely terrible," she said behind her hand as we scurried out of the infirmary.

Dante was the defining image of luxury and grace as he leaned casually against the body of a shiny, black automobile. It was a convertible with glossy black paint and a body with curves like a woman's. His suit was impeccable in every way that screamed gentlemen and wealth—the dark gray tweed of it highlighting the silver of his eyes.

I eagerly pranced down the Academy's steps like a child sneaking out for a joy ride. The hem of my new summer tea gown danced at my ankles.

"Is this yours?" I asked in awe while my kid-glove-clad fingertips traced the edge of a slick curve.

He chuckled and flashed me a perfect white smile. "Of course." He extended his hand toward me. In it was one perfect, white rose.

"And this is yours." He indicated toward the flower. I took it between my fingers and brought it to my nose immediately. It smelled unreal, not like any rose I had ever smelled before. It was as if it had been dipped in perfume. The scent was wonderful but foreign, almost overwhelming.

"Thank you." I raised up on my tip-toes and gave him a peck on the cheek as a reward for his thoughtfulness. Not at all sure if it was socially acceptable for a young woman to do so, but deciding not to care all the same. I was rewarded in return with another beaming smile before he turned to open my door and usher me in.

"You are most welcome. Shall we?" he stated more than asked.

After sliding into his seat, he pressed a small bronze button on the dash and the vehicle quietly came to life.

"Is this vehicle electric?" I asked.

"Naturally." He turned us out of the cobbled drive, down past a set of elaborate iron gates, giving a quick nod at the guards standing by as we exited out to the street beyond. "I wouldn't be caught dead in one of those old, crank-style contraptions. Besides," he continued, stretching his fingers in his black leather driving gloves, "only the best will do for my girl."

My girl?

I was charmed if not slightly put-off by the claiming title of the pet name. After all, we hadn't known each other long and this was our first outing. But perhaps this was possibly considered courting and it was taken more seriously.

After a very short drive, we arrived at our destination. Dante parked at the front entrance and came around to open my door before turning the automobile over to the valet. The elegant, white marble building was far larger than I had expected though, honestly, I didn't know what to expect having never been to afternoon tea before—let alone in Paris. Suddenly my inexperience made me nervous as my finger fidgeted.

Before I could change my mind about the outing altogether, Dante took my arm into his and patted my hand reassuringly. A footman opened the gold-framed glass doors for us and we entered a vast lobby. It appeared to be a hotel or club of sorts. To the right was a set of heavy, wooden doors that peeked open as people came and went, allowing me a glimpse of the dim, lamp-lit space. Smoke from cigars and pipes streamed in its light as men drank dark liquor from crystal glasses, all seated in plush, dark leather chairs around low tables. Occasional laughter boomed through the crack in the doorway until it closed shut.

Steering to the left instead, we approached the entrance of a different-style room. The golden words, Three Birds Tearoom, displayed daintily above the doors. Instantly the maître-d recognized Dante and bowed his head in greeting, addressing him as "Mr. Da Romano," before seeing us to our table.

Despite its namesake, the place was anything but a room, more so resembling a solarium that had been converted to be used for dining. A round, domed glass ceiling spilled light into the space as sun rays peeked through spindling vines that had grown over the roof. Walls bedecked in opulent, floral wallpaper and accented with gold filigree moldings, encased the space. The floor was bedecked in a deep green carpet so lush that the heels of my boots sank into it with each step.

Our table was simple compared to the rest of the space. A round, white-marbled top on a single gold pedestal. The chairs were a matching set, tufted with deep, navy velvet. Dante held my chair out for me before taking his own across the table. He was staring at me from across the table but I couldn't be bothered to return the eye contact as I was too busy taking in all the fanciful elements that surrounded us.

Flecks of gold light caught my eye, the sunlight hitting reflective surfaces, but upon closer observation, I noticed there were, in fact, tiny brass butterflies. They fluttered all around, absentmindedly landing on tea cups, or on the hat of an unknowing diner before flitting off again.

"I suppose they don't have places like this in Peillon," Dante speculated.

I absentmindedly shook my head as my gaze bounced from detail to detail. A waiter obstructed my view with a towering tiered tray ladened with scones, macarons, and delicate finger sandwiches. Beside it he placed a porcelain teapot and set two tea cups on saucers before pouring our cups. Dante dismissed him with the wave of a hand and the young man briefly bowed before silently shuffling off.

"So, you are telling me you have never even heard of this tearoom?" Dante continued over the rim of his cup.

"I don't—"

I was interrupted by the distracting scene of a mechanical, bronze butterfly landing on our sugar bowl. It plucked a sugar cube from its contents and fluttered over my cup before dropping the cube into my tea with a comical plop. I couldn't help but giggle at the absurd whimsicalness of it all. Imagining the butterfly asking, "One lump or two?"

"How?" I asked Dante, beaming like a child from across the table. "How is it so intelligent for something that is just metal and gears?

"Many believe the creator puts a drop of their spirit, their own energy, into their creations, giving it a sort of mock-soul and an illusion of intellect." Dante crooked his finger toward a passing butterfly beckoning it to do the same to his tea.

"No one really knows how it's done though, trade secrets and all. Of course, they are not truly alive either, as you and I are, but it is just enough to make people feel more comfortable around the automatons that are used in the service industry. Such as cleaning one's home or—"

"Or putting sugar in one's tea," I finished for him, before taking a sip from my cup.

He gifted me that perfect, charming smile as he chuckled from across the table. "Yes, I suppose even in dispensing sugar, it makes the experience more enjoyable." He held my gaze for longer than necessary, his eyes falling to my mouth, only briefly, before returning to my own fixated stare. Dante was as beautiful as any sculpture or portrait. He was a piece of art someone could linger on for hours—taking in the tiny highlights of bronze in his curling chestnut locks, or the sculpted planes of his cheekbones and jaw. His perfect balance of masculine and feminine traits that made him appear regal just sitting here, having tea. Like a royal sitting amongst commoners.

And the way he looked at me made me feel as though I was one too. As though just being in his company elevated a person to a higher status of being. Surrounded by diners in their tea gowns and suits, in this beautiful solarium of a tea room, I felt far away from the girl who ran from group homes. The girl who stole to survive and was no stranger to a cold floor for a bed, or a meal from a plastic wrapper.

From across the table something suddenly caught Dante's attention. Dante's gaze darted over my shoulder and before I could turn to see what it was, he stood from his chair and threw his napkin down.

"Sorry to rush you darling, but we really must go now," he said as he took my elbow and guided me to my feet with a half-eaten macron still in my hand.

"But—" I sighed as I glanced back at my still-half-full cup of tea and the wonderful assortment of treats that had been abandoned on our tray. In a blink I was all but dragged behind Dante as I scurried to keep up, shoving the rest of the macron ungracefully into my mouth. Pink crumbs surely fell onto my dress.

"What is—" We halted as soon as we came into the lobby. A doorman was holding the entrance for a gentleman in full military dress. Too many medals and ribbons to count, adorned his red jacket. His features were firm and serious, yet handsome and almost familiar. Though his hair was cut much shorter than Clouden's he had the same eyes and prominent brow. Also, where Clouden's eyes were a warm honey brown—at least sometimes—this man's were cold and calculated. Like dirt thrown on a casket or soil after a storm. Every inch of his gaze reflected death.

My heart skipped a beat at the sight of who followed him. Articus was dressed impeccably in his own crimson uniform. The color warmed his skin and brightened his eyes to the radiance of gemstones. Yet, he wore the same cold calculation as the man before him, giving him the appearance of an inanimate toy soldier.

I froze, unable to speak or move as Dante, and everyone nearby bowed their heads in greeting. Unfortunately, this caught the eye of the older man and he looked over at me with distaste, causing me to quickly curtsy.

"General, if you would like, I have your table ready with a selection of our finest," a man in an impeccable black suit said as he gestured toward the parlor room where the other men laughed and drank. By the time I looked up, Articus passed by me like I was nothing more than a houseplant, completely ignoring my attempts at eye contact. I clenched my jaw against the slap of his rejection.

"Have the others arrived?" the man referred to as "the general" asked.

"Yes, sir. Right this way, sir." The door shut behind them, muffling off the smell of cigar smoke and sounds of rumbled laughter, cutting me off before I could finish calling out to Articus's back.

Dante took me in, a hint of amusement tugged at his lips.

"You are *familiar* with Articus Desaius?" he questioned.

Pink must have flooded my cheeks at the realization of my misstep in using Articus's first name rather than his last, for Dante nearly chuckled before clasping my hand in his. "Don't worry, darling, I'm rather good at being discreet." His gesture and words washed away trace amounts of my worry. If he was willing to look past the slip-up then I could too. And it was almost easy to let the last of my concerns fly away with the wind as it blew through my hair, on our drive back to the Academy.

Chapter Twenty Nine

A STRING OF MILD curses and an abundance of dresses littering the floor greeted me upon my return.

"Where is that stupid, godforsaken, dress?" I heard Kareena huff from her bedroom.

Upon entering, I witnessed another pile of dresses, shoes, and ribbons ladened like a hill on Kareena's bed.

"Everything okay?" I asked softly, but still managed to startle the frantic girl. She popped her head from around the door of her armoire. A tangle of auburn waves fell down her shoulder to her back, lashing with her hasty movements like a curtain caught in a breeze would.

"Oh, it's just ... Father is coming to the Academy for an impromptu inspection and no one thought to even tell me he was in town until less than five minutes ago and he'll be here any moment." She tore another dress from her collection, inspecting it before tossing it in the pile with the others.

"Why are you so worried about what to wear? All your dresses are beautiful. Won't any of them do?" I pondered out loud, hoping I didn't sound rude or intrusive.

Kareena merely chuckled sarcastically without sparing a glance from her task. "When Father comes for inspection of the Academy, he comes to inspect us *all*." She turned, pouting with her hands balled on her hips. "Now, where on earth is that wretched dress he sent last spring?" she asked herself as her eyes roved over her room. Suddenly she gasped with realization and collapsed on all fours before crawling toward the bed.

Arms crossed and head tilted I observed her with curious amusement as she scurried across the floor like a tiny animal in undergarments. She pulled a large box out from under her bed and blew the dust off it before lifting the lid to reveal a dress that appeared more uniform than personal attire.

After several attempts to shake out the dust and the musty smell from disuse and a quick press from a harried staff member, she dressed and we headed down the Academy halls. Along with everyone else it seemed.

Cadets, teachers, and even staff all lined the main foyer to the Academy on both sides. All still, in silent anticipation. Meanwhile, a dull roar emitted from beyond the Academy doors. I looked out a passing window, beyond the Academy's great iron gates just as they were closing behind a black town car. A flood of people excitedly cheered around the stone walls and gate, waving small, red banners and flags, while others saluted. I watched the vehicle slowly roll up the drive to the entrance of the Academy and wondered where Articus was.

"Come with me, Miss Fox," a deep voice commanded, startling me from my window gazing.

Clouden took me by the elbow and led me down the main foyer and out the Academy doors before commanding me with his eyes to stop and stand beside him.

"I will introduce you, do not say a word unless directly addressed. Understood?"

I curtly nodded my head and glanced around to the others standing outside with us. All faces I did not recognize. Most appeared to be Clouden's age—perhaps they were other professors—and all were men, except Kareena, who stood at Clouden's other side, leaning forward to pass me a small, yet sympathetic, smile before turning her attention back to the approaching vehicle.

My gaze wandered from one face to another before landing on a young man with deep umber skin and thick black hair. His honey-colored eyes weren't focused ahead or beyond like the others, but instead were directed toward Kareena, Clouden, and I. We briefly made eye contact before he quickly looked away and straight ahead. He was the man Articus was sparring with the other evening. I couldn't clearly see the fine features of his face then, but I recognized his build. That broad, strong chest clad in a deep red uniform, slightly more decorated than the other cadets. Was he another young instructor like Articus? They looked similar in age which, if so, would make them both far younger than the other professors. Had he seen me watching them that night? Did he recognize me as well? Or was I merely caught in the crossfire of his gaze as he was looking toward someone or something else?

The sound of a car door closing snapped me to attention. The man I previously saw in the hotel lobby exited the car's dark interior, shortly followed by Articus. He was still dressed in his red military uniform from earlier, looking so foreign and distant, like a stranger. Such a far cry from his typical gray vest and white shirt I had grown accustomed to seeing him in. Similar to the general, several ribbons and metals hung from his jacket. He looked far too young to be decorated so thoroughly, but then again, so did the higher-ranking man before him. How young must they have been when they started their military careers?

The two gradually made their way down the aisle of bodies as every head bowed or saluted in greeting. Some muttering, "general" under their breath in acknowledgment. They paused in front of a man I recognized from earlier that week, during mass. He stood in formal black robes, a white band peeking out from his black collar.

"Father Gerard," the two men greeted as one by one they took the priest's hand

and touched their foreheads against it.

"I'm glad to see that the Holy Father has held you in his arms of protection and brought you safely to us once again," Father Gerard said as he smiled fondly at the men reverently bowing before him. His eyes crinkled at the edges as he looked upon Articus in particular. "May he continue to show favor and mercy over you and your family."

"Thank you, Father," they both chanted before rising and continuing their way down the aisle. Following suit with the others, I clasped my hands behind my back and averted my eyes to the ground. Two sets of impossibly shiny black boots appeared in my line of sight.

"Clouden," a confident voice addressed.

"General Desaius," Clouden greeted back and the two men clasped hands in a firm and formal gesture. Side by side it was easier to see the difference between the brothers. Gray peppered the temples of Clouden's chin length strands, while the general's shortcut was perfectly combed back and streaked with gold from the sun. Just as the sun most likely lightened his hair, it had also tanned his skin, causing Clouden to appear paler in comparison. But nothing stood out more than the general's eyes. They seemed to pierce right through everything and everyone they fell upon, making me feel as flimsy as paper as he took me in from head to toe.

"And who is this?" the general asked.

I took a small step forward and curtsied.

"This is Miss Alise Fox, my new ward and assistant," Clouden responded for me.

"Interesting that my lieutenant did not find it necessary to tell me of this before my visit," the general said, accusingly, apparently not liking to be left out of the loop. Articus's jaw ticked. Whether it be to the accusation or the way the general addressed him, I was unsure.

"I didn't find it of any consequence or concern to you, general." Reservation prevalent in Articus's tone.

As though he didn't even hear his words, the general turned his attention to Kareena. He clasped her chin delicately with his thumb and she beamed back up at him with all the devotion of a child.

"Daughter."

"Father." Kareena's soft voice was coated in adoration. I looked Articus up and down. How sadly interesting it was that the general called Kareena his daughter but did not call Articus his son.

I again failed to gain some sign of acknowledgment from him—eye contact, a small smile, anything. Instead, I was met with a cold wall of indifference as he ignored me completely and continued on his way through the Academy doors behind his father.

Within the Academy's grand foyer, a voice called attention and every cadet straightened into formation before saluting the general and Articus as they hastened down the marble floors. My eyes shot daggers in the back of Articus's bleeding red jacket.

"I'm not speaking a single word to you today, and if you know what's best for you, you'll do the same," I said as venomously as possible. I had all but raged the entire rest of the day at his disgusted attitude towards me and spent most of the night tossing and turning in a fit, punching pillows into submission and kicking the suddenly too-rough sheets off my legs every few minutes only to grow cold, yank them back up to my chin, and start the whole ritual over again. Eating dinner alone that night did not help either. While Kareena and Articus dined with Clouden and the general, I was left alone with my thoughts and nothing to distract me from them beyond sorting the vegetables from my stew into organized clusters on my plate.

Here I was to be at Articus's beck and call and yet he couldn't even acknowledge my presence. After all the time I had been forced to work with him. The nights training, the days studying, and giving my body over like some lab rat. Yet, I was somehow a dirty little secret that Articus kept from the general, until his hand was forced it seemed. Merely just a ward working in the kitchens and helping with some filing as far as anyone was concerned.

Articus responded with a mischievous grin at the corner of his mouth. Damn that appealing expression. He seemed to feed off my fuming frustration this morning.

"That's nineteen words so far." He leaned forward with hands stuffed into his trouser pockets—back in his civilian clothes, this morning. "What is the matter, Little Fox?" His stupid, playful smile only grew with my stubborn silence. "Finding it difficult to compose yourself around me?"

I would not get sucked back into one of his games today. Especially not the kind where we tried to get a reaction out of each other and see how far we could go before one, or the other, took the bait, or called for mercy. But my anger got the upper hand.

"I don't want to talk to you after the way you behaved towards me around . . . around . . . that man," I seethed, crossing my arms in an act of defiance. But he saw right through it. My mask was becoming thin around the edges. Hurt leaked through the cracks.

"What are you so upset about now? You're practically pouting like a child."

"You acted like you didn't even know me. Standing there next to him in that . . . that uniform with all those people bowing and saluting you two like some kind of gods," the words stumbled out of me—all the humiliating feelings of yesterday boiling over. "You didn't even acknowledge my presence at the hotel and it just served as a reminder that I don't even truly know you. And why did he call you 'his lieutenant?'"

"But you want to," he called out, ignoring my question and mirroring my crossed arms. "You thought you did and now you're confused and upset that you cannot fit me in a box."

"Maybe I would if you actually wanted to be known, but until then I'm not going to play games with a boy who just wants to toy with my head." I dared a challenging stare in his direction as I laid a raw truth and bitter pill between us. I didn't know him, not truly. Which side of this coin was his true face? Was he the general's son, the cold and commanded killer? Or was he the playfully mischievous and kind boy I only had brief glimpses of before?

An angry crease formed between his brows. "Did it ever occur to you that I had my reasons for creating distance between us in front of the general? That I have my own concerns about things you know absolutely nothing about?" I flinched at his words. His stern tone left me feeling like a child scorned. "And I am in no way a boy, Miss Fox. If you are determined to keep accusing me as such then I'll find myself needing to prove to you otherwise."

I huffed out a breath of disbelief and all but rolled my eyes at his threat.

Where was the stack of heavy tomes when you needed one to throw? I thought, looking over our vacant work desk in the archive.

Without second thought I coarsely retorted, "Please spare me from any primitive actions you men here take to assert your dominance upon women." Articus's face cringed with disgust, as if I had slapped him.

"That's not what I meant and I would never . . ." His eyes trailed off with his words and he bared his teeth, biting down on his words. A heavy weight dropped in my chest, it reminded me of disappointment. But that couldn't be right. I shook my head to clear my thoughts. What was wrong with me?

"Is that honestly how you see me?" Articus's brow relaxed but a muscle in his jaw ticked—a small sign of the rage he buried down. Feeling antagonistic, a small part of me wanted to unbury it. To let it pour out unleashed before images of a pipe dripping with blood came to mind.

"How do you want me to see you? All I know is what you show me," I countered.

"I would prefer to be seen for who I am, rather than your preconceived notions of me and men in general, it would seem."

Articus pointedly sat back down and returned to his work. His armor it seemed, as he pretended to be busy and indifferent. The air in our little alcove grew weighted with tense silence. I could not fault him in wanting to be viewed in such a way. Wasn't that how we all wished to be seen? To be truly seen. But how could we when we were always donning masks to protect ourselves? Always playing games and roles to satisfy others.

"Then show me," I said more to myself than him, barely brave enough to say it beyond a gentle whisper as I turned a page in the book before me, pretending to read its contents. Articus continued on with his work hastily and was most likely unable to hear my near silent request.

The deeper questions haunted me into the night. How would he show me he was a man? What did a real man, per se, even look like outside of physical appearances? And why did I not know the answer? Beyond the shadowed memories of the only father I had ever known, I had no example of a man's devotion. When Kareena spoke of her father it was with fear of criticism and a need for approval, yet reverence shown in her eyes when she gazed up at him, as though there was no one above him. But what did a romantic or even a relationship of mutual respect between a man and woman look like?

Was it the playful embraces from behind that my father would give my mother in the kitchen as she hummed and washed the dirt off carrots from the garden? Or was it something more passionate that burned like starlight behind closed doors where no one could see beyond the glow that remained on lover's cheeks? Perhaps it was whatever one wanted it to be. Whatever was decided, discovered, or settled for. Some settled for less, while others demanded more than they were told they deserved.

I still wasn't sure what I truly wanted and it seemed that was only the first of many problems.

Chapter Thirty

L EANING BACK ON THE soft, white blanket I let the late spring sun melt me into complacency, grateful for the break from my work with Articus and Clouden. After my fight with Articus, and after Clouden requested, yet another sample of my blood for testing, I was more than eager to leave the confines of the dim and cold underground lab for the warmth and vibrancy of the kitchens, where Kareena and I raided the food stores for fruits, jams, meats, and bread to add to our basket. Ms. Hazel all but swept us out the back down with her broom and called us thieving little mice while she simultaneously added a croissant and muffin to our stash.

I was surprised when Kareena led me past the woods that lined the back of the Academy only to emerge into a clearing that overlooked a large pond. Sweeping meadows with tiny flowers in every color signaled the first blooms of spring. The grass looked almost golden in the sun's rays and the light sparkled like diamonds off the pond's rippling surface.

"Our secret spot," Kareena had told me upon arriving and assured me no one would bother us here. I admit I felt honored to be brought to a place considered so sacred to Kareena and my heart warmed with more than just the sun's heat.

After briefly catching up on the latest Academy gossip and how Kareena's most recent shift went with the infamous Nurse Petit, we fell into a companionable silence. I popped a berry in my mouth and offered to refill Kareena's cup with more sparkling lemonade. The bubbles fizzed and popped as I poured her a second glass. The fizzing and growing warmth on our faces, courtesy of the champagne we discreetly mixed into our carafe when Ms. Hazel wasn't looking. Though she would be furious upon discovering the missing bottle, we decided it was well worth the risk of her wrath.

A soft rustling broke my sun and alcohol-induced trance. I peered over my shoulder to see Articus standing behind us. He wore only his gray trousers and white button up with the sleeves rolled up, exposing his strong forearms, cut off where his hands met the inside of his pockets, as usual. He looked at me with annoyance as though I were an unwelcome pest in his house.

"Oh, it's just you," I said flatly before turning back to the beautiful view.

"I'll leave." Articus turned on a heel, but was stopped by Kareena as she burst to her feet and hauled him closer, dragging him by the arm.

"Oh no you don't, Brother. I invited both of you to join me and it would be entirely rude for you to leave just as you have arrived." I scowled at Kareena's omission and she gave me an adorable pleading expression for forgiveness in return. "Now I know you two haven't been getting along lately and I've made it my life's mission to mend things." Kareena pulled Articus down on the blanket beside me, causing him to fall, ungracefully on his backside.

"Alise wishes not to speak any further with me today, dear Sister." Articus lifted the glass of bubbling lemonade and sniffed it briefly before gulping down its contents and pouring himself another glass.

"Nonsense, Alise is my friend and I cannot tolerate having my own brother at odds with her. Please, Articus, it means so much to me that you two get along. Can you not make some attempt to reconcile whatever is going on between you?" Lashes flickered at Kareena's use of Articus's name. It was something I had never heard her call him. Her usual choice being "Brother," was often used as a term of endearment or to taunt and tease instead of his actual name.

Articus sighed reluctantly before turning his attention to me. "The sun looks lovely upon you Miss Fox, and I fear I may perish if you wish to never speak with me again," he deadpanned and rose to his feet, a glass of fizzing lemonade hung casually from his hand as he made his way to the pond's edge.

"That wasn't so hard now, was it?" Kareena called to his back. "I'm sorry, Alise. He tends to get in one of his moods when Father comes around—all brooding and stormy. I wish I knew how to help him out of it." She stared off after Articus as he reached the pond's edge several paces away. Her caring concern for him pinched at my heart.

"You care so deeply for him," I assured, placing my hand over hers. "And I'm certain he does for you, too."

Kareena sighed, looking off towards Articus's silhouette. "He has given everything for me and my happiness. I fear I'd be in a far worse place in life without him always watching out for me. In so many ways he has put me first, above himself, even to his own detriment."

"How so?" Curiosity getting the best of me, I hoped I wasn't treading on sensitive ground. Kareena looked back over to Articus, making sure he was out of earshot before scooting closer to me and leaning in conspiratorially.

"Our beginning was not a happy one, me and Articus's. See when we were little, when I was just a babe, we lived in the same village with our real . . . I mean our birth parents." I swallowed a choking lump down to the pit of my stomach. "When it was destroyed in a border raid, Articus and I were the only ones who remained. He found me and took care of me the best a young boy could and I've been his ever since." A small smile pulled at the corner of her mouth.

"Thankfully, it wasn't long until General Desaius found us and took us in as his own children. Though I was too young to remember my family from before, Articus remembered everything. I know he misses his birth father deeply. He loved and admired him very much."

"Does he speak of him often?" I asked.

"No. In fact barely at all. But I've learned that with Articus, it is the things he loves the most that he finds the hardest to speak of. Perhaps if he did not cherish those precious to him so much, it would be easier for him to not cling so tightly." Kareena looked across the field towards Articus, his back turned to us as he threw back the last of the lemonade from his glass in one swallow and threw the cup into the water beyond.

"When Father officially adopted us, Articus was furious to have his last name changed from Carpenter to Desaius. See, it was all he had left of his birth father and his past. It nearly destroyed him as a young boy."

Dr. Aaron Carpenter.

The name rang in my ears like an alarm bell.

Articus Carpenter.

My chest seized as I tried not to audibly gasp. A small, painful crack broke inside me at the realization that in the First Realm, Articus brought a part of himself with him. A small piece he could no longer have here. A quiet rebellion. A paltry freedom.

"Because I was still a babe, Father wanted to change my name to something more English, but Articus made sure it was kept as is. I guess you could say it was his first gift to me." She looked back at me, eyes shining, but not with their usual joy.

My mind conjured images of a small boy with a baby girl in his arms. A determination in his eyes stronger than any other, to keep her alive and well. To give her whatever he could, even if it was just a name. Something she could keep forever. Something no one would be able to take from her. Kareena grew silent for a long moment and I searched my mind for something to say to break her from the unfamiliar melancholy. But nothing felt like it would be enough.

"I still do not know what deal he struck with Father in order to keep that small piece of myself. He refuses to tell me even to this day about his bargains with him." She sighed deeply. "The general has always been a kind and doting father to me." Kareena fiddled with the lace edge of her sleeve. "He's given me a life far better than any I could imagine, but it has always been different between him and

Articus." She looked up at me, her eyes glistened and I schooled my expression into neutrality, trying to be the strength she needed.

"When my father threatened to send me away, convinced I was becoming a distraction, that we were far too codependent with each other, Articus gave up everything to keep me with him. I remember crying my eyes out when my governess practically dragged me into our car to be sent to boarding school, only to have my father change his mind before we could even leave the grounds and tell me I had my brother to thank for the change in plans."

The small crack in my chest grew at the act of such devotion. What did Articus exchange for Kareena's return? For her freedom from a certainly oppressive future that was not of her choosing.

"It was his words that were able to convince Father that it would be beneficial to the Desaius name if I were to become a doctor, something I have always dreamed of, rather than an Elite's wife. I don't know how he accomplished it, but I am forever grateful and because of it, his happiness means everything to me. I fear whatever deal he made may have been far too sacrificing on his part. Nothing could ever be enough to repay his acts of selflessness, being successful is the least I can do though." I smiled softly back at Kareena's own sad smile.

"It sounds like he loves you very much." I clutched her hand tighter in reassurance. "And I can tell you love him just as greatly." Kareena's free hand swiped a lone tear away before it could fall down her cheek.

"I know. It's just . . ." She hesitated and glanced back towards the pond's edge. "I pray he can find his own happiness someday. That he can find someone who will love him in the ways I cannot and that he'll find someone else worth living for. I want him to have a life of his own . . . so he can finally let me go." The last words trailed off her tongue slowly with a hint of misplaced guilt for her confession.

What she didn't say—what she wouldn't say—rang clear. She wanted to be free. A yearning I was all too familiar with myself. And though Articus had given her the opportunity to do just that, he still held on to her with his loneliness, with his need to protect. With his love. Did he truly not have any romantic relationships? What I saw the other day had me thinking otherwise, but perhaps there wasn't anyone he was serious about in his life yet and that's what kept

Kareena from moving on with her own as well.

"I'm certain he'll find someone, someday." I squeezed her hand again and smiled at her before a dark shadow descended over us.

"I sense the mood has gotten far too serious for such a beautiful day." Articus scooped up Kareena like a child and turned back towards the pond, a kicking and pleading Kareena in tow.

"Don't you dare, Brother!" She squealed as she pounded on his chest.

"Oh, but I shall, sweet Sister," was all he said before tossing her into the water.

Kareena screamed with an air of excitement more than fear as she landed in the pond, fully dressed. Just as quickly she emerged, completely soaked through, a scowl visible through red tendrils of wet hair. I covered my mouth to stifle a laugh and caught Articus's determined stare upon me.

"Oh no. No. No. No," I begged, backing away from him and the pond's shore. He advanced on me quicker than I could blink and snatched me around the waist, hauling me off my feet. My back pressed against his broad chest for the briefest moment before he tossed me like rubbish into the pond's sparkling surface.

Kareena's uncontrollable laughter greeted me at the water's surface as I shot up from its shallow depths.

"How dare you laugh," I teased and splashed her in the face.

"You laughed too! Don't think I didn't see your shoulders shaking." She splashed back.

Suddenly the sound of thunder and an even larger splash washed over our heads. We both turned towards the source just in time to see a shirtless chest and golden hair pop-up with a shit-eating grin.

"Brother!"

"Articus!"

We screeched simultaneously.

"I couldn't let you ladies have all the fun," Articus said before playfully splashing us again.

Kareena and I looked at each other with the same scheme in mind, before languidly stalking in Articus's direction.

"Now, now let's behave like civilized beings." Articus raised his hands in surrender. "There's no need to drown an apology out from—"

His words were cut off as Kareena and I each pushed down on his shoulders, submerging him below the water's surface.

He popped back up and silenced our giggles with a retaliation of his own, tossing us over his shoulder and throwing us—squealing—back into the water one by one. For several minutes we continued, back and forth, in our watery battle of two against one. Though the odds technically weren't fair, they felt more than even when you considered our two, much smaller frames, in comparison to Articus's own muscular build. His bare chest gleamed in the sunlight as we splashed and played like children.

How no one heard our shouts from the other side of the woods I'll never know, but in that moment under the sun, in the water's cool embrace, with nothing but smiles and laughter surrounding us, for once, I knew what I wanted. I wanted this. I wanted to be in that moment forever and to never have to leave the safety and freedom of the three of us unleashed and carefree in our secret, hidden paradise.

Chapter Thirty One

E XHAUSTION TOOK ME QUICKLY that night, but my dreams were unforgiving, and sleep didn't last long. I awoke with a shock. Phantom flames burned my skin and sweat coated my back and forehead. My hands shook as I turned the shower dial on and attempted to ease the tension from my muscles with scorching hot water. But even after several long minutes under the water's forceful stream, I still felt as though I was wound too tightly.

Sickening knots corded my stomach while quick breaths, and racing thoughts caused me to pace around my bedroom, wet strands dripping a trail on the rug. Though I couldn't recall the details of the nightmare, the feel of it wouldn't let me go. I busied my hands by sketching, but they trembled too violently to create lines on paper. Within moments my fingers grew rigid, unable to properly hold the pencil at all. No longer could I ignore the signs of the impending attack.

Locking the door to my room I returned to bed, curling into a tight ball. I pulled a blanket fully over my head as I took in large gulps of air. Tears streamed down my face as anxious thoughts overtook me. Thoughts of being trapped, alone, and unloved, a reel on repeat in my caged mind. Losing complete control of my body and thoughts, I shivered into a fitful abyss.

Unaware of how much time passed, I opened my eyes to darkness. It was not restful sleep I stirred from but some comatose hell where my body lay paralyzed, while terror ran wild. Where the old, familiar nightmares and horrid memories—ones I wished would die—resurfaced. My cheeks were wet from tears and sweat and the bedding damp. A soft knock rasped on my bedroom door as a deep calm voice called my name.

"Alise."

Moments passed as I continued to lay there, searching for the will to move or speak.

"Alise, please open up. The door is locked."

The unrelenting voice in my head translated a thousand alternate meanings from the single line.

Please open up . . . to me.

The door is locked.

You are closed off.

Don't shut me out.

I slowly rose from beneath the dark safety of the heavy blanket, my head immediately throbbing as I pressed my fingers to my temples with a groan.

"If you don't open the door, I'll have no choice but to kick it in and risk upsetting Kareena with the damage."

"One second." The sound of my voice made my headache all over again, despite the soft tone.

"However, I do find it amusing when my sister is cross with me, so perhaps I'll kick it in all the same," he continued, either ignoring or not hearing my reply.

"I'm coming, okay? I'm coming," I shouted as I shuffled as quickly as I could to the door, despite the sharp ache that laced through my skull to do so. Hands fumbled at the lock before releasing on a curse. The door opened to a rather disappointed looking Articus.

"Shame. I was really looking forward to kicking the door down." A smirk grew at the corner of his lips as his eyes took me in. I had forgotten I was still in the robe I put on after taking a shower that night, and the garment was surely disheveled from my fitful rest.

Articus reached up and, with gentle fingers, brushed a lock of pale blonde hair, damp and plastered to my face, away and behind my ear. His hand took its time trailing down its length before drawing its ends between his finger and thumb.

"Too much sparkling lemonade?" he asked, softly. His gaze no longer on mine but on the strand, he let slip from his grasp. Suddenly feeling self-conscious, I gripped the edges of my robe together.

"What do you want, Articus?"

"It's nearly noon, Little Fox. You slept through our morning session." His gaze returned to meet mine.

"To answer your question, no I am not hungover and secondly, you are not my master. I don't owe you or anyone else an explanation for why I slept in." Though the words were true they tasted bitter as they spilled from my tongue. Cutting, as they were much sharper than I intended.

"That would be correct, however . . ." Articus agreed as he stepped into the room and closed the door behind him, the unwelcomed entrance angering me even more. "I was merely concerned and thought to check in on you." The sincerity of his actions threatened to soften my heart but a wave of aching pain batted it back.

"Thanks, but as you can see, I'm fine so if you don't mind you can politely fuck off now," I threw back at him, dropping all pretense of lady-like language.

"Lovely," he muttered under his breath as he shoved his hands in his pockets.

"Also, in case you forgot, I can take care of myself and I sure as hell don't need you pounding on my door with your so-called concern." I stomped off to the bathroom and slammed the door shut.

Turning on the faucet, I hoped Articus would assume I was getting ready and leave. But, before I could even exhale, he came storming into the bathroom uninvited.

"Don't do this, Alise."

"What the hell are you doing? I could have been changing!" My voice grew shrill as I wrapped my arms around myself defensively.

"You didn't bring in a change of clothes," he deadpanned.

"I'll ask you again. What. Do. You. Want?"

"I want you to stop this. Stop pushing me away and tell me what is truly bothering you." His face looked tense. A fine line formed where his full lips would be. Yet, he remained calm and still—his hands clenched into fists in his pockets.

"You ask me what I want, but do you even know what you want, Alise?"

That was the wrong thing to say.

"I do! I want you to stop treating me like a dog that's expected to come at your beck and call. You and Clouden don't own me." Raged bloomed in my chest and inflated my words into something a bit more than the truth and though I knew it, I couldn't stop.

"Your participation was part of our agreement to harbor you here. You agreed to it and I, in no way have, nor have I ever, dreamed of treating you like a dog."

"Harbor? Agreed? You dragged me here against my will!" Voice raising to a shout, I prayed Kareena was on her shift in the infirmary.

"If memory serves me right, you practically leapt into my arms and into the portal with me. Or are you so quick to forget?" Articus fixed me with a dissecting glare, making me feel transparent as glass. Making me hate him even more for it.

"You left a literal bloody mess for me to take the blame for if I stayed. I had no choice but to go with you."

"Correct again." I was taken aback. Was he actually agreeing with me? "There was, and is nothing left for you back there in the First Realm. Only pain and suffering. And yes, though it was I who killed Brenton, if given the choice between you or him, I would do it again. I have no regret or apology for that, Alise. If it means protecting you, I'll kill him a million times over!" I could hear him losing the tight hold of his control.

"You need to face the reality of your situation if you are to ever take control of it. This, here, is where you find yourself and all you can do now is take the hand you have been dealt and work it in your favor like the rest of us must. You're not the first person to get a bad cut out of life and you certainly will not be the last. And until you change your perspective nothing is going to improve." A clenched fist rose and opened before shaking fingers combed through his hair. He tugged a fist full of sandy strands before his chest rose and fell with a deep exhale and rubbed the back of his neck.

"I'm just trying to say, you are not alone in your suffering." He almost looked defeated, standing there before me, but it was too late. I couldn't stop the waves of rage that crashed against me and the poisonous words that spewed from the foam of their crest just for him.

"I hope you're not insinuating that your life is *anything* like mine, because yours is practically dripping in privilege and opportunity. Look at your status here at the Academy—the amount of respect you receive from your peers and men twice your age." I knew it wasn't wholly true, and that he had sacrificed for Kareena, and probably others as well, but it was too late to take it back. My words grew legs and wills of their own as they leapt from my mouth, eager to inflict damage. I knew Articus felt the sting of their cut as he threw me a glare just as hurtful. He stalked like a wolf, before it struck its prey, and cornered me against the wall. Both arms planted on each side of my head.

"You know nothing about my life or the events that have led me to where I am now. No idea of what I must do for the sake of others, and to assume so is entirely disrespectful." But I had known. And that made what I said to him all the worse. Shame glistened in my eyes and formed a painful lump in my throat. I had done to him something I hated when done to me, and all I could do was continue to hide behind a wall of anger.

"You're right. I don't know if what little you have told me is even the truth. I don't know you—this you—at all and I don't want to." I spat, hoping the blow would meet its mark and he would give up on me for good. But my chest clinched at the thought of him being cold and distant from me again. At him no longer trying or caring.

"Go on then," he said as he eased from the wall and stood coolly before me. "Keep bringing the blows, Alise. I can take it. If it helps you get through this storm raging inside of you, here I am." His hands splayed as if to present himself for the sacrifice.

Tears threatened to escape my blurry vision.

"I can't stand you! I hate everything about you!" And though it was said with a tone of fury it came from a place of hurt. For I did not know myself, where I was from, or where I belonged and that was the most painful truth of all. I forcefully shoved him, and made my way to the door, desperate to run, lest he see the tears threatening to escape. To hide the way he affected me. The way he so easily peeled off my armor and exposed the raw vulnerable flesh beneath.

Before I could make it through the doorway, a strong, warm grip wrapped around my waist and tugged me against a solid hard chest. His heart pounded just as quickly as mine as his breath tickled my shoulder.

"Careful, Little Fox, hate and obsession grow from the same root as passion. It only takes one word, one shift in the light to change a perspective of hate to one of achingly wretched love," he spoke the words like a confession in my ear. As though he were all too familiar with the feeling. I slowly turned around to face him. To see if any truth of this could be seen in his eyes.

"It is not hate, but indifference that is the killer of passion." He gently swept a strand of hair behind my ear and grazed his fingers down my jaw towards my lips, before thinking better of it and pulling away.

"I would gladly drown in the ocean of your hate than stand securely on the shore of your indifference." His conviction was sure but lined with pain. It was present in the way his eyes fixed upon me as though he were pleading forgiveness. From me? It wrecked me to see how I was, and had been treating him. Ached to know he would turn himself over to my hurtful words for my own sake and that he found me worthy of the infliction.

Overwhelmed, I stepped back intending to leave the bathroom again, but his gentle hand clasped my wrist, and pulled my closed fist to his chest. His eyes bore into me. Emotions swirled in them in a combination I couldn't decipher.

"What do you need? To hit me? To tear me apart until you lose your voice? Whatever you need, Alise, I will endure for your sake." His tone grew softer with each word. His hand slid idly up and down my spine in calming strokes.

"Cut me down. Destroy me if you must. If it brings you peace, then I'll gladly take it."

The crack in my chest threatened to shatter. The tight grip of rage finally shook loose, making room for so much more to seep out. Tears I had been so adamantly holding back burned my cheeks as they fell.

Articus had become my whipping boy. A scapegoat for every horrid thing that happened thus far. And the shame of the marks I left on him was all too overwhelming. I needed to take responsibility for my life. Though the course of events had spiraled out of control, I could no longer blame others for it. Especially if it meant further harming him.

"I don't want to do this anymore," I whispered, voice cracking under the weight of my guilt. "I want things back to how they were. When you were just Aaron and I was just Alise. I'm exhausted with trying to grasp everything and everyone as they slip from my fingers. I can't keep control of any part of my life or even my sanity and I just can't . . . I need . . ." Articus gently cupped my jaw. His thumb stroked away a trailing tear.

"It will be alright. You are safe, and you are not alone." I clutched him tightly as I wept into his chest. He held me just as tightly back. Several long moments crawled by like that. Running water, the only white noise accompanying my muffled sobs, as I let them wash over me, letting the tension leak out with every tear and every stroke of Articus's hand up and down my back.

"Look at me." Articus clasped my chin with his finger and thumb. My gaze reluctantly lifted up to his pine green eyes and though he was merely asking me to bare my face to him, it felt as if he requested to see my very soul. Worrying my lip, I tried my hardest not to let my gaze stray from his, which appeared lit from within. It appeared brighter in that moment than I had ever seen before. Certainty and light radiated comfort to my aching heart.

"You don't need to run from me anymore."

I exhaled a shaky breath as though his words had released whatever last bit of tension remained.

"Tell me, are the nightmares back?"

All I could do was slowly nod, for they had never left to begin with.

"You don't have to talk about it now if you don't want to, but if you find you cannot sleep, or you just need to escape, you can use my office whenever you like. It's quiet and safe there. I promise."

I merely nodded my head as a weak, "*Thank you*" fell from my lips.

Articus's gaze lowered to my mouth. "That's adorable."

"What is?" I asked, suddenly feeling very self-conscious, again.

"The way you bite your lip."

Realizing I was doing just that I stopped abruptly.

"You seem to do it when you are worried or focused, or sometimes confused." His thumb swiped delicately over said lip as he spoke. His soft strokes sweeping away the throb my teeth had caused as his expression relaxed as though he felt just as soothed and entranced by the act as I was. "But other times, when you think I don't notice, you unconsciously bite it to stifle the longing I suspect is hidden behind your stolen glances."

A warmth flowed over me, caused by more than just embarrassment. I recalled the times when he had touched me in just this way, the sounds of rain hitting the rear window of a station wagon while relaxed eyes looked down on me, echoed in my mind. The warming sensation grew to sweltering as those thoughts trailed to a quiet nook in the library. To Articus's mouth on mine, his lips and tongue following along to a dance that I led. That feeling of having control, of me directing the push and pull of our kisses left me wanting for more. If I leaned in ever so slightly, would he let me take hold of that power over him again? Would he let me have another small taste?

I became hyper-aware of the silky touch of my robe as it moved along my breasts with each breath. Articus's scorching touch melted through the thin material with each stroke up and down my spine.

Before I could find the courage to reach up on tiptoes to meet his mouth with mine, he leaned in for me as his hand slid behind my neck and tipped my jaw up ever so slightly. His warm breath danced on my lips. I thought I felt the words, "*Forgive me*," dance across them before his lips brushed mine. The feather light sensation stole the air from my lungs and though the first caress was so fragile it could shatter, the next was anything but. With one firm press, both his body and lips molded against mine, as my back pressed against the door. A fist clenched the silken material of my robe at the small of my back and his thumb drew down on my jaw, beckoning me to open for him. The velvet touch of his tongue on mine sent a liquid hot sensation through my bones and trailed down every limb in my body to my very toes. I grabbed his collar as a shuttered breath escaped my lips between kisses and the silken robe slid off my shoulder, exposing a small offering of flesh.

Like an animal hungry for a taste, Articus's mouth made its way down. His lips grazed and teeth nipped at my jaw. Rewarding him with a soft moan I arched my back and pressed my chest against him as my fingers found their way up the strong column of his neck and into the silky strands of hair. The angle gave him better access, as his mouth continued to feast down my neck. A combination of soft presses and languid, bone melting sweeps of tongue between teeth dance upon my scorched skin. The strands of his hair tickled the tips of my fingers as I combed and clasped them in a demanding request for more. When his teasing mouth reached the crest of my bare shoulder, he bit down. The pressure skirted just on the edge of where pleasure met pain, and that hot and cold rush of liquid stiffened my spine while simultaneously melting my bones into a puddle of pure, undiluted desire.

My toes wiggled in the small pools and to my surprise I heard a rippling sound in response. I gasped and looked down, breaking the connection between me and Articus in the process. A puddle of water was starting to grow beneath our feet as liquid spilled from the edges of the sink from the faucet I had left on and apparently forgotten all about.

Articus released me, abruptly, as though someone dowsed him in icy water before cutting the water flow off with the turn of a knob. I smiled like a fool behind my hand at the ridiculousness of it all. Articus's shoes squished with the sound of water as they were clearly soaked through. My robe disheveled and parted open, exposing a strip of pale flesh down the middle of my abdomen closing to a point just above my hips. Making evident the fact that one second, we had been at each other's throats and the next, down them in an entirely different way.

Chaos so messy and raw that I could only laugh at the state of us. However, Articus's amused smile vanished as he took me in from head to toe. His eyes swiftly met back with mine and I found a look similar to dread etched in his stare. His fingers gently secured my robe to cover me properly before leaving the bathroom without a word and I was left there, with only confusion and desire for company, in the wake of his warmth. Feeling discarded and cold once again I wrapped myself in my arms and sighed.

Chapter Thirty Two

I ENTERED THE SHARED living space a few moments later, dressed in one of my more comfortable dresses that didn't require help getting into. Articus's back greeted me. In his hand was a small piece of parchment and beside him on the entry table, a box decorated beautifully in red paper with gold foiling and a matching ribbon.

Noticing he was no longer alone, Articus turned to face me before thrusting the note into my direction.

"It's for you," his words were curt. "At least I pray so or I'll be personally overseeing a cadet's exceptionally merciless punishment."

I side-eyed him as I looked down to see what he was talking about. The note briefly read:

I am on my knees, begging you to do me the absolute kindness of saving me a dance at the upcoming Academy Graduation Ball.
Only yours,
Dante

Upon opening the box, I had to hold back a squeal, at the risk of looking like a giddy little girl. An assortment of sweets and chocolates of a mouthwatering variety, sat in tiny tissue paper cups, lining the box's interior. The label inside indicated it was from the same confectionary Kareena and I had visited on our trip into the city, not long ago.

"How original," Articus's cynical words threatened to dampen my glee.

"I know you are not entirely fond of him, but he is kind to me," I said, accusingly.

Articus responded with a disappointed look from the corner of his eyes.

"Kind. Is that all you require?"

I stared back, my eyes bored into his.

"Go on then. Say what you really think of him." He crossed his arms over his chest and scratched his chin in a show of pondering.

"Let me think. Dante Da Romano . . ." He began to circle slowly around one of the suites many Parisian rugs. "Decent marksman, possibly great if he focused more on the skill rather than becoming so easily distracted by wine and women." He paused for emphasis, staring down at me. I huffed and crossed my own arms before frowning back at him.

"Unquestioningly follows orders. A desired trait in any soldier. Not so much in a man of free thought, though. But the one fault I cannot see past is that he's an Elite brat who's never earned a thing for himself and has never been denied a whim. The way he uses those around him is disgusting at best and he feels no remorse for his behavior towards others."

My frown grew. "That's a little harsh—judging him by his upbringing and his family. I think you of all people . . ." My words trailed off and died on my tongue as Articus strode slowly towards me with one of his daring stares. Realizing we had already had this conversation and danced to this tune about assumptions, I decided to shut down the train of thought.

"And what do you know of the beloved Mr. Da Romano?" he asked.

"I'll admit not much beyond what I have been told by others but I like the way he treats me."

"The way he treats you?"

"Yes." My voice cracked under his scrutiny.

"He took me out to tea when no one would so much as glance my way and . . . other things." Things I didn't want to elaborate on to Articus. Like how he made my stomach flutter with butterflies. How when he focused on me, I felt as though I had the sole attention of a prince, and the rest of his kingdom meant nothing more to him than I did.

"I see," was all Articus said after a tense pause. Seeming to have heard enough, he made his way to the door, pausing with the knob in his hand. "Take the rest of the day to rest. We can continue our work tomorrow. Enjoy your chocolates," he added quickly, and with a tone a bit too formal for my liking, before closing the door behind him leaving me with even more confusion as a tangle of thorny vines crawled around inside me.

If I didn't know any better, if I hadn't seen him with that other girl in a secret, and scandalous way, I would have thought him jealous. Or perhaps he was just concerned for me like a friend would be. If it were Kareena receiving gifts and attention from Dante or any one of the cadets, I'm sure he would behave the same if not be in a complete rage. Maybe now I fell into a category of someone he cared for, platonically. It was just my wellbeing he was concerned for. And if he did not see Dante lacking then he would not have had such a reaction to the gifts and the note that came.

But that kiss. If I wasn't being completely delusional, it was him who initiated it. Him who sunk his teeth into me like a man starved for what was before him. Then again, those words I thought I heard before he pressed his lips to mine: "Forgive me." Why would that apology be on his lips if he didn't feel some kind of regret for what he was about to do?

We entered some strange new truce, it seemed. We were beyond aiming for each other's throats at every opportunity, and I knew deep down I did not hold the blame and hatred I once did toward him any longer. Even if it would make my own guilt and self-blame less if I did. But what was between us was hard to define. We had kissed more than once at this point and I couldn't say I loathed or regretted it. And nothing about either time felt platonic. Not in the way he touched and bit at my flesh. It felt hungry and passionate, as though he were just as starved as I was. But wasn't that regret I saw on his face, before he covered me back up and left?

Perhaps it all originated from a place of him being a man alone with a mostly undressed woman in his arms. The act of comfort going just a little too far. I remembered how he laughed after I kissed him in the library. How he shattered what little power and happiness I found at directing his mouth with mine. To him it was all an amusing game. It didn't mean he was necessarily attracted to me or wanted anything more than cooperation or possibly friendship from me. And his less than favorable thoughts about Dante didn't at all reflect how he felt about me. His animosity towards him could have stemmed from a long-standing rivalry.

Whatever this was, it was something other. Something ill-defined and complicated. Which was only fitting considering the way things had been going so far and until I was given reason to believe differently, that's all Articus and I were ever going to be.

Blurry.

Complicated.

Other.

The scent of yeast and browning sugar enveloped me in a trance as I kneaded dough in the warm, lit, kitchen. Every press of my knuckles and fingers messaged away a worry, a thought, until there were none left. All that remained was the task at hand. Though I desperately needed the break yesterday to recenter myself and rest, I found I quite enjoyed working in the kitchen in the early dawn hours before the sun and staff came pouring in from every crevice. The sun had been leaking through the kitchen's only window above the large tub like sink for a few minutes now and so did the staff as they collected dishes and pitchers of juices and water to be brought to the commons for the soldiers and professors.

"You seem to be quite the buzz amongst the staff this morning, girl." Ms. Hazel's words broke me out of my blissful trance.

"Oh, is that so?" I asked, innocently.

"Don't play coy with me, girl. I've heard of the gifts he's been sending to your suite, as well as the outing to tea at The Three Birds with Da Romano."

The shameless gossip.

"Now, if you ask me . . ."

I hadn't.

"That young Dante Da Romano is quite the catch, especially for a girl in your position." It did not get past me what she meant by her choice of words. She meant an orphan with no Elite background or wealth of any kind. And though I was technically an imposture in this realm, her words rang true.

"If you play your cards right, child, you could be expecting a proposal before the start of summer. That is if he can pass you off as worthy to those pretentious Elitist par—"

A loud crash, followed by the shattering of a dish cut off Ms. Hazel's rant. A familiar looking girl with dark hair and doe-like eyes stood with trembling hands in the doorway. The dish that I assume was previously in said hands, lay broken, in a million unsalvageable pieces at her feet as her plump lips gaped open.

"Sabrina! Be mindful. Quickly. Quickly. Fetch the broom and clean up this mess before someone cuts themselves."

As if coming out of a nightmare, the girl snapped to action and quickly started on righting the mess. I felt a little sorry for her having incurred Ms. Hazel's wrath and tried to redirect the furious woman's attention.

"Ms. Hazel, what is the Graduation Ball like?"

"Dear child, it is only the most anticipated event at the Academy. It's held every year before the official graduation ceremony, to honor the cadets who will be leaving to start their military careers. Though it means more work and preparation than I care to have, it is one of the few pleasures the boys get to enjoy here, so we do our best to make it a memorable experience for them."

"It is also the social event of the year," a sweet, lilting voice chimed in from the doorway. Kareena waltzed into the kitchen with all her usual carefree grace before plucking a still-warm, chocolate croissant off its tray. Ms. Hazel, too slow to successfully swat her hand away.

"And it is the only time the cadets are permitted to invite a civilian to the Academy. Receiving an invitation is a coveted privilege. One that invokes bragging rights from girls all across the Colony." Kareena popped a piece of the stolen pastry into her mouth, an audible moan radiated from her.

"These chocolate croissants are divine. Are you certain you are not a sorceress, Ms. Hazel," she teased, causing the older woman to chase us out of the kitchen with a dish towel, like thieving children.

Chapter Thirty Three

W E EXITED THE STAFF quarters and fell into step in the main hallway. Our heeled boots echoed in tandem on the black and white checkered marble floors, while my arm looped casually in Kareena's.

"I heard Dante Da Romano invited you to join him at the Graduation Ball," she stated matter-of-factly.

"I wouldn't say that, he merely asked me to save him a dance."

"Either way, as the ward of Professor Clouden you have every right to be there."

"Will you be attending?"

"Of course! I go every year. It's the one thing I get to hold over the head of those Elitist snobs in the tea rooms. Though I may technically be a lowly, adopted village girl, and not technically from the Desaius bloodline, I have every right to enjoy all the privileges that come with it, and attending the Academy's annual ball is something many of them could only wish for." Kareena held her nose in the air and I knew it wasn't an act of snobbery but one of the small slivers of dignity she refused to let anyone steal from her.

"I noticed you and Articus are not too fond of the ones you call 'Elites?'" I asked cautiously, letting my curiosity get the better of me.

She only hummed in response.

"Why is that, and why are they called 'Elites?'"

"Elites are those who come from wealthy and high-ranking families. They look down on anyone who is not one of them."

"But you two are the general's children and from the way I've seen people act around him I can only assume he is very highly regarded." Highly regarded was an understatement. People all but threw themselves at his feet and sniveled in his presence.

"Yes, but some enjoy letting us never forget that we are, in fact, adopted, regardless of the fact that we are our father's only children. We have had to prove ourselves at every turn in order to keep our pride in tack. Articus even more so than myself."

"You need not prove yourself to anyone. Especially not some stuck-up rich kids," I retaliated, accidently letting my diction slip. Kareena gave me a puzzled look before giggling uncontrollably with a hand pressed to her stomach.

"I absolutely adore your honesty, Alise." I felt her tug me just a little closer as we stepped into the sunlight that shined down on the training field.

"Has Dante ever treated you poorly? Looked down on you or made you feel lesser in any way," I asked, afraid of her answer.

"Oh no, not at all!" she exclaimed and clutched my hand in hers.

"He's always been a perfect gentleman and I hold nothing against him."

"So, it is safe to assume then that not all are bad?" I questioned more than stated.

"Men or Elites?" Kareena teased, stirring a breathy laugh in my chest. "Men are all bad, Alise. Unruly little savages they are, and we must discipline them at every turn less they run wild and rule us all."

I broke out into uncontrollable laughter right alongside her until we clutched our stomachs and gasped for air like school girls.

I was a little disappointed when I read the contents of a note that waited for me in the alcove of the library where Articus and I usually met for our morning sessions. Though he did not sign his name I knew it was from him for it merely stated:

No session today.

Short. To the point. And with no explanation of why. Yes, it was definitely written by Articus Desaius. After not seeing him at all after our talk yesterday, I had to admit I was a little intimidated by the idea of having to find ways to occupy my time once again.

Deciding to roam the aisles, I searched for something interesting to read. Perhaps, a topic of interest to study on my own. The soft murmurs of cadets coming and going, and the rustling of pages was all the company I needed as my eyes trailed over one spine after another.

History of the Rise of the Colony

A Collection of Modern Weapons and Their Progression

Theological Political Structures

Riveting literature indeed.

The ground quaked under my feet, causing me to shuffle slightly. Vibrations reverberated through the soles of my feet to the tips of my fingers. I quickly looked around to the others occupying the archives to see if anyone else felt what I just had.

Several cadets rose from their seats and looked around in confusion. Some whispered to the ones beside them asking if they felt that too and what it possibly could have been. But before they could finish speculating, a loud booming of thunder rattled the library so fiercely, those who rose to their feet including myself stumbled in place. Forced to brace ourselves with whatever was close by, books fell from their shelves and dust sprinkled down from the ceilings.

From one of the many alcoves a voice shouted to anyone who could hear, "It's a raid!"

Several cadets rushed to the windows in a flood of bodies to get a better look, while others stood planted in place, a look of utter terror on their faces. I nudged a cadet by the shoulder, hoping to get a closer look through one of the lead-glass windows. My eyes were met with a scene I couldn't conjure from my wildest imagination.

Airships clogged the sky in a fleet so heavy they blocked out the sun. Silver metal clouds, shaped similar to submarines, with plumes of smoke trailing in their wake, broke from formation. Instead of rain, rogue storm clouds dropped bombs of thunder and lightning upon the Parisian skyline. Each one shook the ground and pulverized entire blocks of buildings in the city beyond. A red dawn of destruction glowed from the carnage.

Every explosion was deafening, forcing me to clamp hands over my ears as my breath quickened. Those same handful of airships changed course and directed their aim towards the Academy grounds. Some onlookers cursed in awe, others in anger as they broke away from the sight and fled the library all together.

Meanwhile, I stood trembling like a scared doe who heard the shots of gun fire. My head clouded with fear.

Is Kareena okay? What about Articus? Should I make my way to the infirmary or find a place to hide?

My chest clenched with every quickened breath, making it harder and harder to get the air I desperately needed. Hands shook to the point of uselessness as I wiped my sweaty palms across my skirt.

I bolted from the window and the scene of impending doom just as another ear-splitting crack of an explosive tore through my skull. I stumbled to my hands and knees, but before I could rise, another shock wave pummeled me back to my knees. The walls of the library were lit with a red glow that poured in from its few windows.

They were getting closer.

Each merciless explosion made it harder to think. To see. To move. A succession of what sounded like cannon fire echoed relentlessly. So groundbreakingly loud, I thought my ears would surely bleed.

Firm hands lifted me from under my shoulders to my feet. I flinched under their touch like a terrified animal and turned to see Clouden, hair and clothes disheveled, and coated in a thin layer of dust. His eyes were wide and his lips moved, forming my name, but I couldn't hear it past the ringing in my ears.

"Alise! Alise! Can you hear me?" He shook me violently. His voice was finally able to break through my shock.

"Kareena! I have to—" I shouted not knowing if my voice was even carrying over the chaos around us as more books and even whole rows of shelves fell to the ground with each explosion.

"I'll make sure she's okay. You need to get somewhere safe and hide." Only one place came to mind. Only one place truly felt safe. The only place I wanted to be at that moment.

"Run, Alise! Go!" My feet obeyed instantly. Run. I could run. Running is what I did best.

Run, Little Fox, echoed in the chambers of my mind with each pounding step. It was Articus's voice that carried my feet. His voice alone pushed me forward. It was a chanting prayer my feet fell into rhythm with.

I hurtled over fallen book shelves with an ease I didn't comprehend despite my steps faltering with each tremble of the earth around me. Every deafening blow sent a sharp pain through my skull as that unnatural thunder filled the air, making it thick with dust and debris. Another immediately radiated through the library, shattering a nearby window. I instinctively ducked and covered my head as shards of glass blasted inwards from its frame.

How close were the ships now? Would they reach the Academy and reduce it to nothing but rubble along with everyone inside?

A falling shelf caught the corner of my eye and I barely dodged it in time, the edge nearly skimming my leg at the last possible moment. Another bystander, however, was not so quick to react. I heard his loud grunt as the shelf hit him in the head before taking him down to the ground with it.

I rushed to him and shook his shoulders in an attempt to stir him. Dust and splinters of wood littered his uniform and hair. Standing out against his dark strands, painting the most likely black locks, a muted gray. As strong as my instinct to run was, I knew I couldn't live with myself if I left him.

"You have to get up!" I yelled over the sound of crashing shelves and the rumble of aftershock as I continued to shake him.

His eyes fluttered open with a moan and I tugged him by his arm. Coming to, he finally realized what I was attempting and pushed himself up on his hands and knees. Just enough to slip out from under the case that pinned him as I tugged him by the sleeve. I slid my arm below his and shouldered what amount of weight I could, almost falling over myself. Blood poured down the side of his face, as fresh sap would from a tree, and dripped onto his shoulder before disappearing into the crimson of his uniform.

"We have to get you to the infirmary!" I shouted not even knowing if he could hear me, or if his ears were ringing as loudly as my own. My voice sounded muffled even to myself, as though we were under water. He merely grunted and let me shuffle alongside him as I shouldered half his weight against my side.

We navigated the maze of the Academy like lost children as others ran by us, all headed in multiple directions. Some had terrible wounds while others seemed unscathed with a look of determined purpose on their faces as they headed off to where they could be useful.

"It must be a rebel attack," I heard one cadet say as he ran by.

"I heard it was our own ships dropping the bombs!" another exclaimed.

"Don't be an idiot," his comrade chided.

"No. He's right," the third of the group said as he caught up to the others. "I saw it myself."

The infirmary was an uproar of utter chaos. Nurses rushed from one patient to the next as more flooded in. Some had minor wounds, while others had gashes so deep they exposed bone. One's leg bent in an unnatural direction as he moaned on a cot. Groans of pain and the shuffling of feet constructed the symphony of panicked energy that fueled the cramped space.

A nurse approached us and swiftly removed the half-conscious boy from my shoulder without question. I had no idea how reliant I was on the warmth of his body at my side until the weight slipped away, leaving a cold empty chill to run rampant through my bones.

My eyes scanned, haphazardly, for any trace of auburn hair. My ears tuned to seek out that familiar voice. But she was nowhere in my line of sight. Unable to discern all the moving bodies from one another as they moved about so frantically, I grew more and more panicked with each second, I did not spot her.

Soft hands gently clasped my cheeks and I flinched despite the warm touch. My eyes clashed with emerald green ones that studied me acutely from head to toe before clutching me in a tight, desperate hug. Relief became so thick I choked on it, causing tears of gratitude to leak from my eyes. Though I did not know the god Kareena and Articus worshiped during Mass each Sunday, I thanked him all the same, with shuttered eyes and silently moving lips.

Thank you. Thank you. Thank you.

"Thank God you are alright," Kareena huffed into my hair. Her hands gripped the material of my blouse as though they'd never let go. Yet, they finally did, just enough to look me over once again as I wiped stray tears from my cheeks and chin.

She nodded in understanding. "It's okay Alise, it's going to be alright."

I nodded along with her even though I didn't completely believe her and more disobedient tears escaped.

It was so close. Too close to losing someone I cared so much for, again. Too close to having my heart ripped out and shattered into a million pieces even though it still had yet to fully recover.

"Listen to me, Alise," Kareena said with all the strength of a confident leader. Not an ounce of fear trembled in her voice. "Go find my brother." Her eyes pleaded though her voice did not waver.

All I could do was nod as I wiped the last of my tears away and turned to flee out of the infirmary. A new sense of resolve brought energy to my aching body as I ran once again.

Chapter Thirty Four

REACHING THE FAR EDGE of the library I gripped the wall's edge as I panted, trying, and failing to catch my breath. A pause between explosions grew into a long tense moment. Time seemed to hold its breath in anticipation. But it never came. Letting my curiosity win out, I dashed to a nearby window. The once approaching ships—the ones that had broken from formation—were being shot down by the other members of the fleet as though punishing their insubordinate brethren.

Some of the ships exploded in midair, becoming enormous balls of fire before falling to the earth, while others retreated beyond the horizon and out of reach.

The aerial warfare dragged away from the Academy and then the city all together. As a rain cloud would clear from the sky, they drifted elsewhere, the fleet moving as one. Only the faint sound of sirens in the distance and the blood-red glow of fire lingered in their wake. Downed airships smoldered like picturesque hills made of burning debris. Their smoke, along with that which burned from the city, blocked out the last of the sun, painting the landscape in a hellish scene of grays and reds. My eyes burned as I dashed away from the horrid scene.

It all happened so fast yet it felt like hours, days. A wave of exhaustion flooded me as my adrenaline started to wane.

I ascended the wrought-iron, spiral staircase one heavy step at a time. The railing under my grip was cold and that corner of the library was especially dark with only one, now cracked and broken, stained colored window to illuminate the landing. When I reached the top I raced to the door, throwing it open wide, only to find it empty of any living thing.

My heart sank at the sight, yet, I still harbored hope that he would find me. He told me I could come up here whenever I needed to escape. That it would be a refuge. He promised.

Dust particles glinted in thin streams of light from the singular window. I stood there and took in every detail of the cozy, masculine space, now littered with books and other items that had clearly fallen from their places amongst the shelves. Yet, the small space still calmed me as I drank it in with small sips, like a freshly brewed cup of tea. From the worn-down, upholstered wingback, to a rather sturdy looking mahogany writing desk. Its surface was scattered with papers of all kinds. I walked around the desk, dragging a finger along its surface, relishing the feel of its smooth polished wood under my skin. My eyes scanned the papers laid haphazardly before me, mindful not to disturb them. There were notes clearly written in Articus's unique hand, books left open, maps layered upon each other, and letters, mostly addressed to Articus, and signed at the end by General Desiaus. Others looked to be in some kind of code or foreign language. Sentences that didn't make sense to me scrawled upon wrinkled parchment. Oddly, they were signed off with the names of animals and birds.

Sincerely, Stork.
Cordially, Black bear.

My attention strayed to the wall behind the desk. It was fitted completely with built-in wooden bookshelves, littered with old leather-bound tomes and dust. I plucked a fallen book from the floor and slid it into place between two others. Along with the volumes were random, perhaps sentimental items.

Bird feathers, empty medicinal amber jars, a spyglass, and a rather ornate, gold leaf box. I felt a tinge of sorrow as I accidently stepped on the shattered pane of a picture frame. A black and white photograph of a young boy and a tiny toddler slid out from the ruined frame. I studied it for a moment. My eyes scanned over the boy's features and the way he held the curly haired toddler in his arms, before placing it between the pages of a book that appeared rather well-loved. Every new discovery was a distraction my anxious mind craved.

The gold leaf box sat, surprisingly, undisturbed from its place on the shelf. It had no lock and curiosity itched at me relentlessly. So naturally, I gently lifted its hinged top, revealing red, velvet lining cradling a beautiful, antique pistol. It was unlike any gun I had seen before. Instead of the typical dark steel of a modern firearm, this one was made of what looked like brass, with an ivory inlay in its grip and an elaborate engraving of a wolf down its barrel. Tiny red rubies were inset in the wolf's eye. The shape of the weapon was curved in an old fashion style. Not daring to touch it, I leaned in to get a closer look, wondering if this gun had ever been used or if it was just for ceremony.

"Beautiful, isn't it?" a soft whisper danced on my skin, jolting me up right. Before I could turn around to face whoever snuck up behind me, an arm barred across my chest gripping my opposite shoulder. A soft breath slid down my neck as I felt a hard broad body press against my back. A rampant heart beat beneath.

Intimate. Isn't that the nature of whispers and secrets?

I relaxed into his hold, letting him pour his secrets into me.

"The general gave it to me as a gift on my twenty-first birthday, shortly after I was promoted to lieutenant. This gun is a legacy," Articus continued. "It represents everything I am to become: The general's pride, his right hand, his weapon. Every day it tempts me to end the fight for my own soul, to return it to my holster and return myself to the life he has paved for me, that he has trained me for since childhood."

I recalled the day I saw Articus in his decorated uniform alongside General

Desaius, with bored disdain on his face, while soldiers saluted. Women waved their handkerchiefs in praise while men bowed their heads in fearful respect. It had all been so perplexing—different and foreign from the Articus I thought I knew. But now I saw the truth. Like a snarling dog on its master's leash, Articus was the creation of his prideful adoptive father.

I slowly turned to meet his eyes, so full of frustration and desperation. He must have felt trapped. A fleeting fox, growing tired and waning in strength, as the hunting dogs closed in.

"I was so worried," he spoke, his voice was raw as his eyes roamed over me. If he was looking for a wound, he would find none on my skin, but several on my heart.

"I came looking for you but you weren't here and I didn't know where else to go so I—"

He hushed me with the gentle touch of his finger on my lips. I swallowed down a painful lump as unshed tears threatened to break in relief. Upon closer inspection, he appeared unscathed and so I thanked his faceless, nameless god once again.

"It's alright," he said, seeming to understand my worry. "I'm still here." His words an echo from a time before.

"Where were you?" I pleaded.

"I was trying to regain control of this situation." He sighed, running a hand through his hair before clamping down on the back of his neck. His soul appeared so exhausted through the window of his eyes. Of course, he would be trying to do all he could to end the air raid. He was a lieutenant of the Colony and a high ranking one, I presumed.

"I'm so tired, Alise." His head dropped to rest on my shoulder. "So tired of playing sides. Of remembering which mask to wear."

My hand reached up and cradled his head of its own fruition. And though I had so many questions, I let him speak uninterrupted. Let him pour his exhaustion over me like a heavy warm blanket. For even that brought me comfort.

"He has requested for me to return to the field. My life will now be completely committed to the military and the Colony's stifling politics. I'll no longer be able to live and teach at the Academy."

My chest ached for him. For the burden felt in every word.

"Is there nothing else you can do? Could you not request to stay and continue your work with Clouden?" I asked in as gentle a tone as possible.

"The general has invested too much in my training to let me go now," Articus replied, head lifting, eyes staring off ahead at nothing. "He has patronized me up until now, only letting me stay under Clouden's guidance for as long as it benefits him."

"Spying on the other realms for him," I stated more than asked.

Articus's stare slammed into mine. I felt just as shocked as his gaze expressed, that I managed to fit the pieces together. It was the only answer that made sense once I learned the risk and consequences of Articus traveling to a realm that was off limits. The visit when we met, clearly had not been his first.

"Yes," he drawled, cautiously. "Clouden convinced him the military could benefit from the intel, though Alise, you must know, that was never my own true intent." He looked down at me with pleading eyes. His hold on my lower back desperately tightened, bunching the material of my ruined dress. He needed me to believe him and see him as more than the general's tool.

How could he not have known that there would be no judgment from me? Someone who knew what it was like to do what you must to survive. Even if it went against every moral fiber in your body. Even if it broke your soul in two.

"I know," I whispered. I inhaled deeply to steady myself, to be the strength he needed in this moment. His other hand lightly cupped my cheek as his thumb grazed back and forth over my bottom lip. A tell of his troubled mind. My breath caught in my chest. My eyes looked up from his hand to those beautifully verdant eyes now glassy with unshed tears.

"I don't want to hurt and kill and manipulate for the general's own ambitions any longer," he murmured.

"I know," I reassured him. My voice grew weaker with each touch of his trailing thumb.

"I've done so many things I regret in order to survive, to protect Kareena, and give us a better life, but I don't want to go back to that version of myself. I can see now, there is too much evil in the world to destroy what little beauty remains." His forehead pressed into mine. His piercing stare closer than ever as though glimpsing my very soul and pleading for me to see his in return.

I could. Never before had it been laid so bare before me and I wanted to burn the world down for every scratch and tear I saw upon it.

My back ached slightly as it hit the bookshelf behind me. The hard wood pressed into my spine and legs. But I didn't care. All I wanted to do was drown in those sad, desperate eyes. To change their sorrow to joy and their pain to pleasure. To let him know I believed in him, I saw him and I . . . cared for him.

I opened my mouth with the intent to utter a reassurance, but my voice failed me as I noticed his gaze lower to my mouth. His hot breath on my lips, the inviting scent of vetiver and parchment surrounded me.

"Alise," he breathed. "You don't truly hate me, do you?" he asked.

"No." I exhaled, and he pulled me a fraction closer. "Not at all." Closing the last of the small trace of space between us, he pressed his full lips against mine.

Chapter Thirty Five

I DIDN'T HESITATE TO respond. I wanted—needed him to know, without a shadow of a doubt that those lies I'd mistaken for truth were long gone. I had never hated him. I hated myself. Loathed every time I pushed him away or blamed him for my misfortune. I let my hurt mold him into the villain, when he was truly anything but. He was my companion on the road to freedom. The only one who believed me when I denied being guilty of the murder of James. The one who met a sick, crazy, flight-risk of a girl and saw more.

Our lips parted, allowing his tongue to delve into my mouth. Each soft, velvet caress sent shivers down my spine and over my skin. My fingertips tingled with the soft, silken feel of his hair. I cherished the feeling, as if it were spun gold in my very palm. The heat of him seared through the material of my dress—melting and relaxing every bone as I molded into him. This time it didn't feel like a game. Or a flinting rush of passion fueled by chemistry alone. It felt like more.

It felt real.

Every kiss was tender and reverent. His touch gentle, that was, until it wasn't. The pace of our kisses quickened alongside our synchronized rushing breaths. Both desperate for more of each other. I wanted to taste more, feel more of him in every way possible and his body reciprocated.

Hungry lips trailed down across my jaw as his hand slid up my waist to my chest. Roughly, he massaged my breast in his cupped hand, eliciting a low moan from my lips. Suddenly, I found myself so grateful I bypassed wearing a corset and the other stifling undergarments a woman would typically be expected to wear under their clothing. I felt his mouth curve up into a soft smile against my throat, seeming to be just as grateful for my little rebellion as well, before continuing his trail of kisses down to my collar bone. He gave it a quick nip between his teeth, sending a rush of liquid heat to my very core, before kissing the spot in tender reverence.

Though worry and reason were all but washed away by the tide of pleasure we were so lost in, intrusive, self-conscious thoughts still threatened in the peripheral. I needed to know for certain.

"Say something," I rasped in between breaths. "What are you thinking?"

Articus paused and took my chin in a firm but gentle grip. Relief soothed like a balm when I no longer saw sorrow swimming in his gaze. Instead, it was replaced by a darkness I did not fully understand as a woman, but I knew came from a place of dimly lit bedrooms and tangled sheets. A shadow that fueled men's desires, and a tiny part of myself relished in the knowledge that it was directed at me.

"I'm not thinking about anything, my Little Fox. Except for how beautiful you are to me right now." He glossed my lips gently with his. A sensation so feather-light, yet it tugged my heart towards his, as if pulled by chains. "And how amazing you taste." The next kiss was firmer, more desperate than the former. Our grips on each other tightened, mine around his neck, tugging him closer.

His at my back. Material bunched in his fist as his other hand slid down my thigh, cupping behind my knee to hitch my leg around his waist. He pressed completely flush against me. Not a single breath of space left between us.

There was no ignoring the long hard length of him. My hips, less than subtly, rocked against him, causing his display of desire to rub against my core. He showed his approval instantly by tugging my hair back and licking up the long column of my exposed neck in one bone melting stroke.

"I can't get enough of it and I don't think I ever will." His voice turned low and harsh.

I hummed in agreement and satisfaction to his omission. His breath against my scorching skin tickled every fine hair on my flesh and my hips rocked instinctively into his again. I surrendered control—handed it over willingly to the man before me. Gift wrapped and addressed to him alone as my body practically begged him to take more. Challenged him to find his fill, if he dared.

As though reading me like one of his favored books he swiftly wrapped my other leg around his waist and lifted me up. My backside held firmly in each of his capable hands as he spun us around and placed me reverently on the sturdy wood desk. At least, I hoped it was as sturdy as it appeared.

Even then his mouth never left mine and I pulled him in deeper, closer, as his tongue explored more thoroughly. Each stroke was a smooth caress that sent shivers down my spine. I nipped at his lower lip then swiped my tongue across the tender spot, eliciting a groan from deep within him.

The faint sound of items clamored to the floor before I felt a warm calloused hand slide up my thigh. Another tangled in my hair.

"Lay back for me," his breathy words commanded and I so joyously obeyed. Smiling up at him I laid my hands above my head and arched my back. My certainly disheveled appearance and growing desire on full display for him.

He bit his lip, making me feel cold and hungry with the absence of his body against mine. I pouted, letting my expression say just how lonely my lips felt without his. His hand grazed gently around my neck as his other slid ever further up my thigh. His thumb circled with every inch it trailed toward my center, causing my eyelashes to flutter with every teasing touch. Mischievous fingers brushed against my bare core and paused.

"You're not wearing anything under this dress, are you?" Articus purred and I shook my head in response while biting my swollen lip with satisfaction. His thumb continued its lazy dance toward the crease of my already soaked flesh, causing my breath to quicken with each torturous stroke.

"Look at you, my pretty Little Fox. Look at how beautiful you are laid out before me." Articus knelt between my thighs and pushed the material of my skirt up to my waist, bearing my needy desire before him, as he kissed a path up my inner thigh. With his mouth mere millimeters from where his thumb rubbed me, he huffed chilling breaths across the damp surface, whispering something that sounded like a prayer. "I'm going to devour every inch of you, Alise. Until the desire I coax out spills on my tongue."

"Yes. Please," I whimpered. The tension coiling inside me becoming too much to withhold.

Articus groaned in satisfaction. A predator toying with its prey before striking a killing blow.

"Such sweet words, Little Fox. Though, I bet you taste even sweeter." I couldn't help but gasp when his mouth closed over me, his tongue instantly finding and flicking over the swollen and sensitive bundle of nerves.

My back arched and hands gripped the edge of the desk as his tongue punished my senses with every merciless swipe. Panting breaths turned to deep and desperate moans. My hips undulated instinctively against his mouth, beckoning him to explore further and deeper like a ship on a rolling tide. This ocean of desire called us both to get lost in its depths. I would gladly lavish it in its drowning waters.

My hand buried into his hair as I rode closer to the edge. Articus's palm slid up to cover my mouth just as a rather loud cry of pleasure tore from my chest. I bit down on the inside of his hand but he did not budge, nor did he slow in his ministrations against my swelling sex. A kind of welcomed panic swept over me with the realization that I was completely, and utterly at his will. But instead of the anxious tightening that normally occupied my chest, a much more pleasant tension grew along my spine and between my thighs. And though I no longer held control of my body, it being, more than willingly handed over to this man who read its language so well—I felt free, liberated, beautiful, and powerful. I never felt more so in my entire life. To have the wolf others saw and the man I did, on his knees before me, making it his one and only desire to please me more than anything else. Knowing that he wouldn't be satisfied until I was driven feral, with passion.

Suddenly, a very familiar and unwelcomed panic pierced through my groggy, desire-ladened haze and I shot up, along with Articus. Seeming to have heard the same sound I thought I did, he swiftly lifted me off the desk and planted me on my wobbling feet.

Thundering foot-steps echoed from the iron steps beyond the office door. I braced myself on Articus's desk in an attempt to regain my balance and steady my breathing while Articus haphazardly threw a bundle of papers into the small stove and slammed the soot coated hatch shut. I smoothed the rumples from my dress as I collected my mettle.

Seeming satisfied with his odd task he came around behind me before saying, "It's the general. He never comes up here so it can only mean he's extremely displeased with me." His hands gently collected mushed hair from off my neck. "Whatever he says, whatever I say, just remember that you know me Alise, the real me. Not the one he wishes me to be." He twisted the gathered strands into a coil. "He bleeds just like any other man. You need not fear him as others do."

I released a breath. "I'm not afraid." I assured him, just as Articus slid a pen into the coil of hair, securing it in place.

"Of course, you're not." I heard his lips part into a grin beside my ear.

The general didn't even knock before entering the cramped office with his mouth already open to speak.

"Articus! Where—" His words cut off as his eyes razored in on me standing behind Articus's desk.

"General," Articus said in greeting with a resolute calm demeanor. However, General Desaius refused to take his dissecting eyes from me. Instead, he scanned every last inch of me and I wondered if he noticed my surely flushed cheeks and swollen lips. My reddened neck from Articus's stubble or any other trace of what just abruptly ended seconds ago.

"What is so urgent, Father?" The term of endearment, most likely used in an attempt to draw the general's attention to himself and away from me, was ineffective. He looked me over one last time with utter disgust before finally directing his attention back to Articus.

"You know very well what brings me to this hovel of yours." The sneer carrying over his every word.

"We have received vital intel on the attack and the Council is holding an impromptu meeting in response."

Articus sighed deeply, fists clenched at his side from behind the table where only I could see.

"And I assume you wish for me to attend."

"At my side, yes. As is expected and as you should." The general made no attempt to disguise his contempt in my presence. I had all but vanished from his plane of existence.

I discreetly tipped my head toward Articus and reassured him in a hushed voice. "It's fine. I'll go now and tell Kareena that I have found you. That you are well and unscathed." The diction of the Second Realm slipping back into place with kid gloves.

Articus made to reach for my hand as I turned away, my head bowed in respect, to scuttle off like the docile lady the general would expect. I did not give his hand time to reach mine, for I knew it was better to not reveal your desires to someone who could use them against you in the future.

A large booted foot stepped into my line of sight, barring me from the exit. I lifted my chin to face the handsome, yet cruel face of General Desaius. His lips kicked up in the corners upon meeting my eyes but the gesture did, in no way, resemble friendliness. Instead, his wicked smile reminded me of a jackal baring its teeth.

"I have seen you before. Correct?"

"Correct," I answered without hesitation and willed my voice not to waver under the weight of his scrutiny.

"You are familiar with my daughter?" Clearly, he was struggling to remember me though it had only been days since we were introduced. But, of course, why would he remember a mere girl as insignificant as I? Perhaps, he needed correcting.

"Alise Fox, sir. Ward to your brother Clouden, and beloved friend to your daughter Kareena." I refused to bow my head this time, as I had seen the others do and this would be the final time I introduced myself to this self-important man. It was one thing to be respected by others, it was a complete other to feel entitled to it.

"And what are you to my son?" His sharp eyes darted between me and Articus.

"I'll leave that for him to define," I said calmly.

"I see," he drawled as he held my stare. If he felt any disrespect to my lack of reverence towards him, he hid it poorly behind a sneer of contempt. I was starting to think this was a common resting expression for him.

After too long of a moment, he sidestepped with one swift clomp of his boot, finally allowing me access to the door. I slid out as quickly as possible. However, after I closed the door gently behind me, I did not make my way down the spiral stairs.

Chapter Thirty Six

"I T IS AS WE suspected," the general continued without a hitch. "The rebels have infiltrated our own military forces under the guise of Colony soldiers." The general's baritone pitch made no attempt to speak discreetly.

"Do we know which faction?"

"They haven't declared themselves yet, but I am certain it will not be long before the bragging starts amongst themselves, causing word to spread of who was responsible. Their pride will make them known, despite their obvious failure."

The fact that he considered the death of, I assumed, several civilians, not including the destruction of businesses and homes, nonconsequential, spoke volumes to how poorly he valued the lives of others. If circumstances were different, I would be internally cheering for those brave enough to take on the power-hungry colonizers that called themselves the Colony. If it were not for the never-ending stream of death that always accompanied war between men. In that moment I prayed, to a god I did not know, that Articus and all the other boys forced into the draft against their will—against their very conscious—would find a way out.

"Until then I require you at my side as we convene with the Council and as I address the Academy on this matter."

"Is that a command, General?" Articus's voice huffed with a sigh of exhaustion.

"It is, Lieutenant. In fact, I'm assigning you to head the search for these rebels. I want you to find these assailants and bring them to justice, seeing as your skills are so well-suited for such a task. We will leave immediately after addressing the Academy."

Justice.

The term was vague at best. Would they be brought to trial? Would they be court-martialed for their crimes, or executed on the spot? Was Articus to be unleashed and commanded to bite by his master?

As the conversation grew quiet, a riot of hushed words exchanged between the two men, I carefully slipped my heeled boots off. Their soles dangled gingerly from my fingers as I tiptoed down the iron steps.

After finding Kareena back in the infirmary and informing her of Articus's well-being, I volunteered to help with the menial tasks of washing bandages, cleaning out bowls of bloodied water, and anything else I could aid in. Yet, too often, I found myself holding the hand of a cadet as he groaned in pain. Nurse Petit claimed my presence soothing after I coaxed the third soldier into a restful state, with merely the stroking of my hand in theirs, while I told them one of the stories my father would tell on stormy nights. Proving that no matter how much bravery the young men managed to call forth, there were still little boys deep inside each one.

By the time General Desaius called a meeting in the commons for all to attend, everyone was exhausted and sore. Either from physical wounds or from tending to those with them, all carried an invisible hurt beneath their skin, a mark that would scar the heart and mind. Most likely both, I feared. I was familiar with such lesions. They oozed into nightmares, made miniscule things that were once so innocent, a trigger of suffocating thoughts and paralyzing fears. How many would flinch at the suddenly painful sound of thunder or a door closed too forcefully? Would confusion set in as their hands shook without recognizing the source of the reaction? Or perhaps the feel of unshed tears would push at the back of their eyes when common dust particles caught the light in a familiarly haunting way.

As I stood beside Kareena, her hand clutched mine in a desperate attempt to anchor ourselves to each other, the general's words fell on my deaf ears. My mind was too preoccupied with observing every face of every soldier and staff member who stood among us. As though by doing so, I could assess the level of damage done to each one. A heavy blanket of sorrow weighed my shoulders down, making my head feel heavy with every pulse of the crowd around us.

As if she also felt the force that surrounded us, Kareena's head tipped to the side and rested on my shoulder. It was a burden I was more than willing to hold for her.

"With that said, after repairs are made, it will be business as usual and we will, indeed, have the Graduation Ball and ceremony as planned." Soft murmurs broke out amongst the others over the general's declaration. "We cannot, and will not, let the actions of a few, delusional radicals cause us to stumble!" The irony of his words were not lost on me. Articus suppressed a cringe as he stood by his side, always the silent portrait of calm calculation and vicious power that General Desaius insisted on carrying alongside him like a lucky totem. "We are the strong arm of the Colony. Its very might resides in you. We must remain as a unified, unshakable force for all to look up to. To cower at!" Hoots and hollers of agreement rumbled off the walls. Several soldiers and professors raised their fists in the air in solidarity.

Articus stepped forward to speak. "Be strong in the face of opposition, brothers. They can only take what you clasp lightly." His voice energized the crowd. Even more chimed in with their own passionate proclamations.

"May the righteousness of the Colony dwell within you," General Desaius declared, his ego clearly nudging him to have the last word. Soldiers, all around us, shouted mantras of power and strength. Their voices became a singular, booming force that could be felt in every particle of space between bodies as Articus and the general turned to leave in swift sure strides. They were, indeed, the embodiment of leadership and certainty that the soldiers needed to see. The façade of an impenetrable wall in living, breathing, flesh.

Just as swiftly as they were able to embolden the crowd before them, they were gone.

The following days were a blur of endless repairs and tidying. Yet, with the help of every staff and soldier the work was done quickly, and surprisingly effectively. Myself and a few cadets volunteered to restock the books that were salvaged from the wreckage. I enjoyed the, mostly, solitary task. Questions about what the other day meant between Articus and I proved to be very distracting and I found myself lost in thought about it all. Sometimes in the middle of conversation with Kareena, I found myself having to apologize for spacing out, once again. Other times late at night, alone, my imagination ran wild with memories so vivid I could almost feel his mouth on my flesh.

Had he not left that day, immediately after attending the speech with the general, I would have addressed the issue with him already. Perhaps I would have told him that I knew about Sabrina and, though I didn't have any delusions of exclusivity with Articus, maybe she did. And to deceive another girl in such a way was something I did not want to be a part of. The same held true for Dante. It seemed we both had someone else, innocently and unsuspectingly, standing on the sidelines of our game and it wasn't fair to either of them.

"I heard it was the Menagerie that claimed responsibility for the bombing." An eager, hushed voice came from a few aisles over, breaking me from my thoughts of Articus.

"The Menagerie? Who would name themselves something so moronic?" A different male voice chided back. Drifting closer to the source, I made sure each step was slow and silent as I approached closer.

"My cousin said it's because of their code names. After you're initiated, they strip you of your real name and give you one that is reminiscent of an animal." Two young cadets were huddled by a stack of cluttered books, seemingly more interested in their conversation than where they were placing the tomes.

"That is one of the stupidest things I have ever heard. It's probably just a drunken tale told at the pub," the slim, red-haired one in rolled-up shirtsleeves said, dismissing his companion's claims.

"It is true!" the shorter, dark haired one whisper-yelled. His friend held a finger to his own lips, hushing the smaller one, in response. "It is true, my cousin met one of them before. Says a member tried to recruit him. Said he called himself 'Black Bear.'"

A heavy tome crashed to the ground as it slipped from my lax arms. I darted behind a bookcase and held my breath. There was a long pause before someone spoke again.

"Keep your trap shut you fool. If anyone so much as suspects he was contacted by a rebel faction, they'll have him dragged out of his bed in the middle of the night and executed by firing squad."

Black Bear.

My mind reeled through memories of where I had heard that name before. No, not heard—seen. The name was written on one of the letters cluttered across Articus's desk. Was he actually corresponding with this supposed rebel faction?

My feet moved before my mind could decide what to do next. They dashed up the spiral staircase to Articus's attic office, though I knew he would not be there. Upon closing the door behind me I quickly looked over the mahogany desk, now cleared of all papers. It was unusually tidy. I recalled the cabin in the woods in the First Realm and how everything was in its place. How it looked untouched and unlived in. A hiding place with no clues to its occupants left behind.

I pulled a drawer open and then another to no avail before removing books from his shelf and shaking them upside down, hoping to reveal any loose contents. But nothing with the unusual animal name signatures could be found.

I wiped my glistening brow with excretion. The air was unusually warm. I looked to the quaint stove to investigate the source, only to find no fire burned within. Upon further inspection, only a pile of ash and the corner of a piece of parchment were heaped in its innards. Plucking the corner of parchment from its burial place, I could see a bit of scrolling that still remained.

ack bear

My hackles raised as I imagined the punishments Articus would endure if even a trace of these letters were found in his possession—possibly even death. And if it were at all in my realm of control, I would make sure that never happened. Just as he had protected me, now I would protect him. I grabbed a match from atop the stove and struck its sulfurous tip, watching the flame spark and fizzle to life. An amber wave consumed what little remained of the paper as I tossed it back into the stove, along with the match, to become nothing but ash with the rest of the evidence.

A heart stopping screech caused me to flinch. The piercing eyes of the goddess, along with my pencils, were abandoned on the damask sofa cushion as I sprinted to Kareena's half of the suite. The door flew open before I could even reach the handle. Kareena joyfully grinned from ear to ear. Her cheeks were rosy and eyes sparkled.

"Come. Look what arrived." She firmly grasped my hand and tugged me into her bedchamber where two wide, powder pink boxes with gold bows sat on her bed.

"One is for you." She squealed as she planted me by the shoulders before one of the beautifully wrapped boxes and started untying the ribbon from her own.

Pulling a golden ribbon loose, I discovered matching, gold leaf lettering embossed upon the box's lid.

Alberta Ferretti

I did not recognize the name myself but from Kareena's reaction—she was bouncier and giddier than ever—I assumed it was a good sign.

"Who is Alberta Ferretti?" I asked, trying not to dishonor the name with my horrible pronunciation.

"Only one of the most talented designers in all of Italy! Her gowns are coveted across the entirety of the Colony! And now, my dear friend, we are so blessed to have one of her designs grace our unworthy bodies."

I huffed at her ridiculous statement.

Kareena lifted her lid first, revealing its treasured contents. Powder blue chiffon, accented with satin trim, and intricately woven beadwork, lay nestled in white tissue paper. Kareena lifted it in one swift motion by its shoulder straps before clutching the gown against herself and twirling in front of the mirror. Its skirts fluttered towards her ankles with all the grace of falling feathers. Layers of silk cascaded over one another like the waves of an ocean. A few anchored with intricate, crystal beadwork designs in indistinct vines and flowers.

My jaw dropped to the floor. "It is absolutely beautiful," I proclaimed.

Kareena's reflection gave me a grateful smile as one hand clasped the gown against her, while the other held her hair up from her neckline.

"Well, go ahead. Open yours and let us see." For a moment I had all but forgotten about my own box at the sight of Kareena's dress. My stomach flipped with anticipation of what could possibly be inside that could measure up to the detail and beauty of her own gown.

Upon lifting the lid, a note, with my name scrolled across it, fluttered atop the folded tissue paper. The handwriting was one that felt familiar. I looked over my shoulder to see Kareena still arranging her hair in the mirror before reading the notes contents.

I know it can't compare to flowers and chocolates, but I suppose it will have to do. My only regret is not having the chance to see you in it as you bless everyone with your presence at the Graduation Ball. Perhaps when I return, we may have an intimate celebration of our own. Just you and I.

P.S. You may also wear this dress to said celebration if you desire, though clothing is optional and not preferred.

As if summoned, my cheeks flushed and recollections of that charming smile and flirtatious wink he would give to those we came across in our travels, came to the forefront of my mind. How desperately I had wanted one of those easy smiles directed at myself and I couldn't help but suspect a dimple tugged at his cheeks as he wrote this salacious note and slipped it into the box.

My fingers gently unfolded sheets of tissue paper to reveal a bodice of ivory silk and crystal beadwork. My chest tightened and eyes swelled at the treasure presented before me. In place of straps were strings of pearls strung together with gold links. I slid my fingers beneath the pearl straps to gently lift and reveal the rest of the gown. Frightened that a single tug could snap the string and send the pearls tumbling to the floor, I used extreme caution as I gently handled the garment.

The silhouette was slim and tapered around the waist through to the hip before flaring out gradually at the knee like a trumpet—certain to create the illusion of curve to my slight frame. The neckline was sweetheart cut and trimmed in rows of transparent beading that sparkled when it caught the light. The pearl straps draped the shoulders and gathered to meet a pearl medallion designed in the way of an intricate flower, in the center of the chest. A single, teardrop shaped pearl dangled below it.

My breath caught in awe of the masterpiece. A knot of gratitude lodged in my throat at the thought that this dress was handpicked or even possibly, designed just for me. The planning ahead Articus must have done to have it ready in time. All while I probably still considered him my enemy. While I still pushed him away at every opportunity and had no qualms in cutting him with my words. Even then he still found me worthy of such a gift, whether I reciprocated his kindness or not.

Feeling like a blubbering fool, I bit my quivering lip and swiped at my damp eyes. Kareena caught my attention in our reflections before turning to me with concern in her expression.

"What's the matter, Alise? Is the dress not to your liking?" My reaction was clearly mistaken for sorrow.

"Oh no, it's not that at all. I love it. It's just that no one has ever given me something so beautiful in my entire life and I'm feeling rather undeserving at the moment." I huffed out a nervous laugh at my own ridiculousness this time.

"Nonsense. You are more than worthy to receive everything your heart desires, my dear friend," Kareena said before clutching me in an embrace that warmed my very bones. For a moment I let myself believe her—let myself forget the lies and manipulations I had weaved. Forget that, every day, I lied to her about who I was, and where I was from, and allowed the joy and warmth of her words to smother my guilt. Only for a moment did I indulge in this falsehood, with my treasured garment pressed between us. She slowly pulled away, giving me a small smile before returning to the mirror.

"Now how should I style my hair? Half up or all up?" Her nose scrunched with ridicule as she mushed her hair atop her head, and a perfectly spiraled tendril of russet fell across her face.

Chapter Thirty Seven

I STEPPED THROUGH ORNATE French doors with Kareena's arm locked in mine as we took in the spectacle of wonder before us. I imagined for Kareena it was not as nearly breathtaking of a sight as it was for me, seeing it for the first time. A scene I could only have conjured in a childlike dream of extravagant ball gowns and gold rimmed crystal flutes that bubbled with pink champagne, came to life around us. The air crackled with the energy of a hundred bodies as they danced like swans in graceful synchronization. Dresses floated in a wave of color across the dance floor as hands, feet and skirts moved as one.

Every detail of the ballroom was wildly lavish with more romantic, delicate elements than that of the more neo-gothic interior of the Academy. Where dark woods and heavy arches bedecked the halls outside of this space, gold and white trim framed delicate, fabric wallpaper and gilded mirrors. The aesthetic, a feminine energy that held no other place inside the Academy walls beyond, except perhaps, in Kareena's suite.

Music from a small orchestra stirred from their place on a slightly raised dais. Some of the instruments were like nothing I had ever seen, while others, I recognized. The violins and piano were familiar in shape, yet they were made with gears and pipes instead of bows and strings. An artist blew into the neck of a violin-looking instrument, like one would a flute, causing the most elegant sounds of humming wind to come forth from it. Meanwhile, the piano was played more like a zither would be. The musician plucked its strings that were splayed before him on a long flat table. Its sound emanated from pipes of different sizes and heights with each pluck of the artist's skilled fingers. Other musical contraptions looked more like a child's windup toys rather than instruments. Yet, the sounds that came to life from them were just as beautiful as the others.

"Champagne?" a young man holding a gold tray of bubbling flutes offered me. A red bow tie and rose were the only colors against his all-white suit, reminiscent of bright crimson blood on fresh snow. We thanked him as Kareena and I each took a glass. Somehow, in all my gawking, we had made it into the throes of the crowd. The room felt warmer with every step we took deeper into its chaos. Some girls greeted us with warm smiles, mostly directed toward Kareena, while others eyed us with distaste before donning a reluctant grin that was so painfully forced, I could see the veneer crack.

"Try not to let them get to you. They are bored, insecure creatures and see anyone beyond their tight circle of relations as a threat," Kareena said softly as a particularly snobby flock of ridiculously puffy chiffon and too many diamonds passed us by with complete disgust written on their overly rouged faces.

"You are easily the most beautiful girl here, wearing a dress from a boutique they could only dream would make a design for them. They are dripping with jealousy." She guided me to a refreshment table ladened with tiered trays of pastries of every kind and my heart grew warmer at the thought that some, if not all, were most likely crafted by Ms. Hazel.

"Funny," I said as I plucked a raspberry tart off a gold tray and placed it on a frilly napkin. "I think the same of you."

Kareena flashed me a sparkling smile before giggling into her glass. "Just promise me you won't hide sewing needles in my boots in a fit of jealousy."

I almost choked on the mouthwatering tart. "They would do that?"

"Wouldn't be the first time." She sighed, taking another sip from her glass. "To this day I still check the soles of my shoes before putting them on."

"Vicious little beasts," I said under my breath.

"Those are the pranks of children compared to what the older ones are capable of. You would be shaken to hear the tale of how Miss Fairchild managed to convince Miss Ravine's fiancé to break off their engagement. Apparently, it broke quite the bond between their families and not a single suitor has called on the poor girl since. Most wouldn't think twice about ruining a life, should the opportunity present itself."

I had no words. These girls were apparently born and raised as serpents with fangs for teeth. Poison most likely dripped off their every word and burned flesh as surely as a flame would.

"Looks as though someone is waiting for his dance." Kareena lifted her chin in the direction behind me. I turned to see a fairytale prince looking more polished and sparkling than ever. His glassy, sterling eyes shined with the shimmering light from the crystal chandelier above. Each curl on his head a glossy spiral and not so much as a speck of lint rested on his immaculate dress whites. Gold frogging laddered up his jacket while a perfectly-ironed crease ran down his starched dress pants, grazing the tops of his oily, polished boots.

He beckoned me with a gloved hand.

"Is it alright if . . ." I asked Kareena, feeling guilty about leaving her alone where a rampaging socialite could stab her with a hair pin at any moment.

"Go. Go." She shooed me with a flick of her wrist. "Have fun. I'll be just fine." She winked before she turned me by the shoulders to face Dante once again and nudged me forward, leaving no room for hesitation.

"You look ravishing, Miss Fox," Dante said behind one of his too perfect smiles as he lifted my hand to his mouth for a chaste kiss.

"I take it you've come to collect your dance from me, Mr. Da Romano," I teased, like the upper-class lady I was anything but. This close I noticed his cheeks were flushed, most likely from the warmth of the crowded room and the layers of his uniform.

"Am I that transparent?" he chuckled as he mocked an injury with a palm pressed over his heart.

"Well, lucky for you, your timing is perfect, for I seem to have been abandoned by my traitorous chaperone."

"I have you all to myself then." He wove his fingers through the hand he still held in his before guiding me onto the dance floor and pulling my body closer to his with the palm of his hand around my waist. I did not know the moves to the dance, beyond the little bit Kareena managed to teach me last night, wearing nightgowns instead of ball gowns and slippers in place of heels. But by following Dante's lead we soon found our rhythm.

Everything, from the way he smiled down at me, to the crystal chandelier above, and the glittering specks of light across the dream-like space, made it harder for me to find my resolve. I had already decided that I would tell him, tonight, that I wanted nothing more than friendship from him. Though I couldn't exactly tell him why, as I was still figuring it out myself, it felt wrong to string him along after everything that happened between me and Articus. Especially if the rumors were true and there was any chance Dante would even consider proposing to me.

An odd sense of trepidation twisted knots in my stomach, making me regret the raspberry tart I, less than elegantly, wolfed down moments ago. But I knew my anxiety was misplaced, because Dante had always been kind and patient with me in our time together, so there was no reason to think he would be upset with my request. In fact, perhaps he would merely laugh and say that friendship was all he wanted in the first place and I would find the rumors were just that and there would be no love lost. If I could only be so lucky.

Before I could find my courage to speak, Dante was backing away from me. Our dance was over too soon for me to say my piece.

"I'll find you later, alright?" he said before turning away to join a cluster of rowdy cadets.

"Sure," I replied, mostly to myself as I stood alone in a sea of bodies.

To avoid being trampled by the other dancers I made my way to a server with a full tray of champagne flutes. The bubbles surely contained all the courage I would need to face Dante once again, then perhaps I would not freeze-up and actually say what I intended to. After tapping the server on the shoulder, I delicately plucked a flute off his gold-plated tray before bringing the fizzy drink to my lips. The bubbles tickled my tongue and throat, as I swallowed rather large gulps.

"You know you're just a toy to him," a sultry voice drawled from behind me.

"Excuse me?" Covering my mouth as I swallowed, I turned to see a group of three, lavishly dressed young ladies behind me. Their gowns were reminiscent of the colorful confections I had seen in the patisserie's window, while out shopping in the city, with Kareena—overwhelmingly frosted and abundantly trimmed. They stood in the formation of a pack of geese in flight. The leader stood at the front, the one I assumed had spoken.

"He's just having a little fun with you now and, if you're lucky, he might even ask you to join him on holiday to his family's summer home in Cannes," she said with insincerity. Her tone laced with mock enthusiasm as though I had won some trivial prize, as her eyes wandered across the ballroom with an expression of utter boredom.

"But you can never hope for it to go beyond that. He would never dream of introducing you to his parents." The flutter of her lace fan wafted her perfume up my nostrils. The robust bouquet of sugared roses made my stomach turn.

"I'm sorry, but you must have me confused with someone else." I smiled just as insincerely back at her and tried to appear as nonplussed as possible as I made to back away.

"That was Dante Da Romano you were just dancing with?" A statement more than a question. "I only tell you all this to spare you the heartbreak you are sure to endure with that one."

For a moment I considered that she could truly be concerned for my well-being. Though only slightly. And this rigid manner was the only way an upper-crust lady as herself knew how to express such an emotion to another. However, the sneer on her companions' faces as they cut me to shreds with their glares had me thinking otherwise.

"Oh, you have no need to worry for me, honey." A bit of my true diction slipped out thanks to the champagne. "Mr. Da Romano and I are just friends." I looked back over my shoulder to the group of soldiers he had joined just in time to see Dante kick back a glass of champagne himself. A curious eyebrow raised in my direction.

The ladies laughed in unison.

"I hope for your sake that is true." As though to migrate to a different hemisphere the flock of geese dressed as baked sweets took flight behind their leader.

"Have a nice night," I sang as the trio sauntered off without so much as a farewell, just as the last dredges of liquid bubbles emptied from the glass into my mouth.

I headed towards another server to replace my empty glass. I was in desperate need of something to numb the prickle of needled glares from the judging eyes of nearly every young woman in the room. Catching up to the server I swiftly traded flutes with a curt, "Thank you." The once sweet tart now turned sour in my stomach, and though the champagne fulfilled its purpose to dull my nerves, it only aided in worsening the chaos in my gut.

"There you are!" a sweet, familiar voice chanted behind me. "I've been looking all over for you."

A sigh of relief rushed from my lips as I turned to find Kareena with her arm locked with a man I never met before. His deep brown eyes were flecked with gold and the gathering of curls atop his undercut were combed back from his face. A tight, stray curl escaped to fall across his brow. His full lips tugged up at the corner as he took me in.

"I have someone I want to introduce you to." Her smile beamed as she looked up to the man beside her. "Alise, this is Dean Hempshire. Dean, this is Alise Fox."

"Pleasure to meet you at last, Miss Fox," Dean said with a small bow of his head. Recognition hit me like a train at full speed. *This* was the same man I had seen sparing with Articus that dim-lit evening. The same who caught my stare the day General Desaius arrived at the Academy.

"The pleasure is mine, Mr. Hempshire." I curtsied in return. I looked between the two. A radiance between them glowed in their intimate smiles, in the way Dean's thumb swiped back and forth across Kareena's hand—a way that could only mean one thing.

"Kareena is this your . . ." I wasn't sure if boyfriend was the commonly used term here. She smiled back at me, giddy with all the excitement of a child seeking approval. Yet, I didn't understand why she felt she needed it from me.

"I planned to tell Brother tonight and hoped the gathering would deter him from causing a scene but alas, he is not here to share in the news."

Surely the rumors of them being seen together would reach his ears when he returned. Yet, why she feared he would cause a scene, I did not understand. Clearly Kareena was happy and I knew that would mean everything to Articus. And from the way I had seen Dean and Articus carry on that evening in the courtyard, I could only assume they were confidants and friends. Why would he not approve?

"Your brother will be elated for your happiness," I assured her.

"Perhaps," Dean chimed in, "but he will certainly have my hide for it either way."

"Don't joke about that!" Kareena reprimanded with a soft smack to Dean's chest, causing the man to burst into robust laughter before bending down to place a kiss atop her head. His lips formed words against her hair I could not decipher. My heart swelled at the display of affection.

A familiar tune carried from the orchestra, snagging my attention. A melody from a different place, far away from here. And though there were no words, they filled my mind just the same as if they were whispered in my ear.

You're just too good to be true, can't take my eyes off of . . .

"Oh, I adore this song!" Kareena bounced on her toes. "Alise, come dance with us." Before I could respond, she abandoned Dean's hold and clasped my hand, dragging me to an opening in the sea of floating gowns. Dean's chuckle followed behind. Several couples, paired together alongside us and shortly after, I was woven into their choreographed line dance. The repetitive moves were easy enough to pick up—a brushing of arms, a few turns, and then a rotation of the partner.

I stumbled in my step at the realization of where I had heard this song before. It was in a moving car. The white noise of tires on pavement, and a crash of adrenaline from being attacked at the rest stop had made me groggy. A low gentle voice I had mistaken for the radio, or maybe it was both, had sung me into dreamless rest.

Suddenly, I saw Articus everywhere. A bit of him in every partner I danced with. A young freckled boy with green eyes a similar shade as his. Another with a mischievous glimmer in his expression that felt all wrong on him, and only made me miss the way it looked on Articus even more. The heated air of the crowded dance floor, a reminder of a warm hand caressing my back. I was surrounded. Engulfed. Drowning in all the ways I thought of him. Even with Articus gone he was everywhere and in everything. My body craved the anchor he had become. I needed the weight of his presence like a reassuring hand placed on the back.

I'm still here.

"I need some air," I said to no one in particular before I dashed from the dance floor, Kareena on my heels.

"Alise, are you feeling alright?"

I fanned myself with my gloved hands. "Too much champagne, I think." Making excuses for my flushed appearance. "I think I'll walk back to our rooms and call it a night. The fresh night air will help, I'm sure of it."

"Let me escort you then," Dean offered.

"No. no." I waved him off. "Please, enjoy your night. I'll never forgive myself if you two were to miss out on my behalf." Kareena looked me over, doubtfully.

"Are you sure?"

"I'll be fine. Just a skip across the gardens and I'll collapse in bed before you know it." I forced a reassuring smile for her sake.

"Promise me you'll go straight to bed." The motherly tone she used on her patients came through.

"Promise." I clasped her hand and squeezed it lightly as I gave my oath.

"Pleasure meeting you again, Dean," I threw out before making my way to the exit. My shoulders scrunched and I instantly cringed at the informal misuse of his name. My façade was cracking with every note that played of the hauntingly beautiful song. Every detail overwhelmed me as I pushed through the crowd toward the ornate doors that promised solitude on the other side.

Chapter Thirty Eight

I TREKKED BRISKLY THROUGH the echoing corridors of the Academy, stopping briefly to take my satin heels off before padding down the marble floors, barefoot and desperate to reach the gardens. The heavy click of heeled boots sounded behind me. Dante, lazily pursued me. In all my distraction and haste to leave I had forgotten what I set out to tell him tonight, and was relieved to see him approaching.

"There you are. I was meaning to discuss something with you," I called, ready to get the whole thing said and over with.

"And I, with you," he drawled back.

I surveyed the wide hall. It felt too exposed for the sensitive nature of what I wished to speak with him about—where anyone could pass by and hear us.

"Come." I beckoned to a dark alcove, lit by small streams of moonlight through a singular, leaded window. "Let's speak over here, in private."

It wasn't until he joined me, leaning against the alcoves archway, that I noticed the shine of a rectangular metal object as he slipped it in his pocket.

"Private indeed," he chuckled, his sultry baritone voice ran across my flesh causing it to prickle.

"There's something I must tell—" my words were cut off as he pinned me against the cold stone wall, an elbow at either side of my head.

"Kiss me," he whispered and he firmly pulled me into him, his lips closing in before I could even take a breath to protest. They pressed onto mine forcefully as he deepened the kiss greedily. The suddenness of it all riddled me with shame. What had I expected to happen after ushering him into a shadowed, secluded nook, alone? I tasted whiskey as he intrusively slid his tongue into my mouth, causing me to clamp down on it with surprise. A yelp of shock muffled behind our pressed mouths. This, however, only encouraged him. He groaned as his hands roamed over me and his body pressed harder into mine. My exposed back scratched on the rough stone wall.

It felt wrong. *He* felt wrong. His lips were cool and wet compared to Articus's warm fire. Where Articus's hands melted flesh and bone, Dante's chilled, causing cold shivers across my skin in an unpleasant way. The sensation was similar to that of a spider in my hair, or a bug crawling under my skin. I cringed as Dante's hand slid under the pearl strap of my gown, that I so loved. Loved because it was from *Articus*. Picked by him especially for me.

Dante's hands were stone cold and too firm. The strap of the dress snapped from its seam, breaking me from my paralysis. This needed to end now.

"Please stop, Dante," I said gently against his mouth. My eyes drew up to the bolsters above as I took a deep, readying breath of courage. But he didn't. Or maybe he didn't hear me. His hand slid over my breast and groped hard as he moaned. His mouth trailed down my neck, giving me reprieve from his suffocating kisses. I made no effort to be quiet or gentle then. I grabbed his wrist and pulled his hand away from my chest, grunting my request for him to stop again as I tried to pull him off me completely. He was so much stronger than me though, and with one swift move a single hand pinned my wrists above my head.

His head came to lean on the wall beside mine as he rasped, "Don't play hard to get *now*."

Panic rose in my chest, squeezing it tightly in a merciless vice. I shriveled against the wall. He thought I was playing? My panting breaths, mistaken for a rush of excitement and not fear-laced desperation. I was nothing but a rabbit whose heart beat out of its chest as the predator cornered it. He licked my ear with too much tongue, the wet feeling leaving a trail of palpable disgust as three glasses of champagne, and a single raspberry tart threatened to rise from my stomach.

"I'm not playing at anything, now stop!" I demanded and thrashed against his hold with no success. This was not the Dante I knew, nor expected, but I had to make it stop. I would have to fight, reason, bargain, whatever I could to end this now before it could go any further. Inhaling deeply, I readied my lungs to scream. His hand was quicker, stifling the cry before it could leave my lips.

"That's not funny," he slurred and shook his head in reproof. His mouth descended to my exposed chest, the broken straps on my gown no longer able to hold the bodice in place through my thrashing. I jerked a knee up to meet his only weakness, but my form-fitted dress did not allow for range of motion. His grip on my wrists tightened with frustration. He "tisked," as though I were a disobedient child and released my mouth to wave a reprimanding finger at me. The mistake was a sloppy one on his part as my mouth was free once again to let out a cry for help. Yet, the scream was cut short by a burning slap across my face.

"No screaming," he scorned, grabbing my chin in a vice grip. "I hate it when they scream."

Tears burned my eyes, fueled by the sting of his slap and the devastating realization that I couldn't get through to him. Couldn't stop him from destroying me in his drunken state of lust. Each tear stung like acid as they rolled down my cheeks.

Before I could attempt to scream again, the only instinct left in me, he pinned my head against the wall with a hard kiss on my mouth. I bit down on his lip in retaliation causing him to pull away. He touched his lip, observed the blood on his fingers and smiled. A completely content, satisfied expression, as if I had served him up exactly the type of fight he wanted from me all along.

"Now that's more like it."

Dread consumed me. Caged, and feeling trapped, I threw my head forward as hard as I could, connecting it with his nose. Reactively he let go of my wrists to cover his face and when he saw the blood on his hands his smile changed into the snarl of a feral beast.

"You little bitch!"

Grasping the opportunity, I leapt from the alcove, but he lunged and grabbed me by the back of my dress, slamming me face down on the hard marble floor. A yelp of pain escaped upon impact. As I tried to crawl away, Dante's boot came down on my back, pinning me in place like an insect. He grabbed an arm and twisted it painfully behind my back, eliciting a whimper as bone was twisted to the edge of cracking.

"I'll take you right here like the little slut you are," he hissed as his legs straddled across my backside. I felt him shuffle as he fumbled with the buckle of his belt. I attempted to squirm free but his weight was heavy and my head dizzy from impact.

Footsteps and laughter came towards us from down the hall and I cried for a whole new reason. Dante leapt off of me in a heartbeat and sauntered down the hall like a village drunk. As though the horrid man who tore me apart and left me limp and aching on the cold floor never existed. Sloppily he leaned on the wall as he made his way down and around the corner until he was out of sight.

Horror and shame rolled through me like waves at the idea of the weak and vulnerable state I was about to be discovered in. Half of my chest was exposed and my skirt was torn clear up to my backside. Blood certainly coated my face. A mix of both mine and Dante's.

Not wanting to be seen, I scurried back to the shadows of the alcove and hid there, until the voices passed by and tapered off to silence once again. I remained huddled for several moments. Dark shadows blanketed my beaten, ruined body. Sobs muffled from behind my clenched fists. I felt violated and discarded. My chest tightened and released with each despairing gulp of air.

It was several long moments before I was able to gather up my tattered dress, along with the remaining shards of dignity and head for my room. The entire way

I slinked into the shadows—my only guardian—and flinched at the slightest of sounds. Then I all but ran through the exposed garden and didn't stop until I slammed the suite's heavy door behind me. Exhaustion wrapped its heavy grip around my legs and I collapsed in a puddle of ruined fabric, torn beadwork, and blood before the mirror on my armoire.

My face and eyes were puffy and exceedingly red on one side, my hair a nest of tangles, and my legs bruised. Cataloging every mark, every assault, and violation I succumbed to tears upon the Parisian rug. My cries of pain were graciously muffled by the carpet's plush fibers. I couldn't stop sobbing, as a parade of one damning thought after another berated me. How could I be so naive? How could I have misjudged Dante so terribly? Why did I lead him into that alcove so removed from the crowd of the celebration? This was my fault. I deserved what happened for being such an idiot.

Even after sleep overtook me, I continued to cry as I fell into nightmares just as painful.

The following days I went into hiding, licking my wounds. At first, feigning a hangover when Kareena came to check on me. The second time she expressed her concern over my solitude, I claimed illness, saying I must have caught something at the ball and would hate to risk giving it to her and thus, possibly her patients. My weak voice echoed in the bathroom as I soaked my ruined gown in the sink. No matter how hard I scrubbed, the blood would not come out and only succeeded in making my raw fingers even more pink.

Later that night, long after everyone was asleep and the grounds were vacant and quiet, I tossed the tarnished masterpiece into the same outdoor oven Articus had burned our First Realm clothing in, before sprinting back across the training field. The sweat on my brow, more of fear than excretion.

After hearing the door to our shared suite close, I mustered the courage to crack my bedroom door open. A silver tray with a matching cover sat on the foyer table. I felt immense guilt each time a meal was brought up for me, or when I fed

Kareena another lie about having an illness or a headache. But the fear of possibly crossing Dante's path, should I venture back through the halls of the Academy, was stronger than my remorse. It was enough to send me retreating back to my room with the tray firmly clasped in my hands. As though even the common area of our suite wasn't safe from his steely gaze. How I had ever found those gray, cold eyes alluring I could no longer fathom. Perhaps, at times, our illusions of who a person is are so strong they blind us to who they really are.

To what they had been showing us all along.

Part Three

A BOOK OF LIES

Chapter Thirty Nine

B y the end of the week, I had gathered enough willpower to stroll the gardens after picking at a small lunch. I chose a time I knew most would be in classes and I would be free to wander alone. Surrounded by woods on one side, the gardens laid separate from the training grounds, connected only by a small gap between the archives of the library, and the structure that housed our suite. Despite my solitude, and the late spring sun warming my skin, I struggled to relax the tension from my body. Every crack of a twig and rustle from the neighboring woods had me flinching and looking over my shoulder. Half-way through my intended reprieve I gave up and headed back towards our suite, making sure not to stride too briskly as to frighten myself with the sensation of being chased. I all but slammed the door behind my back as my knees buckled. About to collapse in my relief to finally be back inside and safe I noticed I was not, in fact, alone.

Two pairs of eyes, in two varying shades of green, widened at the sight of the flustered mess before them.

"Oh, there you are Alise, look who has returned to us." Kareena indicated across the small polished table, ladened with tea cups and pastries of every kind. His pine tree stare never left me as his sister spoke, nor did mine as he rose from his seat and extended an arm to the vacant space between them.

"Please, join us." Articus said and like a drifting boat being pulled to port I floated, without thought, towards him. The sensation of finally releasing a breath that had been held for too long washed through me—as though my heart had been waiting this entire time for something it had lost, now returned.

"How long have you been back?" I asked, my voice barely above a whisper, raw from several days of crying.

What if he had been back for days now and I was merely unaware while sequestered in my room? What if I appeared ungrateful for not finding him myself to thank him for the dress and the other gifts? I had realized, during his time away, that the paper and graphite had also been from him and not Dante, as I previously, and wrongfully assumed.

"I returned to Paris this morning. Tart?" Articus's question broke through the fog of swirling guilt as he extended a small plate with tarts of every flavor piled upon it.

"Oh, yes thank you." I placed the plate before me, not touching its contents.

"How are you feeling?" His question startled me. "Kareena has told me you have been quite ill during my absence. Are you feeling any better?" Though kind, his concerned inquiry made me cringe with guilt.

I offered him a weak smile I hoped was convincing enough before lying, "Yes, very much so. Thank you for asking."

Articus raised an eyebrow at my curt and formal response, his gaze finally breaking to look me over. For once I felt thankful for the modest fashions of the Second Realm. Long, muslin sleeves covered the bruises on my wrists, and full skirts covered the ones on my shins and knees.

"Were these made by Ms. Hazel," I asked, imitating a cheerful tone, in an attempt to take his focus off me, though the question was stupid and the answer, obvious. I suspected he saw right through it.

"Of course," Kareena replied. "Apparently she still thinks you are a scrawny, growing boy in need of gaining a pound or two, Brother." Indicating the excessive number of sweets before us.

Articus chuckled before swiping a chocolate-filled pastry from the tray and popping it into his mouth whole, all decorum forgotten between us as he reached for another.

"Who's to say I'm not," he replied. Kareena swatted at his hand while mumbling something about swine under her breath. Articus swiftly dodged her waving hands and plucked another confection from the towering tray, popping it in his mouth as well, before he leaned back in his seat. My breath caught in the middle of a breathy laugh, as calloused fingertips glossed over the tops of mine. I glanced back up to Articus, but he was zeroed in on his sister as our fingers laced together, under the table and out of sight.

"As for you, *Sister*. I believe I heard a rumor that you were seen slinking out of weapons storage with Dean Hempshire, the other night." His expression turned vacant of all its previous playfulness.

Kareena's teacup paused mid-way to her mouth, her eyes fluttered several times before she swallowed deep and slow.

"I don't know what *rumor* you are referring to but you should know better than to give any stock to such things," said the girl who frequented the kitchens for more than just morsels of sweets.

"Then I should assume that it is also just manufactured gossip that you were seen by all at the Graduation Ball with him leashed to your arm the entire night?" The air grew so still, I could hear the click of the trap being set. Articus's fingers stopped their worrying dance across my knuckles and I hoped my own expression and the sudden tension in my grip did not give Kareena away. This was something she would need to tell her brother herself, and I felt sorry that the timing was forced upon her by the loose lips of others.

The two stared each other down across the tiered tray of pastries. A type of communication going back and forth between them that I could not hear.

"Don't you dare," Kareena hissed before slamming her tea cup down on its matching saucer.

"My own damn sister," he breathed. His brow creased and eyes blazed as he rose, my hand forgotten and left to grow cold in my lap. Before I could even exhale, he was out the door, Kareena fleeing behind him. Her muffled protests for him to wait, carried down the hall.

I shuffled behind like a curious puppy down the Academy halls, as I observed the exchange between the arguing siblings. A few other curious heads popped out from behind closed doors as the bickering rose in volume. Articus's gait quickened and became more and more leaded with each curt step.

"You must know he is a gentleman, nothing uncouth has happened between us," Kareena barked at Articus's back. Her feet scurried to keep up with his wide strides. He refused to so much as turn to acknowledge her as she stammered behind him.

"If I'm not mistaken the bastard is instructing in the weapons room this time of day," he mostly muttered to himself before sharply turning a corner.

"You are such a dumb brute!" Kareena shouted at his back before gathering up her skirts to more effectively catch up.

"I never claimed I wasn't," Articus replied without stopping.

"He seemed rather nice when I met him," I shouted ahead, hoping to reassure and ease some of the tension. But Articus did not so much as hesitate a step in his determination, and Kareena only shook her head while giving me a pleading glance over her shoulder. Decidedly I would continue to keep my mouth shut.

"Brother, I beg of you, stop!" Kareena pleaded, just before Articus paused in front of a heavy wooden door and kicked it open upon entrance.

I peered around the doorframe to see several shirtless cadets with wooden poles in their hands stare in shock as Articus yanked one from the closest soldier's hands and bellowed to the rafters, "Dean Hempshire, I've come to defend my sister's honor!" I tried not to laugh at Kareena's dramatically mortified expression as she all but melted from embarrassment upon the polished wood flooring. Her face grew pinker by the second from beneath her hands.

A familiar form broke from formation upon Articus's call. Sweat glistened on his chest and furrowed brow. In one last desperate effort, Kareena tugged at the back of Articus's shirt. His jacket had been abandoned some ways down the hall.

"Don't do this," she hissed.

"Art, what are you—" Dean began to ask.

"If you have any honor, you will join me outside, now!" Articus barked.

Dean looked between the two siblings with confusion before understanding settled in. His expression grew serious as he curtly nodded at Articus and followed him out. His booted feet echoed in the tense, still room for just a breath before a burst of cadets discarded their rods to follow behind. Some announced a fight as they paraded down the marble halls. Their voices boomed down the corridor, while others murmured amongst themselves, betting on who would prevail: the fierce lieutenant or the weapons apprentice. I couldn't help but roll my eyes at the ridiculous dramatics, and though Kareena was seeming to take the event quite seriously, biting her nails as we shuffled behind the hoard, my own shoulders shook with silent laughter.

From the windows of the dorms and library, faces pressed against glass to get a better look at the training field below, while Kareena and I stood on a stone bench at the back of the tight circle of bodies. Articus brought his cane down with a force driven entirely by anger. A loud *crack* caused me and several others to flinch as Dean's block snapped his staff in two. Dean tossed the pieces aside.

"We were going to tell you when she was ready," Dean panted. "I was only respecting her wishes." Articus discarded his cane as well. "If it were up to me, I would have confessed my feelings immediately after our first kiss." I cringed at Dean's words. As expected, they only aided in angering Articus more and he charged recklessly at his opponent.

The two grappled, arms linked at an impasse.

"You kissed my fucking sister?" Articus growled. Dean must have had a death wish, for his lips tugged at the corner in a smug smirk.

"Technically she kissed me." His smirk was swiftly wiped away with Articus's fist. Dean stepped back and rubbed his jaw.

"Alright, I probably deserved that but listen to—"

Articus had collected the discarded cane in the seconds it took Dean to recoup from the blow and used it to deliver another to the back of Dean's knees. A move I had seen before between the pair, bringing Dean to collapse on all fours. The crowd's hoots and cheers grew louder, making it harder to hear the exchange between the two. My ears were only able to glean a word or two here and there as they continued to tussle about.

"*My friend*" and "*backstabbing*," were all I could make out. Beside me Kareena clutched my arm just as fiercely as she clenched her jaw.

"She is a woman now, Articus." I heard over the chaos of the crowd. Kareena groaned and nuzzled her face into my shoulder in an attempt to hide her embarrassment. "And I consider it a blessing she has chosen me!"

I rose on tiptoes, trying to see over the heads that blocked our view.

From between the gaps of moving bodies I could see Dean had somehow gained the upper hand. Articus's lip was swollen and blood was speckled upon his shirt. Dean gripped the two broken pieces of his staff in each hand so tightly the dark skin around his knuckles lightened. The crowd roared and clustered together tighter, blocking my view once again.

"Alise," Kareena's voice muffled into my sleeve. "Let's go. I can't stand to witness another second."

In the emptiness of the vast colonnade, while the crowd bellowed from beyond the stone walls, I couldn't help but wonder what made Kareena have a change of heart when it came to relationships, especially with a man from the Academy. It felt like just days ago that we had scoffed together at the ridiculousness of men and when Kareena confided in me that she would rather pursue her own ambitions than be a bride.

"Kareena, if it's not too bold, may I ask what swayed your feelings toward affection for Mr. Hempshire?" I cautioned. I didn't want her to think I was at all doubting the genuineness of their love, for it was apparent to even one such as myself, who had little to no experience with romantic relationships.

"Well, if you must know, Dean and I have always been friends, being that he's Articus's best and truly only friend here at the Academy. And he has been here for nearly as long as we have, as well as his similarity in age to Articus. I guess you could say their friendship was a given, especially when you consider their shared affinity for weapons, and since I had no other young girls my age to play with, I naturally just tagged along." A small smile quirked the corner of her lips at the recollection of what must have been a cherished childhood memory, and I was glad I could distract her from the chaos in the training yard.

"Honestly, it wasn't until the beginning of the new year that I started to see Dean in a different light, and since we were already such good friends, I guess you could say emotions developed rather swiftly between us." The apples of her cheeks pinked slightly with her confession.

Opening my mouth to give some form of reassurance I was abruptly cut off by the cheers of victory, and moans of disappointment approaching behind us, through the Academy colonnade.

"I thought for sure he had him," one cadet said to another as he reluctantly dropped a few coins into an outstretched beret. Clearly losing out on a wager placed between the two friends turned opponents. Their conversation disappeared around the corner with them.

"That was brutal," another said as a group of three others passed by. He paled as he rubbed at his face.

"There's a reason they call him the Wolf of the Colony," his friend said before throwing a quick side eyed glance our way.

"I meant for my pocket book," the distraught one replied. "I bet fifty pounds on Hempshire."

His friends erupted with laughter, as one playfully punched him in the shoulder before calling him an idiot.

I looked over my shoulder in time to see two bleeding fools leaning against each other. Idiotic smiles on their faces that did, in no way, reflect the tone of the fight that had just occurred. *Who beats their best friend bloody and then embraces and laughs about it a moment later?* Men are truly beasts in human skins. Kareena ran to Dean and looked him up and down, taking in every cut and bruise.

"Did you have to rough him up so badly?" Kareena chided at her brother. Her hands continued to explore Dean's body. "Boys and your immature rituals." I thought I heard her mutter as she continued to look Dean over with a trained eye.

"I'm fine, I'm fine, Kareena . . ." Dean gripped Kareena's wrists to pause her fussing. "We have worked it out and he has given his blessing." Dean beamed down at her.

Kareena's mouth gaped open as her head darted toward her brother—his body straight and stoic with all seriousness.

"Truly?" she asked.

Articus curtly nodded and Kareena erupted with a squeal of joy before throwing her arms around Dean and kissing him firmly, almost taking him down as he stumbled and clutched her firmly against himself in return. My heart warmed at the sight. Kareena had secured her happiness and they had both fought to keep it, in their own ways.

Giving the adoring couple some privacy, I turned away just in time to see Articus's shadow bend around the corner.

Chapter Forty

ARTICUS LOUNGED IN A worn, wingback as I had seen him do many times before in the quaint attic office—our solitude from the Academy and all its bustle beyond. This time though, no book lay waiting in his hands. Instead, a handkerchief was pressed to his bleeding lip. He looked adorably vulnerable in his rumpled and bloodied shirt and his hair mushed wildly about. With him utterly disarmed, it somehow made it easier to speak than it had been in the days since he left. Since . . .

"You completely humiliated your sister. Are you truly that upset about her and Dean being together?" Though my words were a reprimand, my tone was gentle.

"I felt betrayed, yes." He removed the cloth from his lip to examine it. I closed the space between us and plucked the handkerchief from his raw and bloodied hand. With no other chairs in which to sit, I knelt on my knees beside him and gently blotted his bloody knuckles. He flinched at my touch, or perhaps in surprise at the demur gesture, I could not tell. His pine-forest eyes widened as I looked up, signaling him to continue.

They shuttered as he looked away to the only small window in the space.

"He is my best friend—my only friend, truly. And I believed there were no secrets between us."

I cautiously hummed in response, for fear that if I spoke too soon, he would retreat back into himself.

"To be honest though, I'm glad it is him that she has chosen for herself rather than the general marrying her off for political gains," he confessed.

"She's free in that way," I caught myself saying under my breath. Articus ceased my tending to his hands, removing the cloth from my fingers and clutched my palm in his. With a coaxing tug I rose and fell into his lap as he brought my hand to his lips.

"I know that must be important to you, freedom." His lips glossed over my knuckles, sending a shudder through me. All I could do was nod, forgetting what all I needed to speak with him about.

"I missed you," he whispered against my skin. "Did you think of me much while I was gone?" An eyebrow raised while his mouth tilted up to one side, in a teasing expression. He bit down lightly on a digit causing me to squirm in his lap and tug my hand away. He swiftly captured it back and pulled me closer against him so his lips could tickle the ridge of my ear.

"I thought of you often and relentlessly. At first it was insufferable—distracting even." Fingers grazed the sensitive skin of my neck in equally soothing and jarring strokes. "I found it a nuisance at first, but then I found myself seeking out my memories of you. Of your face when I touched you—tasted you." I shuttered as he nipped at my earlobe and immediately pressed a tender kiss against it.

"But it just made me even more miserable in your absence." Articus swiveled my head to face toward his and without hesitation pressed a tender, and equally consuming, kiss against my lonely lips. I leaned into him and my hands gripped the collar of his shirt like a life raft as his lips seared through me.

For reasons unbeknownst to myself, my brain thought it excellent timing to bring up images of Articus with the dark haired, doe-eyed girl. With the thought of him kissing her as he did me, I jolted back, breaking our connection. An expression of hurt and concern creased his brow.

"What's wrong?"

"This was a mistake," I sputtered hastily.

"A mistake? Why do you say that?" His brow furrowed even further, gaze growing cold.

"What about Sabrina?" I asked while crossing my arms and closing myself off. I wouldn't be his secret, or do Sabrina the disservice of being his. No. I'd quite had it with men who thought they could do as they pleased with any and all women with no consequences.

"What about her?" was all he said. His scowl seared unmercifully into me. It was enough to almost make me want to back down. Almost.

"I saw you two together, hidden in the shadows of one of the alcoves." I made to leave his lap.

"And what is it you think you saw?" Firm hands grasped my hips and pulled me back down. His refusal clear. He would not make this easy.

"I saw you whispering into her hair." I worried my lip with unease. His hands became a blaring distraction on my hips. "Her arms were wrapped around your neck and she kissed you." And though I technically didn't see her lips meet his, a fire grew in my belly all the same. It gave me the conviction I needed and strengthened my resolve.

"Did she now?" He raised his hand to cover a smile. A single dimple revealed, giving away how utterly unconcerned he was about this all.

"Yes!" I proclaimed with more certainty than I truly had. "Is she your lover?" I rushed out before I could think better of it.

He paused for a moment. His eyes strayed to a vacant corner of the room. "I'll admit, we had a romantic relationship at one time." My spine went rigid. "Many years ago, when we were much younger. When I was a reckless and angry boy, and she was alone and out on her own for the first time." His expression cleared of all humor. "But it is probably not as you think and I can say for certain, you did not, see her kiss me, with your own eyes. In that, you are mistaken. What you stumbled upon was nothing more than a desperate plea for forgiveness and a conversation between platonic friends."

That only firmed my grip on my crossed arms. "Forgiveness for what?"

Articus sighed and ran a hand through his disheveled hair. "It really isn't your concern."

Squirming in his lap, I attempted to rise again. "Then perhaps I tell you I don't believe —"

He tugged me by both arms back down. "Sit," he emphasized. "I will tell you anyway, because I trust you to keep what I say between us." I froze. Shocked at his willingness to share. I nodded for him to continue.

"A close friend of hers has found herself in a compromising position for a woman in this realm. She was wooed by one of the Elites and then abandoned after becoming pregnant. Sabrina thought to help her friend by stealing the medicines needed to terminate the pregnancy from the infirmary." I felt my eyes grow wide.

"When the blame for the missing items fell upon Kareena, Sabrina felt immense guilt and came to me to confess what she had done for the sake of her friend in need. Though her guilt was unnecessary and misplaced, she did nothing wrong." I thought of how she dropped the dish that morning in the kitchen. It was when Ms. Hazel and I spoke of Dante and the Graduation Ball.

"Who was the man who abandoned her friend?" I asked.

"She wouldn't say."

"He doesn't deserve their protection, whoever he is," I muttered with disgust in the pit of my stomach.

"I agree, Little Fox." His hand clasped my cheek and his thumb smoothed over my frown, melting it away with each swipe. My gaze drew back to his. I felt foolish for assuming the worst of Articus, yet again. "Do you still think letting me kiss you was a mistake?"

I shook my head as my cheeks surely pinkened from recollection of the last time we were alone in his office. Articus chuckled low and deep at the sight of it and didn't hesitate to pull my mouth down upon his.

This time there were no doubts, or thoughts of others holding me back, while his lips glossed across mine. My fingers made swift work of his shirt buttons. They were greedy to touch the plains of his chest and trace the ridges of his abdomen while his own hands kneaded my waist and hips. They undulated instinctually against him in return. Relishing the power and control he gave as I controlled the pace from atop, I parted my swollen lips in response to his tongue's gentle request to enter and was rewarded with lush, limb tingling, strokes against my own. My hand desperately clung to his shoulder, while the other clutched silky hairs at the nape of his neck, beckoning him to give and take more.

"God, you're so beautiful like this." He smiled against my lips. His hands gripped my back side and lifted me swiftly with him. My legs instinctively wrapped around his waist as my arms clung to his neck until he laid me down reverently on the same chaise that occupied many of my fantasies. In my mind, I squealed with anticipation while outwardly, all I could do was marvel at the desire darkening Articus's deep and hungry stare. That I could inspire such a reaction within him, emboldened me to sit up and slide his shirt from off his shoulders. A trail of kisses given to each inch of exposed flesh as he uttered my name with a shuttered breath. His fingers grazed my hairline and stroked the still-tender lump on my scalp, causing me to hiss involuntarily.

"What is this?" he questioned as I shot my head up. My mind stumbling to put together a lie, an excuse, anything.

Sensing my hesitation, his brow furrowed as he made to part my hair from the tender spot. Shame chilled every nerve ending and smothered every trace ember of desire, at the thought of what he would discover.

He noticed the shiver that rushed through me as I made to pull back. Noticed the way my hands tugged at my clothing, as though they did not cover me thoroughly enough. He noticed everything. His eyes scanned my face for answers before he asked, "What happened?"

I had never taken the time to build a plausible story. Never imagined he would be this physically close to me again, to need one.

"Nothing," I weakly lied as I grasped at any explanation my addled mind could conjure up.

Articus gripped my arm before I could protest and pulled my sleeve up to reveal a bruised wrist.

"I can't fucking believe . . ." he muttered at the sight of the night I longed to forget. I opened my mouth to say more but words betrayed me. As if he knew exactly where to look next, Articus slid my skirt up over my knees. I scrambled to shove the material back down before he could get a good look at the bruises on my knees and shins. But I was too late.

"Tell me the truth, Alise," he demanded.

"I fell."

"The whole truth."

"I tripped and fell," I replied defiantly, crossing my arms in an attempt to mask my growing shame and unease. My eyes were unable to meet his and they found an item on the shelf beyond to burrow into. Terrified he would see the unshed tears threatening to make an appearance, I hoped he wouldn't read the rest of the truth on my face.

"Whoever it is you are trying to protect, I can tell you, is not worthy of the favor." I knew he wasn't. How fervently I knew he wasn't. Dante wasn't worthy of a damn thing, let alone my time or protection. It was my own pride that was getting in the way. What happened was humiliating. Especially after all the months of training Articus poured into me. All the effort he made to prevent something just like this from happening. My vision blurred. I wasn't ready yet, to face the ugliness of that night. I had decided to forget it all in order to continue living with myself. In fact, I considered myself lucky that I got away when I did. Knew that even worse things could have happened had Dante not been interrupted by the random passersby, who unknowingly granted me salvation that night.

Articus tipped my chin up gently to face him. "You can tell me, Little Fox. Whatever happened wasn't your fault." The affirmation cracked the shell I encased around my heart. Was it the truth? Didn't I know that it was? Perhaps. But for some reason it didn't feel real until he said it. And I had no idea until that moment how much I needed to hear him say so.

A dam cracked far and wide as tears and bottled-up emotions spilled out uncontrollably, washing away any remaining hold I had on them.

"I'm so sorry," I pleaded. "I tried to fight him off, just as you taught me, but that stupid, beautiful gown made it impossible and—" I stopped abruptly as his eyes widened with understanding and then narrowed again. He looked away, seething with disappointment and rage.

"It was the night of the ball," he stated more than asked. Raw anger glazed his eyes and red rose up his collar.

"I'm fine really. There were people coming down the hall and it scared him off before . . . before anything else could happen." I trailed off, realizing every word only made his temper worse. Fingers twisted in my skirt and I bit my lip. Though I tried to be as vague as possible for his sake, it was also for my own. The thought of what Dante almost did, what he tried to take from me, drunk or not, made me feel sick to my stomach. I pressed a hand on the twisting knot that grew painfully inside my abdomen as nausea rolled through me.

"It's okay. Honestly, I'm—"

"Stop," he commanded, calm and sharp as a blade. "Not another word." Articus bit down on a curse before rising and storming out of the room. The wooden door creaked in protest to the forceful slam as it shut behind him.

I didn't have the strength to chase after him, to try to further explain. I couldn't even muster the will to stand as I collapsed to my knees and stared at the vacant wall. Shame and disgust assaulted me again and again. Wave after wave threatened to break me further, to crumble me into a heaping mess of shattered pieces. Something I feared I would not be able to piece back together, again.

Articus must have been as disgusted and disappointed with myself as I was. And that was the most debilitating truth of all. I couldn't stand to endure his pity. For him to see me as weak and helpless despite all his efforts. A lost cause at worst. Trembling hands wiped away burning tears before they could fall. A different kind of beast tightened its claws around my throat for letting myself be so affected, so hurt and vulnerable at the hands of another. Determined not to become a broken puddle of tears, left discarded, ever again, I rose to my feet and paced across the small attic office like a caged panther. Hands gripped my hair at the root as my sorrow grew into burning anger. Each step became more ladened than the next as if I could smash all my wild emotions beneath my feet. A tension twisted so relentlessly in my body I felt I would shatter if I didn't scream or fight or . . .

Grabbing the closest thing within my reach, I blindly threw it across the room with a primal shriek. The ink pot shattered, leaving a black splatter across the once blank wall. A misshapen, gaping dark void glistened and winked back at me. A miniature replica of the star strung portal that deposited me into this hell.

Chapter Forty One

I HAD MY FILL of boys. They only wanted to chase, trap, and consume. Once their game of cat and mouse is over, and the prey has surrendered their body to their insatiable hunger then the hunter becomes bored and is off again in search of sweeter, fresher meat with no remorse held for leaving a broken, used-up heart in their wake.

Standing before my reflection I adamantly appeared more hunter than prey. All pretense of softness had been exchanged for the sharp cut of a black-fitted jacket over a crisp, white blouse. I refused to surrender myself to anyone. I would let them believe I played at their game, unbeknownst to them that I added rules of my own. They would pursue me until they decided I was too difficult and gave up. If they call me a prude, a tease, a whore, then so be it. It doesn't matter because in the end I knew I won, even if it was by default and my heart and soul still belonged to me. The mantra poured into the cracks and sealed like a resin over the wretched, beating organ. I pinned my hair into a simple bun and took in the black and white contrasting form I had become—one I felt more comfortable in than any gown. Not that I didn't love my new collection of dresses I had required since arriving, but today I felt like making a different kind of statement and this one, donning my frame, shouted it loud and clear without me having to waste a single breath.

I was not to be fucked with.

There were times I was, in fact, called all those demeaning things and then some. Usually after I rejected unwanted advances, tried to turn someone down gently, or even ignored them altogether.

Little bitch.

I'll take you right here like the slut you are.

A knock at the door broke me from the cutting memories and I opened the door to our suite to find a demure looking girl, holding a small tray with a letter on it. "Message for you, ma'am," she said, as she gave a small dip at the knee.

"Thank you." I retrieved the folded parchment and gave her a small nod in response. After reading the few short lines, I huffed a disbelieving sound.

"Please notify the other messengers that I will no longer be accepting missives from this sender," I requested before storming off towards the archives.

The egos of men are so large, yet so very fragile. Why was I so foolish to believe things would be any different in this realm?

"You're quite right," Articus stated, bringing my focus to him. Had I said that last part aloud?

He leaned against the wall across from our usual table, in the privacy of the shadowed nook. Arms crossed as he observed me. "Only a boy would be so reckless with something so precious as your heart." Determination lit his gaze.

I knew it to be true, in some minuscule way I couldn't properly grasp and keep hold of. But years of experience told me otherwise. How is one to believe themselves to hold any worth when the world has constantly shown them otherwise?

"If you want to be chased, then it would be an honor, undeserving to most men, to pursue. If they were wise to see your value, they would play whatever game you constructed, for as long as you wanted." My eyes were drawn to his fingers that mindlessly traced the spine of a book as phantom ones danced along mine. "And if you ever decided they were worthy of you—and I mean all of you—not just your body but your heart and soul as well, Alise, then they should consider themselves blessed." His voice tapered off to that of a soft almost growl as his fingers stilled on a tome. I looked up from the entrancing dance of his digits to see him staring back. Unabashed. Unwavering. Steady and sure of himself. A part of me knew, as much as I wanted to deny it, that he wholeheartedly believed every word he spoke. I hated how it frightened me and thrilled me in equal parts.

Truthfully, I didn't hate it at all.

Articus wielded his words like a knife that mercilessly cut away at lies. In other moods, his speech dripped like honey from his lips and beckoned me to taste and I never knew which to expect. Sometimes, such as now, it was a bit of both.

"You truly believe women are worth such an effort?" I couldn't help but ask. My fickle mind's addiction for reassurance, reared its ugly head.

"The right one, yes," he replied. His verdant stare was unrelenting.

"How would one know she was worth it all?" My hands and heart stilled, reside to wait and receive more.

"A true man knows when he sees her." There was a sense of complete, and all-consuming seriousness in his tone, his merciless stare, even in his posture. I was a student again in the lecture hall, absorbing and digesting every word, as I was presented with new and perspective-altering information.

A long, tense stretch of silence was snapped like the delicate stem of a flower.

"Speaking of boys with delicate temperaments," I said as I fished around in my pocket for the note I had crumbled into a lump earlier.

Articus crossed his arms over his chest and shook his head as he refused to touch the note I had received, seemingly written in haste, from Dante. It said, in the shortest of terms, that he wished to speak with me in order to formally apologize for his actions of late.

"It's the least he can do," Articus stated as though he already knew exactly what the note contained. "I'll go with you."

"No," I snapped. He raised an eyebrow at my swift, curt reply. "Please. It would only humiliate me further and I want to handle this myself." He opened his mouth as though to protest.

"You've already done enough," I said, interrupting his thought with a smile I hoped reflected my gratefulness towards him. "I deserve an apology and it can't just be because you're standing over my shoulder glaring at him."

"If that is what you wish," he agreed, to my surprise. "But take this." He reached into a brown, leather messenger bag and handed me the hilt of a sheathed dagger. "Don't hesitate to stab the Elitist pig if he so much as touches you." I smothered a chuckle at his absurdness, knowing he was quite serious, as my shoulders shook. "I'm surprised it's not a gun," I managed between breathy chuckles.

"I would prefer it, but I've witnessed first-hand how much more proficient you are with a blade." A small hitch tilted his lips as he handed me the leather sheath. "Even plastic ones." The mysterious dimple appeared with satisfaction.

I accepted the knife with steady hands. If it would give him, and honestly myself, peace of mind to carry it, then so be it. I doubted I would actually need to make use of it though. Dante was, after all, drunk when he attacked me. Based on the time we had spent together before, I assumed his actions were out of character and he wouldn't have done what he had if he was of sober mind. Though I would never give him the chance to do something like that again, and after this conversation with him was over, I planned to never speak to him ever again, as well.

"Well, I have to admit I'm surprised that you actually came." Dante rubbed the back of his neck, grinning sheepishly from the doorway.

"You wanted to talk?" I replied curtly from the hall, just outside his dorm room. He paused, taking in the pants and blouse I was wearing. Unusual for most women here to wear unless riding horses, I had gotten many a look from passersby, including Articus when he thought I wouldn't notice, and Clouden who nearly dropped a glass vial, at my appearance in his lab this morning. They wisely both choose not to say a word about my unusual choice of attire.

"Yes, of course. Please come in." Seeming to remember himself, Dante stammered as he held the door to his room open for me.

"I'd rather not," I said, crossing my arms over my chest.

He sighed deeply. "Oh dear, how I have ruined things." He looked up from his low-hanging head. Those stone-gray eyes peered through the dark, thick lashes I used to pine over. Now, everything about him repulsed me. His once handsome features were now too perfectly constructed and lacked originality. His once charming words were now too sweet and shallow for my taste.

"I'm so humiliated by my previous behavior, Miss Fox. Could you do me this one last underserved kindness and let us speak in private?" He gave me his most charming and pleading smile.

I took stock of the apparent wounds on his face and it brought me some small, sick satisfaction that he hadn't been left unscathed after all. A bandage lay across his nose, most likely from my head butting into his face, that night. I hope it at least cracked if not broke from the impact. I also noticed a cut puckered red and swollen on his lip and a greenish tint of a developing bruise around his eye. The latter two could not possibly be from my doing. Could they?

Reluctantly I stepped inside, as Dante closed the door behind him and I heard the soft click of a lock. My stomach plummeted with immediate regret. I would let him say his apologies and then get out as quickly as possible.

Feeling grateful for the knife in my boot I asked, "What is it you feel you need to say to me?"

Dante's sheepish grin suddenly turned savage. The beaten humiliated boy, now a cocky, arrogant Elite as his entire demeanor shifted before my eyes—a wolf shedding its sheep skin. Or in Dante's case, a snake.

"I am sorry events transpired the way they did the other night. I will admit I perhaps drank a bit too much and became . . . clumsy. I did truly believe you were being playful at the time, though." It was the worst apology anyone had ever given me. Was he seriously apologizing for being sloppy? Anger flared inside me. The heat from the flame fueled my resolve.

"There was nothing playful about what you did, Dante—drunk or not," I said as my hands balled into fists.

"I must have misunderstood you," he continued. "See, Brenton shared so much about his debauchery with you that I couldn't help but assume . . ." Blood roared in my ears.

Brenton.

He knew Brenton? What did Brenton tell him?

Dante moved closer, looking down at me through lowered lashes. Surely, all the blood drained from my face and gave me away. After looking down on me a moment longer he stepped aside to reveal the contents spread across his bed. There were photos of me that I clearly was not aware were being taken at the time, as well as a notebook, left open to showcase scribbled pages of text, lying like a crime scene upon his sheets.

"Have a closer look," Dante beckoned, gesturing to the offering he wished for me to poke and prod at for proof of its authenticity.

I collapsed to my knees and started rummaging through the photos, my hands shaking as I lifted a picture of James and I. I had no idea how much I truly missed his smile and his presence until that moment, and I had to swallow to choke back the knot in my throat. The last thing I wanted was to be vulnerable in front of Dante. Stealing a quick glance over my shoulder I found Dante looking rather bored at his fingernails, before slipping the photo that contained James in my pocket.

"Every time he came back from his little trips away, he would write in that godforsaken journal of his and quickly hide it away if anyone so much as glanced at it." As he spoke, I leafed through pages, catching sentences here and there that mentioned me, some truths and some lies. Every word revealed the past between us, and the delusions he conjured up as well.

"One night when he hadn't yet returned, I snuck into his room and finally got my hands on it. You can believe my shock when I found those pictures as well. Do all First Realm citizens dress so poorly? I've never seen such odd fashion."

The words struck and venom paralyzed.

First Realm.

He knew.

Chapter Forty Two

MY FISTED HANDS TREMBLED as I rose on less than stable footing. What, all, did the journal entail? It didn't matter. He knew enough. He knew too much.

"However, it seems you First Realm girls are far less inhibited, compared to our own righteously rigid females." His tone, which indicated a sense of entitled claim of ownership over said-girls of the Second Realm, further curdled my blood.

"I think you're confused Mr. Da Romano, whoever that is in those photos, although she bears a striking resemblance is not me. I told you I'm from Pellion.

I'm here as a ward to Professor Clouden," I insisted, trying my best to keep my words from stumbling on the shaking ground beneath my feet.

"Right, right." He scratched his chin in mock speculation. "Speaking of Pellion, when I took you to the Three Birds Tearoom, you said you had never been to or seen such a place. That is quite curious considering my family owns all three of the locations, including the one in Pellion, Miss Fox." My stomach dropped as my mind stumbled to counter what he was insinuating. "Quite the attraction, I'm told, the jewel of the town."

"I didn't frequent town much. My family kept to themselves." Sometimes it was easier to lie when you told the truth about someone else.

"I contacted my family in Pellion," he countered immediately, as he approached me, causing me to step back several inches until the back of my knees met the frame of his bed.

"The Riccis claimed to have never heard of you, let alone the Foxes." My heart raced in my chest. I opened my mouth to counter his claims to deny everything, to say something, but I could see the certainty in his eyes. He made myself and the whole room feel smaller as he closed in. He didn't give me a chance to speak before reaching around me to flip open a page in the journal.

"Read it," he demanded.

When my eyes took in the words written on the page I wanted to vomit and cry all at once. To fight and rage against it all and to flee until I was nothing but dust. Anything to get away from the sight of my name written over and over again on those pages. Line after line of "Alise Fox" written in a desperate and possessive hand. The letters indented into the paper with a firm press the further they trailed down.

"As you can see, Miss Fox," he emphasized, "there's no denying it. You are the girl in the photos, you are not from where you say you are, but are, in fact, from the First Realm." His words were another kind of attack. I ran out of lies. Ran out of excuses. I found myself floundering like a fish but nothing would come out.

"Entering the First Realm is highly illegal, Miss Fox. Not to mention the many inter-dimensional laws that were broken by smuggling a First Realm citizen into another realm. And I think I know exactly who helped you get here." With those last threatening words my heart froze over, as cold as his silver stare. I couldn't believe I once thought him handsome. That I didn't see the snake behind that perfect smile. Cold calm washed over me, making my posture firm as a statue.

"I found my way here myself," I said without an ounce of feeling. Every wild emotion herded into a pen I slammed and locked shut.

"But see, I don't believe you, and it would certainly be in both you and Articus's best interest if you convinced me otherwise." Confirming his implications, I didn't hesitate.

"What do you want?" I asked coldly, ready to do anything I needed to keep Articus out of this mess Brenton and I created. If I were to get caught, I refused to drag him down with me. Unlike myself, he had a future and a sister who loved him. I couldn't take that from him and I couldn't let Kareena lose someone so precious to her again.

Dante inhaled deeply as he circled before me. "No girl here has ever been up to par with my somewhat, unique tastes, so you can imagine how exceedingly jealous I was that Brenton Drexar, of all people, had found someone like you. And in the forbidden First Realm, none the less. I think the fool had it in his mind that he was in love with you. He was quite possessive," he purred the word and it took everything in me not to be sick on his boots as he grazed a knuckle down my cheek. My head jerked away from his touch. "In fact, when he didn't return, from one of his little trips, I figured it meant he ran off with you for good."

The echoes of gun fire and a flash of dead eyes, crying tears of blood, reverberated in my mind, rattling what little stability I had left.

"You're confused Dante. I was never—"

"His journal is quite specific in what you two partook in. I must say he could have had a future as a romance novelist the way he lavished on about your sexual encounters."

I swallowed back bile at the thought of the fantasies, delusions, falsities that must be written on those pages, and what Dante's mind conjured up upon reading them. Rage blossomed like a slow blooming rose in my chest as Dante continued rambling on.

"I thought I was cursed to forever only bed these dull girls for the rest of my life—to suffer knowing something better was out there, just out of reach. That was, until you showed up." A devilish smirk carved his mouth. He eyed me like a pleasantly-wrapped gift that had fallen into his lap. The filth of his stare coated my skin like oil that would take several searing hot showers to cleanse.

"And with Articus Desaius of all fucking people and no Brenton in sight. I could only assume then that the worse had befallen my poor little colleague, and Articus's unpleasant visit the other day only confirmed my suspicions in his involvement." His stare pinned me down. I became a moth on a display board to later frame and hang like a trophy.

"Articus has nothing—"

"However," Dante drawled, interrupting me once again. The walls were closing in and desperation filled my chest to bursting. Tension strung me tightly through my limbs.

"I could be convinced otherwise," he offered, proving further, just how much of a snake he truly was. The poison in his words did their work to burn a path through me, so intense I could barely see through the glaze of rage.

"Get to it already," I hissed through clenched teeth. My hand flexed at my thigh, ready to strike. I quickly glanced over Dante's shoulder, at the door that was, indeed, locked.

"I think you know sweetheart," he drawled as he further cornered me. My calves touched the bed but as he pressed in, I refused to collapse upon it.

"Give me a taste of that First Realm charm Brenton wrote, so endearingly, about. Feed this desire in me the Second Realm girls cannot satiate and when I'm satisfied, when I'm convinced . . ." He pushed me down on the mattress with a commanding shove.

"Only then will I forget all about your illegal origins and Articus's role in it." He leaned over me and purred the words in my ear.

I sat up quickly, making myself less vulnerable. Dante grabbed my knees and yanked them apart, spreading my legs before him. He whispered as he continued with his demands. "If you ride me hard enough sweetheart, I may just forget about my missing friend as well. Deal?"

My chest tightened. He was asking for more than he realized. He was bartering for far too much of me. Whatever Brenton's journal said was obviously a lie and extremely exaggerated and I was drowning in the weight of it. Dante couldn't, wouldn't see that. He already had an image in his mind of who I was long before he ever met me. It was sealed in him like that sick desire he had spoken of, and I knew he would never let me go. No amount I gave over to him would be enough. He would never be satisfied because I wasn't the girl in that journal. I wasn't who Brenton or Dante thought I was, just as they were not who I thought either. Dante would always hold the truth of my origin, or Articus's suspected involvement, over my head like dangling bait on a line, to get what he wanted from me.

Both Brenton and Dante turned out to be more a pair of snakes than I could have ever imagined. One an insecure, boasting, liar. The other a selfish, greedy, spoiled boy who was never told, "no."

Until now.

"No," I relished my response with a smile.

"Pardon?" he said, taken aback.

"I said no deal." Taking advantage of his shock I leaned back and kicked him square in the groin—just as he deserved. I leapt off the bed and ran for the door as he groaned, doubled over in pain.

My fingers fumbled at the lock as Dante tried to muster up enough strength to stand up right. As I went to pull the knob, a hand grasped my hair and yanked my head back away from the door. He threw me down on the floor and I quickly scrambled away from him until my back hit a wall. My hands reached for the wall to stand but his boot came down and kicked me in the lungs, forcing all the air from my chest. Taking advantage of his upper hand he yanked me back up on my feet by my hair. A yelp of pain escaped my lips. He then threw me towards a table and smashed my face against it so that I was bent over at the waist and once again vulnerable.

Through the panic I tried to think, to remember what Articus taught me about getting out of the hold of someone who could easily overpower me. Suddenly, I remembered the concealed weapon I carried in my boot and reached down, past the table. My fingers flexed and wiggled to no avail. It was too far from my grasp to reach the hilt.

Dante leaned over, pressing into me and I didn't hesitate. I reached behind me and dragged my nails down the side of his neck. He groaned but only budged slightly. Yet, it was all the space I needed to roll out from under him and connect my booted foot to his stomach, using the leverage of the table to launch more added force than I could deliver alone. He stumbled back, hands coming to his midsection as he groaned. Blood dribbled down his neck and onto his collar. Without hesitation, I ran to the door, throwing it wide before running full out. Never once did I dare to look back.

It felt too easy this time.

I couldn't help but feel as though any moment Dante would reach me, and haul me back to his room, kicking and screaming. I was certain of this and it fueled every hazardous, pounding step. Not caring who saw me or the blood on my shirt from Dante's neck, I dashed around a shadowed corner and finally paused to catch my breath. My lungs protested with each cutting inhale and my heart, hammered against my ribcage, begging to be freed. After several moments with my ears attuned to any sounds of approach, I realized Dante was not pursuing me, or perhaps had lost my trail.

The light trickle of relief was short lived as halfway to my room a shadow of dread overtook me, swallowing whole. What had I done? Dante was going to talk now that I refused him. Tell whatever Elite ties he had about Brenton missing, my arrival from the First Realm and worse, who brought me here. Though he asked for too much, more than I could ever give without becoming a broken, empty shell, it would be for Articus. Articus who so selflessly did the unthinkable for me. He unleashed that monster his father created inside of him to protect me and I couldn't even give Dante my flesh in exchange. One after another anxious thoughts bombarded my rattled mind.

Would they put the pieces together and discover what Articus had done back in the First Realm? And if they did, what would be his punishment? I knew. An eye for an eye. A life for a life taken, seemed to be the perspective of justice in this realm. He already risked so much by bringing me here just for me to make a mess of this intended refuge. And what of Kareena? She would be destroyed if Articus was so brutally ripped from her life. No. I couldn't risk letting that happen. I couldn't let Dante reveal what he knew and what he thought he did. But I couldn't very well turn around and plead for him to reinstate his previous offer. Besides I knew, in the end, I could never meet his terms, could never live up to the delusion Brenton painted of me. Even if I agreed to be what he wanted, to play the part, it would not be long for him to go back on his half of the *arrangement.* To go back on his word to keep quiet. One could never trust the dealings of a serpent.

I changed course. There was only one person I could trust to help me. Who more than likely, had the means and connections to help me. Who already knew the truth.

Crashing like wreckage into Clouden's office I tried to catch my breath, grateful to see his scowling glare at my intrusion. He took one look at my tousled hair, the desperation on my face, and the blood under my nails and rose from his desk, his annoyance fading to concern.

"I'm so sorry," I huffed out between panting breaths. "I didn't know where else to go and I . . . I have to protect him. I have to protect Articus." Tears that had built up in my eyes, threatened to fall as I could not choke them down any longer. The pent-up emotions shattered the confines I locked them in and ran rampant inside me.

Clouden swiftly scanned the landing before closing the door behind him. The sound of the lock clicking in place broke me. The weight of everything crashed into me and upon me, and I sank into its drowning waters.

"Dante," I started, trying to explain through short quick breaths. "He knows. He's going to tell them everything and . . ." My body trembled; limbs turned ridged. "I couldn't, I couldn't give him what he wanted. I—" I was hysterical as Clouden pulled me into his warm embrace. Crumbling, I cried into his chest. Stained his shirt with my tears and Dante's, still-fresh blood.

"Please," I begged, shoulders shaking as I sobbed uncontrollably. "What do I do?"

His hand stroked my back like a father would soothe his child. In a hushed and calming voice, he spoke against the top of my head, "Tell me everything."

J.O. ELLIS

Chapter Forty Three

ARTICUS

WHERE IS MY LITTLE FOX?

My knee bounced from below my mahogany desk, and my pen tapped restlessly in an insistent rhythm. My eyes scanned the reports before me for what felt like the hundredth, useless time. Letters melted and molded together. They abandoned their strict formations on the parchment to form the curve of her lips. Periods and commas made up the freckles of her pale shoulders and nose. I should have been ecstatic for the victory of my brothers—of rebel forces successfully holding the Austria-Slovenia border against the Colony. But even a triumph of that nature could not hold my attention. The enthusiasm fell flat in my chest, instead of the swelling pressure it should have been. The fruits of our labors tasted dull in comparison to the sweet after taste her lips left on mine.

It held no comparison to my recollection of her pure, unadulterated, taste on my tongue. The way her mouth parted for me, so willingly, like a knife cutting into the soft skin of a ripe peach. The satisfaction of entrance was just as delicious as the flesh inside. The smooth feel of her creamy thighs in my firm grip and . . .

I was a man distracted.

Restless . . . obsessed . . .

Enthralled.

I waved away my errant thoughts and checked my watch for the time—half past noon. She was late. Beyond the platonic love I held for my sister, I had never experienced anything other than the occasional lust, seemingly made more frequent as of late due to a certain heart-stopping pain in my side, who was most likely doing something utterly reckless, once again.

At least today she was dressed appropriately if such an incident for her to fight or escape should arise. Those form fitting riding pants were nearly the death of me. Every curve of her, usually hidden beneath oversized clothing or full skirts, was on display. The shape of her twisted my stomach every way imaginable as the restless pressure to capture and consume grew stronger with each sway of her enticing ass. It was all I could do to stuff my fists into my pockets in her presence. To deny the urge to fill them with her substance, with any piece of her that she would offer me. If I hadn't treated her like some paltry token from my explorations in the First Realm, perhaps I wouldn't have to steal touches like a thief pickpockets coins. A clasped wrist here, the brushing away of an errant strand there.

Intent to torment myself no longer, I removed my reading glasses and rubbed the bridge of my nose before pulling out a drawer from my desk and lifting a false bottom to store the letters for later reading. A forceful tug pulled at the core of my chest as if to command, "Come here. Come find me." Sure, steps made quick work of leaving my only small slice of solitude in this godforsaken Academy.

Certainly, there would be no harm in stopping by the cadet dorms to make sure she was alright. I'll just make up an excuse for my intrusion. For she would certainly pout that succulent lip out in retaliation for my checking in on her. On second thought, I'll gladly endure that bratty attitude if it means I'm to be blessed with such a sight. No excuse needed. Not that I don't think her capable. My Little Fox has claws and teeth she wields mercilessly when cornered. Weapons she is more than adequately skilled in using to cut a man down. To make him bleed. Sometimes with only words alone. As I am first-handedly acquainted with this specific talent of hers.

No. I would just be passing by to follow-up on the healing of a certain cadet's injuries caused by my rageful fists meeting his conniving face. It is the least I could do.

I slipped a mask of cold indifference into place and slid my fists into the pockets of my trousers as I turned a corner, no longer a passionately obsessed young man, but a levelheaded lieutenant, into the halls that made up the cadets living quarters.

I didn't bother knocking gently or even wait for permission to enter as I threw the door to Dante's dorm room wide open. The door slammed against the adjacent wall as I took in the chaotic scene before me and the grumbling Elite with a bloody cloth held to his neck. My mouth threatened to kick up a corner at the sight.

"Bit off more than you could chew, soldier?" With a pointed brow raised in his direction, I indicated his lack of protocol was not well received. He shuffled from his bed and clumsily stood at attention.

"Lieutenant Desaius. To what do I owe the pleasure, sir?" Though his words were formal, they held the bite of disdain I had grown numb to over the years as a high-ranking officer not much older and sometimes even younger than the soldiers I commanded and taught.

"Just following up to see if the point of our lesson the other day had sunk in thoroughly." A bit of the wolf grinned at the sight of blood slowly dripping from his handkerchief. A twisted, sick part of me, weaned on pain, aroused at the thought it was Alise who was responsible for the fresh wound.

Down boy.

"Am I correct in assuming it has?"

"Yes, sir," he said with none of his usual vigor.

"Excellent." I made to turn away and slam the door behind me but the muttering of words from behind my back, delayed my exit. "Something you wish to say, Da Romano?" I threw over my shoulder with a sneer. Though corporal punishment wasn't my favorite method of correction, I was more than eager to take advantage of the allowance of it in this particular soldier's case.

"When you see Alise, tell her if she begs nicely, I'll reconsider the terms of our deal." An arrogant smile attempted to tug his lips before thinking better of it and backing away a step with his head lowered. Those knife-like eyes glared up through a mess of curls.

My lungs became void of breath.

No.

Little Fox, what did you agree to with this bastard?

Though I knew Da Romano was not above lying through his venomous teeth, I had to be sure. If the chaos of his dorm was any indication of how his meeting with Alise went, then it wasn't a civil discussion that was had. Though I wanted to discipline Da Romano right then and there, wanted to lock the door to his escape and tear him limb from limb it would have to wait. I had to be certain she was safe and whole first. Vengeance could come after.

Kareena sobbed into her hands. The ink on the parchment she held blurred with her tears as it bled into black blotches. After discreetly looking her over, I concluded this was only an injury of the heart. Though a great one at that and thus, I predicted, mine would also be wounded presently and far worse. I crouched down beside her and patted her head in soft strokes. Kareena, my sun, the northern star in my sky looked up at me with gray storm clouds in her usually bright eyes.

"She's gone."

If I had thought my heart would stop beating before, it surely did under the vise of Kareena's words. I rushed to Alise's adjoining bed chamber and threw the door open. Clothes hung haphazardly from open drawers, items scattered and broken as though in haste or rage. The chaos of the scene reminded me of the shattered ink pot upon the wall in my office. The oozing pain it displayed in the wake of its creator. I checked her night stand knowing for certain she wouldn't leave without her sketchbook and pencils. My lungs clenched and breath left my very soul to find the drawer empty. In my rush to be certain I pulled out all the drawers from their hinges. All found void. I clutched my hair at the scalp and grunted out a curse.

Oh, Little Fox, how you run.

Kareena's presence formed behind me as warmth blanketed my back. "Brother," she pleaded weakly. "It's for you." She knelt and plucked a folded piece of parchment from the floor, most likely shuffled in my hast, before handing it to me with trembling hands. My name was written on the front in the same handwriting that was permanently etched in my brain. The result of all those days and nights pouring over the pages of the journal she kept at the asylum. The hook of her a's the curve of her c's as familiar to me as the components of a pistol.

As I read, I noticed the ink was smeared in places and I devoured every line of text despite the voice of self-preservation screaming for me not to. I thoroughly ignored the shouting in my skull that pleaded for me to no longer subject myself to the pain of losing her. But in truth, she was already gone and I was indeed a fiend for suffering.

Articus,

He knows.

Dante knows about Brenton and where I'm truly from, and that you helped me and he's going to tell. I can't live with myself if you are punished for saving my life because you did, in fact, save my life. I understand that now and I'm sorry I didn't acknowledge your sacrifice in doing so, before. I'm sorry I fought you and pushed you away with every word. I didn't know it then, but I was determined to hurt myself.

Every shove bruised my heart. Every cut of a sharp word cut me just as deep.

I refuse to take you away from those that love you so, I'm leaving instead. I'm taking the blame for it all. It's already been done and now . . . now I'm going to do what I do best. I'm running. But this time it will not be easy or even desired, because this time I'll be leaving so much I love behind.

I never properly thanked you for the dress and the graphite, and sketchbook. For teaching me to defend myself and for never underestimating me. For standing up for me when I was too weak to do so and standing your ground when I needed it. But most of all I want to thank you for showing me what selfless love looks like.

I see you, Articus Carpenter. Who you truly are. And I don't hate any part of it. My only regret is that I didn't tell you sooner. . .

Illegible scribbles smeared with what were most likely tears, at the letter's footer, making the rest of the words unable to decipher. My jaw ached as my teeth clenched to the point of shattering. She was going to take the fall for it all and throw away any chance of having a life here in the Second Realm with us. For us. For me. I bit back a sob and clenched my fist to the point of pain. I let it distract me from the growing ache in my chest and the knot in my throat. For certainly if I broke down here, now, in front of Kareena, it would only worsen her own suffering.

A soft hand rested on my shoulder. Her voice resolved and certain as she said, "Go to her."

My head whipped toward Kareena at my side.

"I will not leave you," I stated with as much conviction as I could muster through my tight jaw.

"And you won't be, but soon I will be leaving you." She gave me a weak smile as she read the confusion written on my face.

"I was going to tell you and Alise today." The name sliced as surely as a blade to bone. "I was accepted into the medical program at a university in Poland. I'll be going this fall and Dean is coming with me. We are going to start a new life there—far away from Father and the Academy." Joy flickered like a starved ember in my chest for my sister's success. And if the circumstances of her announcement were different, I would have lifted her off her toes and spun her into dizzying circles until she begged for reprieve or I collapsed with delirium. She truly had made her own way, where she could, and built a future for herself. One I never could have given her alone.

The babe that clung to my pant leg for balance was now a young woman, breaking the clasp of her hand from my own—from the one she depended on for so long—that I had grown accustomed to its weight. What would it feel like to not have that comforting burden upon my shoulders any longer? What would keep my feet grounded once she was gone as well?

"I know you care for her, dear Brother, and I know she does for you as well. You have both tried to hide it from the world, from yourselves, but it has always been clear to me. I see the stolen touches and the way you both pretend not to look."

"Kareena, I . . ." I started to counter but for once, I could think of nothing.

She merely smiled, weakly, up at me. "Now, go. Chase after her or both you and I will regret it for the rest of your miserable life."

I swept her up in my arms and buried my face in her hair. Breathing her in for what felt like the last time, I memorized the scent of her, the feel of her warmth and pattern of her breath. It trembled and I set her down just as she swiped away tears with frantic fingers and gave me her most convincing shining smile.

"I'll be alright. I promise. Now go!" Her hands gave an unconvincing shove against my chest.

Goodbye did not exist between us. Not for this piece of my heart that stood shaking, yet sure before me. I wanted to thank her, to tell her I loved her, but I knew words would fail me. Instead, I kissed the top of her auburn head with one long, lingering inhale and hastened out the door, unable to look back for fear of crumbling my resolve.

There was only one other person whom Alise could turn to for aid. Only one who knew our secrets. And I didn't care how uncharacteristically desperate I looked as I ran past onlookers towards the archives of the library.

Chapter Forty Four

ARTICUS

"**W**HERE IS SHE?" I barked at Clouden as the door to his office slammed open. As was the standard for the day, it seemed. He looked uncharacteristically distressed but nonplussed by my sudden appearance.

"Sit down, boy," he commanded without looking up, only infuriating me further and dragging me toward that sharp edge of desperation and action.

"Tell me, now!"

"She wished for me not to tell you for just this reason. Respect her wishes in sparing your life and forget you ever knew her."

Forget I ever knew her?

I wanted to spit. How could he ask such a thing of me? Didn't he know? Couldn't he see through the façade of my rage that I was crumbling without her? If I went another minute without her, I would become reduced to nothing but primal pain and bitter ash to be carried away by a mere draft and left an empty shell. A body with no soul and no beating heart left with it.

I charged without thought and slammed him into the wall, gripping the collar of his shirt till my knuckles turned white. The wolf inside bared its teeth as I seethed in his face.

"Tell me where to find her, or I'll rip your fucking throat out."

Clouden stared plainly back at me. The scar down the side of his jaw, a sliver of the moon crested below his glaring eyes. Before me was the only man who wasn't fearful of what the wolf could do to him but rather, what it could do to the man it dwelled within.

My hands trembled and vision blurred the longer we stood there in tense silence. Ragged breath flooded my ears. Though my cheeks stung, I didn't dare wipe the burning tears away, for they were caused by the fear and pain of losing her. They were precious and I would hoard every single one.

Clouden's glare softened as his eyes trailed the evidence dripping from my chin. "You truly do love her," he murmured with disbelief.

Disarmed, I loosened my hold on his torn collar until I released him altogether with one, achingly, deep sigh. "I understand now." He sidestepped me and leaned over to open a drawer from his desk, removing a fresh piece of parchment. My body trembled with restless anticipation as he quickly wrote and then sealed a letter with melted wax, then stamped it with the Desaius insignia before handing it to me.

"She's at the docks, boarding a merchant ship to the Third Realm. She left about twenty minutes ago." He glanced at his watch. "If you leave now, you might be able to get there before the ship—"

I sprinted out of the office before he could finish, with his letter violently stuffed in my pocket.

Chapter Forty Five

T HE MISTY BREEZE OF the sea ruffled my hair, and loose strands freed themselves from my braid and danced across my face, tickling my lips and cheeks. I licked my lips and tasted the subtle hint of salt and sun. I was more than a little disappointed that the ship Clouden had arranged for me to board was a water vessel and not one of the airships I marveled at since my time in the Second Realm. However, since the bombing raid upon the city, they didn't hold quite as much awe and allure as before.

The city around the port was still in need of small repairs but, in general, had seemed to recover swiftly from the recent attack. Black soot, stained white washed walls, and roofs donned tarps of varying sizes, to cover suspected holes. Windows were being replaced and debris carried away. My ride in the summoned town car gave me an up-close view of it all on my journey to the docks and I wondered if such attacks were a common occurrence to those living in the city?

I thought of the letters I found in Articus's office and cursed my luck for not having the chance to implore him further about them. Did he have affiliations with the Menagerie and did he play any role in the bombing of the city? I remembered what he had said to me that day, how things had gotten out of control.

Beyond the political climate and the aftermath that surrounded me, I grieved the fact I would never get to ask Articus anything ever again and that I never got to properly say goodbye. I was not even able to finish the letter I had written to him. Tears made my vision blur beyond sight and my hands shook uncontrollably as I tried to spill my heart out on paper—as I tried to cram weeks worth of things left unsaid in the space of a few sentences. He would never know how I truly felt and that truth stung the most. The truth of it cut into my soul with a million tiny stings I'm sure would linger for the rest of my life. I had fearfully hidden my feelings from him and fully suffered the consequences of doing so. But maybe it was better this way. Maybe it would be easier for him to let me go by not knowing the truth of how I felt. I would carry the burden alone. I had no lack of familiarity with storing up secrets, but this time it would be my own that destroyed me.

"Miss Fox," a booming voice called behind me, startling me from my thoughts. I turned to acknowledge the man who called me. Dressed in a bright white uniform with brass buttons and a hat to match he looked every bit a sea captain. His skin was tan from obvious time spent in the sun, his eyes a glistening blue, much like the waters surrounding us.

"My crew and I welcome you aboard my ship. I am quite honored to be entrusted with the ward of Clouden Desaius upon her travels." A handsome smile splayed across his face.

"My master and I thank you, and your crew, for graciously providing safe passage, Captain," I curtsied small and briefly. Though it was more of a bow in riding pants and boots.

"Come," he beckoned. "Allow me the honor of giving you a tour of the ship before we launch." He extended an elbow for me to grasp and I reached out to accept—appreciative of the distraction.

"Halt!" a voice bellowed from the ramp below.

"Sir, this is a private trading vessel, you cannot—" the shout was suddenly cut-off by a low grunt.

"Alise!" someone shouted and I instantly recognized the voice. It sent a bolt of hope through me, so strong, it momentarily froze my feet in place. It couldn't be. He wouldn't.

I swiftly released the captain's arm and dashed to the ship's railing, leaning over to look below. Articus stumbled as two guards clasped his arms behind his back. He threw his head back, his skull meeting the nose of one of the guards who swore and released him to clamp a hand over his face. With his free arm he swung and landed a punch in the face of the other who held him, knocking him straight on his backside.

"Articus!" I shouted, though I still couldn't believe my eyes.

His wild gaze shot up to meet mine across the expanse of dock and crew between us. A wild tendril of hair blew across his brow in the sea breeze. I inhaled a large breath before scampering down the ramp to the docks below. With only a few inches remaining between us I threw my arms around Arrticus's neck and all but leapt into his arms as I buried my face in his chest. Inhaling deeply, I absorbed his vetiver and parchment scent and sealed it to my memory for safe keeping. His heart hammered in my ear, harder than I had ever felt it beat before. His arms instantly wrapped around me and held me against him desperately, as though he were grasping at the very wind itself.

"Stay close now, Little Fox," he murmured into my hair. My eyes shut tight against the burning his words summoned, against the jagged knot in my throat. His panting breath slowed and I felt his lungs expand in one long inhale as his cheek rested against the top of my head.

"Lieutenant Desaius, to what do I owe the pleasure of your visit?" I heard the sea captain's voice ask. Around us, crew members murmured amongst themselves, in response to the announcement of the infamous lieutenant.

Realizing the scene we were surely putting on for all to see, I reluctantly unclasped myself from the depths of Articus's hold and turned to face the spectators surrounding us.

"I'm here on behalf of my uncle's request." Articus removed a letter from his pocket and handed it to the sea captain. The parchment was crumpled and creased.

The captain accepted it willingly, with a small smile and a weather-worn hand. "Another favor from my presumptuous friend, it would appear."

Articus chuckled lightly. "I'm afraid so. I have been asked to escort Miss Fox to the Third Realm and to ensure her safety during her travels."

I gaped up at him.

"But, you can't. What about . . ."

Articus caught my glance with the side of his eye and cocked his lips into a disarming grin, revealing that single dimple I so loved. Then he winked. It was a silent communication, one we hadn't used since our time in the First Realm all those lifetimes ago.

Play along.

"Well, it would appear so," the captain said after reviewing the letter's contents. "Welcome aboard Lieutenant Desaius. I will consider myself doubly honored to have both you and Miss Fox aboard my ship." He nodded his head swiftly before heading back up the ramp and onto the deck above.

Now alone, I swiftly turned to Articus, ready to bury him in a pile of questions and demands.

"You know I'm not planning on coming back, right?"

"I know." He smiled fully looking down at me. His fingers mindlessly swept a strand of hair behind my ear.

"But, what about Kareena? You can't leave her. You might not ever see her again." I chewed on my lip and looked down at my fidgeting fingers.

"I know," he repeated, "and Kareena understands as well. She practically threw me out the door to come after you and she made it very clear that if I didn't, she would never forgive me for the rest of my life." A fist playfully knocked my chin up to face him. "Look at me, Alise."

I lifted my eyes to meet his and nearly drowned in the emotion I found in his pine-green stare. Desperation and longing swirled with relief and adoration, stealing my breath and yet grounding me all at once.

"Wasn't it you, all that time ago, who told me that what I want should matter. Well, I'm finally taking your advice and doing something utterly selfish. I'm coming with you, Alise. Because being with you is my greatest indulgence." His other hand clasped my waist and pulled me in closer. "You are so brave Little Fox, but you don't have to do this alone. Let me stay by your side. Let us figure this out together." My eyes welled with unshed tears as I nodded—my throat too tight to release words.

He was here. Despite all he had to lose, and despite the free pass I had given him, he still refused to let me go. Never before had anyone stuck with me so adamantly through such tumultuous circumstances. Had protected, lied and even killed for me. Yet here he was. Willing to give it all away for me.

I stood on my tiptoes and planted my lips on his. Reassuringly, his hands pulled me closer against him, as though he hungered for every kiss, every touch, I was willing to part with, big or small. The sea breeze tickled our cheeks in unison and the crew around us hooted and cheered at the spectacle we were certainly putting on. I giggled against Articus's mouth, becoming self-conscious in the best kind of way. He let me pull away, just enough to gaze back into that comforting forest of greens that reflected back down at me.

The familiar shades never ceased to remind me of the trees that grew behind my cabin home in the fading and few happy memories of my childhood. They were brought back to life by this boy before me. In this man who had, on more than one occasion, chased me through a maze of redwood and pine.

Who taught me what I was capable of and never batted an eye at any ungraceful or unseemly part of me.

"Where are your belongings? Did you not bring anything for our journey?" My brow furrowed as I glanced around.

"I didn't really have the mind to pack," he rasped, swiping his thumb over my cheek bone before ultimately deciding to steal another warm and radiant kiss from my already lonely lips.

Spectators be damned.

Chapter Forty Six

ARTICUS

O NCE BOARDED, ALISE AND I quietly discussed the intricacies of Clouden's plan and the details of our story, should anyone ask. Clouden had indeed made arrangements for us to travel to the Third Realm, but under the pretense that we were collecting research on his behalf with our return date, undetermined. However, what truly happened once we arrived would be up to us. In the meantime, Clouden would be gathering information of his own on Dante Da Romano, with help from the tips that would come to him about Dante's family, possibly, being involved in the cover up of one, or more, illegitimate children of their sterling son's, and several other unwilling pregnancies as well. All information given anonymously, of course, yet just as damning to the family, and the council members reputation, should it be proven true. A helpful and daring piece of leverage given from a dangerously unassuming girl.

"Dante said something to me that I found concerning."

Alise turned her attention from the churning waters beyond to assess me.

"He said he would reconsider the terms of the deal you two struck. What did you agree to, Alise?" Her cheeks pinked and it wasn't from the sun's warmth alone.

"He wanted me to provide him with something that . . . that I couldn't give," she paused and she didn't need to specify for me to understand. My hands clenched into the railing with disgust until my knuckles turned white. The thought of him touching her in such a way was enough to have me vomiting over the side of the ship's haul, if not for my clenched, rigid jaw.

"But I imagine he realized his disadvantage after he noticed this missing." She untucked the hem of her blouse and lifted a small journal from the waistband of her pants. "It's Brenton's journal. He had it all along, before I even had a chance to search Brenton's dorm room. He left it on his bed when I went to speak with him, as well as photos of me in the First Realm." She eyed her prize with a smirk of victory. "Guess he never imagined a frail girl, such as myself, could be capable of stealing it from right under his pretentious nose."

My clever Little Fox.

"Nor capable of making him bleed," I added with a jesting raise of my eyebrow, thinking to myself, "I see the claws you try to conceal and they are a stunning sight to behold."

"They always underestimate me," she pondered thoughtfully with a playful glint in her eye while a finger tapped her chin. At the image of her beautifully ferocious, violence I had to command my knees not to fall to her feet in reverence to this goddess before me. The sound of her twinkling laughter caught on the wind to float away into the wake of the ship. The city's outline grew smaller on the horizon behind.

"Are you planning to read it?" I asked. She breathed deeply and closed her eyes as she turned her face toward the sun. Its beams lit upon her crown like the salvation she was.

"No," she breathed. "I think I already know enough about Brenton Drexar than I care to." And without hesitation she flung the journal overboard, into the churning drink. We watched as it floated a great distance away before soaking through and sinking into the ocean's depths. Alise sighed with relief or regret; I could not discern.

"My only regret is that I was unable to get ahold of the pictures as well." And her face waned with defeat. I wrapped my arm around her waist and pulled her against me, my chin rested perfectly atop her head, bringing more comfort to me than she could know.

"You did well, Little Fox."

More so than she could ever know.

"Though I was able to get just this one." She reached into the pocket of her riding pants and pulled out a photo creased where it had been folded multiple times over.

In it was the image of Alise, clearly in the First Realm with torn pants bedecking her long legs, scuffed tennis shoes on her feet, and an oversized t-shirt draped over her shoulders. Her long, cornsilk hair flowed freely beside a taller, tanner figure. Brunette waves fell across his brow as he leaned in, as though conversing. A thick and decorated strap held a guitar at his back instead of a bag like the one Alise carried. They appeared to be in some kind of greenspace, surrounded by others similar in age, though their faces were blurred with movement. From the distance and angle, it appeared the photo was taken unbeknownst to the occupants in the image. As though they were captured and immortalized in the candid scene of everyday life.

"Is this James?" I dared to ask as I handed the photograph back to her.

Her gaze locked longingly on the small piece of glossy parchment for one long moment before replying, "Perhaps it's time I let him go." And before I could stop her, her fingers unfurled and the photo was snatched by the wild wind and carried out of reach.

"You didn't have to do that," I reassured her.

She sighed deeply as she watched the wind's stolen prize drift from view.

"It was time," was all she said before nudging between my arm and the ship's rail, pressing her side flush against mine.

The sun was setting low over the water's horizon. The vibrant display of reds and oranges stirred a longing in me that had me wondering how many more kisses I could steal from Alise's lips before the crew started their jeering again and she pushed away from embarrassment at our public display. Resolved to find out just that, I lifted a hand to cup her face and turned that soul piercing sky blue gaze to face me.

"Prepare ship for portal entrance!" a crew member called out, interrupting my pursuit.

"Already?" Alise looked around perplexed.

"Yes, Miss Fox. It is a short day's journey to the receiving portal and then from there we will be flying," the captain said as he manifested beside us. He lifted a pocket watch from a golden chain connected to his breast pocket. When he opened it, four round disks rose in tiers, each displaying a different skyscape on its face in conjunction to the realm it represented, showing the time of day or night it was in each. A series of hour and minute hands all pointed to different roman numerals. The watch face representing the Second Realm, displayed a twilight sky and the clock's hands indicated it was approximately eight in the evening.

"We will enter the portal to the Third Realm under the cover of night," the captain declared before snapping the watch shut and returning it to his pocket. "The skies are clear tonight. You are in for quite a treat," he added and threw a wink at Alise before continuing across the deck to give orders to his crew.

Alise stared gaping at the sea captain's back. "What was that . . . that device and how—" but before she could organize her words the ship shifted with a jolt and she stumbled into my arms. I marveled at her awe as a large balloon filled with air at the ship's center slowly rose higher above us. A sail then swiftly released at the bow to catch the wind and jolted the ship forward once again. I leaned down to whisper in her ear, my arms braced across her chest and waist.

"Come. See the best part." I directed her wide eyes back towards the railing and over the side of the ship. The vessel lifted higher and higher from the water until its hull was revealed completely. Once mere inches above the water's surface, a set of framed canvas wings jutted out of the hull's side and caught the wind in its sheet.

Alise gasped at the sight. It must have been something truly out of her realm of imagination to witness firsthand. I had noticed how she stared longingly at the airships from the windows of the Academy, how she poured over the diagrams in an attempt to understand the design and science behind their operation.

"What are you thinking?" I breathed into her hair.

"I . . . I still don't understand it, but . . . but it's even more amazing in person." Her hands held tight to the arms around her.

The air had chilled as the sun made its final descent. Stars twinkled into existence around us and below as they reflected off the water's, now distant, surface.

"Portal ahead!" another voice bellowed in warning. Alise's head swerved toward the front of the ship.

"Where? I don't see it?"

I lowered my head to her shoulder and pointed my finger down her line of sight.

"There, where the stars and ocean vanish." Because it was night the portal was nothing more than a vacuum of darkness. Stars in the sky and their reflection below disappeared around the rim of the portal's gaping entrance. Much like the ink stain left on my office wall, no light could be seen within its deep bowels. It was simply a smear of black across a speckled sky. As we sailed nearer, the winds changed as the portal's pull lured us forward. The rushing of water quickened beneath the airship as the portal drank in the ocean like a parched god. Alise sucked in a breath—possibly reminded of her first, less desirable experience with portal travel.

"Here," I said as I grabbed a piece of rope tied to the mast closest to us and wrapped it around our middles before tying it again to the post. More an assurance to her than a true safeguard. Her nails slowly relaxed their stinging grip on my arm but she did not wholly let go.

"Entering portal. Brace yourselves!" the captain called.

As the ship's bow entered the vast, black stain on the ocean's horizon, it vanished into complete darkness as though consumed and erased from existence. Inch by inch the darkness claimed more and more of the airship and its crew.

I recalled the clumsiness of our first and rather hasty expedition through a portal together. How Alise clung to me and held her breath as we floated through a universe of infinite stars just to find ourselves drowning in a lake of bones. Just as before I hadn't known where exactly this portal would dispense us. But I knew whatever met us on the other side, we would greet together with Alise securely in my arms and a hope I carelessly let burn too brightly.

Chapter Forty Seven

THE DARKNESS WAS COLD and suffocating as it crawled across the deck toward my feet and up my legs. I clutched Articus's arm, tighter than ever before. His warm broad chest was a reassurance I wished to hide in as the portal slowly consumed us. This was so different from my first leap into the discarded portal in the First Realm. That time was sudden and impulsive, whereas this was torturously slow and deliberate. An illicit shiver tingled from my head to my toes at the sensation of being shrouded by darkness. There were no stars to greet us this time, nor did I feel as though I was plunged into water. There was only stillness and nothing. No sound came from the creaking ship nor the rest of the crew.

And the eerie nothingness of it all terrified me.

"Breathe," a warm soft voice hushed against my ear. Suddenly, I was reminded of the strong arms around my chest and waist. Of the steady heartbeat at my back. The same beat that anchored mine and beckoned it to mimic its calming rhythm.

"Alise."

"Yes," I replied into the nothingness around me, my voice disappearing just beyond the reach of my lips.

"Will you promise to stay close to me this time?"

His question was loaded with so much meaning yet, I didn't need to dissect it or think my response through. I had followed this man to the ends of my known world and swam through the depths of his. This time we would leave it all again and enter a place foreign to both of us. And though I should have been fearful of the unknown, of the seemingly never-ending dark engulfing us, I found I was not. No trace of lingering regret laid in my chest, nor did my resolve waver as he held me close—exactly where I wanted to be. No. There would be no room for fear and doubt with Articus at my side.

He held me as though I was a missing piece of himself. A piece he was trying to fuse back together, as I replied, "I promise."

Epilogue

*E*XCERPTS FROM THE MISSING *journal of the missing person, Brenton Drexar.*

September 12th, 1990

I've made contact!

After months of casting out messages through my father's old contacts, sleazing in lowbrow pubs in seedy port towns, I've finally received a response. I wasn't certain I would ever hear back, considering how old the information I stumbled upon in my father's dusty belongings was, but through the web of messages I sent out, one struck its target. Though it wasn't directly from my late father's mysterious benefactor from years past, it was nonetheless a message. Which was more than I could hope for and even more so, he has a job for me. A task, you could say. One that, if completed, will be rewarded greatly with enough currency to reinstate the prestige and ranking of the Drexar name for generations to come.

Though his promises are lofty, if Father's recounting is accurate, then this man is the most wealthy and powerful of the Four Known Realms. If anyone can make good on it, it is him. Once and for all I could wipe away the stain my father left on the Drexar family tree and possibly erase it from history all together.

October 6th, 1990

He wants her back desperately.

I can see it in his messages, despite the line of hands and mouths it has passed through before reaching me over these past weeks. For years I've been familiar with this type of desperation. Enough so to recognize when a man covets, envies, truly wants what is just out of reach.

It burrows into my chest every time another Elite gives me a cold shoulder or doesn't invite my mother and I to a gathering because of our last name. If I were a Da Romano or a Fairchild, things would be different, but instead I'm cursed by the less than pristine path my father chose to take. His actions now follow my mother and I like the plague.

If we were from any other class of citizen, a mercenary would be an understandable position for someone no longer enlisted. Though dangerous, it pays handsomely for the risk. But in high society, from a family of class, it is considered degrading and tactless. A misstep I'm reminded of by society everyday. It was only through pity and my mother's pleading letters to some old family friends that I was accepted into the Academy and I'm never left to forget it.

I'm starting to think no amount of money will ever place my mother and I in good standing again.

October 26th, 1990

A part of me thought that if I could see it on paper, my mind could better process what's been happening, because there's no way this is humanly possible.

He sends a message. A time and place. Always remote, usually at night. When I arrive at the predetermined location, on the time he has given me, on the dot, a portal opens. An uncharted portal!

It's as if he somehow knows the chaotic pattern of their comings and goings. Or even wields them to open himself, from afar, in whatever realm he now dwells in. It's . . . it's impossible, I know and to even write it down makes me feel ludicrous, but there's more. Not only is he navigating, or possibly even bending the laws of physics to produce portals that open and close on command, they all access the First Realm—the forbidden realm.

To even write this down is to risk discovery and be punished with death. However, the statements alone are so fanciful, if discovered, this entry would most likely be determined as one of a mad man or simply a piece of fiction. For what god wills the elements to control such chaotic things as portals?

This powerful man, whoever he is, has me gathering intel on her whereabouts. On that girl he so desperately wants back. Through old clues my father left behind about where he left her, and dusty First Realm newspaper articles, I'm getting close.

November 21st, 1990

I found her.

She's beautiful in an ethereal way and perhaps that's part of why he wants her back. Surprisingly though, he wants me to wait. To stand down and merely observe until the time is right. I don't understand why but when I returned to find my mother crying with joy over a ten-million-pound inheritance we received, from an uncle we knew nothing about, I decided I don't get paid to think.

Perhaps I'll use some of the money to find a more competent physician. The headaches from realm travel have been growing worse. Some nights they become so unbearable I've considered crawling on all fours to one of those underground opium dens to stifle the pain. Lord knows I have more than enough money now to maintain any habit I so choose. Perhaps a little more will finally be enough to set things right.

December 30th, 1990

HE CAN'T HAVE HER!

Over the weeks I have grown to fully, and truly understand where the eagerness in his previous query came from, why he's spent so much money and effort to have her back in his grasp. For I care about nothing more than having her all to myself. Every second with her, even just in her orbit, is bliss.

When I purposely bumped into her at the university, causing her belongings to fall from her arms and helped her gather them, the look in her eyes as they met mine was one of pure destiny. I saw the universe and all its possibilities in those eyes. Which is how I know she must think just as much about me.

Every bite from a spoon, drawn in and out of that luscious mouth, every sip from a cup, I know she's thinking of me between those lips. Every smile she directs toward that talentless musician is stolen by his gaze.

Those smiles are mine!

Snatched away and stored in my collection. And quite the collection it has become, but nothing in it will ever compare to when she's finally nothing but mine. If he wants her so badly, he can come get her himself, the coward, because now I have a plan of my own.

I'll play along for now until I'm finally rid of all obstacles and my path is cleared directly to her. Until I hold all the power, something I've found I very much like the taste of. It's amazing what money can accomplish in the First Realm. What others are willing to look past for the right price. They are cheap and getting what I want there is easy.

Soon she'll be my pretty bird in a cage that only I hold the key to.

Acknowledgements

Firstly, I'd like to give glory to God for instilling his creativity into his creation and always refilling my cup and guiding my path with his sound discernment. I dove headfirst into self-publishing with only my faith in his goodness and a very rough manuscript and here I am now with a story to share and more readers than I could have ever hoped for. Thank you, Lord for always reminding me who I am.

Special thanks to my editor Friel for helping me put together my blurb when I was struggling to sum this story up. I went from hating it to giddy with joy with what we had created. Who knew writing a blurb would be harder than writing a whole book? Thank you, my friend.

I would also like to thank my copy editor Caitlin for not only traversing the complicated world of grammar with me but for also going above and beyond in lending me her honest opinions and developmental input as well. Lord knows I could never keep track of all the rules of grammar, punctuation etc. Not only did she make herself open and available to me and understand the balance of life as a working mother, she took this raw oyster of a story and helped me crack away to the pearl inside and for that I am eternally grateful.

To my cover artist Jade, I would like to thank for being on the miraculous level of telepathic when it came to my vision and what I wanted for this book's cover. It was as though she plucked the very image form my mind and made it a reality. Not only did she lend her amazing talent to me but she was also on top of any technical issues I came across and remedied them with an ease I could not posses myself and for all of that I am thankful.

I would like to thank Blythe, Courtney and Leigh Ann for being my sound board, my beta readers and my biggest cheerleaders. Their honesty and encouragement mean the world to me. I don't know how I would have made it through the imposture syndrome without them to lift me up and remind me of the excellent writer they believe I am. Where would I be without my best friends to talk about ACOTAR fandom theories and if the multiverse is possible with while later crying about the stresses of self-publishing and mom guilt? Definitely not sane and not sharing my writing with the world and I love them for it.

Thank you to the others who have supported me along this journey with their sage advice and encouragement. My author friends, Emma, Marilyn, and Caity for always being there to answer my questions and guide me with their experience. I appreciate you all dearly. And thank you to my other beta readers Lauren and Brooke for going above and beyond just reading my manuscript by lending me their editing eye and telling everyone how much they loved my writing. And also, thanks to my family who all instantly ordered a signed copy without even knowing what this book was about and told everyone they knew, about the author in the family.

Furthermore, thank you to my husband Chris who, every day, believes in me more than I believe in myself. Who saw me working on a story I had trapped in my mind and said, "Let's publish it," without hesitation. Who poured his own time and resources into making that a reality for me so that I could maintain control of my art and still share my story with the world. He said, "If only one person reads it and loves it, it will be worth it." Here we are with way more than just one happy reader or soul touched. Without his unwavering belief in my abilities and his handy technical side I would never have had the courage to release this story into the world. I'm sorry its not eight pages of written gratitude my love, but it will have to do for now.

Lastly, but gratefully I would like to acknowledge my son, who despite how the world views him, sees only adventure and discovery with a set of fearless eyes. Thank you for modeling that fearless courage to me every day so that I may learn how to embrace it myself in a world that says you can't. You can my little prince and so I must.

About the Author

J.O.Ellis is an author living in the piney woods of Texas with her veteran husband, autistic son and two dogs, not including the several other animals she brings into her home on a regular basis. When she's not writing she can be found lost in a pile of books, advocating for the inclusion and rights of the neurodiverse, thrift shopping or befriending a woodland creature.

Visit paperbackhartpress.com for more information about upcoming releases and other works.

Printed in the USA
CPSIA information can be obtained
at www.ICGtesting.com
LVHW040255060124
768269LV00030B/1370/J

9 781088 096895